Praise for Margaret Daley and her novels

"Margaret Daley writes an entertaining story with believable characters in *The Power of Love*."
—*Romantic Times BOOKreviews*

"Margaret Daley takes a candid and inspiring look at a child severely wounded and the two people who'd do anything to make her happy in *A Family for Tory*."
—*Romantic Times BOOKreviews*

"*When Dreams Come True* has a unique plot with realistic dilemmas. Margaret Daley gets to the heart of family issues and Dane's struggle to reconnect with his wife and children."
—*Romantic Times BOOKreviews*

"Many romances deliver basic love-at-first-sight plots, but nuance is key in Margaret Daley's *Tidings of Joy*. Chance and Tanya gradually discover friendship and love in a book that offers strong family values."
—*Romantic Times BOOKreviews*

MARGARET DALEY
The Power of Love

The Courage To Dream

Steeple
Hill®

Published by Steeple Hill Books™

STEEPLE HILL BOOKS

Steeple
Hill®

ISBN-13: 978-0-373-65122-1
ISBN-10:   0-373-65122-8

THE POWER OF LOVE AND THE COURAGE TO DREAM

THE POWER OF LOVE
Copyright © 2002 by Margaret Daley

THE COURAGE TO DREAM
Copyright © 2003 by Margaret Daley

All rights reserved. Except for use in any review, the reproduction or utilization of this work in whole or in part in any form by any electronic, mechanical or other means, now known or hereafter invented, including xerography, photocopying and recording, or in any information storage or retrieval system, is forbidden without the written permission of the editorial office, Steeple Hill Books, 233 Broadway, New York, NY 10279 U.S.A.

This is a work of fiction. Names, characters, places and incidents are either the product of the author's imagination or are used fictitiously, and any resemblance to actual persons, living or dead, business establishments, events or locales is entirely coincidental.

This edition published by arrangement with Steeple Hill Books.

® and TM are trademarks of Steeple Hill Books, used under license. Trademarks indicated with ® are registered in the United States Patent and Trademark Office, the Canadian Trade Marks Office and in other countries.

www.SteepleHill.com

Printed in U.S.A.

CONTENTS

Books by Margaret Daley

Love Inspired	Love Inspired Suspense
The Power of Love	*Hearts on the Line*
Family for Keeps	*Heart of the Amazon*
Sadie's Hero	*So Dark the Night*
The Courage to Dream	*Vanished*
What the Heart Knows	*Buried Secrets*
A Family for Tory	*Don't Look Back*
*Gold in the Fire	*Forsaken Canyon*
*A Mother for Cindy	
*Light in the Storm	
The Cinderella Plan	
*When Dreams Come True	
*Tidings of Joy	
**Once Upon a Family	
**Heart of the Family	
**Family Ever After	

*The Ladies of Sweetwater Lake
**Fostered by Love

MARGARET DALEY

feels she has been blessed. She has been married more than thirty years to her husband, Mike, whom she met in college. He is a terrific support and her best friend. They have one son, Shaun.

Margaret has been writing for many years and loves to tell a story. When she was a little girl, she would play with her dolls and make up stories about their lives. Now she writes these stories down. She especially enjoys weaving stories about families and how faith in God can sustain a person when things get tough. When she isn't writing, she is fortunate to be a teacher for students with special needs. Margaret has taught for over twenty years and loves working with her students. She has also been a Special Olympics coach and participated in many sports with her students.

THE POWER OF LOVE

And we have known and believed the love that God hath to us. God is love; and he that dwelleth in love dwelleth in God, and God in him.

—1 *John* 4:16

This book is dedicated to the staff at
Jenks High School and all the students
I have had the privilege of teaching.

Chapter One

"What now?" Rebecca Michaels pulled back from the peephole, a frown marring her tired features.

When she opened her front door to the large policeman, tension whipped down her length. Standing next to the stranger was her son. The policeman's solemn expression told her the next few minutes wouldn't be a welcome-to-the-town exchange. She braced herself. "Is there something wrong, Officer?"

"Ma'am, is this your son?"

She nodded, her throat tightening.

"I found this young man behind the grocery store, loitering. He should be in school."

"That was where he was supposed to be." Rebecca directed her attention to her nine-year-old, whose features were set in a sullen expression. "What happened, Peter? You left an hour ago for school."

He dropped his gaze. "I didn't wanna go."

"That's not an option." Rebecca looked toward the policeman. "I'm sorry to have inconvenienced you. I'll make sure he gets to school when my baby wakes up."

The man stuck out his hand. "I'm Gabriel Stone. I haven't had the opportunity to welcome you to Oakview yet. Sorry it had to be this way."

Rebecca shook his hand, comforted by the firm feel of his fingers around hers. His handshake conveyed an impression of directness and no-nonsense that was refreshing. "I'm Rebecca Michaels." She relaxed the tense set of her shoulders.

"Well, ma'am, if you don't mind, I can take your son to school for you."

"I wouldn't want to put you out."

"No problem. That's part of my job, making sure the kids stay in school."

Grateful for his offer, she smiled. "Then great. My other son, Josh, just went down for a nap, and I hope he sleeps for a while."

The policeman returned her smile, the lines at the corners of his eyes deep as if he smiled a lot. "If you need any help, don't be a stranger. I live on the next block. I've known your grandmother for years."

As her son and Gabriel Stone turned to leave, Rebecca called, "Come right home after school, Peter. We need to talk."

The pout that graced her son's mouth made her wonder if she would have to go out looking for him after school. She started to say something further when

Gabriel Stone said, "He'll be here. I'll make sure of that, ma'am."

Rebecca leaned against the doorjamb and watched her son and the policeman walk to the squad car. Gabriel Stone might bring Peter home this afternoon, but who was going to give her the strength to deal with this new problem? She squeezed her eyes closed and wished for the wisdom she would need to handle her eldest. He hadn't wanted to come to Oakview. He'd let her know that he hated his new school and wanted to go back to his old school in Dallas.

Had she made a wrong decision about coming to her grandmother's to live? She hadn't had much choice after her husband walked out on her and the children. Taking a deep breath of the spring-scented air, she relished the quiet of the moment, only the occasional sound of a bird in her grandmother's large oak tree breaking the silence.

"Rebecca, who was that?"

"Gabriel Stone." She closed the front door and turned toward her grandmother, who came from the back of the house, her cane tapping on the hardwood floor. She stopped, and with her shoulders hunched leaned on her cane, something she only did when she was really tired. Granny had been up part of the night with her and Josh. The doorbell must have awakened her. "Everything's okay. You should go back to sleep, Granny."

"I needed to get up. I never sleep past seven, and here it is nearly nine."

"You probably never stay up to all hours of the night, either. I'm sorry Josh was so fussy."

"My child, never apologize for that." Her grandmother waved her hand toward the door. "I wish you had asked Gabriel in for some coffee. I don't get to see him nearly enough, especially now that he's the new police chief."

Police chief? She'd had no idea she had been talking to the person who ran Oakview's small police department. He hadn't said a word. "He'll be back this afternoon."

"Did he come over to welcome you to Oakview? That would be just like the boy."

"No." Rebecca wished that had been the case. "Peter skipped school."

"I knew he wasn't happy, but I never thought he would do that." Rose Bennett headed for the kitchen. "I think you could use a cup of coffee. You've been up quite a while with Josh."

Massaging the tight cords of her neck, Rebecca followed her grandmother into the most cheerful room in the house. Sunlight from a large bay window bathed the kitchen. The yellow and powder-blue flowered wallpaper, the white cabinets and the polished hardwood floors lent a warmth to the room that Rebecca loved. She remembered spending a lot of wonderful childhood days in this very kitchen, listening to her grandmother's stories of her family during the Oklahoma land rush. If she could, she would spend most of her time in this room, cooking. She rarely had that kind of time anymore.

Granny retrieved two mugs from the cabinet and brought them to the pine table situated in front of the bay window. "Sit before you collapse. You look exhausted, my dear."

Rebecca started to argue, then realized her grandmother was right. Weariness clung to every part of her. She could easily slump over on the table and go to sleep. She needed the caffeine to keep her awake so she could finish unpacking. Even though they'd been in Oakview for two weeks, they were still living in boxes. Peter would never feel as though this was his home as long as he had to get his things out of cardboard boxes. She was determined to have them settled completely as soon as possible. Then maybe they would begin to feel like a family again.

Granny poured coffee into the mugs, then took a seat next to Rebecca. "First, how's Josh? You must have finally managed to get him to sleep."

"You know Josh. He rarely complains. But his ears are still bothering him. He eventually went to sleep, I think out of pure exhaustion. I worry that his ear infection will spread to his lungs. You know the problems he can have with his breathing."

"He's such a sweet baby." Granny sipped her coffee. "Of course, I'm not sure he's considered a baby any longer. He'll be two soon. I wish I could help you more with him."

"Granny, offering to let us stay here has…" Rebecca swallowed hard, but the tears returned to plague her.

"Child, this is your home, too. Always will be." Rose patted Rebecca's hand. "You're family, and next to God, family is the most important thing in our lives."

"I wish Craig thought his family was important." Rebecca remembered a time when their small family had been important to Craig—before Josh was born. When they had been first married, he'd wanted children, but over the years his feelings had changed.

Rose pinched her lips and snorted. "That man will regret leaving you one day, only by then it'll be too late."

"We've been divorced a year yesterday."

Rose placed her hand over Rebecca's. "I know, child. I'm sorry. With faith and time the pain will go away."

The feel of her grandmother's small, gnarled fingers over hers comforted Rebecca. "Time might help, but I don't know about faith, Granny. I think God stopped listening to my prayers long ago. I've tried so hard to keep this family together. My sons need…" She couldn't continue. The heartache of the past few years overwhelmed her, robbing her of her voice and capturing her breath in her lungs.

"It may seem that way, child, but He hasn't. He has a plan for you. You just don't know what it is yet." Rose squeezed Rebecca's hand. "You're here with me now. Things will start to look better."

Drawing in a shallow gulp of air, Rebecca swallowed past the tightness in her throat, determined to hold her family together somehow and reach her eldest son. "Peter's so miserable. He has never been openly hostile and defiant to me until lately. He used to love school. Now, I have to force him to go."

"Wait until he makes new friends. He'll forget all about Dallas."

Rebecca took several sips of her lukewarm coffee, wishing she had the faith that her grandmother had. When Craig had walked out on them eighteen months ago, she had prayed for help and guidance. None had come. Josh had to have surgery on his heart. The bills stacked up and Craig was slow to help pay for his children's upbringing. She had to sell the only home Peter had known and finally admit she couldn't make it in Dallas by herself. She'd returned to the town she'd grown up in Oklahoma.

Rebecca reached to pour herself another cup of coffee when she heard Josh's crying. Glancing at the time, she realized he hadn't slept more than half an hour. She pushed to her feet. "I'll see if I can't get him back to sleep."

Her grandmother caught her arm to stop her. "Honey, when God closes a door, He opens a window. Moving back to Oakview is a fresh start for you and your family. This is a wonderful town to raise your children in."

Rebecca leaned down and kissed her grandmother's wrinkled cheek. "If that's correct, then you're my window, and I appreciate you opening your home to me and my children. Ever since my parents died, you have been my anchor."

Josh continued to cry. Rebecca hurried upstairs to her

bedroom, where he slept in a crib next to her bed. She looked at her youngest who had managed to turn over—finally, after twenty months. His face was beet red, and his short arms and legs were flailing.

"How's my little man?"

He turned his head toward her, his big brown eyes, slightly slanted at the corners, filled with tears.

"Nothing can be that bad," Rebecca said, scooping her son into her embrace. He fit in the cradle of her arms, his length no more than a one-year-old's.

Tears misted her eyes. Blinking them away, she began to sing Josh's favorite song. He cuddled against her, sleep slowly descending. She would not feel sorry for herself or Josh. That was wasted energy—energy she couldn't afford to waste.

Gabriel entered the clothing store and strode toward the elderly woman, sitting in an uncomfortable-looking chair with a young man standing over her with a scowl on his face.

When Ben Cross saw him approach, he waved his hand toward the white-haired woman and said, "I want her arrested. She tried to take a watch."

The elderly lady bristled. "Nonsense. I was admiring the watch, stuck it in my pocket to buy after I had looked around and forgot all about it."

"Ma'am—" Gabriel began.

"Bess Anderson. You can call me Bess, Officer. All my friends at the home do."

"Shady Oaks on First Street?"

"Why, yes. You know the place where I live?" She straightened her shoulders, clutching her purse handle with both hands.

The elderly woman reminded Gabriel of a typical grandmother of yesteryear. She was dressed in a floral print dress with sensible walking shoes and a felt hat on her head. All she was missing were white cotton gloves. "Ma'am, how—"

"Bess, please. Ma'am makes me sound so old, which I refuse to be."

"Bess, how did you get here?" Gabriel ignored the glares Ben was sending him.

"Why, I just walked out of the building and headed for town. I like to shop and haven't been in a while."

"Then let me take you home." Gabriel turned away from Bess and whispered to Ben, "I think this was all a misunderstanding. I'm inclined to accept her word that she just forgot about the watch being in her pocket. Is that okay with you?"

Ben pursed his lips, his eyes pinpoints.

"She's at least eighty. I can't see locking her up, Ben."

The young man sighed. "Okay. This time. This better not happen again."

Gabriel escorted Bess Anderson to his squad car. While the elderly woman gave him a rundown of her afternoon outing, he drove her the few blocks to the Shady Oaks Nursing Home. As he walked her toward the main building, the director came out the front door, worry carved into her expression.

"We've been looking all over the place for you, Bess. Is everything all right?"

"My goodness, yes. I just had a lovely stroll into town, and this nice gentleman offered to bring me home." Bess continued past the director.

Gabriel shook his head as he watched the old woman disappear into the building. "Bess Anderson is certainly an interesting character, Susan."

"And a handful. She's only been with us for a few weeks, and this is the second time she has walked away from the home. I don't know how she gets out. Thank you for bringing her back. Do you want to come in for some tea? It's almost four. We were about to have it in the main lounge."

"I'll take a rain check. I have a date with a young man at the school. In fact, if I don't get moving, I'll be late."

Quickly Gabriel headed toward the elementary school. He pulled into a parking space just as the bell dismissed the children for the day. He climbed from the squad car and leaned against it, his arms folded across his chest, and waited for Peter Michaels to appear. Gabriel waved to several students coming out of the school, but he kept his gaze focused on the door. He wouldn't put it past the boy to try to sneak away. Peter hadn't been very happy this morning when Gabriel had deposited him in the principal's office before having a brief word with the man.

When the last student filed out of the school, Gabriel straightened and decided to head inside to see if Peter had given him the slip. He took two steps and stopped. Coming out of the building at a slow pace was the child in question. The sullen look on his face underscored the reluctance the boy felt.

Gabriel relaxed against the car and waited. He had a lot of patience, and he had a feeling he would need every bit of it to get through to Peter.

"Glad you could make it," Gabriel said, and opened his car door.

"This is dumb. I can walk home. It's only two blocks."

"I told your mother I would give you a ride."

The boy's frown deepened as he rounded the back of the sedan and climbed inside.

Gabriel started the engine and slanted a look toward Peter. He stared straight ahead, defiance stamped in his features. No small talk on this trip, Gabriel thought, and backed out of the parking space.

A few minutes later Gabriel pulled into Rose Bennett's driveway, and Peter jumped from the car before Gabriel could even switch off the engine. The boy raced for the house and disappeared inside so fast that Gabriel had to admire the child's quickness. He would be great on the baseball team. An idea formed and grew as Gabriel ambled to the house to pay his respects to Rose and maybe get to see Rebecca Michaels again.

All day he had been unable to shake the image of her

wide eyes as she had stared at him. Deep in their blue depths he had glimpsed a vulnerability that touched him to the core. He hated to see someone hurting, and Rebecca was definitely in pain.

Even though Peter had left the front door open, Gabriel knocked on the screen, not wanting to ring the bell since her baby might be sleeping. He heard the sound of Rose's cane tapping against the floor as she shuffled toward him.

"My goodness, Gabriel, why are you standing out there? Come in. Are you through for the day?"

"Yes, ma'am."

"I just made a fresh pot of coffee, and I know how much you like my brew." Rose reached into the mailbox at the side of the door and retrieved several envelopes.

"No one makes it quite like you."

He stepped inside and glanced about him at the warmth of the house. Rose was determined to bring the outdoors inside. In every room there were vases of cut flowers from her garden and pots filled with green plants. The house's clean, fresh scent reminded him of a beautiful spring day.

"Now, that will definitely get you a second cup. I was in the kitchen trying to decide what to fix for dinner. Since Rebecca's moved in with her boys, we eat early. Why don't you stay and eat with us tonight?"

"I don't—"

Rose paused at the entrance to the kitchen, clasping both hands on the cane, her sharp, shrewd gaze directed at him. "I won't take no for an answer, son. I know for a fact you usually go home at night and eat by yourself in that big empty house of yours. Tonight you can eat with me and my family."

"Put that way, I can't refuse. I'll stay on one condition. You let me help with dinner." He enjoyed being a policeman in this Oklahoma town. The people had taken him into their hearts and made him feel a part of Oakview when he had moved here ten years before. They had comforted and shared in his pain, too. He would never forget their support.

"I'll let you share cleanup duty with my granddaughter. Cooking is one of my favorite things. Cleaning up isn't."

"It's a deal."

Gabriel sat at the kitchen table while Rose retrieved a blue mug from the cabinet and poured him some coffee. The aroma filled his nostrils, easing some of the day's tension. There was something in Peter's rebellious expression that concerned him, causing a warning to go off in his brain.

"I noticed you brought Peter home," Rose said, slipping a look at him while she stood at the stove and browned some ground beef. "Did he say anything to you?"

"Not a word."

"That's what I was afraid of. That child doesn't say much, and when he does he's always angry."

"Yep, that about sums up my experience with him." Gabriel took a long sip of his coffee, relishing the delicious taste of the rich brew as it slid down his throat.

"I've been trying to get him to church, but last Sunday I think he deliberately made himself throw up so he didn't have to go. I don't know what to do about him, and Rebecca is as lost as I am." Rose placed the wooden spoon on the counter and began cutting up an onion.

The aromas of cooking meat and fresh coffee reminded Gabriel of the home he used to have when his wife was alive. Now he usually heated up frozen dinners or grabbed something at the diner in town by the police station.

"What's he angry about?"

"He didn't want me to move to Oakview."

Gabriel peered over his shoulder at Rebecca, who stood in the doorway, that haunted look in her eyes again. His natural curiosity was aroused by this woman as he took in her petite build. Short brown hair framed an oval face, and her smooth, creamy complexion was devoid of any makeup. She wasn't beautiful, but there was something pleasing about her appearance.

"What did Peter say about skipping school?" Rose added the onion to the ground beef and stirred.

"Not much."

"Is Josh asleep finally?"

"Yes, but I don't know how long that will last. I hope the antibiotic takes effect soon."

"What's wrong?" Gabriel asked, finishing his coffee.

"An ear infection. Can I help, Granny?"

"No. I asked Gabriel to dinner, and he'll help you

clean up. Sit and relax for a few minutes. You've been going a mile a minute since this morning."

Rebecca followed her grandmother's advice and took the chair at the opposite end of the kitchen table from Gabriel. Closing her eyes, she rolled her head and moved her shoulders. "Well, in between taking care of Josh, I did manage to empty a few more boxes. Only a dozen left."

Gabriel walked to the coffeepot and filled his mug. The scent of cooking onion saturated the air and made his stomach rumble. "Are you staying long?"

"I'm not sure what my plans are." She picked up the mail and flipped through the stack of letters.

"Did you receive your check?" Rose turned toward Rebecca, concern in her expression.

Frowning, Rebecca tossed the letters on the table. "No. He's late again. I don't know what I'm going to do."

"Is there something I can help you with?" Gabriel took the seat across from Rebecca, an urge to protect inundating him. In his line of work he often helped strangers, but this was different. He didn't like to see distress dull her eyes and wished he could erase it.

"No." Her gaze found his. "There isn't anything that you can do. My ex-husband is late with his child support. That's all." She shrugged as though it were nothing.

Gabriel seriously doubted it was that simple, but he saw the do-not-trespass sign go up and he didn't pursue the topic. Instead, he said, "I'd like to have Peter come out for the baseball team. I think he has potential."

"Baseball?"

"He's quick, and the guys on the team are a great bunch of kids. I help coach a Little League team after school."

"I doubt you'll get him to agree. All he wants to do lately is stay in his room and listen to music."

"Does he like music?"

"Yes."

"Maybe he could join the church choir. I'm the director. The children perform at the early service and the adults at the later one."

Rebecca stiffened, her jaw clenching. "You sound like a busy man. When do you have time for yourself?"

"Baseball and music are things I do for myself."

"Rebecca, you should see the children perform at church. Ever since Gabriel took over a few years back, the crowd of people attending our service has doubled. The choir is wonderful, and Gabriel's quite a singer. Rebecca used to be in her church's choir in Dallas."

He dropped his gaze from Rebecca's face, feeling the heat of a blush tinge his cheeks. He had never been comfortable with compliments. Singing was a gift God had given him, and he wanted to share it with others, use it to spread His word. God had been his salvation when he had hit bottom after his wife and child died.

Gabriel shifted in his chair. "We could always use another voice. Even if Peter doesn't want to sing, you're certainly welcome to join the adult choir."

Rebecca came to her feet. Feelings of being railroaded into doing something she wasn't ready to handle overwhelmed her. She had forgotten about how small towns were. All she wanted to do was hide and lick her wounds. She was afraid people like Gabriel wouldn't allow her to. "I think I hear Josh crying," she murmured and rushed from the room.

"I didn't hear anything," Gabriel said, frowning, not sure what had just happened.

Rose opened a can of kidney beans and one of tomatoes, then dumped the contents of both into the skillet. "I guess I shouldn't have pushed. Rebecca's faith has been shaken ever since Craig left her. I know I'm supposed to forgive that man for what he did to my family, but I'm having a hard time. He walked out on Rebecca, Peter and Josh when they needed him the most. All he left her was a note on her pillow. She woke up one morning, and her marriage of twelve years was over." Rose snapped her fingers. "Just like that."

How could a man walk out on his family? Gabriel wondered, continually surprised by how easily some people discarded their children and wives when he would give anything to have a family. Memories of his loss engulfed him. Pain constricted his chest, making it difficult to breathe. In a few seconds, three years before, his whole life had been changed because a man had decided to drink and drive.

Gabriel started to say something when he heard footsteps approaching the kitchen. When Rebecca entered, she held a baby in her arms close to her chest. She placed the child in a swing set up in the corner, adjusted some tiny pillows to prop the boy up, then started it. When Gabriel saw Josh's features, he knew something was wrong.

Rebecca caught him staring at the child. "My son has Down's syndrome. His second birthday will be in six weeks, and yet he doesn't look a day over one."

Gabriel didn't know what to say to her announcement. She made it sound almost a challenge. Was the child the reason her husband had left? If so, how could he turn his back on one of God's creations? He would have given anything to be able to hold his own son, to cradle him to his chest. That wasn't possible, never would be.

"I hope you're planning a big party. Birthdays are important to children," Gabriel said, as though he was an expert on children when he had never really experienced the joys of fatherhood. His son had only lived a few hours. A tightness gripped his throat.

Rebecca went to the cabinet to get bowls. "I haven't thought that far ahead. I've been a little preoccupied lately with the move and all." She heard the defensive tone in her voice and winced as she withdrew the bowls and closed the cabinet door.

"If you need any help—"

"No, I'm fine." She cut in, not wanting to hear his offer of assistance when she had never been able to get Craig even to change Josh's diaper. Again she experienced the stifling need to be alone to deal with the emotions threatening to overpower her. If it had been possible, she would have been better off staying in Dallas where she could get lost in a crowd.

"Rebecca!" Granny turned from the stove with the wooden spoon in her hand and a frown of disapproval on her face.

Rebecca immediately regretted her cool interruption. She attempted a smile that she knew didn't reach her eyes and said, "I'm sorry. It's been a long day."

"Go get Peter. Gabriel will set the table for us," her grandmother interjected.

Thankful to escape the kindness she glimpsed in Gabriel's dark eyes, she rushed from the kitchen and didn't slow her step until she was upstairs and outside Peter's bedroom. Pausing, she inhaled a steadying breath, then knocked on his door.

All she heard coming from the room was the blare of music. She knocked again, louder.

The door swung open, and Peter scowled at her. "I'm not hungry."

"Then you don't have to eat. But you do have to come down to dinner and sit while we eat. We have a guest tonight."

"Who?"

"Chief Stone."

Her son set his mouth in a firm line. She didn't know if she had the strength to fight him if he refused to come downstairs. She did need help, but she was alone in this world except for her grandmother whom she didn't want to burden with her problems. Granny wasn't in the best of health, having suffered a mild stroke several years before.

Peter pushed past her and stomped down the stairs.

Rebecca released her pent-up breath, then took a deep breath and blew it out through pursed lips. She needed to believe everything would work out, but each day she felt the weight on her shoulders growing.

Tears sprang into her eyes. She swiped at one that rolled down her cheek. She didn't have time to feel sorry for herself. Both Josh and Peter depended on her. Somehow she would hold this family together.

When she entered the kitchen and saw Gabriel sitting at the head of the kitchen table, she came to a halt inside the doorway. He looked at home, holding Josh, supporting his small body in the curve of his arm. Her heart slowed, then began to race at the sight of him smiling at her son. Josh smiled at Gabriel. The large, muscular man dwarfed her son, but the picture of the two of them seemed so right that Rebecca blinked as if she had been caught daydreaming the impossible.

For a few seconds Rebecca allowed herself to wonder how it would feel to have a man like Gabriel Stone supporting her emotionally, loving her children. She shook the thought from her mind. She could only depend on herself to keep this family together.

Chapter Two

"He wanted out of the swing when it stopped," Gabriel said, looking at her.

"Thank you for taking care of him," she murmured, retrieving her son from Gabriel and putting Josh into his high chair, again propping him with pillows so he could sit up. He was starting to support his weight, but he was still having trouble maintaining his balance for any length of time.

"There's a child in the church choir with Down's syndrome. He loves music."

"Josh does, too." Rebecca snapped on his bib.

Rose sat at the other end of the table, forcing Rebecca to take the chair next to Gabriel. "Let's join hands. Gabriel, will you give the blessing?"

Rebecca took Josh's tiny hand and Gabriel's larger one. The touch of Gabriel's fingers about hers sent warmth up her arm. The link felt natural and right. That surprised her.

"Heavenly Father, we come to this table to offer our thanks for this wonderful food. Please watch over us and give us the strength to deal with our problems."

The devotion in his voice gave Rebecca a sense of peace for the first time that day. She relished the blessing and wished she could feel that kind of love and faith again.

While Rose spooned chili into a bowl, then passed it to Peter, Rebecca fed Josh his baby food, mashed bananas and roast beef, two of his favorites. She introduced another food, strained carrots. He made a face and spit the carrots out. She dabbed at the orange that ran down his chin.

"Way to go, Josh. I hate carrots, too," Peter said, the first enthusiasm he had shown all day.

"So far, I haven't been able to find too many vegetables he likes." Rebecca tried another spoonful of carrots, which Josh immediately rejected.

"Have you tried mixing the bananas with the carrots and seeing if he'll eat that?" Gabriel set a chili bowl in front of Rebecca.

"Well, no. I suppose it wouldn't hurt." Rebecca dipped her spoon into the bananas and scooped some into the carrots. She wrinkled her nose at the mixture of light yellow and orange swirls.

When she fed Josh some of the new mixture, he kept most of it in his mouth. She gave him another spoonful, and he ate that, too.

"This might work with other vegetables, too. Thank you for the suggestion." Rebecca looked toward Gabriel.

His dark gaze caught hers and held it. "Anytime."

"Do you have any children?" she asked, realizing she knew nothing about this man and in many ways wished she did.

"No. Judy and I always wanted a whole house full." Pain flitted across his features for a few seconds before he managed to conceal his emotions.

"Judy is your wife?" Rebecca glimpsed a wedding ring on his left hand.

"She died three years ago." He touched his wedding ring, twisting it on his finger. "We had hoped to start a family when we moved here. It never happened."

"But he's determined to make up for that. He takes every child he can under his wing." Rose sipped water, her eyes twinkling.

Here was a man who had wanted children but didn't have any while her husband hadn't wanted to care for his two sons. Life wasn't fair, Rebecca thought, a constriction in her throat making it impossible to say another word. She dropped her gaze and continued to feed Josh.

A few minutes later Gabriel asked, "May I try that? You haven't had a chance to eat any of this great chili yet."

Rebecca hid her surprise at his request. She had always been the one to feed Josh. It was her responsibility, and she hadn't asked anyone else to do it. "I guess so."

"I've been watching you. I think I've got your technique down," he said with a sparkle in his dark brown eyes.

She blushed at the idea that he had been watching what she'd been doing. The thought unnerved her more than she cared to think about.

"Eat while I finish up with this roast beef and banana-carrot combo."

Rebecca delved into the chili, filling her bowl with the delicious-smelling food. She was starved and hadn't realized it until she started eating. While she savored her meal, she watched Gabriel make a game of feeding her son. Josh smiled and cooed. Why couldn't this have been Craig enjoying his child?

"You know, Peter," Gabriel said while pretending to be a dive bomber coming in for a landing in Josh's mouth, "I noticed how fast you were running into the house. Have you ever thought about being on a baseball team?"

"Nope. I have better things to do after school."

"It does require a lot of time. It takes quite a commitment for a young man."

The challenge in Gabriel's voice dared Peter to accept. Her eldest straightened, his eyes becoming pinpoints. Peter didn't say anything, but he studied the police chief as though he wasn't quite sure what to make of the man.

At the end of the meal Gabriel wiped Josh's mouth. "Rose, that's the best food I've had in a long time. Thank you for inviting me to dinner."

"You're welcome." Rose gripped her cane and struggled to her feet. "Josh, Peter and I are going to retire to the living room while you two clean up. Peter, will you carry him for me?"

"Sure, Granny." Peter carefully picked up Josh and followed his great-grandmother out of the room. "It's time for us to practice, Josh, my man."

Rebecca started taking dishes to the sink. "You don't have to help. I can take care of this mess if you need to leave."

"No. I told Rose I would help, and I always follow through on what I say." Gabriel brought several bowls and glasses to the counter.

While she rinsed the dishes, he put them into the dishwasher. They worked side by side in a silence that Rebecca didn't find awkward. A sense of teamwork eased any tension she experienced from his nearness. She usually felt the need to fill the void in a conversation with chitchat, but for some reason she didn't with Gabriel. Another surprise, she thought.

When she was through with the dishes, she noticed that it was dark outside the window over the sink. She reached to pull the shade down at the same time Gabriel turned toward her. Their arms grazed. Again that sense of warmth fanned from his touch. Startled by the brief contact, she flinched.

"Sorry. I didn't mean to bump into you," he said with a smile that crinkled the corners of his eyes, lending an appealing attraction to his tanned features.

"No problem." Rebecca yanked on the cord to lower the shade, then wrung out the washcloth to wipe the table and counters.

She felt Gabriel's gaze on her while she worked.

The thought of him watching her made her heart beat faster. The silence between them hummed with alarming undercurrents. Her battered emotions were too raw for anything but friendship between them, if even that.

"I'm just about through in here if you want to go into the living room and join the others," she said, aware that her hands quivered.

He lounged against the counter, his stance casual, relaxed. "I'll wait. Can I help with anything else?"

She shook her head while she hurried the cleaning, the nape of her neck tingling where she imagined him staring.

"May I ask you a question?"

She pivoted toward him, clasping the edge of the kitchen table she had been wiping. Her legs felt weak, as though the strength had suddenly been siphoned from them. "Shoot." She laughed nervously. "Maybe I shouldn't say that to a policeman."

That warm smile of his touched his mouth again. "Josh doesn't just have Down's syndrome, he has something else wrong with him, doesn't he?"

Her grip tightened until her knuckles turned white. "Yes. He has spina bifida. His spine isn't developed. The doctors told me that he would never walk, talk or do anything."

"I'm sorry. That has to be hard on you."

Rebecca stared into his troubled gaze for a long moment, then shoved away from the table and draped the washcloth over the edge of the sink. "It's harder on Josh," she finally said as she headed for the living room.

She came to a stop in the doorway, aware that Gabriel was right behind her, looking over her shoulder. Peter clasped Josh under the arms and was helping him across the carpet. Tears returned to block her throat. Every night Peter practiced "walking" with Josh. Her oldest son was determined that Josh would one day play sports with him. That, according to the doctors, would never happen, and she didn't have the heart to tell Peter.

Gabriel set his hands on her shoulders and leaned close to whisper, "You're lucky to have such a nice family."

The wistful tone in his voice made Rebecca ache for what he must have lost when his wife died. His words helped her focus on what was right with her life. "Yes, thank you for reminding me of that."

When he dropped his hands, she immediately missed the warmth of his touch.

Through the fog of sleep, Rebecca heard the doorbell ringing. She dragged herself out of bed, slipped on her robe, then hurried to the front door. She peered out the peephole and saw Gabriel Stone. Why was he here at this hour? Then a thought struck her, and she quickly opened the door. Standing next to the police chief was Peter, for a second time in one day wearing a defiant expression on his face.

"Sorry to bother you at such a late hour, but I found your son running from a house that had just been egged."

"Whose house?"

"Mine."

"Peter Michaels, what do you have to say for yourself?"

Her son looked away, his frown deepening, his mouth pinched as though he wouldn't say a word no matter what.

A chill swept her. Rebecca pulled her terry-cloth robe tighter about her and stepped to the side. "Please come in. I don't want to discuss this out on the porch for the whole town to hear."

Gabriel made sure that Peter entered the house before he came inside. "I'm willing to forget this incident. Since tomorrow's Saturday Peter can come by my house to clean up the mess."

"He'll be there. And when he's through cleaning up the eggs, he can do some other chores for you."

"I'll take care of my mess, but that's all." Peter crossed his arms over his chest, his features arranged in a stubborn expression.

Rebecca drew in a deep, bracing breath, so tired from no sleep and unpacking that all she wanted to do was collapse into a chair to have this discussion with her son. She gripped the banister, using it to support her weight. "That's not debatable." She looked toward Gabriel. "What time do you want us there?"

"Eight will be fine, if that's not too early for you."

"Are you kidding? I'm up at the crack of dawn with Josh."

"You can't make me!" Peter shouted, running up the stairs. "I won't go!"

Rebecca's first instinct was to hurry after her eldest, but when she heard his bedroom door slam shut, she winced and decided it wouldn't do any good. She might say something she would regret, because at the moment her patience was worn thin.

"I'm sorry, Rebecca. I hated to have to bring him home this way and at such an hour."

She shook her head. "You did the only thing you could. I didn't even know he was gone. He's never sneaked out before." She attempted a smile that she knew faltered. "At least not that I'm aware of. I'm afraid lately I don't know what my son is thinking or doing." She ran her hand through her hair, suddenly conscious of the fact that she must look a mess.

Gabriel smiled. "He'll come around when he gets used to Oakview. It's hard moving to a new town."

"We used to be very close until…" Rebecca couldn't finish the thought. She was tired of thinking about the past and what used to be.

"You don't have to come tomorrow morning. I'll make sure Peter does what he needs to do and I'll put him to work after he cleans up the eggs."

Rebecca straightened from the banister. "Peter's my problem, not yours. We'll be there tomorrow morning at eight sharp."

"If you need any help—"

"I appreciate the kind offer, but I'm fine." Rebecca walked to the front door and opened it.

Gabriel paused in the entrance and turned to say something but stopped when he saw her standing so proud and untouchable. She didn't know how to accept his help, and he wouldn't make things worse by saying anything else to her. She had enough to deal with. But it didn't stop his desire to wipe the sadness from her eyes.

He nodded, murmured, "Till tomorrow," and strode away from her house.

He climbed into the squad car and sat for a few minutes staring at a light in one of the upstairs bedrooms. The silence of the night soothed him, and he bowed his head. "Please, Lord, give me the guidance I need to help Rebecca and her children." He closed his eyes, drawing strength from the knowledge that He would be with him, that He would show him how to help Rebecca, Peter and Josh.

When Gabriel started the car, he felt calm, at peace as he always did after he communicated with God. He started to back out of the driveway when the radio sounded in the quiet. He responded to the call from the station, knowing it wouldn't be good.

"Stone here."

"There has been some vandalism at the school baseball field. Thought you might want to know, sir. I called your house, and when there wasn't an answer, I thought you might be out."

"Thanks, Bob. I'll head over there and take a look."

When Gabriel arrived at the baseball field, he immediately noticed the large window on the side of the main building was shattered. Taking his flashlight, he checked the area outside before shining the light through the smashed window, glass shards glittering on the concrete floor. Relieved to find the inside undisturbed, he headed for the front to have a closer look around. By the door he stepped on a broken egg in the gravel.

Peter Michaels. Of course, he had no proof the damage had been done by the boy, but he would stake his career on it. Peter might not realize it, but Gabriel could tell when someone was crying out for help and he intended to give the boy that help, starting first thing tomorrow morning.

Rebecca pushed the bell again and heard its blare so she knew it was working. Suddenly the door jerked open, and she automatically stepped back. Gabriel with messed-up hair and a day's growth of beard greeted her with a puzzled look.

"What time is it?" he asked, combing his fingers through his conservatively styled black hair.

"Eight." She curled her fingers around the handle of the stroller that held Josh, staring at the overpowering man who had haphazardly dressed in a pair of jeans, a white T-shirt but no shoes.

Gabriel glanced at his watch. "I must have slept through

my alarm. Sorry. Got to bed later than usual last night. There was a break-in at the baseball field." He directed his gaze toward Peter, who stood next to Rebecca.

She looked from the man to the boy, wondering if something was going on. Could Peter have been involved with the break-in? She hoped not, because if that was the case she had a bigger problem than her child not liking Oakview. "Peter, did you do anything else last night besides egg Chief Stone's house?"

The boy's bottom lip stuck out, and he stared at a point by his shoes. "What do you think I am? Stupid?"

"No. On the contrary, I think you're very smart," Rebecca replied, realizing her son hadn't answered her question. From his expression she also realized she wouldn't get an answer out of him.

"Come inside while I put some coffee on. I have to have at least a cup before I can start functioning in the morning." Gabriel moved to allow them entrance into his home.

Rebecca hesitated. She had only come with Peter to make sure he showed up. After a confrontation in his bedroom, she couldn't be sure of anything with her son.

"My coffee isn't as good as Rose's, but it's not too bad." Gabriel waved them inside.

Rebecca picked up Josh and followed Peter into the house, trying to dismiss her eldest son's anger. When she'd grounded him for shouting at her earlier, he had laughed as though what she had said meant nothing to him.

"Have you all had breakfast?"

"Granny won't let anyone leave without a proper

start to the day, as she refers to breakfast." Rebecca held Josh close, comforted by his presence.

"Has she fixed you her cinnamon rolls yet?"

"Last Sunday. When I woke up, the house smelled of cinnamon and baking bread."

"What a wonderful way to start the Lord's day."

Rebecca glanced around at the house as she walked toward the back. His living room looked comfortable, with a navy and burgundy plaid couch, large pillows and stacks of magazines and books. She pictured him stretched out in his navy blue recliner, reading a book while a fire blazed in the fireplace and soft music played in the background. His home reflected the man, comfortable and laid-back.

"Have a seat while I put the coffee on."

Rebecca settled herself at the kitchen table, made of sturdy oak with enough chairs to seat a family of six. She placed Josh on her lap, pleased to see her youngest son show interest in his surroundings. Light streamed through the large window over the sink. She smiled, thinking it was appropriate for a lawman to decorate in red, white and blue.

Peter remained by the doorway into the kitchen, such anger on his face that Gabriel wished again for a magic answer on how to help the Michaels family. *Keep the faith. God has His own timetable,* he reminded himself as he sat across from Rebecca. *The answer will come when the time is right.*

"If you want to get started on the cleanup, Peter, I have a bucket and a scrub brush in the garage through there." Gabriel pointed toward a utility room.

Peter shot Gabriel a look full of anger, then stomped toward the garage, muttering something that Gabriel was glad he wasn't privy to. There was a limit to every person's patience, and with Peter he was afraid he would need an extra dose.

Gabriel looked at Rebecca, who was watching her son leave. The sadness in her eyes contracted his heart. "Physical labor will help him get rid of some of that hostility."

While her gaze connected with Gabriel's, Rebecca hugged Josh closer, as though he could shield her from heartache. "He's so full of anger. I've tried talking to him about it, but he won't say anything." Again the scene in her son's bedroom swamped her with feelings of inadequacy. Peter was a different child from the year before.

"Have you tried counseling?"

"Yes. He just sat there, determined not to say a word to the woman."

"How about the minister of your church?"

Rebecca shook her head.

"Ours is very good with young people."

"No." She answered so quickly she surprised even herself. "I'm sure he wouldn't respond to a stranger," she offered in explanation.

Gabriel noticed the firm set to Rebecca's mouth, the tension transmitted in the rigid lines of her body, and knew she would reject any coaxing to get Peter or herself to talk with Reverend Carson. "Then let me try to help."

"I can't accept—"

Gabriel held up his hand to stop her flow of words. "I'm worried about Peter. I think he might have vandalized the baseball-field house. I found a broken egg by the front door. I don't believe in coincidences."

Rebecca closed her eyes for a few seconds. She adjusted Josh in her arms and kissed the top of his head, drawing strength from her youngest. "He might be innocent. You don't know he did anything."

"What do you think in your heart?"

She rubbed her cheek against Josh's hair, then peered at Gabriel, her eyes glistening. "What do I do?"

"Let me help. I've dealt with troubled children before, and not as a lawman."

Again she shifted Josh in her arms, looking away from Gabriel.

"May I hold Josh?" The need to hold the child ran deep in him. Gabriel had missed so much with his own son.

Her gaze returned to his, confusion deep in her eyes. She hesitated, then rose and handed Gabriel her child. Josh's big brown eyes focused on his face. A tightness threatened to close his throat as he stared at the small boy in his embrace. He supported Josh in the crook of his arm. Smiling at him, Gabriel found himself making silly faces to get the child to grin. And when Josh did, Gabriel's heart swelled with pride.

"How are his ears today?"

"Last night he slept through the night for the first time in several weeks. I think the medicine is finally working. At least I hope so."

Gabriel tore his gaze from the child and looked at Josh's mother. Holding Josh only underscored for Gabriel what he was missing. The emptiness inside pushed to the foreground.

"So do I. It's not easy going without sleep," he finally said, realizing an awkward silence had descended.

She sighed. "Something I'm quickly finding out."

"What are your plans now that you've moved to Oakview?" He had dealt with his loss and didn't want to renew the feelings of anguish.

"I need to get a job soon."

"You know I might be able to help you with that."

A closed expression settled over Rebecca's features. "You've already done enough."

"Nonsense. What are friends for? Let me ask around. What are your qualifications?"

When she laughed, there was no humor in the sound. "I don't have any."

"Everyone has qualifications."

"I've been a mother and wife for the past ten years. I suppose I can clean houses, chauffeur and organize PTA meetings." She snapped her fingers. "Oh, and I have some computer skills. We had one at home."

"What will you do with Josh when you go to work?"

She cocked her head. "Frankly, I don't know. I can't

keep staying at Granny's house and not contribute to the finances."

"I'm finished. Can we go now?" Peter announced from the doorway into the utility room.

"You still owe me some of your time."

Peter folded his arms. "How much?"

"I'll take you home in the early afternoon." Gabriel glanced at Rebecca to make sure that was all right with her.

She nodded, then stood to take Josh from Gabriel. "We'd better be going. I want Josh to take a nap in his own crib."

"I have baseball practice this afternoon, so Peter should be home by two. I'll feed him lunch."

"Fine," she mumbled as she started for the door. When Gabriel rose to escort her, she added, "I can find my own way out. Finish your coffee."

Peering at his mug, he realized he hadn't taken a sip of his cold coffee. He dumped the brew into the sink and poured some more into his cup, steamy whiffs of the hot liquid wafting to him.

"What do I have to do?" Peter asked in a surly voice.

Gabriel brought the mug to his lips and took a long sip of the coffee, purposefully waiting a good minute to answer the boy. "This is my Saturday to do yard work at the church. You're going to help me."

Peter opened his mouth to reply, then snapped his jaws together, his teeth making a clicking sound.

"Why don't you go check on Lady out back?"

"Lady?"

"My dog. She has puppies. See if there's enough water for them while I get ready." Gabriel watched the child stalk to the back door and yank it open, anger in every line of the boy's body. The next few hours could be very long.

"Peter, this is David Carson. He's going to help us." Gabriel opened the door to the church's shed and went inside.

"You're the new kid at school," David said with a wide grin.

"Yeah. What of it?"

David's smile vanished. "Nothing. Just making conversation."

Gabriel heard the wonderful start to the exchange between the two boys and wasn't so sure it was a good idea to have David here helping. He had thought introducing Peter to some nice kids his age would make the situation easier.

Gabriel handed David a plastic lawn bag. "First, we need to pick up any trash, then pull weeds in the gardens."

Peter crossed his arms and refused to take the bag Gabriel held for him. "I don't pick up trash."

"There's a first time for everything." Gabriel stood his ground.

Peter narrowed his eyes and stuck out his lower lip. Then when Gabriel thought Peter would run away, he yanked the bag from Gabriel's hand and stomped off toward the nearest garden.

"What's his problem?" David asked, jerking his right thumb toward Peter.

Gabriel watched Peter yank up a plant that wasn't a weed. "He needs a friend. I thought you might help me out there."

David's eyes grew round. "Are you sure? At school he isn't very friendly. Keeps to himself."

Gabriel clasped David on the shoulder. "You've grown up here. Everyone is familiar to you. What do you think it would be like if that wasn't the case?"

"I guess, scary."

"My point exactly." Gabriel squeezed David's shoulder briefly, then added, "Let's go see if we can save some of the plants."

Two hours later Gabriel stepped back to inspect their work, pleased. He had managed to save most of the plants, and the gardens looked great. He took pride in maintaining these beds as though it was his statement about the glory of God to the world. The flowers showcased the beauty He was capable of.

"Let's take a break and go inside to get some sodas." Gabriel took the plastic bags from the two boys.

David headed for the door. Peter stared at the church, hesitating.

"I'll stay and do some more work," Peter said as Gabriel started to follow David.

"Even God declared a day of rest. You worked hard. You deserve a break."

Peter blinked as though Gabriel's words surprised him.

"He welcomes everyone into His house." Gabriel walked toward the church, hoping that the child would join David and him. But he knew he couldn't force Peter. He had to want to come inside the Lord's house.

Gabriel selected a soft drink after David, then propped himself against the wall and sipped his soda. His disappointment grew as the minutes ticked by and Peter didn't appear.

Gabriel had half finished his soft drink when Peter shuffled into the alcove outside the large meeting room. "What do you want to drink?"

Peter scanned the choices in the machine. His eyes lit up for a few seconds. "Strawberry cream soda."

"Hey, that's my favorite. No one else at school likes it." David tipped up his can and emptied it.

"They just don't know a great drink when they see it." Peter took the can from Gabriel, then moved back, keeping his distance.

"This is probably the only vending machine in town with strawberry cream sodas. Dad keeps it stocked for me."

"Dad?"

"He's the minister here."

"Oh. Isn't that kinda hard on you?" Peter asked as though it were a disease to have a father be a minister.

David laughed. "Nah. Dad's pretty cool about things."

Peter tipped the can to his mouth and nearly drained it in one long swallow. "Mmm. I haven't had one of these in a while. Mom couldn't find it at the grocery store last week."

"Now you know where to come if you ever run out at home. The church is always open." Gabriel tossed his empty can into the trash. "Ready to get back to work?"

"Sure. We've got baseball practice later today, and our coach is a real stickler for being on time." David slid a glance toward Gabriel, then crushed his can and aimed for the trash bin several feet away. The can landed in the container. "Yes! I haven't lost my touch since basketball season."

Peter frowned. "You play a lot of sports?"

"Yeah. You should come out for the baseball team."

"I don't play baseball." Peter dropped his can into the trash and shuffled out of the alcove ahead of Gabriel and David.

When Gabriel stepped outside, he said, "That offer to come out for the team still stands. We take newcomers all the time." He knew he was taking a risk by extending the invitation again. He didn't particularly want to spend another late night cleaning up the field house.

"Yeah, we need someone who's fast," David said, hurrying to catch up with Peter.

"I don't run, either." Peter came to a halt in front of the shed, his frown firmly in place.

"I've seen you in gym class. You're fast. Even our teacher said something about that the other day."

Peter slanted a look toward David. A thoughtful expression replaced Peter's frown. "Nah. She just wanted to make me feel welcome." He dug the toe of his shoe into the dirt.

"Not Mrs. Hinds. She loves to point out a kid's bad points. She's the regular terror of our school."

Peter laughed. "Yeah, I kinda figured that the first day."

Gabriel walked into the shed while the boys discussed the gym teacher who had been at the school thirty years, prodding children who preferred to sit in front of a television into exercising. Hearing Peter's laughter firmed his resolve to help the boy. He again said a silent prayer for assistance.

Several hours later, at the local diner, Gabriel and the boys ate hamburgers and fries. After their lunch Gabriel took David home, then Peter. As Gabriel pulled into the driveway, he saw Rebecca sitting on the porch swing and couldn't resist the urge to say a few words to her.

As he approached, he noticed Rebecca's brow knitted in worry, her hands clutching a letter. He wanted to ask her if he could help, but remembered her reaction when he had. She felt she had to struggle alone.

"Something wrong?"

Rebecca lifted her head, squeezing her eyes closed for a few seconds. Seeing the sheen of tears, he fought the urge to hold her close.

She swallowed several times, then looked toward him. "An overdue bill from the hospital."

Gabriel eased beside her on the porch swing. He remained quiet, allowing her to set the pace and tone of the conversation.

"You know, I tried to explain to them that I'll pay when I can. You can't get blood out of a turnip. It's not like I don't put something toward the bill each month." She shrugged, trying to smile but failing. "I guess they didn't like the small amount this month. I need a job *now.*"

"If I hear of anything, I'll let you know right away. Of course, since this is a small town, you might have to go to Tulsa to look for a job."

"I know. I hope not." She balled the bill in her hand. "How did Peter do?"

"Not bad. He enjoyed playing with my mutt, Lady. She has three puppies that are all over the place. He was in the midst of them when I went out back to get him."

"Craig would never let Peter have a pet."

The more he heard about Rebecca's ex-husband, the more he was glad the man didn't live in Oakview. Gabriel was afraid the man would test his faith. Some people didn't know how to appreciate what God had given them. "After a rocky start, Peter and David Carson got along pretty good."

"I'm glad to hear that. If Peter could make a friend, I think that'll help his adjustment."

"That's the plan."

With her head tilted, she stared at him. "Thank you. I appreciate the help."

Gabriel realized her admission had been difficult, and that made it all the more special. He smiled, pleased to see her return it, her eyes sparkling with a vivid blue. He was determined to show her she wasn't alone, that God was with her, and if she would accept him, he was too.

Chapter Three

"Well, my man, I hope you're ready for bed because your mother sure is. These late nights are killers," Rebecca said, picking Josh up and cradling him close.

She sat in the chair by the crib and began to rock. After she'd sung two lullabies, Josh closed his eyes and relaxed.

Rebecca heard her grandmother approaching the bedroom. She looked up to find Granny standing in the doorway. "I hope my singing didn't awaken you."

"Never. I love hearing you sing. I had to go to the bathroom, heard you up and thought I would check to see if Josh was asleep yet."

"Yes." Rebecca pushed to her feet and carefully laid her son in his crib. "I think tonight he'll sleep through to morning once again. At least I hope so." She came into the hallway.

"Peter didn't say anything at dinner about going to Gabriel's. Did he say anything afterwards?"

"He said something about a dog with puppies, then grumbled about pulling weeds at the church. That's all I got out of him." Rebecca sighed, remembering the one-word answers she had received from her eldest at the dinner table. The only time he had been a part of the family that day was when he had worked with Josh after supper.

"I'm glad he was at the church today. Gabriel usually works there on Saturdays, along with some of the young people. I hope Peter met some kids he could be friends with. That's what he needs, church and friends."

"He needs a father who will care about him. Craig hasn't called him in the two weeks we have been here. His birthday is coming up, and I know Peter will want his dad here to help him celebrate. What should I do?"

"Have you talked with Craig lately?"

"No, not since our move."

"Call him and let him know the importance of Peter's birthday to the child."

Rebecca rolled her shoulders and kneaded the tight cords of her neck. "I'm not sure my call would help the situation, but I'll try." She started for Peter's bedroom. "Peter's been unusually quiet this evening. No loud music from his room."

Rebecca opened the door and peered into the darkened bedroom. The window was up, allowing a soft breeze to stir the curtains, the scent of the outdoors to fill the room. A shaft of moonlight streamed through the opening and across Peter's empty bed.

"He's not here." Rebecca flipped on the overhead light and scanned the area. "Oh, no. He sneaked out again."

"He might be downstairs. Check the house first before you get too upset."

Rebecca inhaled deeply, but nothing alleviated the tension building inside. "You're probably right. He's downstairs watching television as we speak."

She made her way to the first floor and went from room to room. Finally, ten minutes later, she had to acknowledge that Peter wasn't in the house. She checked the front porch then the yard, and there was no sign of her son.

Granny appeared in the kitchen. "Gone?"

Rebecca nodded, her throat tight with suppressed emotion. She was scared. What kind of trouble was her eldest getting into at this very moment? Where was he? She sank onto a chair and buried her face in her hands. She felt so alone.

Her grandmother put her hand on Rebecca's shoulder. "Call Gabriel. He'll help."

She remembered Gabriel's suspicion about Peter vandalizing the field house. "But he's the police chief. What if—" Rebecca couldn't voice her fear that Peter was getting into trouble, the kind of trouble the law would be interested in.

"Gabriel is a friend of this family. Ask him to help."

She hated asking anyone for help, but fear compelled her to reach for the phone. Her hands trembling, Rebecca dialed the police chief's number. In less than twenty-four hours this man had become part of her new life.

Gabriel climbed into his squad car and gripped the steering wheel. Staring out the windshield, he tried to come up with another place Peter might go. The boy hadn't been at the usual hangouts or behind the store where Gabriel had first seen him.

Gabriel closed his eyes and bowed his head. "Dear Lord, please help me find Peter. He's hurting, and I want to help."

As he turned the key in the ignition, he suddenly knew where to find Rebecca's son. He backed out of the parking space at the rodeo grounds and headed for the high school baseball field. When he pulled into the lot next to the stands, he saw someone sitting in the bleachers, his head buried in his hands, the slump of his shoulders emphasizing his dejection.

Gabriel switched off his headlights and quietly climbed the stands. He hung back until his eyes adjusted to the dark and he could see who the person was. Relieved at finally finding the boy, Gabriel made his way toward Peter.

Gabriel hated sneaking up on someone but knew the boy would run if given the chance. He laid his hand on Peter's shoulder. The child gasped and turned.

"Easy, Peter. It's just me, Chief Stone." He kept his voice even, calm.

Peter started scrambling away. Gabriel's grip on his shoulder strengthened.

"Leave me alone. I didn't do anything wrong."

"Well, for starters, son, you're trespassing."

"I'm not your son!" Peter twisted and finally managed to slip from Gabriel's grasp.

The defensive anger in Peter's voice tore at Gabriel. "Don't make this any worse. Come on. Let's go to my car."

"No! I didn't do anything wrong," Peter shouted, so loudly Gabriel was sure the people who lived nearby heard him. "This baseball field belongs to the public, and I am part of the public."

Gabriel decided to change tactics. "Okay. If you want to stay, I'll stay." He sat down and waited, resting his elbows on his knees and loosely clasping his hands.

In the dim moonlight Gabriel saw the boy's mouth twist into a deep frown, his hands clenching and unclenching at his sides. Finally Peter took a seat and tried to ignore Gabriel. That was all right with him. He knew dealing with Peter would call upon his patience, and thankfully God had given him a huge reserve. Peter slumped and rested his chin in his palms.

"Your mom's worried about you," Gabriel said a few minutes later.

Peter stiffened, bringing his head up.

"Don't you think we should at least give her a call and let her know you're all right?"

"She doesn't care about me."

"Well, she certainly had me fooled earlier on the phone. I could have sworn I heard her crying."

Peter remained silent, leaning forward, his chin on

his fist, as though settling in for the night. He fixed his gaze on the baseball field, illuminated by the three-quarter moon.

Gabriel retrieved his cell phone from his shirt pocket and dialed Rebecca's number. "Peter's okay," he said when Rebecca answered on the first ring, and quickly filled her in on where he'd found Peter.

There was a moment's hesitation, then she asked, "Is there—did he cause any problems?"

"No," Gabriel said, not sure if Peter had vandalized the field house or not. His brief inspection on his way to the stands had revealed nothing wrong. "I'll bring him home soon."

"Thank you, Gabriel. I don't…" Her voice trailed into silence.

"You're welcome, Rebecca. Peter and I will see you in a while."

"Is she mad?"

Gabriel remembered the silence at the end, a vulnerable pause in her sentence while she tried to gather her composure. "She's more worried than anything."

"She's always worried."

"What about?" Gabriel asked, wanting to keep the fragile conversation going but realizing he wanted to know so much more about Rebecca Michaels than he did.

"Josh, Granny, money—me."

"I find that moms worry a lot. I think that's part of being a mother. Mine still worries about me, and I'm thirty-six years old and have been away from home for seventeen years."

"Yeah, well, I can take care of myself. I don't need nobody to worry about me."

Gabriel smiled at Peter's tough-sounding voice and remembered once there had been a time he'd thought the same thing. God had proven him wrong. God had shown him he wasn't alone in this world.

"Even when you're able to take care of yourself, it's nice to know someone is there for you."

"I don't need nobody," Peter said, the strength in his voice lessening slightly.

For a brief moment Gabriel felt himself hurled back twenty years. He had declared that same thing to his mother after his father had died, leaving him the man of the house with three younger siblings. In his anger he had nearly lost his way until his grandfather had shown him the power of the Lord's love. That power had been strengthened when Gabriel had lost his wife and son—a son who wouldn't be much older than Josh. Emotions he thought were behind him surfaced, knotting his throat. He had so wanted a family.

"It can get mighty lonely going through life by yourself," Gabriel finally said, twisting his wedding ring as memories of the day Judy had slid it on his finger seeped into his thoughts. He had never taken it off.

"But at least no one can let—" Peter snapped his mouth closed.

"Let you down?"

In the moonlight Peter tensed, his jaw clamped tight.

"Who let you down, Peter?"

"Nobody!" Peter shot to his feet. "I can find my own way home."

Gabriel rose. "No, I told your mother I would bring you home, and I'm going to do what I promised. You'll find that I always do."

"Fine!" The child shoved past him and hastened to the squad car.

Gabriel peered heavenward, noting the clear sky, the stars glittering in the blackness. The spring air was warm, the light breeze carrying a hint of honeysuckle. Perfect— except for the storm brewing at the Michaels's house. He felt Peter's anger as though it were a palpable force, reaching out to push everyone away. The child was determined to stand alone no matter who got in his way.

When Gabriel slid behind the steering wheel, he turned to Peter and asked, "Why did you come to the field tonight?"

The boy shrugged.

"Have you been thinking about my offer to join the team?"

"No way." Peter answered so fast Gabriel knew the opposite was true.

"If you don't want to play, I could use an assistant."

"I'm sure I won't be able to do anything for a while. Mom's gonna ground me longer for leaving the house. I'll probably not be able to do anything till summer."

"Then why did you do it?"

"'Cause I felt like it."

Gabriel heard the pout and stubbornness in the child's voice and again thought of how he had been after his father's death, so angry at the world. "What if I can get your mother to let you come out for the team?"

"Sure, why not. It beats staying in that old house. But I ain't gonna play."

Gabriel started the car, careful to keep from grinning. Once he had Peter at the baseball field, he would get the boy involved in the team as more than an assistant. Of course, he had to convince Rebecca to allow Peter to practice after school. Normally he wouldn't think that was a problem, but with Rebecca, he didn't know what to expect.

Rebecca answered the door on the first knock, throwing her arms around Peter's stiff body and pulling him against her. "Don't ever scare me like that again." She stood him away from her and inspected him as though afraid he had been hurt. "Why did you leave?"

Her son shuffled back a few steps and looked at his feet. "I needed some fresh air." He lifted his head and fixed his gaze on her.

Rebecca wanted to shake some sense into him but knew anger wouldn't bring about the peace she so desperately needed. She balled her hands at her sides and counted to ten. When she still wasn't calm, she started for one hundred. "We'll talk about this in the morning."

Peter's chin went up a notch. "Why not now? You're just gonna ground me."

Her fingernails dug into her palms. "I don't know what I'm going to do. I do know that I need to calm down first or I might regret what I say."

"Tell him—" Peter nodded toward Gabriel "—that I'm grounded and won't be able to help with the baseball team after school."

"Why, that's a great idea, Peter. You should become involved with a sport."

"Oh, good grief." Her son tramped across the entrance hall.

"Peter, I'll see you Monday right after school at the field. Wear your tennis shoes," Gabriel called as the boy fled up the stairs.

At the top her son stopped. "I might be busy. Mrs. Harris wants to see me."

"Then come as soon as you can."

Peter frowned, started to say something else, then stalked toward his bedroom.

"Mrs. Harris wants to see him?" Rebecca stared at the place her son had been standing. "That's the first I heard of it. Of course, that doesn't surprise me. Lately, there's a lot I don't know about my son. We used to be so close." She massaged the muscles in her neck and shoulders to ease the tightness. "I can't believe you talked Peter into going out for the baseball team."

"I didn't, exactly. He's going to be my assistant."

"Assistant? That's even more of a surprise."

Gabriel chuckled. "I sort of backed him into a corner."

Rebecca slanted another look up the stairs, her heart beating normally again. Her vivid imagination had conjured up all kinds of trouble for Peter. "Did he say anything to you about why he left the house?"

"No, not exactly. For a second I thought he was going to tell me about someone letting him down."

"No doubt me for moving here."

"I think it's someone else. Talk to him tomorrow. Maybe he will be ready to tell you."

"Maybe," she murmured, knowing in her heart that her eldest wouldn't talk to her about what was troubling him. In the past year their relationship had unraveled, and she didn't know how to stop it from coming completely apart. "Thanks again for all your help."

"It's part of my job. I'm just glad it ended okay."

"Yeah, but you've lost several nights of sleep because of my family."

"I wasn't in bed yet. I was trying to read a book and not getting very far." He started to turn away and stopped. "I was going to call you anyway tomorrow."

"You were?"

"Jenny, our file clerk at the station, decided to elope last night. I got a call from her late this afternoon. She and her new husband are going to live in Oklahoma City. We could use a new file clerk, sometimes a dispatcher. It doesn't pay much, but I hope you'll apply."

"File clerk? I think I can handle that."

"There's some computer work involved, too."

"That shouldn't be a problem. If I don't know your programs, I should be able to pick it up quickly."

A smile flashed across his face. "Then call the station and set up an interview with my secretary, Mabel."

Rebecca watched Gabriel stroll away, both elated and apprehensive. With a job on the horizon, she had to work out child care for Josh. She didn't want to leave him, and yet she had to earn some money to support her family, to pay the bills. Craig wasn't reliable, and Josh's care was expensive. If she got the job at the police station, at least she would be staying in Oakview. As she closed the front door, she pushed her doubts to the background and made a promise to herself. Gabriel Stone would not regret giving her this chance.

Chapter Four

Rebecca heard the back door slam. Peering into the kitchen, she saw Peter go to the refrigerator. He took a jug of ice water out and poured himself a tall glass.

"How was practice today?" Rebecca came into the room, hoping that her son would finally say more than two words to her. She'd never had the talk with Peter because he'd avoided her, and she knew the uselessness of having a conversation with him when he was in a rotten mood.

"Just great," he mumbled. "One of my favorite things is to run laps around a baseball diamond." The frown carved into his features belied his words.

"I thought you were the assistant."

"Yeah, well, it seems the assistant runs along with everyone else, even the coaches. Something that Coach Stone forgot to tell me the other night."

"I guess you couldn't very well stand there watching everyone run."

"Right, and he knew that I'd feel awkward." Peter's frown deepened as he trudged to the sink and put his glass in it.

Rebecca looked at her son's dress shoes. "Where are your sneakers? You didn't run in those, did you?"

"Yes." Peter stared at the sink as though he had never seen it before. "I forgot them, but *he* didn't believe me. He made me run anyway."

"Did you really forget them?"

Peter whirled. "Yes, of course!"

"But you never wear your dress shoes to school."

"Well, I wanted to today." He glared at her, daring her to disagree.

"Let's talk, Peter."

"Now? I'm beat."

"Then have a seat at the table." Rebecca gestured toward it. "We've put this off too long. We need to talk about Saturday night." She made her voice firm, no-nonsense sounding.

Peter loudly sighed but walked to the table and plopped into a chair, slouching against its caned back.

"Chief Stone thinks that you're upset because you feel someone has let you down."

"He should mind his own business," Peter mumbled, picking at the bright yellow place mat in front of him.

"Lately you have been his business. When you disappeared the other night, you became his business."

"Only because you called him." He stabbed her with a defiant glare.

"I was afraid something bad would happen to you. Nine-year-old boys don't go out at midnight."

"I'm gonna be ten soon." Peter dropped his gaze and began to roll the place mat at the corner.

"Ten-year-old boys don't, either."

"I'm not a baby anymore."

Rebecca grasped his hand. "I know that. Both Josh and I depend on you, honey. That's why I can't have you leaving the house late at night. I don't know what I would do without you." Emotion welled in her throat.

Peter kept his head down, his shoulders slumped.

"Promise me you won't do that again."

He mumbled what she thought was a yes.

"And as long as you're involved with the baseball team, I won't extend your grounding. I think it's important you do something like that." She realized the second she said those words that she might be dooming Peter's participation with the team. Lately he seemed to go out of his way not to do what she wanted. "Now, speaking of your birthday, what do you want to do for it? We could have a party and invite—"

Peter's head shot up, and he yanked his hand from her clasp. "I don't know anyone in Oakview to invite. All of my friends are back in Dallas."

"Then what do you want to do?"

Chewing on his lower lip, he glanced away then at her. "I want to go fishing with Dad like we used to."

The tightness in her throat spread. Her lungs burned. Craig and Peter used to go fishing at least once a month.

Her son loved to fish and hadn't been since Craig had left them. "Then we'll call him and see what we can set up."

His face brightened. "We can?"

"Yes, let's call this evening after he gets home from work."

"Great!" Peter jumped to his feet. "I'd better go do my homework."

As he ran from the kitchen, her grandmother came into the room. "My, who lit a fire under that young man?"

"Granny, I'm so afraid he's going to be disappointed."

"Why, child?"

"He wants Craig to take him fishing on his birthday."

"Oh." Granny sank into the chair that Peter had occupied.

"I told him we'll call him tonight and see if he can. I shouldn't have. What if—"

"Rebecca, have faith. Everything will work out for the best. You just wait and see." Her grandmother patted her hand, then pushed to her feet. "Now, if I don't get moving, we won't have dinner tonight."

"Let me check on Josh and then I'll be back down to help. I think my little man has finally decided to catch up on all the sleep he missed this past week."

Rebecca climbed the stairs to the second floor. She peered at Peter's bedroom door and noticed that it was open. Lately he always closed it when he was in his room. She started to look in, to see if everything was all right with her eldest son, when she heard his voice coming from her bedroom.

She paused in the doorway. Peter had Josh on the bed, changing his diaper and making funny faces at him.

"Okay, big guy, that ought to fix ya right up. Tonight we'll practice extra hard on our walking. Don't want to slack on the job. I want ya chasing me around this house before the year is out. Think of all the things I can teach ya to do." Peter lifted Josh high in the air, then swung him from side to side.

Josh's giggles blended with his older brother's laughter. The sound pierced Rebecca's heart. She cleared her throat.

Peter whirled, surprise evident in his expression. "I heard Josh and thought I'd better check up on him."

How could she tell Peter his dream wouldn't come true for his little brother? The pain in her heart expanded. "Will you watch Josh while I help Granny with dinner?"

"I guess," Peter said, replacing the surprise on his face with his usual sullen expression. But he held his little brother close as though protecting Josh from the world.

Crossing her legs, Rebecca smoothed her black calf-length skirt. Her heart pounding against her chest, she clasped her hands tightly in her lap.

"Chief Stone will see you now," a short, gray-haired

woman announced when she appeared in the reception area of the police station.

Rebecca rose, took a deep, calming breath and entered the office the older woman indicated with a wave.

Gabriel came around his desk, offering his hand for Rebecca to shake. "I'm glad you applied. Since the pay isn't much, I wasn't sure you would."

"How could I refuse? Your offer is the only one I've had."

He grinned. "I have to admit there aren't many jobs in Oakview, but we aren't too far from Tulsa where I'm sure you can find a better-paying job."

Warmth flowed through her at his smile, warmth meant to put her at ease, and it did. Her tension evaporated as she responded to his compassion. "I can't spend anymore time away from Josh than is necessary. Driving to and from Tulsa would add an extra hour and half to my work day as well as eat into my salary."

"Who's going to take care of Josh?"

"Granny, until I can come up with a more permanent solution. Peter will help when school is out in a few months and Ann, next door, has volunteered to help Granny until then."

"Josh is welcome here if you get in a bind."

"Then I have the job?"

"Yes. I wish it were more."

"It's a job, and as you know, I need one."

Gabriel sat on the corner of his desk, his stance casual, openly friendly. "When can you start?"

Rebecca noticed him absently twirling his wedding ring on his finger and marveled at the depth of love he must have had for his wife. What would it be like to have a man love her that much? "Tomorrow if you need me," she finally answered after clearing her throat.

"Jenny hasn't been gone more than a day, but her work is already stacking up. If you can start tomorrow, that'll be great." Gabriel rose and headed for his office door. "How's Peter today?"

"Limping around. He hasn't done that much exercise lately, and his muscles are protesting."

"I'm sorry. I didn't realize he was so out of shape." Rebecca recalled her eldest groaning as he descended the stairs that morning for school. "Don't be. This will be good for him. I don't think he was too upset by the sore muscles. I didn't hear a word of complaint from him at the breakfast table this morning, and he took his tennis shoes to school today. Believe me, lately he's the first to complain if he's upset about something."

"Good. I know it wasn't comfortable for him running around the baseball field in loafers, but everyone who shows up participates. I didn't want him to be any different."

Gabriel brushed against her as he reached to open the door at the same time she did. Rebecca stepped away, nonplussed by the casual touch. Their gazes linked for a few seconds before Gabriel swung the door open and called, "Mabel, I believe you've already met Rebecca Michaels. She's our new file clerk. Rebecca will be starting tomorrow at eight. You'll be working closely with Mabel, helping her with her job."

"Welcome aboard." Mabel pumped Rebecca's hand several times.

"She used to be in the Navy," Gabriel whispered so loud everyone within a few feet could hear.

"And proud of it. I run a tight ship." The older woman's hair was pulled back in a severe bun, her clothes crisp and clean and her stance ramrod straight as though a board were stuck down her back.

"It's nice to meet you, Mabel." Rebecca resisted the urge to rub her arm after its vigorous workout. Even though she hadn't had a job since high school, she knew it was important for her to start out on the right foot with a co-worker. "I'll see you tomorrow."

"Eight sharp."

Rebecca smiled, but she was worried. She knew the value of being on time to a job, especially a new one, but with two children, plans and schedules didn't always work out as she wished. She would just have to get up earlier tomorrow morning. She was determined that Gabriel's faith in her would pay off.

"Mom!" Peter yelled from the top of the stairs. "I can't find my tennis shoes. I have to have them!"

Rebecca hurried out of the kitchen, carrying Josh in her arms. "Where did you put them last?"

"If I knew that, I would know where they were."

She stopped at the bottom of the steps and tried to

think where Peter would have put his shoes. Nothing came to mind except the fact she only had twenty minutes to get to work. She was not going to be late the first day. "Okay, retrace your steps yesterday when you came home from practice."

"Mom, I've already done that. I can't remember. I was so tired—" Peter's face lit up, and he spun on his heel and raced for his room. A minute later he reappeared, wearing his tennis shoes. "I kicked them under the bed."

"Why?"

"I was angry at Coach Stone."

"Why?"

"Just was."

Her son's expression closed, and Rebecca knew she wouldn't get an explanation from him. That left Gabriel. She intended to ask him when she got to work *on time*.

Rebecca hurried into the kitchen to finish feeding Josh his breakfast. She propped her youngest in his high chair and started to spoon some cereal into his mouth.

"Here, let me do that, Rebecca. You still have to get ready for work."

Rebecca looked at her grandmother, then at the clock on the wall. She had fifteen minutes to get to work.

Rushing into the small bathroom under the stairs, she ran a comb through her hair and then raced out. Only seven minutes to get to work. She hoped all the police were at the station, because she found herself pressing her foot on the accelerator more than she should. She

could imagine the headline in the local newspaper—
Newest Member of Police Staff Caught Speeding.

She brought the car to a shrieking halt in a parking
space right in front of the building, happy some things
were going her way. Hurrying inside, she glanced at her
watch and was glad to see she was only two minutes
late. She had made it on time—well, practically on
time—for her first day of work.

"You're late, Mrs. Michaels. Try to be here on time
in the future. There's a lot of work that needs to be
done." Mabel stood behind her desk outside Gabriel's
office, her expression stern, her stance reminding
Rebecca of a drill sergeant.

Rebecca stopped halfway across the room, aware of
Gabriel to the side, talking with one of his officers. He
turned toward her, a scowl on his face, and her heart sank.

A smile transformed Gabriel's face almost immediately. He said a few more words to the officer, then
headed toward Rebecca, his eyes warm with a welcome.
"I wanted to be here to greet you your first day at work."

Everything would be all right, Rebecca thought, forgetting other people were nearby while she basked in
the warmth of Gabriel's greeting.

He slid a glance toward Mabel, who stood behind her
desk watching them, and lowered his voice. "She's tough
on the outside but soft on the inside. Give her time."

Rebecca eased her tense muscles and returned
Gabriel's smile. "I didn't think I should get a speeding
ticket my first day on the job. Probably wouldn't look

very good." She peered at Mabel, who was tapping a pencil against her desktop. "But then, maybe I should have."

"Just between you and me, no one's out patrolling at the moment so you'd have been safe. In fact, trying to catch speeders isn't a high priority for this department. But I don't condone that kind of behavior, so don't let anyone know," Gabriel said in a tough voice while merriment danced in his eyes.

"Wild horses couldn't drag it out of me." Rebecca pressed her lips together to emphasize her point, caught up in Gabriel's playfulness. He had a way of wiping away her worries, of making her see this job was a start to a new part of her life.

"Now don't be alarmed, but Mabel is heading this way with a look of determination on her face. I realize her nickname is Dragon Lady, but I don't know what I would do without her. She's been here so long that she knows where the skeletons are buried."

Rebecca turned toward the Dragon Lady, who came to a halt right behind Rebecca. Smile, she told herself, and forced her mouth to curve upward, drawing comfort from the fact that Gabriel was next to her. He made her feel she was capable of doing anything. He made her want to lean on him when she knew she couldn't.

Rebecca stuck her hand out to Mabel. "I'm so glad to be here—"

"Mrs. Michaels," Mabel said, ignoring Rebecca's outstretched hand, "we have a lot of work to do today.

With Jenny gone these past few days, things have been piling up. If you're through chitchatting, come with me."

"Yes, Mrs...." Rebecca realized she didn't know Mabel's last name, and somehow she was sure the woman wouldn't want her to call her by her first name.

"*Ms.* Preston." Mabel pivoted and marched toward a desk in the far corner.

Rebecca threw Gabriel a helpless glance, then followed Mabel, all the while eyeing her new desk, which faced a wall with old brown paneling. A pile of folders threatened to topple. Papers scattered across the battered desktop mocked any sense of order.

The older woman waved her hand toward the papers. "I don't like to talk ill of anyone who isn't here, but as you can see, Jenny didn't work much these past few months, ever since she started dating her new husband. I won't tolerate that from you."

Dating or not working? Rebecca wanted to ask, but diplomatically kept her mouth shut. "How long did Jenny work here?"

"Not long, and frankly, even if she hadn't left for Oklahoma City, she wouldn't have been here much longer." Mabel gestured toward the pile of folders. "These cases haven't been filed in a month. This wouldn't have happened if Gabriel hadn't made me take a vacation. I don't tolerate slackers on the job. It's just you and me keeping this place running. And a police department must have order and efficiency to work properly."

Rebecca wondered what the woman did tolerate, but kept her mouth shut. She needed this job, and even though Gabriel was the police chief she suspected Mabel ran things around the station. "I'll do my best."

"You better, or…"

The unfinished sentence hung in the air between Rebecca and Mabel. Rebecca swallowed past the sudden constriction in her throat.

"Now." Mabel placed her hand on top of one stack of folders. "The first thing you need to do is log these into the computer under complaints, then file them over there." She pointed across the large room to a bank of file cabinets. "When you're through with that job, I'll explain what else you need to do."

After Mabel gave her the password to get into the computer files, she strode away. Rebecca released a slow breath while she scanned the messy desk, so out of place in the orderly station. She heard a cough behind her and looked to see Mabel waiting for her to get busy. Rebecca scrambled into the hardback chair and switched on the computer, hoping she knew the software program. She didn't want to ask Mabel for help. She only had so much bravery for one day. Thankfully the computer was similar to the one she'd had in Dallas.

As she checked the hard drive, trying to find a place to log in cases, she couldn't help feeling like a fish out of water. She looked up from the computer and stared at the brown paneled wall in front of her. It must have been part of the station since the sixties. Noticing at least a dozen nail holes in the paneling, she thought about bringing some pictures to hang and maybe some flowers from home to brighten her work area.

"Mrs. Michaels, is there a problem?"

Wincing, Rebecca clicked on an icon and found what she was looking for. "No, Ms. Preston. I've got everything under control."

Two hours later Rebecca regretted saying she had anything under control. She frowned at the offending computer screen, wondering what Mabel would do if she threw it at the brown paneled wall.

"It can't be that bad." Gabriel leaned against the desk, gripping its edge, while he stared at her.

The minute Rebecca saw his face crinkled in a grin, a sparkle in his eyes, the past few hours' troubles vanished. She relaxed in her chair.

"What's wrong? You've been staring at that computer for the past hour as though you're gonna do bodily harm to it. I have to remind you, ma'am, we're in a police station, and that kind of behavior is frowned upon."

"Did anyone bother to check how competent Jenny was with the computer?" she asked with a laugh. "Nothing's where it should be. I've spent the past hour moving files from one folder to another. I haven't had a chance to log in any of these yet." Rebecca trailed her hand up the foot-high stack taunting her. "And to make matters worse, Ms. Preston has been coming over here every fifteen minutes and watching what I do over my shoulder. I can feel her breathing down my neck. I'm sure I have scorch marks on my flesh."

Gabriel's grin widened. "Mabel's just trying to make sure another Jenny doesn't happen." He bent forward, invading her personal space. "You see, Jenny is the mayor's daughter, and we sort of had to hire her. But I don't think Mabel has forgiven me for that yet. Everything will work out."

His clean pine scent washed over her, and Rebecca imagined a spring day spent hiking in the woods. "Easy for you to say. I don't see her dogging your every step. I'm even afraid to take a bathroom break. By the way, where is it?"

"Come on." He grasped her hand and pulled her to her feet. "You haven't had a tour of the station yet, and every new employee deserves at least that."

With his touch, again Rebecca visualized walking in a pine forest, the sun streaming through the trees, bathing her face in radiance much as his smile did. *Everything will work out.* In that moment she believed those words.

Chapter Five

"This is the jail where we harbor hardened criminals," Gabriel said, touching the small of Rebecca's back as he guided her toward a door. A tingling awareness of his nearness flooded her senses. Her throat tightened, and her pulse sped.

Rebecca noticed all the cells were empty. "Often?"

"On the weekend it picks up. A few people who can't hold their liquor. Occasionally there's a fight. If we're lucky that's all. I'm proud to say there hasn't been a serious crime in Oakview in a year."

"How many police officers do you have?"

"Twelve besides myself. Today you should meet some of them. When you get settled in, Mabel will show you how to dispatch messages to the patrolmen out on the beat." He led her into the main room and pointed toward his office. "That's mine, but you already know that."

Rebecca's gaze fixed on Mabel's desk, which stood guard outside Gabriel's office. "Who gave her the nickname Dragon Lady?"

Gabriel chuckled. "A man who wanted to see me, and she kept telling him that I was busy."

"Did he get to see you?"

"No. He had to come back later. Mabel has her pluses."

"You didn't want to see him?"

"He was a salesman, and he had a hard time understanding the word no. Mabel helped the poor guy with its meaning."

Gabriel gestured toward another door. "That leads to the rest rooms and the courthouse. Now you've been on the grand tour such as it is. Any questions?"

"When's lunch?"

"Don't let Mabel hear you ask that question on your first day."

Rebecca ignored the twinkle in his eye and said, "I have to let Granny know when I'm going to be home for lunch. She'll need to keep Josh up so I can do his physical therapy with him after I eat."

"Mabel goes to lunch at noon, so you can go before or after her, whichever works best for you."

"I'll try one today, and see if that works best for Granny and Josh."

"Just let Mabel know—"

A commotion at the front door caused Gabriel to turn. He sighed and strode toward an officer, a small, elderly woman and a young man with a beet-red face who appeared as though he would have a stroke at any moment.

"Ben, what can I do for you?" Gabriel asked, eyeing the cuffs on Bess Anderson. "I think, Officer Morris, we can remove those. I doubt Bess is a flight risk."

"She's a menace to society." Rebecca recognized the man speaking as Ben Cross, the owner of a clothing store. "She took a bottle of perfume this time." Anger was in the young man's face as well as his voice. He stepped forward until he stood only a foot from Gabriel. "I demand that something be done this time. You promised you would take care of her."

Gabriel plowed his hand through his hair and drew in several deep breaths. "Now, calm down, Ben. Why don't you come into my office and we'll talk about this?"

"No!" Ben stiffened, his hands balled at his sides. "I want satisfaction this time."

A picture of the young man dueling at dawn popped into Rebecca's mind, and she clamped her lips together. When she couldn't contain her grin any longer, she covered her mouth with her hand.

"Mabel fixes a great cup of coffee. Come on into my office and have a cup while we talk this over."

"No! I can't have this—" Ben floundered for a word to describe Bess "—woman in my store. If people hear I let her get away with this, I'll be robbed blind."

Gabriel rubbed the back of his neck. "Then by all means fill out a report on Bess Anderson. I wouldn't want anyone taking advantage of you."

Ben glared at Gabriel. "Are you making fun of me?"

"I wouldn't do that. A crime has been committed, and you have a right to report it."

Rebecca observed Bess standing next to the officer who had brought her in. She whispered something to the young policeman, then brushed a piece of lint off his navy blue shirt. Next she pulled out a handkerchief and began to polish the officer's badge, all while Ben demanded justice in a loud voice.

"Where's the paper I need to fill out?"

"Come into my office, and I'll fill it out for you."

"What are you going to do about her?" Ben jerked his thumb at Bess, who continued to rub the policeman's badge.

"My staff will make sure she's processed."

While Ben stalked into the office, Gabriel hung back and said, "Make sure Bess is comfortable, Officer Morris. She can sit at Rebecca's desk." Gabriel gave Rebecca a look that spoke volumes. This was not a part of the job he enjoyed. "Rebecca, please get Bess something to drink until I can have a word with her."

When the door to Gabriel's office closed, Officer Morris motioned for Bess to follow him. "Ma'am, you need to have a seat over here."

"Where will you be, young man?"

"I need to fill out a report on this incident."

"You're going to leave me alone?"

Rebecca moved forward. "No, I'll keep you

company. Chief Stone wanted me to get you something to drink. What would you like?"

"Tea, with honey and lemon, if you have it." Bess sat in Rebecca's chair, placed her black pocketbook on her lap, then straightened her white gloves and gripped her purse handle.

"Now if I can only find where to get the tea," Rebecca mumbled and plodded to Mabel's desk. "Excuse me. I hate to bother you, but where can I get—"

"Through that door next to the women's rest room is a kitchen. There should be hot water and some tea bags. I don't know about the other stuff. Most of the people around here drink coffee, black." Mabel pulled open a drawer in the bottom of her desk and rummaged through her purse until she produced a packet of honey. "Use this."

"No lemon slices in that purse?"

Mabel almost smiled. "Afraid not."

"Thanks." Rebecca made her way to the kitchen, amazed that the Dragon Lady had a heart, after all.

Five minutes later Rebecca entered the police station with a cup of tea minus a lemon slice but sweetened with honey. As she crossed the room, she heard Ben's raised voice followed by Gabriel's soothing one and cringed. Evidently Gabriel was having a hard time calming the man down.

"Oh, my, that young man is really angry at someone." Bess took the cup Rebecca handed her.

"He says you took some perfume from his store,"

Rebecca said, pulling up a chair next to Bess in hopes of being able to get some work done while the older woman was at her desk.

"Oh, my, why would he say that? I'd never steal a thing from anyone. Goes against my beliefs."

Rebecca peered at the high pile of folders that still needed to be logged in, shrugged and replied, "Perhaps you didn't realize it."

"Not realize I stole something? Oh, my."

The hair on the nape of Rebecca's neck tingled. She peered at Mabel. The Dragon Lady shot her an exasperated glare. Rebecca sent her a look that silently asked Mabel what was she to do, toss Bess out of her chair? Rebecca glanced away before she received her answer.

"Maybe you forgot you had it." Rebecca concentrated her full attention on Bess, determined to ignore the look she was receiving from Mabel. Rebecca chose to remember the packet of honey Mabel had given her. That gave Rebecca hope that just maybe she and Mabel could get along.

"I so like to shop, and the home won't let me go to town."

"They won't?"

"No." Bess sipped her tea, her pinkie finger sticking up in the air, her posture prim and proper.

"I wish we had a lemon."

"Why, my dear?"

"Because you asked for it. All we had was honey."

"This is fine. You should come to the home and have afternoon tea with me sometime."

"I would love to. May I bring my grandmother?"

Bess smiled, took another sip of tea and said, "That would be nice." Then she leaned close to Rebecca and whispered, "I don't hear any more shouting coming from that office. Do you suppose the young man has calmed down?"

"I hope so. If anyone can calm him, it'll be Gabriel."

"That man with the nice smile?"

"Yes," Rebecca answered, remembering Gabriel's smile and deciding that was the nicest thing about him. When he directed one toward her, her insides melted and her stomach fluttered.

"People shouldn't waste their energy getting mad. It's so much nicer if people got along with each other. Don't you think so?"

"Yes." Rebecca turned toward Mabel and blew out a relieved breath. The woman was busy working at her desk, her attention on the computer screen in front of her.

"We sometimes have to work extra hard to win some people over, but it's worth it in the long run. I need to bake that young man a chocolate cake, then maybe he won't be so angry."

Rebecca chuckled. "Chocolate works wonders on me."

"Then I'll bake you one, too. How about Sunday afternoon?"

"You don't have to bake me a cake on Sunday."

"No, to come to tea, since you work during the week."

"I'll have to check with Granny, but that sounds fine to me."

"Good. I love to have company. Since moving to the home, I haven't had many people stop by."

Rebecca heard the loneliness in Bess's voice and vowed she would be at tea on Sunday afternoon if she had to bring the whole family, which might not be a bad idea.

The sound of Gabriel's office door opening brought Rebecca to her feet. She chewed on her bottom lip and tried to relax, but in a short time she'd started to care what happened to Bess. She didn't want to see the woman locked up like a common criminal.

Gabriel shook Ben's hand. "I appreciate the compromise."

"Just make sure it doesn't happen a third time, Chief. I'm only doing this because we're friends."

"I understand."

As Ben left the station, Rebecca waited next to Bess, her hand on the back of the woman's chair. Gabriel spoke to Officer Morris. The young policeman nodded, then tore up the paper he had been writing on. Finally Gabriel traversed the room and came to a halt in front of Bess, a neutral expression on his face. Rebecca rested her hand on the woman's shoulder.

"Ben will drop the charges if you'll agree not to go into his store ever again."

"But he has such pretty things."

"Bess, I promised him you wouldn't. In fact, I don't think you should do any shopping for a while."

"I like to shop."

"What if she had a companion with her when she went shopping?" Rebecca squeezed Bess's shoulder.

Gabriel snared Rebecca with his sharp gaze. "Who?"

"Me. I could work something out with the nursing home to take Bess shopping once a week."

Gabriel took Rebecca by the elbow and pulled her to the side. "Are you sure, with all you have going in your life?"

Rebecca tingled where his hand touched her. His scent of pine wrapped her in a cocoon of contentment. "Yes, very. Bess needs someone now. What happened to her? Where's her family?" she asked, forcing herself to concentrate on Bess's problem, not her reaction to Gabriel Stone.

"I don't know. I need to take Bess to the nursing home. Come with me, and we'll talk with Susan Wilson, the director."

Rebecca lifted an eyebrow and glanced over Gabriel's shoulder at Mabel. "Are you sure?"

He chuckled. "Contrary to popular opinion I still do have final say around here." He asked Bess, "Are you ready for me to take you back to the nursing home?"

Bess finished the last of her tea and set the cup on the desk among the mess. "It looks like you could use some help here. I could stay if you needed me to."

"Thanks for the offer, Bess, but I think we have everything under control."

Mabel snorted and mumbled, "That's debatable."

"Come, ladies." Gabriel helped Bess from the chair, then guided her toward the front door. "Mabel, we'll be gone for about half an hour."

"Sure, boss."

"I do believe that was sarcasm coming from Mabel," Rebecca said when the door closed behind them.

Gabriel's laugh filled the spring air. "I do believe you're right."

Rebecca slid into the back of the squad car while Bess rode up front. On the short drive to the nursing home, Rebecca listened to Gabriel chat with the older woman with affection in his voice. He had a way with Bess that touched Rebecca. The people in his town were more than just names to Gabriel. Being the police chief was more than just a job to him. He cared about the townspeople, and they knew it.

"You know what I miss the most since I moved to Shady Oaks?" Bess asked Gabriel when he pulled up to the nursing home.

"Your garden?"

"No. I hate getting my hands dirty. I miss my dogs. I had three of them. My niece gave them away when she brought me to the home."

"Why?" Rebecca asked, sliding from the car and opening the door to assist Bess.

"Because dogs aren't allowed in nursing homes. You

know, child, animals love you unconditionally. That's the best feeling. Nothing like it. Well, maybe, if you're lucky enough to have the love of a good man." Bess looked right at Gabriel then at Rebecca. "If you know what I mean?"

Rebecca blushed and averted her gaze from Gabriel. She felt him look at her and wished Bess hadn't said anything. They were friends. That was all she wanted, all she could handle right now.

As they entered the nursing home, Rebecca saw several elderly people in the lounge area off the foyer. One, in a wheelchair, watched a big screen television. Two ladies played a card game in the corner. Bouquets of flowers brightened the area, and their scent pushed the antiseptic odors permeating the building into the background. The place felt homey, Rebecca thought.

Susan greeted them in the foyer, her head shaking, displeasure on her face. "I'm sorry, Gabriel. She got away from us again. Bess, they're playing bingo in the main lounge. Why don't you join the others?"

"Oh, bingo. Next to shopping that's my favorite thing to do." She ambled toward the lounge.

"Don't forget about Sunday afternoon. I'll be here around two," Rebecca called.

Bess paused at the entrance into the game room. "Sunday afternoon? What's happening Sunday afternoon?"

Rebecca blinked, at a loss for words. "I'm coming to visit you."

"Oh, that. Good." Bess disappeared inside the room.

"May we have a few words with you, Susan," Gabriel said, "in your office?"

The director indicated a door on the other side of the large foyer. "Did she shoplift again?"

"Again?" Rebecca asked, following the two into Susan's office.

"Ben caught her taking a watch last week."

"No wonder the man was so upset."

"Have a seat." Susan pointed to two wing chairs while she sat behind her desk. "I think we've figured out how she's escaping."

Rebecca frowned. "You make it sound like she's in a prison."

"A lot of the people staying here would wander off and not know where they were if we didn't lock the doors to keep them inside. Many of our residents have problems with their memories." Susan turned to Gabriel. "I've fixed the door in the kitchen. It shouldn't happen again."

"I hope not. Ben forgave her this time. I don't know if I can talk him into a third time."

"She didn't remember taking the perfume. I don't think she did it on purpose," Rebecca interjected, thinking how close in age Bess and her grandmother were.

"I agree with you, Rebecca, and that's why Ben finally calmed down. Ben isn't an ogre, but he does have a family to support and lately there has been some shoplifting going on at his store. I think it's kids. He's extra sensitive about it at the moment."

"May I make a suggestion?" Rebecca asked, straightening in her chair as though she were readying to do battle. If need be, she would. "I'd like to take Bess shopping with me once a week. I'll keep a close eye on her and make sure nothing's taken that isn't paid for. She needs someone to care about her. What happened with her family? Her niece?"

"Her niece moved to New York City," Michael said. "That's why she placed Bess in Shady Oaks. With Bess's memory problems, she didn't think the big city would be a good place for her aunt."

"I'll have a word with her niece, but I doubt she'll object to you taking her out for an afternoon. This might help Bess. She seems so lost right now. Her niece had to give her dogs away. I want to give her something to look forward to."

"I have an idea, Susan. My dog had puppies last month. I'll be looking for homes soon for them. I'd like to give Bess one of the puppies to take care of."

"A dog? Here?"

"It's not unheard of to have pets in nursing homes. It would be wonderful therapy for Bess, for all your residents. Bess summed it up when she said animals love unconditionally. That's the best feeling in the world, Susan. If memory serves me, you've got a dog and a cat."

"But if I let Bess have a dog, the others will want a pet."

"Maybe that isn't such a bad idea. Think it over. I'll see if I can get you some literature on it. I'll hold a puppy for a while until you make up your mind."

"I don't know, Gabriel. I can't imagine it staying inside all day."

"You have a fenced yard out back. All I'm asking is that you think about it."

Susan rose. "Fine. Send over any information you have on it, and I'll see. I'll talk with the doctor and nurses and get their opinion."

"That's all I ask." Gabriel opened the door for Rebecca. Outside Shady Oaks he took a deep breath and released it slowly. "Susan does a good job with what she has, but still I wish there was another way to take care of our old people."

"The puppy for Bess was a great idea. I hope Susan approves it." At the squad car Rebecca caught Gabriel's gaze over the roof. "Have you given any of your puppies away yet?"

"The kid next door wants one. Why?"

"I wonder if I could buy one for Peter for his birthday next Saturday."

"No, you can't."

Rebecca climbed into the car, trying to keep the disappointment from showing on her face. "Then do you know where I can get a puppy for Peter?"

"Yes." He smiled. "I won't sell you a puppy, but I'll give you one."

"You will?" Relief flowed through her.

"Lady isn't any fancy breed, but she's a good dog. She wandered into my life not long after Judy died. Just appeared on my porch one morning, cold and shiver-

ing. I think the Lord sent her to me to help me mend.
She was starving and near death. I nursed her back to
life and in the process found a reason to go on."

Tears lodged in Rebecca's throat. Had the Lord sent
her Gabriel to help her heal?

"I'm home," Rebecca called as she walked into the
kitchen from the garage.

Rose cradled Josh in her lap while she fed him.

Rebecca rushed to take Josh from her grandmother. "I'm sorry I'm late, but I was bound and determined to get all the folders logged on the computer
and filed away."

Rose waved her away. "I can handle this. You know
I raised three children. Sit and relax. You've been
working all day."

Rebecca arched a brow. "And you haven't?"

"Taking care of Josh isn't work. It's God's gift to me.
He keeps me young."

Rebecca sank into a chair next to her grandmother
and stroked Josh's arm. His cooing eased her weariness.
Her children were the reason she was working so hard.
They were worth it.

"Where's Peter?" Rebecca asked as she tickled
Josh's stomach and relished the sound of his laughter.

"He's still at baseball practice, but he should—" The
sound of the front door slamming interrupted Rose. "It
looks like he's home."

"Or we have a very loud burglar."

"My gosh, child, work at the police station one day and you're already thinking the worst of the good citizens of Oakview."

Peter entered the kitchen and headed for the refrigerator. "I'm starved. When's dinner?"

"Six." Rose placed Josh over her shoulder and patted his back.

"How was practice today?" Rebecca asked, watching her eldest son pour a large glass of orange juice and nearly down it in one swallow, then refill it.

He shrugged. "The usual."

"Which means?"

"The team practices catching and batting." Peter rummaged through the cabinets until he found a box of crackers.

"I don't want you to eat too—"

"Mom, I could eat everything in this kitchen and still be hungry. Don't worry. I'll eat dinner. Have you called Dad yet?"

"No, I just got home myself."

"Well, then, what are we waiting for?" Peter took the phone and punched in his dad's number.

While Peter talked with his father for a few minutes, Rebecca steeled herself. She remembered the devastation she had experienced when she had discovered the note Craig left, saying he couldn't take any more and he had to leave—for good.

"Mom! Mom!"

Rebecca blinked and focused on Peter, who was

holding out the phone for her. Her hands shook as she took it. "Hello, Craig."

"Peter said you had something you needed to talk to me about. I don't have much time. What is it?"

Rebecca heard the impatience in Craig's voice, and the sound of people's voices in the background. She wondered what their call had interrupted. "Peter and I were hoping you could come up for his birthday next Saturday. He wants you to go fishing with him like you two used to." A long pause on the other end sent her heart pounding against her chest. "Craig?"

"I'm thinking." Another long pause, then he said, "Okay. I can come for a while. I'll be there at seven in the morning. We can spend a few hours together before I have to get back to Dallas."

"Peter will be glad to hear that," Rebecca replied in the most cheerful voice she could muster, while inside she wanted to yell at Craig. *Don't put yourself out for your own son. After all, his feelings aren't as important as yours. He doesn't need to see his own father.*

"I'll have to leave by noon."

"Fine. We'll see you at seven then." She hung up the phone.

"Dad's coming?"

Rebecca nodded, her throat clogged with emotions she couldn't express in front of her son. She laced her hands together to keep them from trembling.

"This is gonna be great." Peter snatched up the box of crackers and the glass of orange juice and left the kitchen.

"Everything isn't as great as Peter thinks?" Rose asked.

Rebecca took her son from her grandmother, needing to hold him close. Burying her face against his hair, she breathed deeply, relishing his baby scent. "No. There were other people at his place, and I could tell he wasn't too pleased by our call."

"Have faith in the Lord, child. Everything will work out."

Rebecca remembered Gabriel saying those same words to her earlier that day. She wanted to believe them. "Granny, I'm trying." She tightened her hold on Josh, drawing strength from her youngest who had been through so much in his short life.

"You haven't told me about your first day on the job," Rose said as she opened the refrigerator to remove some sliced chicken.

"Interesting and challenging."

"Challenging?"

"Not the actual work so much as how to get along with my co-worker." Rebecca started to tell her grandmother about Mabel when the doorbell rang. "I'll get this then tell you."

She swung the front door open and found Gabriel in cutoffs and a sweatshirt. He filled the entrance with his overwhelming presence. She greeted him with a smile, pleased to see him. Her spirits lifted.

"What brings you by?"

"I wasn't there when you left today, and I wanted to

know how the rest of your first day on the job went." His gaze trekked down her.

"Checking for scorch marks from the Dragon Lady?"

He chuckled. "Are there any?"

"One or two. Come in."

"I'd better stay out here. I'm in desperate need of a shower after running laps with the team."

"How's Peter doing? Giving you any trouble?" Rebecca came out onto the porch.

"No, he hasn't complained since that first day. Actually he ran next to David today. For the first lap they carried on a conversation."

"Good, because this morning I was concerned something happened at practice yesterday."

"Why?"

"He came home and kicked his tennis shoes under the bed."

Gabriel chuckled. "Probably because he's done more work these past couple of days than he's done in a month's time." He raked his fingers through his sweaty hair. "I have to give him credit. He's done everything the team has done." Leaning against the railing, he folded his arms across his chest. "Okay. How was your day?"

She sat in the swing and turned Josh in her lap so he could see Gabriel. "The job's fine. I'll win Mabel over. I think she was shocked that I wasn't out the door right at four-thirty. I think I further shocked her by staying until all the files were logged and put away."

"I bet you did. When I first came to work as the police chief, I had to win Mabel over, too. Just because I was the boss meant nothing to the woman."

"Since you're still the police chief, there's hope for me."

"There's always hope, Rebecca. I think that's one of the messages the Lord was giving us when He sent us His only son."

Fear nibbled at her. Dare she have hope? Rebecca thought about Peter's birthday. She prayed that Gabriel was right.

Chapter Six

The crack of the bat against the ball echoed through the park. Rebecca leaped to her feet and yelled as David Carson headed for first base, then pushed on to second. A runner came in to home plate, and everyone in the dugout rushed to greet him with high fives and cheers.

Rebecca found Peter among his teammates, huddled around the boy who had come in for the tying run. A huge grin was plastered on her son's face. Seeing Peter with the others, excited and part of the team, gave her hope that soon he would come to accept their move and maybe even grow to like living in Oakview.

With that thought, Rebecca searched the crowd filing into the dugout for Gabriel, the one partially responsible for this change in her eldest son. When she spotted him bending over and speaking low to the next batter, she smiled at the intense expression on Gabriel's face. He didn't take this game lightly. He was an all-or-nothing kind of guy. He had taken Peter under his wing and was determined to make her son part of this town. Her heart warmed at the thought.

She relaxed and drew in a deep, calming breath. The scent of recently mowed grass permeated the air. Spring was definitely here, she thought, shedding her sweater. She lifted her face to the sun and savored its warmth.

The next batter came to the plate and swung two times to no avail. The third pitch flew past the ten-year-old, low and outside. The ump shouted, "Ball."

"I think I have bitten off every fingernail I have," the woman next to Rebecca said.

Rebecca tilted her head to look at the young mother sitting on her left. "Is that your son at bat?"

"No, David is my son. He's on second."

"Then you're Mrs. Carson."

"Please, call me Alicia."

"I'm Rebecca Michaels. My son is the team manager." She pointed toward Peter, who was placing bats in holders while his gaze was fixed on the batter.

"David has mentioned Peter. They worked at the church a few Saturdays back with Gabriel. My husband said they accomplished quite a bit. We always appreciate any help we can get. Keeping a church up outside is as much work as inside."

Rebecca wasn't going to mention what had led her son to "volunteer" to clean up the church that Saturday. "I know what you mean. The same applies to a house. But then the church is the Lord's house."

"That it is."

The sound of the bat hitting the ball riveted Rebecca's attention to the scene in front of her. The ball sailed toward right field. A member of the other team positioned himself under it and readied himself to catch it. If he caught it, they would go into extra innings. She held her breath.

The boy fumbled the ball. It plopped to the ground and rolled toward the fence. He scrambled for it while David headed for third. The boy in the outfield retrieved the ball and threw toward the pitcher. David rounded third for home plate. The pitcher lobbed the ball toward the catcher as David slid in for the winning run.

"Safe," the ump called.

Rebecca released her pent-up breath, jumped to her feet and shouted, "Way to go. You did it!"

Alicia threw her arms around Rebecca and hugged her. Joy transformed Alicia's plain face into a radiant one. Rebecca pulled away, beaming with her own bright smile.

"David was so worried about this game. The Hornets were the best team in the league last year. This is a big victory." Alicia lowered her voice. "And if the truth be known, Samuel, my husband, told me that Gabriel stayed up most of last night worrying about this game."

"Men and their games," Rebecca muttered and searched for the man in question.

Gabriel stood in the midst of his team, receiving congratulations from the boys and giving them his. Then he quickly had the team form a line to greet the

Hornets on the field. He turned to make sure everyone was in front of him. He saw Peter putting equipment away. He walked over to her son and said something. Peter appeared surprised but followed Gabriel to the end of the line, then planted himself in front of Gabriel as everyone walked onto the field.

Rebecca's heart ached as she watched her son being included in the celebration, giving high fives to all the Hornets who filed past him. Tears crowded her eyes, and she quickly blinked to rid herself of them before someone saw her.

"David says your son is a fast runner. We're one man short. Has he considered going out for the team?"

Alicia's question drew Rebecca's attention. "Gabriel's working on Peter."

"Then it shouldn't be long before he's playing with the Cougars. Gabriel can do just about anything he sets his heart to. And he has such a way with kids. Too bad he doesn't have children of his own. He and Judy were so much in love. If only Judy—"

"Mom, did you see me?" David ran to his mother, smiling from ear to ear.

Rebecca thought about Alicia's comments. She agreed that Gabriel would make the perfect father. Why couldn't Craig be more like Gabriel? Peter and Josh deserved a father who loved them and accepted them as they were. And, Rebecca thought, I deserve a man who loves me and—

Hold it, Rebecca Michaels! What are you thinking?

She had no right even to contemplate a relationship with Gabriel. She didn't want to become involved with any man outside friendship, and she certainly didn't have the emotional strength to fight a ghost for a man's love. Gabriel was still deeply in love with his deceased wife, or he wouldn't be wearing his wedding ring.

"Are you and Peter going to come to Pizza To Go with the rest of the team?" David asked.

Rebecca concentrated on what the child was asking her instead of on the man walking toward her. "I don't know. Peter hasn't said anything." Out of the corner of her eye, she saw Gabriel come to a stop a few feet from her. Her heartbeat quickened.

"You've got to. Everyone goes after a game."

Gabriel greeted Alicia with a smile, then said, "I insist on Peter and you coming to Pizza To Go. It's an unwritten rule that every team member must be a part of the celebration afterward."

"Peter can but I'm not a team member," Rebecca said with a neutral expression, desperately trying to keep her pulse from racing so fast that she became dizzy. That was what she deserved for even considering Gabriel as a potential—a potential what? Oh, my, as Bess would say. Rebecca felt heat suffuse her cheeks and wished she was anywhere but where she was.

"I could always make you an honorary team member, if that's what it takes to get you to the pizza place."

She brought her hand up. "Stop right there. I can't hit a thing and I certainly don't run fast. And worse, if

I saw a ball coming toward me, I'd run the other way. You wouldn't want me on your team."

"But you're already part of my team." His eyes gleamed.

Her heart hammered a mad tempo against her chest. "I am?"

"You work at the police station, don't you?"

"Yes," she answered, mesmerized by the warmth dancing in his eyes, all directed at her. Oh, my.

"Then I rest my case. You're a member of my team."

Alicia laughed. "Rebecca, give up. You won't win this argument. Once you're a friend of Gabriel's, you're a friend for life."

"That you are."

His grin reached out to Rebecca and enveloped her in a sheath of empathy. Yes, they were friends, Rebecca acknowledged, but that would be all and she had to remember that.

"Well, put that way, I guess Peter and I will be there."

"It's out on the highway."

"Yes, I know. Peter has already conned me into going there once."

"What kid doesn't like pizza? Come on, let's get everyone moving toward the parking lot. I've worked up quite an appetite."

"Gabriel Stone, you always say that." Alicia tousled her son's hair. "Right, David?"

"Yep, Mom. Coach, I don't think it'll take much to get us moving."

Gabriel chuckled. "David, I don't think it will, either." He cupped his hands to his mouth and announced in a loud voice, "Time to celebrate. We have a party to go to."

Everyone on the team cheered, then scrambled to get their belongings and hurry to cars with parents following more sedately.

Alicia walked with Rebecca. "I'll see you at the pizza place."

"I have to first swing by and get my grandmother and my youngest son."

"Then let me take Peter with me and David."

Peter came to Rebecca's side at the car. "That's okay, Mrs. Carson. I need to help Mom with Josh."

Rebecca gave her eldest son a perplexed look but said, "We'll be there soon." She climbed into her car and waited for Peter to slide in on the passenger's side. "I can get Josh and Granny by myself, hon, if you want to go with David."

"Mom, I know you don't care that much for pizza, so if you want to stay home, that's okay by me."

"Since when are you passing up a pizza? What's going on here, Peter?"

"It's not my victory. I'm just the team manager. I didn't do anything, so I don't feel like celebrating." Peter hunched by the window, drawing in on himself. He averted his face and stared at the passing landscape.

"Hon, you can always play. Chief Stone would love to see you do that. But you're wrong about not being a member of the team. You're an important part."

"I'm not hungry."

Rebecca didn't have to see her son to know his bottom lip was sticking out. "We promised Chief Stone we would be there."

"You just want to see him. He's always at our house. You work for him now."

"Is that what this is about? Do you think I have romantic feelings for Chief Stone? He and I are friends, Peter. That is all." If she said it enough, she might begin to believe it. On Gabriel's part, that statement was true. On her part she wasn't sure anymore. He jumbled her feelings all up into a tight knot that was solidly lodged in her stomach.

"Yeah, sure, whatever."

"Hon, I think we should talk about this. I work at the police station because that was the only job available right now. I was lucky to get work in Oakview."

"Mom, I said I'll go. Don't make a big deal out of it."

"But you said—"

"Forget what I said. Coach Stone is okay by me."

Rebecca pulled into her grandmother's driveway, turned the engine off and faced Peter. "I love you, honey. You never have to worry about that. No one will ever come between us."

Peter bit his lower lip, his eyes shiny. "I know, Mom."

Gabriel saw a couple entering the pizza place and frowned. Where was she? Rebecca had said she was coming. Alicia had told him she was going to stop by and pick up Rose and Josh. She should have been here by now. Gabriel glanced at his watch for the tenth time in the past twenty minutes. His worry grew. What if she had been in a wreck? What if—

"She'll be here soon," Alicia said from across the table. She winked at her husband, who had joined them a few minutes ago. "Isn't that right, Samuel? Traffic can be beastly at this time of night."

"Yeah, seven o'clock on a Friday night in Oakview we often have traffic jams. You should know that, being the police chief and all."

"Funny, you two," Gabriel said over the noise of thirteen boys all waiting for their pizzas to be made. "I'm just concerned that something might be wrong. She works for me. I think I have a right to be concerned."

Alicia barely contained her smug smile and the twinkle lightening her eyes. "Of course, Gabriel, you have a right since she is your employee."

Gabriel scanned the crowded restaurant. Half the patrons were team members and their families. The players sat at two tables close together, and every boy was talking at the same time. The noise level didn't bother him. The cramped chairs pushed together so everyone could sit in a group didn't bother him. But not knowing if Rebecca was all right bothered him—a lot.

When had he started to care so much?

The minute she had opened the door the first day he

had met her. He'd looked into her big blue eyes so full of sadness and he'd longed to erase that look from them. He was always a sucker for someone who needed comfort. Ever since Judy had died he felt it was his mission to help others through their pain. That was the only reason he was so concerned about Rebecca, he told himself, twisting his wedding ring.

"Ah, she's here," Alicia announced and scooted her chair around so there would be room for Rebecca, Rose and Josh.

David called Peter to his table and made room for him while the waitress delivered four large pizzas to the boys. Gabriel stood as Rebecca and Rose approached him. Gabriel pulled a chair out for Rebecca, while Samuel did the same for Rose. When they were seated, the reverend whistled to get the boys' attention. They all bowed their heads. Gabriel slanted a look at Rebecca, who held Josh against her.

"Lord, bless this food we are about to partake and thank you for the win this evening." Samuel sat again, laughing. "I hope He can forgive me for saying such a short prayer. I didn't know how much longer the boys would have waited."

"It was to the point." Rose placed her napkin in her lap. "Here, Rebecca, let me hold Josh while you get settled."

"That's okay, Granny. I have everything under control."

Gabriel suspected Rebecca had forgotten how to ask for help. He knew Rebecca's husband had done little to assist her with Josh and Peter. Was that why

Rebecca insisted she had everything under control when Gabriel felt that she was being pulled in different directions?

"I haven't gotten to see this little tiger in a few days. Come here, Josh." Gabriel didn't give Rebecca a choice. He reached out, took her youngest from her and swung him high. Josh's giggles were music to his ears. His smile and bright eyes were a balm to Gabriel's soul. When he settled Josh in the crook of his arm, he felt content, complete, as though something missing in his life was found. Was he letting his feeling toward Josh and Peter influence his growing feelings toward Rebecca?

Gabriel chanced a look toward Rebecca and wasn't surprised when he saw her mouth slightly open, her eyes round as saucers. "I'm a take-charge kind of guy. Sorry." He shrugged but didn't give Josh back to her.

He knew she felt she should hold Josh, take care of him throughout the meal, perhaps not eat, so she could see to Josh's needs. Gabriel was determined not to let her hide behind her son.

She opened her mouth to say something. Gabriel stuck a piece of pizza into it. "Isn't that delicious? They make the best, I believe, in the state of Oklahoma."

She mumbled something around the food and sent him a glare that told him he didn't want to know what she had said.

"I'm glad you agree with me. I'll let Harry know how much you like his pizza." Gabriel sent her an innocent look and cuddled Josh closer.

While Rebecca finished the large bite she had been fed, Gabriel played with Josh, giving him a bread stick to hold. Her son grabbed at the new plaything and gripped it for a few seconds before dropping it.

Rebecca saw the exchange between Gabriel and Josh. She scanned the faces at the table to gauge their reaction to the fact her son had a hard time holding onto objects. Alicia smiled at her. Samuel was busy talking with Rebecca's grandmother.

"You have the most adorable son. How old he is?"

"He'll be two in a month." Rebecca waited for the reaction that usually followed that announcement.

"Oh, great. I love planning a birthday party. I hope you'll let me help."

"You'll have to stand in line, Alicia. I have first dibs." Gabriel took a bite of his pizza, still cradling Josh.

"Here. Let me hold him so you can eat." Rebecca wiped her hands so she could take Josh.

"You get to hold him all the time. You've got to learn to share, Rebecca. He's happy right where he is. Enjoy your dinner."

"I could always call the police chief of this town and put in a complaint that you've kidnapped my son. I've got connections. I work for him, you know."

"I like to live dangerously. Want me to dial the station for you?"

Rebecca laughed. "No. It would be hard to hold a baby, eat and dial a phone all at the same time. Something would have to give."

"Have you all noticed how quiet it is?" Alicia asked, glancing at the tables full of Cougars.

"Thankfully, they are practicing good manners and not talking with their mouths full. There's hope after all." The reverend finished his pizza and patted his stomach. "Delicious. If I wasn't watching my weight, I would finish that last piece on the platter."

"That's okay. I'll take the temptation away so you won't suffer." Gabriel reached for the last slice and plopped it on his plate.

"A true friend," Samuel said with a chuckle.

"My duty as a policeman is to protect you, even from yourself." Gabriel lifted the pizza to his mouth. "I take my job seriously." He bit into the slice and chewed slowly.

As the boys finished eating their food, the noise level in the restaurant skyrocketed. Rebecca ate her portion, having to agree that the meal was good even though she wasn't a big fan of pizza. Suddenly the room grew quiet. Rebecca looked up and saw the waitress bringing out a big cake with ten candles lit on it.

Gabriel started singing the happy birthday song, and all the boys followed. When they got to the name, they shouted Peter's, and Rebecca thought she would cry. Tears welled into her tight throat as she watched her eldest son struggle to keep his emotions under control. He was speechless when the woman placed the huge cake with his name on it in front of him. He looked at Rebecca with a question in his eyes. She shook her head and shrugged.

"Guess it's time to give you Josh back," Gabriel said, and transferred her youngest to her arms.

Gabriel rose before she could question him about the cake.

"Peter, when the team found out it was your birthday tomorrow, they wanted to show you their appreciation for joining us with this little celebration. The fact we won tonight makes this party even sweeter." Gabriel moved to the counter and retrieved a package. "This is for you from us." He handed Peter a large, long gift, wrapped in blue paper with a baseball motif on it.

Stunned, Peter took the gift and held it.

"Open it!" The chant filled the restaurant.

Peter tore into the package. When he lifted the leather baseball glove and bat for everyone to see, Rebecca wiped the tears coursing down her cheeks with the back of her hand. Her grandmother gave her a handkerchief that smelled of roses, Granny's special fragrance.

"Isn't that sweet," Rose whispered to Rebecca. "I bet Gabriel was behind this."

Rebecca knew he was. He was determined to show her son he was a part of the team.

"Speech!" The new chant came from the thirteen boys sitting around Peter.

Peter opened his mouth then clamped it closed, a stunned expression on his face.

"I think he's speechless," David said.

Peter mumbled his thanks while cradling his two gifts to his chest.

Gabriel sat again. Rebecca reached over and took his hand, squeezing it. "Thank you." She couldn't say another word. A huge lump in her throat prevented her from speaking.

He laid his hand over hers. "Anytime. A lot has happened to him this past year. I just wanted him to know he was special to us."

"Well, I don't know about everyone else, but I want a piece of that cake. If I know Gabriel, it's chocolate on the inside and from the bakery at the supermarket. They bake the best cakes in town. To die for." Alicia moved to the boys' table to take charge of cutting the cake and handing out slices.

"I'm afraid the cake I baked is gonna look puny next to that monster." Rebecca reluctantly withdrew her hand from Gabriel and immediately felt bereaved.

"Yours doesn't have to feed a score of people. I do have to admit I went overboard when I ordered it. There may be some leftovers."

"Some? Try half." Rose took the piece passed to her and started eating.

"That's our police chief. He never does anything halfway," the reverend said, and popped a forkful of cake into his mouth. "Mmm. This frosting is wonderful. Melts in your mouth." He ran his tongue over his upper lip. "Remember the time you chased those robbers into the next county?"

"I got my men."

"Yeah, but you nearly caused a wreck out on the highway."

Gabriel paled. "Oh, please don't remind me of that folly. Occasionally I see red when someone takes what isn't theirs."

"One of your pet peeves." The reverend ate another bite.

"I'm trying to practice restraint. It just doesn't always work."

"We all have our faults. The Lord didn't make us perfect." Samuel paused, then said, "Speaking of not being perfect, George is getting out of prison soon."

Gabriel stiffened, all color gone from his face. His hand shook as he placed his fork beside his plate. "I know."

"You have to forgive him sometime, Gabriel."

"No, I don't." Gabriel rose. The sound of his chair scraping across the wooden floor permeated the silence that hung at the table of adults. "If you'll excuse me—" He pivoted and left the restaurant.

"Who's George?" Rebecca asked, aware of the strain at the table.

"The man who drove the car that killed Gabriel's wife and son. He was drunk." Samuel Carson looked at the door Gabriel had disappeared through. "I should go talk to him. This wasn't the right time to bring that subject up, but I thought being among friends would lessen the pain."

Alicia patted her husband's hand. "Let Gabriel have some time alone before you approach him."

Rebecca's heart broke. She wanted to go to Gabriel and ease his pain, as he had hers these past few weeks. But she didn't have a right to, and she realized she wished she did.

Gabriel drove his fist into the punching bag hanging on his back porch. Again and again he hit the imagined face of the man who had robbed him of his future. Sweat poured off him, clinging to his T-shirt and shorts, but still he worked out his anger and frustration until exhaustion made it impossible for him to lift his arms.

He sank to the porch floor, rid himself of his gloves, then buried his face in his hands. He could still see the wrecked car with Judy inside. She had died on the way to the hospital. The doctors had done an emergency C-section to try to save his son, born two months too early.

George McCall was responsible. Gabriel wished he could rid himself of his hatred toward the man as easily as he had his boxing gloves. He couldn't, and he felt as though he had let God down. He had tried. The anger was still embedded deep in his heart, and he wanted the man to remain behind bars. Judy and their unborn child had been Gabriel's life. He went through the motions of living, but he knew something had died in him that day along with his wife and son.

"Our Father, who art in heaven, hallowed be thy Name. Thy kingdom come. Thy will be done, on earth as it is in heaven. Give us this day our daily bread. And forgive us our trespasses, as we forgive those who trespass against us. And lead us not into temptation, but deliver us from evil. Amen." Gabriel murmured the Lord's Prayer. It should be a guide to him in his forgiveness of the man who had killed his wife and child. "Please, dear Lord, give me the strength to do what I must."

"Mom! It's after seven," Peter called from the living room.

Rebecca cleaned Josh's face after more of his breakfast ended up on him than in him. She placed him in his swing and went into the living room. "It's only fifteen minutes after seven. Your dad lives several hours away. He's just late. Relax, Peter. Watch some TV until he comes."

Peter gave her a look that said she must be crazy, which might be true. She didn't like him to watch much television, and here she was encouraging him to.

"I don't want to miss him when he pulls up." Peter turned to the window and stared out.

Rebecca saw her son's new fishing gear—a gift from Craig—stacked in the corner by the front door. She noticed he had on his lucky fishing jacket. Worry nibbled at her composure. If Craig didn't come, she didn't know what she was going to do.

When she walked into the kitchen to clean up the break-fast dishes, she glanced at the clock over the stove. Craig had often been late. She hoped this was one of those times.

But twenty minutes later, she resolved to call him. At least that would end her son's ordeal.

Quietly she lifted the receiver and punched in Craig's number. On the third ring he picked it up, and Rebecca's grip tightened on the phone until her knuckles were white.

"You haven't even left yet?" she asked, instead of saying hello to his greeting.

"Sorry. I overslept."

Rebecca heard no remorse in his voice. She inhaled a deep, fortifying breath, then blew it out through pursed lips. "Are you coming?"

"Nah. Too late. I have to be back this afternoon. I have plans."

"Plans that are more important than being with your son on his birthday?"

"Tell Peter I'll call him later. Did he get my present?"

"Yes. He has all his gear packed in the new tackle box and it's by the front door while he waits at the window for you. Please talk to him."

Craig mumbled something under his breath, then said, "Put him on."

Rebecca went to the door to the living room and said, "Your dad wants to talk to you."

Peter frowned. "Is he on his cell phone? Did his car break down?"

To spare her son's feelings, for a second she thought about lying. "No, he's at home."

"But—" Peter hung his head and shuffled into the kitchen to pick up the phone.

Rebecca listened to her son's one-word replies, watching his shoulders sag. She put her arms around him and held him against her while he mumbled goodbye to his father. Peter dropped the receiver, missing the cradle. She tightened her arms about him. When a beeping sound blared, Rebecca put the phone where it belonged.

"He's not coming. He doesn't know when he can see me," Peter finally said, his body shaking.

Rebecca kissed the top of his head. "He'll come as soon as he can. We'll have a great day, anyway."

Peter wrenched himself from her embrace. His face turned red, and his eyes narrowed. "My birthday is ruined! I don't want to do anything!"

He raced from the room, and Rebecca heard him run up the stairs and slam his bedroom door. She sucked in deep gulps of air, trying to calm the thundering beat of her heart. *Lord, why are You doing this to my family? Peter is an innocent. He doesn't deserve this from his father.*

When the sound of Josh's swing stopped, she started toward it to take Josh out but halted halfway across the room. Her youngest son had grasped the bar and stalled its movement. He held his grip for a good twenty seconds before letting go, the swing falling backward.

Tears flowed down Rebecca's face. In the midst of Peter's disaster, Josh had done something he never had before. Even though tears streamed down her cheeks, she smiled and picked up her youngest son. Maybe God hadn't deserted her family, after all.

"Where did you learn that, my man?" she asked,

surprised by the strength he'd shown. She hugged Josh to her, listening to his cooing, relishing his baby scent.

She held him in front of her, staring into his sweet face. "Your big brother isn't happy. What do you think we should do?"

Josh made some more sounds, his eyes bright.

The puppy! She would ask Gabriel to bring it over early. Maybe that would take Peter's mind off his father.

With Josh in her arms Rebecca placed a call to Gabriel, realizing as she listened to his line ring that she hadn't seen him since he walked away from the restaurant the night before. She started to hang up when his gruff voice said, "Hello."

"Gabriel, is this a bad time?"

"Rebecca? No, I was just working out. A little out of breath. What's up?"

"Peter's dad backed out of coming today. Is there any chance you could bring the puppy over this morning?"

"You bet. I'll shower and be right over."

As she put the receiver in its cradle, Rebecca wondered what Gabriel needed. When she had last seen him, he had been devastated by the news of George's release. That had been twelve hours before. He was always coming to her aid. Today she was determined to come to his and help him. If he would let her.

Chapter Seven

"Rose let me in," Gabriel said as he entered the kitchen and placed a cardboard box on the floor.

"Thanks for bringing the puppy. I know it's early. I probably interrupted you, but—" The words died in Rebecca's tight throat. She swallowed, but the dry ache deep inside her threatened her fragile composure.

"Don't you worry about interrupting me. That's what friends are for. To be there when others need them." He studied her from across the expanse of the kitchen.

She saw the evidence of his sleepless night in his face and suddenly wanted to comfort him. "Gabriel, about last night at the pizza place."

"Forget last night. This is about you. About Peter."

The gruffness in his voice, the pain that briefly flashed in his eyes closed off that topic of conversation. He could comfort, but he didn't want comfort. A seed of hurt buried itself in her, and she had to shut it down before she was caught up in a different kind of pain.

"Did Craig say anything about why he couldn't come?"

She shook her head. "I don't understand how he can do this to Peter. He's just a little boy." Tears glistened in her eyes, blurring her vision.

He came to her and drew her into his embrace. "I'm sorry, Rebecca."

She had done so well until he touched her and held her close. The comfort of his arms, his soft, soothing words, opened the dam holding her tears. They spilled out unchecked. She cried, soaking his shirt, the faint thump of his heartbeat close to her ear, a rhythmic sound enticing her to find peace. She felt the calming stroke of his hand on her back and couldn't shake the sensation that she had come home, that this man would protect and support her.

When there was nothing left inside her, she pulled back slightly and looked into his face. It was filled with compassion, and there was a touch of sadness in his eyes. She smiled.

"You seem to be coming to my rescue a lot lately." A whimpering sound came from behind Gabriel. Rebecca peered around him and saw the white and brown puppy trying to get out of the carton.

"What do you think? Will Peter like her?"

"She's beautiful." Rebecca disengaged herself from Gabriel's arms and knelt next to the box, scratching behind one of the puppy's ears, which flopped over.

"Beautiful? More like a funny mix of several breeds

that weren't meant to go together. But if she's anything like Lady, she'll be perfect as a boy's pet."

"It's all in the eye of the beholder." She lifted the puppy out of the box and held her up. The whimpering stopped. Big brown eyes stared at Rebecca, and she was lost. She hugged the warm, cuddly animal, finding its scent as appealing as a baby's. "If she doesn't help Peter forget his troubles, I don't think anything will."

"Where is he?"

"Upstairs in his bedroom."

Gabriel swept his arm out. "Lead the way. We have some cheering up to do."

Cradling the puppy in her arms, Rebecca walked through the living room, checking to make sure Josh was asleep in the swing. As she climbed the stairs to the second story, she sensed Gabriel's gaze on her, and a blush flamed her cheeks. She remembered the feel of his arms about her, and the blush deepened. A warm, tingling sensation left goose bumps all over her body. If she wasn't careful, she would come to depend on him too much.

She knocked on her son's door, waited for him to say come in, and when he didn't, she eased it open a crack. "Peter? Someone's here to see you."

Peter leaped off his bed. "Dad?"

Her smile died. "No, honey, you know he won't be able to come. Chief Stone is here with something to show you."

"I don't wanna see anyone." He plopped down on the bed and turned his back to her.

She opened the door wide and entered. "He brought you a gift."

"I'm not—" The puppy made a noise, and Peter twisted around to look. His eyes widened, but he stayed on the bed, almost as though he were afraid to move for fear the puppy would vanish. "Whose dog is that?"

"When Chief Stone heard you always wanted a pet, he thought you might like one of Lady's puppies." Rebecca approached the bed and sat, extending the animal toward Peter. "That is, unless you don't want her."

Something snapped in her son's eyes. He swung his legs around and sat up, taking the puppy into his arms and burying his face against her small body. "She's mine?"

"She's yours if you promise to take care of her," Gabriel said, coming into the room. "I don't give just anybody one of Lady's litter."

Peter looked at him, a serious expression on his face. "Oh, I'll take great care of her. I promise." A beaming smile split his face as he focused his attention on the puppy wiggling in his arms.

"What are you gonna name her?" Gabriel asked.

"I don't know. I have to think on that," Peter answered as though it was a grave matter. The puppy licked his finger, then began to gnaw on it.

"It took me a week to decide on Lady's name."

"It did?" Peter got on the floor with his new pet and let her waddle around.

"Hon, she isn't housebroken."

"She won't do anything, Mom."

The puppy proceeded to urinate on the throw rug. Rebecca watched Peter wince as he snatched his pet in midstream and got wet.

"Ugh! Mom!" Peter threw her a beseeching glance.

"I'll go get something to clean up both of you."

Rebecca left the room. Gabriel knelt on the floor next to Peter, who held the puppy at arm's length. "You know animals, like people, don't always do what we want."

"Yeah, I see."

"They can disappoint us." Gabriel removed a handkerchief from his pocket and gave it to Peter.

The child wiped his arm and hand. "Tell me about it."

"Do you want to talk about your dad not being able to make it this morning?"

Peter frowned. "No, there's nothing to talk about. My dad was too busy to come see me. It happens." Shrugging, he brought his pet to his chest and stroked her.

"Yeah, it happens, but that doesn't mean it doesn't hurt us when it does."

"I'm okay. It was just a dumb old fishing trip. I didn't want to go that bad, anyway."

"That's a shame. I was hoping you wanted to go fishing. I know a great place we could all go. We could take a picnic lunch, do some fishing and go hiking in the woods. There are several nature trails we could take."

Peter continued to pet his puppy, but his movements slowed as though he was thinking on what Gabriel had said.

"Of course, this is my own special place. You'll have

to swear to keep it a secret. I don't want too many people knowing about it, or all the good fish will be gone."

Peter slanted a look at Gabriel. "Where?"

"I have to show you."

"Can Josh and Mom come, too?"

"Yeah, sure, even Rose."

Peter tilted his head and thought for a long moment. "Can I bring my puppy?"

"I don't see why not. If she's like Lady, she'll love the outdoors."

Peter scrambled to his feet. "Then let's go. Before it gets too late."

Gabriel laughed. "How about this?" He gestured toward the wet spot on the throw rug.

"Oh." Peter grinned as Rebecca came into the room, carrying a spray bottle, paper towels and a sponge. "Mom will take care of it."

Rebecca thrust the cleanup items into her son's hands while taking his pet. "No, Mom will not. You might as well learn now how to do it."

"But we—"

"No buts, Peter Michaels. If your dog messes, you clean up."

Peter knelt and placed a paper towel over the puddle, muttering something about not having the time.

While her son worked on the mess, Rebecca looked toward Gabriel. "What's going on?"

"We're taking his birthday party to a little spot I

know. How quickly can you prepare a picnic lunch and get ready to enjoy yourself outdoors, fishing, hiking and whatever else we fancy?"

"Where?" Rebecca asked, never one to go blindly anywhere without details.

"Mom, it's a secret. Coach won't say. He has to show us his special place," Peter said, spraying the spot on the rug with half the bottle's contents.

"Hon, I think that's enough." Rebecca took the cleaning liquid from Peter.

"We need to get moving. I want to show Mrs. Wiggles the outdoors. I know she's gonna love going on hikes with me."

Rebecca held a squirming Mrs. Wiggles for Peter to take. "It might be a while before she can go on long walks. I don't think her legs will take her very far."

"I'll be her legs until she can follow me." Peter slapped on his ball cap and started out the door.

Rebecca stared after her son. "What happened here?"

"I made an offer he couldn't refuse?"

Rebecca folded her arms and quirked one brow.

"Okay. People love other people's secrets, and I told Peter I would show him where my secret place was."

"How secret?"

"Oh, probably only about half the county knows."

"Only half? So how many others are going to be joining us at this *secret* place?"

"No one, at least I hope not. It's on a piece of property I own outside of town."

"I didn't know you owned land in the country."

"There's a lot you don't know about me, Rebecca Michaels."

"Aren't you the man of mystery?"

"There's a lot I don't know about you, too."

"True."

"But that's the fun of new friends. Getting to know them." Gabriel walked past her and out the bedroom door.

She followed, watching the casual way he moved, not a wasted motion. *Friends*. That's what they were. Nothing else, Rebecca thought, trying to ignore the bittersweet pang piercing her heart.

Rebecca used her body to shut the door on Gabriel's four-wheel drive, then lugged the two bags of food they had brought on to the plaid blanket spread on the ground. She set the food beside a cooler that was filled with soda and ice. Surveying all they had brought, she had to laugh. Josh sat propped in his swing so he could see his surroundings. Granny sat in her lounge chair, and Gabriel and Josh headed for the stream with their tackle boxes and fishing poles.

Rebecca adjusted the awning on Josh's swing. "I think we have half our house here," she said, sitting in the chair between her youngest and Granny.

Her grandmother patted the arm of her lounger. "All the comforts of home. That's the way I like to commune with nature."

The sound of the stream flowing over rocks and the

birds in the nearby trees soothed Rebecca, and she closed her eyes and let the sun bathe her face. She inhaled a deep breath, the scent of the woods behind her filling her nostrils with pine and earth, a potent reminder of the man responsible for them being here.

Gabriel had given her son a reason to celebrate on his birthday. Peter's laughter filled her with joy. "This is heavenly."

"That it is, child. God knew what He was doing when He created this spot."

Mrs. Wiggles yelped. Rebecca opened her eyes to find the puppy trying to escape the leash that confined her movements. Her son's new pet saw him on the bank, casting his line, and wanted to be with him. "Getting Peter a dog was the best thing I've done in a long time." She rose and untied Mrs. Wiggles, who scampered after Peter.

"I can think of a few more things you've done that were just as good."

"What?"

"Becoming friends with Gabriel. Letting him help you. Child, you don't let people help you often."

"Why, Granny, that's not true. I came to live with you."

"But you insist on doing everything. I have to practically arm wrestle you to hold Josh, to feed him."

"I don't want to be a burden to anyone, especially you, after you were so gracious in opening your home to me and my children. Besides, you're taking care of Josh while I work—at least until I can come up with a more permanent solution."

"You're family. Family is meant to rely on each other. Don't you know that?"

Rebecca found her floppy white hat and put it on. "I suppose I do in here—" she touched her head "—but not in here." She laid a hand over her heart.

"You've closed your heart."

"I can't afford to be hurt again like Craig hurt me. I can't let my family be hurt like that. It's safer not to depend on anyone but myself."

Again Peter's laughter drew Rebecca's attention. She looked at her son reeling in his line, and knew he laughed because of the man next to him. She owed Gabriel a lot. She wished she didn't owe anyone a thing. Owing meant ties, and ties meant emotional involvement, which could leave her open to being hurt again.

Peter held up a small fish for her to see. "The first one, Mom. But we're gonna throw it back because Coach says it's too small to eat. You only keep fish that you'll eat."

"Then you'd better get busy. I'm mighty hungry for fish."

"You don't like fish."

"Well, any fish you catch, I'll eat."

"Promise?"

"Yes."

Peter cast his line into the water, then sat on the bank next to Gabriel, listening to something he was saying. Her son's head was bent toward Gabriel, and she could tell what Gabriel was saying held her son's interest.

"You know, Granny, Gabriel may be good at helping others with their problems, but has anyone helped him through his?"

"What problem?"

"His wife's untimely death."

"Gabriel has dealt with that."

"Has he? Remember last night when Reverend Carson mentioned George McCall was getting out of prison? Gabriel went pale and excused himself. He didn't come back. That isn't the action of a man who has completely dealt with his wife and child's deaths."

"I see what you mean. Maybe you could be there for him. The Lord sends many messengers to do His work."

"I'm not a messenger for the Lord. My life's in such a shambles. I wouldn't know where to begin to help another when I'm struggling with my own problems."

"Nonsense, child, you're very capable of helping others. Come to church tomorrow with me, if not for yourself, then for your children."

"Peter went with you last week. I have to stay home to take care of Josh."

"It's not what you say but how you act in life that has a lasting impression on children. Josh can stay in the nursery while you go to the service."

"But—"

"Others can take care of Josh. He's not a burden. He's a delightful child. Just because Craig wouldn't have anything to do with him doesn't mean others won't."

Gabriel gave Peter his fishing rod and rose. He walked to Rebecca. "I'd like to show Josh how to fish."

He hadn't worded it as a question, but he waited for her to say something before picking up Josh.

"He'll have to wear his hat. I don't want him getting sunburned." Rebecca rummaged in the tote for Josh's cap, found it and gave it to Gabriel.

"See what I mean?" Granny asked when Gabriel took Josh to the stream and sat with him in his lap.

Rebecca watched Gabriel place Josh's hands on the pole then cover them with his larger ones. The man was constantly doing simple things to make her care about him. He probably wasn't even aware of what he was doing. She needed to put some emotional distance between them or she would be lost, her heart broken for the second time in her life. She only had to look at Gabriel's ring finger to have that confirmed.

"You're right, Granny. It isn't fair to my children to impose my feelings on them. I'll go with you to church tomorrow, but I'll feel better if I take Josh to the service. He should be pretty quiet."

"Suit yourself, but our nursery staff is quite capable of taking care of him."

"I'll think about it."

Peter leaped to his feet, letting out a yell. "This has got to be a big one."

Her son struggled to reel in the fish. Ten minutes later Rebecca groaned, realizing she would be eating fish for lunch.

"Look what I caught!" Peter displayed his catch, his chest thrust out in pride. He marched to a second cooler filled with ice and put the fish in it. "You're gonna be so lucky. Coach says his pan-fried fish is to die for."

She smiled at her son. "That's what I'm afraid of."

"I want to take Mrs. Wiggles for a walk."

"I don't want you to go far. I know this is Chief Stone's land, but—"

"Oh, Mom, Coach said I would be okay on the trail. Quit babying me. Why don't you fish for a while until I get back? Keep my spot warm."

"Good idea, Rebecca. And I'll take Josh and feed him his snack. I think he's probably worked up quite an appetite fishing."

Rebecca arched an eyebrow. "Granny, you can stop right there," she said while Peter scooped up Mrs. Wiggles and started for the path that led into the woods. "I know what you're up to."

"More fish. That one in the cooler is for you. There are three more of us that would like some fish for lunch."

"I'll gladly share mine."

"No need for that. Go get us some more."

Her grandmother smiled too sweetly as she followed Rebecca to the stream and took Josh from Gabriel.

"I think Josh was getting the hang of fishing. I had to let go for a second, and he still held onto the pole." Gabriel watched Rebecca sit, his eyes shadowed by the low brim of his baseball cap. "Have you fished before?"

"Once when I was a child." She picked up Peter's pole and looked at the end of the line. "What do I bait it with?"

"This." Gabriel thrust a wiggling worm at her.

She shrieked.

He chuckled. "Obviously I'll have to do the dirty work."

"If you want me to fish." She wrinkled her nose and eyed him while he slipped the worm on the hook. "I thought fishermen used lures nowadays."

"Peter and I had too much fun digging around for worms."

"So that was what you two were doing in the backyard while I was slaving away getting all the food ready."

Rebecca settled on the rock with Gabriel next to her and her line in the water. She slid a glance toward him. "You haven't done very well so far."

"That's a challenge if I ever heard one. Okay, if I get the next fish, you have to do something I want. If you get it, I'll have to do something you want."

"Nothing against our beliefs? Nothing illegal?"

Gabriel pressed his hand over his heart. "Rebecca Michaels, I'm shocked you would ask. After all, I am the police chief." He winked. "You're just gonna have to trust me."

His chuckles were as warm as the sun caressing her skin, leaving her tingling all over. His familiar male scent of pine again reminded her of the woods behind her. His eyes glittered with a carefree promise. "Okay. I'll trust you. It's a deal."

As he focused on his pole, there was nothing casual about him. He was a man on a mission, and Rebecca began to have doubts about the wisdom of agreeing to the challenge. She turned her attention to her fishing rod. She needed to win the challenge. That look in his eyes should have alerted her to the danger of agreeing to the dare.

When she got a nibble a few minutes later, she scrambled to her feet, beaming, and began to bring in her line. "I haven't quite decided what I'll have you do, but—"

The line went slack. Rebecca opened her mouth to say something and closed it without speaking. "It's gone," she finally said when she reeled in the line and saw the empty hook.

Gabriel baited it for her. "Easy come. Easy go."

Rebecca sent the line flying through the air, determined to win. Her thumb slipped. When she glanced at the rod, she saw a tangled mess, and realized it would take hours to unravel the snarl she'd made of Peter's line. She pulled the hook in by hand. The best she could hope for was that Gabriel wouldn't catch anything, either. At the moment she would settle for a tie.

She sat on the large boulder they shared, her body only an arm's length away from his. "Well, at least I got a nibble. You've been there all morning and haven't gotten one bite."

"Is that disappointment I hear in your voice? You hadn't even decided what you'd have me do, whereas I know exactly what I want you to do."

"You do?" she murmured, picturing in her mind Gabriel cupping her face and leaning down—

"I've got one."

He rose with the intention of making sure his fish didn't get away. His every move was full of purpose as he reeled in his line. Rebecca's mouth went dry as the minutes to her defeat neared. When Gabriel swung the fish out of the water and onto the bank, beads of sweat popped out on her forehead. Anticipation and dread mingled to form a knot in her stomach.

Gabriel did short work of taking the fish off the hook and putting it in the cooler. Then he turned to her with a predatory gleam in his eyes. He stalked toward her. She took a step back and almost lost her footing.

"Watch it, Rebecca. I know it's spring, but that water is cold."

Rebecca glanced at her grandmother, who was happily feeding Josh and talking to him. No help there.

Gabriel stopped in front of her. "What in the world do you think I want?"

Her voice refused to work. She shook her head.

Laughter glinted in his eyes. "What happened to that trust you said you had?"

She gulped. "It's there—somewhere."

He clasped her upper arm, deliberately prolonging the suspense.

"Enough. What do I need to do?"

The corners of his mouth lifted. "I want you to come with me Wednesday night to choir practice. Rose says you have a great voice. We could use another singer in the church choir."

The picture of them kissing dissolved into disappointment. Rebecca felt the heat of her embarrassment at what she had been thinking. She was sure it had been written all over her face, too.

With laughter still in his eyes, Gabriel leaned close and whispered, "When we do kiss, it won't be on a bet. That you can be sure of."

He released his grip on her arm and pivoted, leaving Rebecca shaken to the core. "What time do you want me there?"

"I'll pick you up at six forty-five," he said without looking back.

Her trembling hands clasped in front of her, she watched him retrieve the two fish from the cooler and begin to fillet them. She pulled herself together and walked the short distance to the bags holding their food. She needed to keep busy. She couldn't believe she had wanted him to kiss her right there in front of everyone. She was setting herself up to be hurt. This evening she would have to have a strong talk with herself about that. She couldn't take much more of this seesawing back and forth with her emotions concerning one Gabriel Stone.

Peter bounded out of the woods, Mrs. Wiggles in his arms. "I saw a baby deer."

"Was its mother nearby?" Gabriel pulled out a frying pan and placed the fillets in it.

"Yeah. They heard Mrs. Wiggles yelp and fled. Can I help build the fire?"

"Sure. We need twigs. Can you gather some?" Gabriel made a fire pit in the sand and put a ring of stones around it.

Peter brought back enough twigs to start a fire. Gabriel showed him how to lay the twigs properly, then he lit them, blowing on them to get the fire started.

As Gabriel and Peter worked, Rebecca observed them and couldn't shake the feeling Peter's father should be showing him this. When the twigs caught fire, Gabriel set the grill and pan over the flame.

Was Gabriel involved with her and her family because of her or because of her two sons? Were Josh and Peter a substitute for the son he lost? The questions came unbidden into her mind as she stared at the two of them working together. There was something going on between her and Gabriel. But what was it?

Peter watched Gabriel for a few minutes, then headed for the stream with Mrs. Wiggles in his arms. When her eldest son saw his fishing pole, he said, "Mom! It's ruined."

Gabriel glanced up. "Nah. I can fix it later. I was hoping, though, that we could throw the ball some."

Peter's frown evaporated. "Okay. But I'm not very good."

"Is that why you don't want to come out for the team?"

Peter stared at his feet but didn't say anything.

"I can help you with throwing and batting, Peter. We can start this afternoon if you want."

Rebecca held her breath. In Dallas Peter had always been active, playing with his friends. She hated to see him alone.

Peter scuffed the toe of his tennis shoe in the dirt. "It don't look like I'll be fishing anymore, so I guess so."

Rebecca relaxed her tense muscles and continued arranging food on the blanket. When she lounged on her haunches and eyed the lunch before her, she smiled, pleased at what she had managed to throw together on the spur of the moment. Several bags of chips—corn, potato and tortilla—a fruit salad, rolls, pickles, carrots, celery sticks, a three-way bean salad and a chocolate sheet cake with chocolate icing adorned the blanket.

As the aroma of frying fish mingled with the scents of fresh water and forest, her stomach rumbled. Her son had caught a fish, and Gabriel was cooking it. She couldn't ask for a better way to have one of her least favorite dishes.

"Come and get it," Gabriel announced to the group.

Rose propped Josh in his swing, then set it in motion. Rebecca passed out paper plates, plastic forks and napkins.

After the fish was served and the other food dished up, Gabriel said, "Lord bless this food and watch over the people here today partaking in this wonderful feast. When things seem the toughest is when we need You the most. Give us the strength to see beyond our own lives and to be a messenger for You."

When Rebecca glanced up after the prayer, she found him staring at her with an intense look that took her breath away. She'd felt a sweep of emotions today, from joy to despair. She'd witnessed a small miracle when Josh had grabbed the bar on his swing with enough strength to hold it for twenty seconds. Had she given up on the Lord too soon? Was there some purpose only God knew behind all her family had encountered this past year?

She knew what she would have asked Gabriel if she had won the challenge. She wanted him to trust her with his feelings regarding his wife and George McCall. She wanted him to lean on her for a change.

She observed him laugh at something her grandmother said, then fork a slice of fish into his mouth. By the expression on his face he enjoyed every bit as he chewed then took another bite. His eating reminded her that Gabriel was an all-or-nothing kind of guy. He had given his heart once. Could he give it again?

Chapter Eight

Peter held Lady's last puppy close to his chest as he sat next to Rebecca in the lounge of the nursing home the following afternoon. Bess strolled into the room, surprise brightening her expression when she saw Rebecca, Peter and Gabriel on the couch.

"Oh, my, they told me I had visitors. I had no idea so many." Bess crossed the room. "What have you there, young man?" She stroked the puppy in Peter's grasp.

"A gift for you."

"Oh, my, for me." Bess pointed at herself. "May I hold him?"

"It's a girl." Peter held the puppy up for Bess to take.

"I can't believe she's mine." Bess eased into the chair across from them and brought the puppy to her face, breathing deeply. "I've missed this smell. I don't know what to say." She shook her head. "That's not true. I know exactly what to say. Thank you." She looked from

Rebecca to Peter, then finally to Gabriel. "I hope you can stay for tea."

Rebecca swallowed several times before saying, "My grandmother wanted to be here, too, but Josh, my youngest, fell asleep, and she decided to stay home with him. She hated missing meeting you and seeing you get your new pet."

"She's really all mine?" Bess's eyes were large, her hand continuing to stroke the puppy as though reassuring herself the animal was real.

The wonder in Bess's voice gave Rebecca a sense of satisfaction she hadn't felt in a long time.

Gabriel shifted on the couch. "Bess, there are some ground rules I told Susan you would follow concerning your pet."

Bess rubbed her cheek along the puppy's fur. "What?"

"She'll have to stay outside during the day in the garden area. She can sleep in your room at night as long as she doesn't disturb anyone. And Susan wants all the other residents to enjoy her, too."

"But what about bad weather?"

"Peter and I are going to build you a doghouse so she'll be fine during bad weather."

"You're going to do that for me?" Bess stared at Peter.

He nodded, his shoulders thrust back, a pleased look on his face.

Gabriel leaned forward, resting his elbows on his knees and loosely clasping his hands. "Bess, this is for a trial period. If this doesn't work, I'll have to take the puppy back. Susan wasn't sure if this was a good idea, but I know it is."

"Of course, it is. Peepers and me will do just fine." Bess straightened in her chair with the puppy curled in her lap. "Now, young man, tell me about yourself. Do you have a dog?"

For the next hour Rebecca relaxed and enjoyed herself, sitting between Gabriel and Peter and listening to them talk about the best breeds of dogs. When it was time to leave, everyone had decided that a mutt was the best breed.

On the drive to her grandmother's, Peter inundated Rebecca with questions concerning the nursing home and Bess Anderson. Finally she held up her hand and said, "Peter, I think you should volunteer at the home. I know you and Gabriel are going to build the doghouse for Peepers, but I bet some of the people would love to have you read to them. Some of them have poor eyesight and can't read anymore."

Peter leaned forward, a puzzled expression on his face. "But, Mom, when? I need to work on my batting and throwing and then there's the team practices several times a week."

"Hon, if you want to do something, you'll find a way. Think about it."

He relaxed, suddenly quiet. When Gabriel pulled into her grandmother's driveway, Peter scrambled from the Jeep and hurried toward the house.

Rebecca laughed. "I have a feeling before long he's going to hate leaving Mrs. Wiggles, especially for school."

"Then there's practice after school," Gabriel said, turning the engine off and twisting so he faced her.

"Such dilemmas for him."

The mellow atmosphere in the car shifted. Rebecca was acutely aware that she was alone with Gabriel—if a person could call being in a car in broad daylight on a fairly busy street alone. His particular scent wafted to her and swirled about her, drawing her into his sphere of influence.

"In the past few days I've seen some of the old Peter coming through. Thank you for your help." Rebecca flattened herself against the passenger side door and rested her left arm along the back of the seat.

"It was nothing."

"Nothing? Gabriel Stone, you have a way with people. You genuinely like them, and they in turn like and respect you—even my son. That is nothing? You're supposed to say you're welcome and accept the praise graciously."

He shrugged and smiled sheepishly. "I suppose that's one of my downfalls. I get uncomfortable when someone says something nice about me." His grin widened. "But you're welcome, Rebecca. I appreciate your kind words."

"See. That wasn't so bad. You didn't choke or anything." She looked at her hand loosely curled in her lap then into his warm gaze. "I would like to return the favor. I want to help you." She was finding the word *want* was too mild for what she was feeling. *Need* was more like it.

"I don't need any help. Everything's fine."

"Is it? For the past two days we have avoided talking about Friday night at the pizza place."

A cloud moved into his eyes—dark, ominous. "There's nothing to talk about. We ate. We went home."

"And we talked about George McCall."

Gabriel stiffened, all casualness gone from his expression. His brows slashed downward. His eyes narrowed. "What do you want me to say? That I'm afraid of what I'll do when I see the man? That my thoughts are anything but Christian?" He gripped the steering wheel, his knuckles ghostly white.

Rebecca waited for a long moment before she answered. "I want you to talk to me. Let me help you through this pain you're feeling. If not me, then at least talk to someone else. It's eating you up inside, this anger you're feeling."

"It's not anger, Rebecca. It's guilt."

"Guilt?"

"Yes. I saw George driving earlier in the day. I didn't pull him over or anything. If I had, my wife and child would be alive. Do you know what that does to a man?" Gabriel yanked open his door and bolted from the Jeep.

Rebecca sat with her mouth slightly open and watched him storm down the street. The anger in his body wasn't directed at George, but at himself. She realized mixed up in that anger was a deep, soul-wrenching pain that was tearing him up inside. She hurriedly climbed out of the vehicle and ran after him.

Rebecca grabbed his arm to halt his escape. "Gabriel Stone, how dare you drop a bomb like that then go stalking off down the street."

He rounded on her, a war of emotions playing across his face. "I have nothing else to say. You wanted to know what was going on. Now you know." A neutral expression finally settled in place as though nothing of importance had happened a few minutes before.

She released her grip on his arm and stabbed her thumb toward his vehicle. "And what do I do about your Jeep in my driveway? I may have plans for later today. I don't particularly relish trenching my grandmother's front lawn in order to get my car out."

He glanced toward the vehicle in question. "Oh."

"Oh, is right."

He strode toward the Jeep. Rebecca hurried to keep up. At the driver's side she threw her body between Gabriel and the door.

"We need to talk about this."

"Why do women always want to talk?"

"Why do men always want to ignore what they're feeling?"

He glared at her, his arms rigid at his sides. "Because talking doesn't always help."

"Then listen," Rebecca said, trying to breathe normally. His nearness made her heart beat way too fast. She had no one to blame but herself. She'd placed herself in this position, so close her hands itched to touch him.

He arched a brow. "Listen?"

"Yeah. Hindsight is always one hundred percent. How could you know what George was going to do later in the day? Was he driving recklessly at the time you saw him?"

His scowl darkened. "I thought you only wanted me to listen."

"Was he?"

"No, but I knew about George's drinking problem."

"The accident wasn't your fault. Period."

"Easy to say. Hard to believe."

"I can't make you believe that, but you're beating yourself up over something you had no control over."

"Kinda like you?"

She pulled herself up straight. "What do you mean?"

"Did you have any control over your husband leaving you?"

"No."

"Did you want him to leave?"

"No."

"Then why are you beating yourself up over something you couldn't control? We can't control everything around us. And hiding from life won't give us any more control over it."

Gabriel stepped so close she could feel his breath on her face. She sucked in a deep swallow of air that did nothing to relieve the tightness in her chest. She pushed him away and slid from between him and the Jeep. "You have a way of turning things around. You're good at avoiding discussions about yourself."

"Boring subject."

"Only to you," she said, without thinking through what she was admitting.

"You think I'm interesting?"

"I didn't say that."

"But you implied it." He grinned. "Admit it, Rebecca Michaels."

She glared at him. "Yes, I think you're interesting."

His grin broadened.

"But then I think all my friends are interesting or they wouldn't be my friends."

"Right. Friends."

She wanted to scream. "What do you want me to say? We *are* friends. I'm not ready for more, and you certainly aren't either."

Leaning against the Jeep, he folded his arms across his chest. "Why do you say that?"

She wasn't sure what drove her to touch him, but she did. She took his left hand and held it in front of his face. "This. A man who wears his wedding ring isn't ready to move on."

He stared at his ring finger then at her, surprise flittering across his face, as though what she had said was news to him. "You're right," he admitted slowly.

"And all of my energy has to be directed at holding my family together and getting back on my feet."

"Then I guess it's friends." He thrust his hand toward her to shake.

She took it in hers and felt a jolt streak up her arm. "Yes," she declared in a strong voice, while inside she felt as if she were lying to herself—and him.

Wednesday night Rebecca sat in the front pew, listening to the choir sing. Their voices rang loud and clear in the church, filling it with beautiful music. She was glad he won the fishing challenge and wanted her to come to choir practice.

When the song was over, Gabriel said, "We'll take a ten-minute break, then finish practicing for the Sunday service."

He strode to Rebecca. "Well, what do you think? Care to join us?"

She shook her head. "I don't sing for other people anymore."

"Then who do you sing for?"

"Myself. Sometimes Josh."

He eyed her. "Are you shy, Rebecca Michaels? If so, there's nothing to be shy about. You'll be one of many. I promise I won't have you do a solo unless you want to." He held up his hand as though he was swearing in court.

"I don't think—"

Alicia sat next to her on the pew. "Oh, come on, Rebecca. We can always use another voice. Besides, we have the best seats in the house."

"But I'll have Josh with me during the church service."

"I know Rose wouldn't mind taking care of Josh during the service." Alicia patted her hand as though everything was settled, then called to another choir member and hurried over to her.

"Gabriel, I can't ask Granny to take care of Josh on Sunday. She does during the week."

"Then there's the nursery. Mabel is in charge of it, and she does a great job."

"Mabel!" Rebecca could picture the nursery, all the babies lined up as though they were in the military.

"Now, Rebecca, Mabel's wonderful with the children. There's a side of her you haven't seen."

"I think I'll pass."

"All I ask of you is to try it one time. If it doesn't work out, not another word."

"Is that a promise?"

"Yes."

"One time and then you won't say another word?"

"Yes."

She smiled sweetly at him, intending to suffer through one half of a practice and one service. Then that would be it.

Gabriel took her hand and pulled her to her feet. "Come on up and join us. We're gonna practice 'Oh How I Love Jesus.'"

By the time the choir practice was over thirty minutes later, the group had made Rebecca feel welcome. She stood by Alicia, who talked to her between songs and introduced her to everyone. When

Gabriel wanted to put Rebecca in the front row, Alicia insisted Rebecca would be better off in the back. He hadn't argued.

"Good night, Rebecca," Alicia said and waved goodbye to her.

Once all the members had left, the sudden quiet in the church seemed disconcerting after all the noise. Rebecca watched as Gabriel turned out the lights. The only illumination that streamed into the sanctuary came from the large door she held open. He approached her. She plastered herself against the paneled door to keep it open. She suddenly realized they were alone. Everyone else had cleared out fast, wanting to get home to their families.

She licked her lips and forgot to breathe as he waited for her to walk out of the church. He fell into step beside her, taking her hand.

"I'm glad you didn't mind walking tonight, Rebecca. I just couldn't pass up such a beautiful night."

She relished the strong feel of his hand holding hers. Staring at the dark sky with stars beginning to glitter in the blackness, she had to agree. "Walking's nice. I wish I had more time to exercise. I used to a lot before—" Her words trailed off.

"Before what?"

"It's not important. I just decided I need to stop thinking about my life in terms of before my divorce and after my divorce."

"Explain."

The softly spoken command mingled with the sound of the insects chirping, compelling her to open up to Gabriel. She felt the comfort of her hand nestled in his. She smelled the scent of a spring night, laced with honeysuckle growing nearby.

"I'm not sure I can."

He stopped in the middle of the sidewalk and drew her in front of him. He took her other hand. "Try, please."

"Before Craig walked out on us, my life revolved around trying to please him, trying to be the perfect wife and mother. I would spend hours keeping the house clean and making sure the meals were just what he wanted. I forgot who I was in the process. After he left, I was forced to discover the person I am. I'm still working on that." She attempted a smile, which wavered. "Being a single parent is hard. It's doubly hard when deep down you're not sure who you are."

"Rebecca, that's where the Lord can help. Turn to Him. Seek answers from Him."

"I'm not sure it's that simple."

He shook his head. "I never said it was simple. Really become a part of the church and you'll see the way."

A car passed, and the driver honked. Rebecca used the distraction to step away from Gabriel. He waved to the driver, then turned his attention on her again.

She wished the moon wasn't so bright. She could read the question in his eyes and didn't have any answers for him. She was still trying to figure out who she was. How could she commit herself to God when she was floundering so much?

"Come on. It's getting late, and I know we both have to be at work early."

"And I can't be late. After being on the job for two weeks, I finally got Mabel to smile at me today. I almost brought out the confetti but was afraid of her reaction when I started throwing it."

"See? I told you she was a pussycat," he said with a chuckle and began to walk again.

"More like a tiger."

"Ah, I have faith in you. You'll learn to handle her in no time."

A warmth suffused her at his words. *I have faith in you.* If she could only restore her faith in herself. Maybe then she could believe in the power of God again.

Rebecca held Josh, not wanting to turn him over to Mabel. Maybe she should forget singing in the choir today. Or maybe she could hold Josh while she sang. That shouldn't be too difficult. He only weighed a little over twenty pounds.

"Mrs. Michaels, are you going to leave your son?" Mabel asked, waiting at the door to the church nursery.

"Please call me Rebecca, at least at church," she said, delaying. Her mind frantically came up with one excuse after another not to leave Josh.

"There are other parents behind you." Mabel's voice softened.

Rebecca glanced over her shoulder and offered the two couples behind her a smile. "Sorry. First-time jitters."

She stepped to the side and let the other parents drop off their children. She noticed they had no qualms about giving their babies to Mabel. Rebecca knew that the church would be careful to whom they entrusted their children, but she hadn't left Josh with a stranger—not that Mabel was really a stranger, but to Josh she was.

After the other parents walked away, Rebecca faced Mabel again and thrust Josh at her before she talked herself out of it. Mabel took Josh in her arms, cradling him in such a tender way that Rebecca was speechless. She tried to form words, but she couldn't. She watched the Dragon Lady coo at Josh and grin like any grandmother. The smile that graced Mabel's mouth transformed her face into a countenance Rebecca wouldn't have believed if she hadn't seen it with her own two eyes. The Dragon Lady was a different person when she smiled.

Mabel peered at Rebecca, a softness in her expression. "Do you have his bag?"

Rebecca blinked, breaking the trance. "Yes. Here." She handed the tote to Mabel, who placed it on the floor next to the door.

"Are there any instructions…Rebecca?"

Hearing her name on the woman's lips for the first time surprised Rebecca. Yes, she realized she had asked Mabel to call her by her given name, but she had honestly thought Mabel would ignore the request. "He likes to watch people. He just needs to be propped up with pillows, in case he loses his balance while sitting, or you can put him on a pallet on the floor or in a crib. Whichever works for you. I'll be back immediately after the service."

"You aren't going to the adult class after the service?"

"Yes, but I'll take Josh with me."

"Why? He'll be fine here with me and the other children."

Rebecca wasn't sure how to answer the woman. She had been forced to leave Josh with her grandmother five days a week to go to work. She felt bad enough about that. Josh required so much care, and she hated others having to do it. She never wanted her son to feel she had abandoned him.

Someone touched her on her shoulder. She pivoted to find Gabriel standing behind her. Her heart raced at the sight of him. She smiled.

"Church is going to start soon," he said, returning her smile. "Ready for your debut?"

"You make it sound like I'm going to sing a solo." She slanted him a look. "I'm not, am I?"

"Of course not." He began walking toward the sanctuary. "I'm glad to see you here, dressed in your choir robes. I wasn't sure you would join us."

"I said I would." She thought about her moment of faltering at the nursery door and decided not to tell him how close she had come to backing out.

"Josh will be fine with Mabel."

"I know in my head that I need to share my care of Josh with others. That's a fact that has come home quite a lot lately. It's just hard to convince my heart. I have protected him from the day he was born. He has always known I was there for him no matter what."

Gabriel paused at the door to the sanctuary. "Who have you had to protect him from?"

"Some people find it hard to accept a child with special needs."

"Who?" He looked deep into her eyes. "Your ex-husband?"

Rebecca laid her hand on his arm. "Craig never tried to harm Josh. He just wouldn't have anything to do with him. He completely ignored Josh, as though he didn't exist from the day he was born. It broke my heart to see it."

"I'm sorry, Rebecca. Not all men—people are like that."

"I've just learned to be protective when it comes to Josh. As he gets older and he's more aware of people's reactions to him, it will hurt him."

"He's one of God's children. It won't happen here." He covered her hand and squeezed gently. "Not if I'm around."

Basking in his words, Rebecca connected with Gabriel on a level that startled her, her gaze trapped by the fervent appeal in his. He made her feel special, important. If only that were true, she thought, and slipped her hand from his arm. He had been pulled into her family because of her children. He was drawn to her two sons. She was thankful for that, but she realized she wanted more.

Rebecca followed Gabriel to the front of the church where the choir sang. She passed her grandmother, Peter and Bess, who had come with them. Bess waved at her. Rebecca waved back, responding to the woman's joy at coming to the service with Rebecca's family. Peter whispered something to Bess, and the older woman smiled, patting his leg. Rebecca wished she had thought about inviting Bess to the church, but it had been Peter's idea. Her son felt a bond with the woman. Their pets were sisters, he'd told her this morning.

The service flew by. She started singing her first song, and before she realized it, she sang her last note. Listening to Gabriel's solo performance had moved her beyond words. She had heard some of it in practice Wednesday night, but for some reason after Reverend Carson's stirring sermon on God's forgiveness, Gabriel's tribute had touched something deep inside her. She remembered their conversation earlier in the week about George McCall and wondered if it had struck Gabriel as deeply as her.

As the congregation filed out of the sanctuary, Rebecca hung back. When only a couple of women were left, she sat in the pew and savored the quiet serenity. She felt at peace—as though God had reached down and blessed her. Could it be possible that there was a reason for all that had happened the past few years? That He hadn't forsaken her and her family?

Slowly she rose and walked from the church, reluctant to leave. In the foyer she noticed some people milling about, but most were making their way to their Sunday school classes. She hurried to get Josh.

At the nursery she stopped in the doorway and watched Mabel cuddling her son in the crook of her arm while she read a story to the other children who weren't sleeping. Her animated voice surprised Rebecca. Mabel threw her whole self into the story, making it come alive for the children. Even Josh was listening and looking at Mabel. Quietly Rebecca backed out of the nursery, her assessment of Mabel changing.

"See? Didn't I tell you Mabel was good with the kids?" Gabriel whispered in her ear.

Rebecca sucked in a deep breath. She felt his breath on her neck and shivered. She edged away from the nursery before replying, "You were right. I'll stop worrying about Josh."

"No, you won't, but then mothers are supposed to worry about their children."

"Not just mothers."

The mischievous gleam in Gabriel's eyes dimmed. "No, fathers should, too. And most would."

Rebecca knew there were injustices in this world. Gabriel not being a father was one of them. "You can still be a father, Gabriel. You're a young man," she replied to comfort him, then blushed when she realized what she had said. "I mean—"

He placed his finger over her mouth. "Shh. I know what you mean."

Do you really? she wanted to ask. There was a part of her that fancied rescuing Gabriel and another part that wanted to run as fast as she could away from him and what could be if circumstances were different in their lives. But circumstances weren't different. He was still in love with his deceased wife, and she was scared to commit to another man.

Chapter Nine

A gentle breeze blew as Rebecca stepped onto the patio and breathed deeply of the flower-scented air. She threw her head back and relished the sun's rays on her face. After several days of rain, she welcomed this perfect seventy-degree weather. A perfect Saturday. Staring at the cobalt blue sky, she noticed not one cloud.

The sound of hammering lured her attention to the two guys in her backyard. They had been working diligently for the past few hours. Peter's head was bent over a board, intense concentration on his face. Gabriel studied a sheet of paper, a frown marring his expression. They both wore cutoffs and white T-shirts with tool belts about their waists.

"Ready for a break?" she called.

Her son hit a nail one last time, then stood, the hammer dangling from the tool belt Gabriel had given him at the beginning of the doghouse project. "Mom! Come look at what Coach and me have done so far."

She made her way toward the pair. Her son looked like a small version of the guy who used to build and remodel homes on the public broadcast station. Gabriel rose, too. He looked like a larger version of the same guy. Like father, like son. The phrase popped into her head, and she stopped short. Were Peter and Josh replacing Gabriel's deceased son? Were her two boys the reason he hung around so much? She shook the disturbing questions from her mind, determined not to let anything disrupt their evening.

"It's starting to look like a doghouse. I see three walls. Is that the roof over there?" She pointed to two pieces of plywood.

"I'm going to ignore that teasing tone and take your words at face value. I never said I was a builder, carpenter or anything remotely in that industry, but Peter and I are two intelligent guys who can surely figure out these blueprints." Gabriel held up the instructions he had purchased from the hardware store.

"I have all the confidence in the world in you two. I fixed some lemonade, and Granny baked some chocolate chip cookies. Peter, you can go get some if you want."

"Oh, great," Peter said, racing toward the back door, the hammer slapping against his side.

"I guess we're ready for a break since my helper has deserted me."

"Mention chocolate chip cookies and my son is a lost cause."

"This guy isn't much different. Where are those cookies?"

"Have a seat on the patio. I'll bring you a plate, if there are any left, and some lemonade."

"You tell Peter if I don't have my share of cookies there will be extra laps at practice."

Rebecca laughed as she went into the house. "I doubt that will make a bit of difference."

"That's what I was afraid of."

In the kitchen Rebecca quickly retrieved two tall glasses from the cabinet and filled them with ice. She noticed her son had taken, by her estimate, at least six cookies and gone off by himself to enjoy them. Peter must be protecting his territory.

After she placed the tray with the cookies and lemonades in the middle of the patio table, she sat across from Gabriel, who rested his head on the bright yellow cushion, his eyes closed, his legs spread as though he was exhausted.

"Tired?" Rebecca took a sip of lemonade.

He pried one eye open and said, "It's hard work trying to maintain an image in front of an impressionable boy. I don't want him to spread the word around town about how inept I am at putting together anything."

"You can always bribe him with your share of chocolate chip cookies."

Gabriel sat up, shaking his head. "Can't do that. I guess I will just have to suffer the slings and arrows of my fellow townspeople."

"Have you had any success in getting Peter to play on the team?"

Gabriel took a bite of cookie, leaving only half of it. "We're gonna practice some later. He's getting a lot better. When he feels comfortable enough, he'll play. I've seen him study the batters. I think he wants to try but is afraid of making a fool of himself."

"Not too different from his coach."

"Hey, I take offense at that remark." He popped the last half of the cookie into his mouth and washed it down with some lemonade. "I'm gonna have to tell Rose she has outdone herself with these cookies."

"She'll love hearing that. Cooking is one of her favorite things. Actually I think that's who I got my love of cooking from. My mother never enjoyed even the simplest task in the kitchen."

"Do you get to cook much?"

"Are you kidding? Granny barely lets me into her private culinary retreat."

"You can always come over to my house and practice. Wouldn't want you to lose your touch."

"And you'd get a home-cooked meal."

"Yep. Can't blame a guy for trying any way he can."

"I might just take you up on that offer."

He leaned forward and snatched another cookie off the plate. "When?"

Suddenly an underlying tension weaved its way into their exchange. "Well." She fumbled in her mind for an answer. "I don't know."

"We could call it a date." He slanted a look at her that melted her insides.

Thankfully she was sitting or she was afraid she would have collapsed. "A date?" She squeaked the words.

"Yes. You know, where a man and a woman go out together to get to know each other."

"One of those," she murmured. She hadn't had a date in over twelve years. She wasn't sure how one was conducted anymore.

"Of course, I know it's a bit unorthodox to have your date cook dinner, but I'm sure it's done in some circles."

"You don't know?" she asked, purposefully putting a teasing note in her voice. She needed to lighten the mood quickly.

"I haven't dated in fourteen years."

"I haven't in twelve. So we'll be the blind leading the blind."

"Should be an interesting date."

"Okay, for argument's sake, say I accept this date."

"There's no argument here," he said with a grin and a wink.

She threw him a frown to quiet him. "If you'll let me finish. What do you like to eat?"

"Just about anything I don't have to fix."

"So if I prepare liver and onions, you'll be happy and eat every little bite?"

"Just about anything except liver and onions. The onions I don't mind, but the liver I can pass on."

"You know you really aren't helping me. Let me rephrase the question. What is your favorite food?"

He tapped his chin with his forefinger and looked skyward as though he were in deep thought. "Nothing beats a thick T-bone steak."

"Grilling is the man's job."

"How about I grill the steaks and you fix everything else—whatever you want? Surprise me."

She narrowed her eyes, pretending to consider his proposition carefully. "This might be my time to get back at you for that challenge you won when we went fishing."

His grin widened. "I'm banking on your sweet nature and the fact I'm the town's police chief."

Rebecca couldn't resist the laughter bubbling inside her. Since meeting Gabriel, she had smiled and laughed more than she had in two years. "Okay, I guess you have me over a barrel."

"Now, that's a sight I need to think on."

"What sight, Coach?" Peter pushed open the back door and came outside.

Rebecca started brushing cookie crumbs off her son's chest and face.

"Ah, Mom." Peter tried to step away.

Rebecca grabbed his arm and held him still. "I don't mind you eating the cookies, but I do mind you wearing them."

Peter stood next to her while she finished her task, but his arms and feet didn't stop fidgeting.

"How about me? Do I have any crumbs on my face?"

The teasing tone in Gabriel's voice made her blush. She shot him an exasperated look. "You have a smudge of chocolate right here." She reached out and wiped some from the corner of his mouth with her finger.

Gabriel blinked, surprised by her action. The teasing gleam faded from his gaze to be replaced with astonishment and something else Rebecca didn't want to analyze.

"Coach, ready to go back to work?"

Gabriel shook his head, trying to rid his mind of one recurring thought. Her touch was dynamite. Maybe he should eat another cookie and leave chocolate on his face.

"Coach?" Peter waved his hand in front of Gabriel's face.

Gabriel blinked again. "Oh, sorry. Just thinking. Ready to work?"

"If I'm not mistaken, Granny is expecting you to stay for dinner, unless you would rather eat alone at home," Rebecca said while she gathered up the plate and glasses.

"Nah. If you all insist, I'll stay. It's a dirty job, but someone has to do it."

"The way Josh eats, it certainly is a dirty job." Rebecca headed for the back door.

Gabriel watched her leave, a warmth mellowing him when he thought about their earlier bantering. He hadn't done that in a long time. He had forgotten what it was like to flirt with a beautiful woman and for her to flirt back.

"Hey, Coach, ready?"

"Yes, Peter, I am."

He clasped the boy around his shoulders and walked with him to where the pieces of doghouse littered the yard. Spending the day with Peter confirmed how much he wished he were a father. He wished he were Peter and Josh's father. That realization snatched his next breath, leaving him struggling for air. He had always been involved in children's lives, but with these two boys he had taken it a step further. Was Rebecca the reason?

"What should we do next, Coach?"

Gabriel focused on what needed to be done. "Let's get all the walls up, then take a look at that roof."

"When we're finished, I want to paint the house."

"What color?" Gabriel cocked his head as though that would help him read the directions better.

"I guess since Peepers is a girl, let's paint it something girly. I can't see pink, though. How about yellow?"

"Sounds good to me." Gabriel held the directions at arm's length then brought them close. He knew they weren't written in a foreign language, but it sure did seem like it when he was trying to figure out what they meant by place knob A into notch D. He wished he had paid more attention in shop.

"You know, Coach, I've been thinking about Miss Bess and the people at the nursing home."

"That's great." Maybe if he held the directions upside down they would make sense.

"I think the team should volunteer once a week to read to the old people there. What do you think?"

"Old people?" Gabriel turned his attention to Peter.

"Yeah, I was thinking we could each adopt a grand-mother or grandfather and read to them or play a game with them. I thought I would adopt Miss Bess. She needs me. She reminds me of Granny, and Granny has us. Miss Bess needs us, too."

Gabriel's throat thickened. A month before Peter had been angry at the world. Now he was starting to look at other people's needs and problems and coming up with solutions that made a lot of sense. Gabriel had read somewhere that the more connections a person had, the longer the person would live.

What would happen if suddenly he lost this family? That was a question he never wanted to discover the answer to. He realized he had come to depend on them to feel needed.

Gabriel swallowed several times and said, "Sounds like a doable plan to me."

"Then you don't mind if I say something to David and the others at practice on Monday?"

"Go right ahead. I'll let you organize it, and if you need anyone to help, ask for a volunteer."

"I think David will. I'll call him tonight and ask him if he's interested."

Gabriel wadded the directions into a ball and tossed them toward the trash pile. He could understand his brother-in-law's frustration when he tried to put his niece's dollhouse together last Christmas. Gabriel would never say another word to the man about how hard could it be to put a little old house together. Nope, not a word.

"Tell you what, Peter, let's take a break and practice some ball for a while. When we come back, we'll put our two heads together and come up with a way to finish this doghouse."

"Are you sure?" Peter scanned the lumber scattered across the yard.

"No, but don't tell anyone I don't have the foggiest idea what I'm doing when it comes to tools. However, I have faith we can manage something. Peepers will need a place to sleep. Rest assured, the Lord will provide a bed—" he glanced at the walls of the doghouse "—of sorts."

"Do you need anything in here?" Rebecca asked Bess as they walked toward the drugstore on Main Street the following Saturday.

"Some hair dye."

"Of course. How long has it been since you dyed your hair?"

"Oh, ages. My dark hair is starting to show."

Rebecca held the door for Bess. "Dark hair? Isn't that what you want?"

Bess headed for the aisle where the dyes were and homed in on the silver. "I refuse to fight Mother Nature. Years ago when I noticed my hair turning gray, I decided to help it along. I dye it every few months to keep the nice silver look, but with everything happening lately I've not kept up."

Rebecca chuckled. The more she was around Bess, the more she liked the way the woman looked at life. She didn't always make sense, but when she did, it was beautiful.

"Ladies, what brings you out on a Saturday afternoon? I saw your car parked out front, Rebecca, and decided to check on my two favorite ladies."

"Why, Chief Stone, what a nice surprise." Bess's eyes twinkled, and her face wrinkled into a bright smile. "Peepers is enjoying her new house."

"Then it's still standing?"

"Why wouldn't it be? You made it."

"Just checking."

Rebecca rolled her eyes. She had seen what Gabriel and her son had gone through. She wouldn't disillusion Bess on Gabriel's ability at carpentry. But the test would come when the first thunderstorm hit, which shouldn't be too far in the future.

Gabriel followed Bess to the cashier, and Rebecca followed Gabriel. He glanced at her and smiled as though he was giving her a private greeting. Rebecca felt the heat in her cheeks and was glad when Bess said something to distract him.

"We were about to get something to drink at the café. Care to join us, Chief Stone?"

"Only if you call me Gabriel, Bess."

"I like calling you Chief Stone."

He nodded. "Then by all means do."

They walked the few steps to the diner next door, and

Gabriel held the door open while Rebecca and Bess entered. In the middle of the afternoon, the café was deserted except for one customer who was finishing his coffee and a piece of pie.

Bess paused and watched the man slide the last bit of pie into his mouth. "That's what I want. I love desserts. The more calories and fat there is, the better it is." She sat in the nearest chair and waved for the waitress.

"Young lady, I'll have a large piece of pecan pie with vanilla ice cream on top. Now, no skimpy slice for me." Bess wagged her finger at the waitress. "And I'll have some hot tea, too, with a slice of lemon and honey."

After Rebecca and Gabriel ordered iced tea minus any slices of pie, Bess sighed and placed her purse carefully on the floor next to her chair. Then she took off her white gloves and laid them beside her fork and napkin, one on top of the other. The waitress returned almost immediately with their orders.

"You know, Rebecca, a piece of pie would fill in a few of those curves. I always found curves draw a man's attention."

Rebecca almost choked on her swallow of tea. The liquid went down the wrong way, and she tried to catch her breath. Gabriel pounded on her back. Her eyes watered as she coughed. Slowly she managed to draw air into her lungs.

He leaned close to Rebecca and whispered, "So does nearly choking to death."

Rebecca sent him a *be quiet* look and returned her attention to the older woman across from her. "Thanks, I'll remember that, Bess." She squeaked the words out in a breathy voice.

"Just trying to help. Those boys of yours need a father, especially Peter. Such a fine boy."

"But they—"

Bess waved her words away. "Don't tell me they already have one. Rose told me, and he doesn't count. He's never around. Peter told me about his birthday."

"He did?" Rebecca asked, stunned. Her son wasn't one to open up to just anyone. She knew Peter had visited Bess several times, but she hadn't known they'd become confidants.

"Of course, he did. We talk about everything. Your boys need someone right here in Oakview." Bess cut a large bite of pie, popped it into her mouth and chewed slowly, closing her eyes as though savoring every delicious bit of the dessert. Then she took a sip of tea.

Rebecca heard her stomach rumble. She licked her lips and wished she could enjoy a dessert. But just being in the same room with such a rich pie could add pounds to her body, Rebecca thought with a last wistful look at the near empty plate in front of Bess.

Bess pointed her fork at Gabriel. "And, Chief Stone, you've been alone long enough. You're too good a man to waste. Get back into the thick of things."

"Bess, I am—"

"No, you aren't. You still wear your wedding ring.

That screams 'Do not approach, taken,' to any woman interested." Bess ate another bite of her dessert, smacking her lips. "This will certainly go right to my hips, but then at my age I don't have to worry. By the time the fat could kill me, I'll be dead anyway. One of the advantages to being old."

Rebecca felt Gabriel's astonished gaze on her. She was afraid to look at the man. She was sure her face was beet red. Bess had forgotten what the word tact meant.

"So when are you two going out on a date?"

Gabriel nearly spewed his tea all over the table. He managed to recover quicker than Rebecca did, but his eyes were wide and his mouth hung open slightly.

"Chief?" Bess quirked a brow at him. "I never took you to be a foolish man."

Rebecca glanced at her watch. "Oh, look at the time, Bess. I have to get you back to Shady Oaks."

"I'm not leaving until I finish this last bite and get an answer to my question." Bess stared hard at Gabriel.

"Bess, Rebecca and I already have a date."

"We do?" Rebecca said before she realized Bess would pounce on that comment.

"Remember last weekend when I was building the doghouse and we talked on the patio?"

"When are you going out?"

"Tomorrow night," Gabriel said.

At the same time Rebecca answered, "Sometime soon."

Bess arched a brow. "Which is it?"

Rebecca peered at Gabriel and let him get them out of this mess. "Rebecca, will you go out with me tomorrow night?"

"But I haven't shopped for any of the food I'll need."

"Ah, are you going to cook him something to eat? My mother always said the way to a man's heart was through his stomach, and my Ralph certainly proved her right."

"I'll meet you at the grocery store after you take Bess home."

"Well, in that case, Rebecca, let's shake a leg. You've got plans to make."

"We don't have to go out," Rebecca said as she walked next to the shopping cart Gabriel pushed down the meat aisle. "We probably need to put our foot down or Bess will think she can manipulate us into doing anything she wants."

"I'm not arguing with this plan." He grinned. "I get a home-cooked meal out of it. Why should I disagree."

"I know I should take offense, but I get to cook a meal—finally."

"So we both get what we want."

"Just two happy campers."

"Right." Gabriel stopped at the case that held the steaks and carefully inspected each package before placing one in the cart. "I have my part. Where do you want to go?"

"The produce section first."

As Rebecca strolled next to Gabriel, she couldn't shake the feeling that their relationship was shifting, whether it was Bess's doing or not. Yes, friends cooked for each other, but this felt as if they were more than friends. She should put a stop to this date before things got out of hand, before Bess did something else to throw them together. But she wanted to cook for Gabriel. She loved to cook, and Craig never had appreciated her efforts. For some reason she felt Gabriel would be different, and she needed that.

"Well, isn't this a surprise?" Alicia nearly locked carts with Gabriel when they rounded a corner simultaneously from opposite directions. "Shopping together? Anything I should know about?"

"Not if we don't want the whole town to know before the sun goes down," Gabriel replied, stepping to maneuver around Alicia.

"Gabriel Stone, I do not gossip."

Both Gabriel's eyebrows shot up. "That's news to me."

"Okay, so I like to talk a little. But no one will hear about this from me." Alicia started down the aisle.

Gabriel watched Alicia disappear. "Don't count on that, Rebecca. Tomorrow in church, I'm afraid, you'll be inundated with questions about us."

"Just me?" She ignored the words *about us*. It made them sound like a couple.

"No, I'm afraid I will, too." Gabriel headed for the checkout.

"I keep forgetting how small towns are. Will the

gossip bother you?" She wasn't sure how she felt about being linked with Gabriel romantically. No, that wasn't quite the truth. She was terrified because she was starting to care a great deal about the man, and she didn't think he was ready for another commitment. She wasn't sure she could handle another commitment emotionally after Craig had hurt her so badly. And she was positive she didn't want her children to suffer anymore.

"I'm a man in the public eye. Gossip follows me."

"It does? I haven't heard a word of it."

"You mean you haven't heard about Calvin and me? Or Annie and me?"

Rebecca put their items on the checkout counter. "No, what about them?"

"Oh, nothing." Gabriel took out his wallet to pay the cashier.

Rebecca was aware of the young woman behind the counter listening intently to their conversation. Rebecca refrained from saying another word until they were outside. She followed Gabriel to his Jeep, handing him bags to place inside. He closed the back door, then went to the driver's side.

Rebecca stopped him with a hand on his arm. "Oh, no, you don't. You can't casually mention some little tidbit then not say another word. I'm human and I want to know about Calvin and Annie."

"It isn't about Calvin and Annie. It's about Calvin and me and Annie and me. Two separate stories." He grinned and slid behind the steering wheel. "Two stories

I'll save until we have dinner tomorrow night." He started the engine and backed out of the parking space, leaving her standing in front of the grocery store.

Who was Annie? It was all Rebecca could think about as she drove home. When she pulled into her driveway, she was determined to have the answers before tomorrow night. No one knew the townspeople better than her grandmother.

Well, Granny had been able to tell her who Calvin was, but Annie was still a mystery. Rebecca approached Gabriel's front door. The warm evening air with a hint of mowed grass permeating the light breeze reminded her that summer wasn't far away. She pushed the bell and listened to it chime, tapping her foot on the wooden porch. Calvin had turned out to be a farmer outside town who had a habit of shooting at anyone who came onto his property—until Gabriel cured him.

But who was Annie?

The door swung open, and Gabriel filled the entryway. "Right on time." He looked around her. "Did you walk?"

She nodded. "It's hard to pass up a day like today. Summer will be here all too fast, and with it the heat. I like to take advantage of the nice weather when I can." She stepped inside his house. "Okay, I'm here. Who is Annie?"

He laughed. "You know about Calvin and me?"

"He could have hurt you."

"I knew he wouldn't."

"How?"

Gabriel shrugged. "Just did."

"But to keep walking toward him as he shot at you? I'm sure that isn't in the police chief manual."

"I wasn't the police chief at the time, but I think the good people of Oakview felt they had to give me the job after that incident."

"Yeah, anyone crazy enough to let someone shoot at them must be crazy enough to be a police chief."

"Right. Someone had to call the old man's bluff. Besides, he was shooting at the dirt around me."

Rebecca walked toward the kitchen. "Okay, now that we know about Calvin, what about Annie? Did this involve a gun, too?"

"Oh, no. Annie couldn't have held a gun if she had wanted to—which I doubt she would have, since she was a cow."

"A cow!" That certainly wasn't the picture she had conjured up on the walk to his house. Rebecca pivoted toward Gabriel and saw the amusement deep in his eyes.

"Of course, at the time I knew her she was a calf, and I was her rescuer." He swept his arm wide. "My kitchen is your kitchen." He started for the back door.

"Hold it! How did you rescue her?"

Gabriel came to a stop and turned slowly toward Rebecca. "The story would be better on a full stomach."

She fisted her hands on her hips. "There will be no full stomach if there's no story."

"Blackmailing me? The town's police chief?"

"You bet."

He lounged against the counter. "There really isn't much to tell. Annie got stuck in a bog, and I had to get her out. Of course, after she got out, I ended up stuck in the bog up to my thighs and had to wait for help to arrive—three hours later. Not one of my finer moments, if you ask me. I think I was the punch line for a few jokes after that."

Rebecca pressed her lips together, but the corners of her mouth twitched. Finally she couldn't contain her laughter any longer. "You mean Annie didn't go for help?" she asked, wiping the tears from her eyes.

"Actually she did wander back to her owner, but sadly she couldn't say where she had been."

Her laughter settled into a huge smile. "Life in a small town is certainly different from a big city. I can't say I ever heard of that happening to the police chief of Dallas. But then I doubt he got out much."

"I'm a hands-on type of guy. I wouldn't want to be stuck behind a desk."

"As opposed to being stuck in a bog?" The laughter bubbled up again, and she found herself unable to stop. She collapsed into a chair at the table, picturing him with mud up to his thighs, trying to take a step forward and unable to.

He waited until she ceased and said, "I'm glad you find the situation amusing."

"You don't?"

A smile cracked the stern expression on his face. "Now I do. Not at the time. All I wanted to do was slink home and not come out for days."

"Were you able to?"

"No. I had a steady parade of people pay me visits that evening on one pretext after another. The only things they really wanted to know, however, were the gory details."

"Which you supplied?"

"Yes. It was either me or the person who found me, and I didn't want her to."

"Who?"

"Mabel."

"You're kidding? That's rich. She pulled you out?"

"You have to remember she was in the Navy once, and she's quite strong for a small woman."

Rebecca held up her hand. "Okay. Okay. I don't think I want any more details. I'll just let my imagination work overtime."

"That's what I'm afraid you'll do." He pushed away from the counter. "Have fun with it. I'm starting the fire."

When the door closed behind Gabriel, she moved toward the refrigerator to get the ingredients for twice-baked potatoes and broccoli-cheese casserole. While she washed the potatoes, she spied Gabriel on the patio, cleaning the barbecue.

Since she had met him, she had laughed more than in the past few years. He enjoyed life and lived it to the fullest. His faith had sustained him through difficult times and made him a stronger man. As she observed him fill the pit with fresh charcoal, she couldn't deny her feelings any longer. She was falling in love with Gabriel Stone.

Chapter Ten

"You may cook for me anytime. You have a gift."
Gabriel wiped his mouth with his napkin and folded it
next to his plate.

Rebecca's hand shook as she picked up her glass and
drank cool water. All she had been able to think about
during dinner was that she had fallen in love with
Gabriel. And she knew neither of them was ready for
another commitment. She wanted a total commitment
from a man. He had to love her for herself, not the
ready-made family she would give him. If Gabriel could
commit, would it be for the right reasons?

"I'm glad you liked my food," she finally murmured
after putting the glass on the patio table.

"Especially your dessert. Your chocolate eclairs were
wonderful, mouthwatering, rich—"

She chuckled. "I get the picture. You can have the last
one."

He pounced on it, taking his time devouring it, a huge grin on his face. He licked every morsel of chocolate off his fingertips. Transfixed, Rebecca watched. How was she going to protect her heart? She knew it was too late. Gabriel wouldn't mean to hurt her, but make no mistake, she would be hurt. He was an honorable person who would realize a commitment had to be based on love between the man and woman, not on the fact he wanted a family.

Gabriel stretched his long legs in front of him and relaxed in his chair. "I don't think I'm gonna be able to move for a while."

Rebecca looked up and noticed some clouds racing across the moon. She took a deep breath and smelled rain in the air. "I think a storm's building."

He rested his head on the cushion and stared at the darkening sky. "That might not be good news for Peepers. Thank goodness she'll be inside with Bess tonight if it does storm."

"It's bound to happen during the daytime. Then what?"

"Pray, and if that doesn't work, buy a doghouse ready made, which is what I should have done in the first place."

"But you wanted to spend some time with Peter."

He raised his head and fixed his gaze on her. "Was I that obvious?"

"No, I don't think Peter suspected a thing. Even if he did, he loved every minute of you two building that—doghouse."

"You're too kind. I'm not sure that's what I'd call the thing we built."

"Mothers look at their children's creations with rose-colored glasses."

Gabriel laughed. "At least I got some good news out of him while we worked. He told me he wants to join the team as a player and participate in our next game. He wants to start working out with the others at practice. Actually he already has, to some extent."

"Now I'm really gonna be nervous when I watch the games. It's so much easier when your child is the manager. No pressure."

"But it's so much more exciting when he hits the ball and gets a run."

"Do you think he has a chance?"

"Yes. I'm his coach. He's more than ready. He was from the beginning, but Peter feels he must be perfect in order to be valuable to the team."

"It's because of his dad. Craig always pushed Peter to do everything perfectly. If he didn't, Craig wouldn't say anything to encourage him, or he would make sure Peter knew everything he had done wrong."

Gabriel straightened, all casualness gone from his expression. He clenched his jaw, and his hands curled tightly around the arms of the wrought iron chair. "Is that why Peter's afraid to try anything new?"

Rebecca nodded, afraid to speak for fear her voice would crack.

"I've been trying to get him to join the children's

choir. He keeps telling me he doesn't sing very well, but I've heard him. He has a beautiful voice."

"You've gotten him to do more than I thought you would be able to. Give him time. He'll come around."

"He has all the time in the world with me. I'm not going anywhere. Some day he'll realize that."

But I might have to go somewhere else, especially when it becomes too painful to be around you and not be fully a part of your life. She immediately pushed the thought of moving into the background, not wanting to put a damper on the evening. "I'm glad you care for my son."

"I care for both your sons, Rebecca. They're important to me."

"The family you never had," she said before she realized the meaning of what she was saying.

Gabriel flinched as though struck.

"I realize you always wanted a large family. With your wife's death that was taken away from you." She sat forward, deciding to broach the subject that had been bothering her since she realized her feelings for Gabriel were deepening. "Are you using my sons as a substitute for the family you lost?"

"You don't pull any punches, do you?"

Rebecca rose, restless. "I try not to anymore. I did once. I'm beginning to care for you as more than a friend." She pivoted toward him. "I don't want to be hurt again. I won't be the only one to suffer. My boys will, too."

Gabriel surged to his feet and covered the distance

between them but kept his arms at his sides. "I would never hurt you or the boys. Never."

"Not intentionally. But—" Rebecca reached out and clasped his left hand "—things turn out in ways we never intended."

"I'm not going to kid you, Rebecca. Yes, I wanted a family with lots of children with Judy. And I still want that family. I have never tried to hide that fact from anyone who knows me."

"But can you love the woman who will ultimately bear your children as she needs to be loved?" Rebecca ran her finger over his wedding ring. "Can you move on?"

He looked at their hands. "I don't know." He brought his troubled gaze to hers. "That's the best answer I can give you right now."

"Then that's the only one I want. I want no lies between us. I've had that. Never again."

"Give me time." He lifted his hand and stroked his thumb across her lips.

The first drop of rain splattered Rebecca's head. She glanced up, and another splashed her forehead. "We'd better get these dishes inside before it really starts to pour."

Gabriel cupped her face and peered into her eyes. "You're special, Rebecca Michaels." Combing his fingers through her hair, he lowered his mouth toward hers.

The sky opened, releasing a deluge of water and forcing them apart. Rebecca hurried toward the table to grab as many dishes as she could. Gabriel stopped her and pulled her toward the house.

"I'll get them when it stops."

"Are you sure?" she asked as the back door slammed. She turned to look out and could hardly see the table.

"Very," Gabriel said close to her ear.

The tickle of his breath caused goose bumps to rise on her skin. She stepped away. "It looks like it'll rain for a while. I think I need to bum a ride home."

"It's early."

"But tomorrow's a workday, and I need to make sure Peter has his homework done."

"I think you planned this to get out of doing the dishes."

"Clever, wasn't I? But then all you have to do is let the rain do your job for you."

He glanced out the window. "If they aren't washed away." He grasped her hand. "Come on. Let's dig up an umbrella and get you home."

Several days later Rebecca eased the door to the police station open and peeked in to see if Mabel was at her desk. Sighing heavily, she quietly shut the door and knelt by Josh, who was in his stroller.

She ran her fingers through his baby-fine hair. "I know Gabriel said to come on and bring you in today, but—" Drawing in a deep, fortifying breath, she stood. "I have to get my courage up. I was hoping to get here early enough to sneak you past Mabel. No such luck. I think the woman sleeps at the station."

"No, but she sure beats me most mornings."

Rebecca gasped and whirled to find Gabriel lounging

against the door with his arms crossed and a smile on his face. His eyes made a leisurely trek up her body. "Good morning, you two."

"Are you sure this will be okay? I know Mabel took good care of Josh at the church nursery, but you know how she feels about the workplace."

"If you hadn't been able to bring Josh with you to work, would you have stayed home?"

"Yes."

"Then that's the tactic we take with her. Your grandmother isn't feeling well, and your neighbor, Ann, is in Tulsa for the week. You don't have anyone to take care of Josh."

"Maybe Alicia—"

"Stop. This will work out. I promise. And I never renege on a promise."

She offered him a tentative smile. "That's one of the things I like about you. Lead the way."

Gabriel opened the door for Rebecca. Mabel glanced up from the keyboard and frowned. Then Josh cooed, and her frown dissolved into a smile. She rose, crossed the room and scooped Josh into her arms.

"Is your grandmother sick?" Mabel asked, blowing softly on Josh to get him to laugh.

"Her sinuses are really bothering her, and she has a bad headache."

"Well, I see we won't get much work done today," Mabel murmured to Josh and carried him to her desk. She sat with him in her lap.

"I think someone kidnapped Mabel Preston," Rebecca whispered to Gabriel.

"I knew she liked children, but if this doesn't beat all."

Rebecca wasn't sure what to do. She stared at Mabel while the woman explained to Josh the inner workings of the computer.

Mabel looked up. "At least one of us should get busy."

And in Rebecca's mind she knew exactly to whom Mabel was referring. Rebecca pushed the stroller to her desk and parked it next to her chair. She hurriedly began logging in the incident reports from the evening before. Thankfully there weren't many.

When she was through, she peered at Mabel. The woman and her baby were gone. Rebecca leaped to her feet and searched the large room. Then she noticed the door to the courthouse was ajar. She went in pursuit of them and found Mabel showing off Josh to several of the secretaries in the building.

"You need to let others enjoy your son as much as you do." Gabriel came up behind her.

"But he's…"

"Disabled?"

She nodded.

"Is that any reason someone couldn't love him? When I look at Josh, I see a child with the sweetest face and the biggest brown eyes. He's so trusting and innocent. As an officer of the law I forget sometimes what that means, and he always reminds me."

Rebecca went into the police station. She felt adrift, even though she had work to do.

"I'm going to see Ben at his store. It seems someone is shoplifting again."

"At least Bess is in the clear."

"Thank goodness. He thinks it's some teenage girls who were in the store last night. He feels they're putting pressure on each other to shoplift."

"I hope I won't have to deal with that. I know how difficult peer pressure can be. Thanks to you, Peter's getting to know some good kids. David was over at the house yesterday after school. They did their homework together, then practiced some baseball."

"The kids your child hangs with are important. I'm glad I could help." Gabriel paused at the door. "When I get back, I want to take you and Josh on a picnic at lunchtime. The day's too beautiful to eat inside."

Before Rebecca realized it, it was almost one. Josh was stirring from his nap in his stroller, where she'd placed him while Mabel went to lunch. Through the doorway, Rebecca saw Gabriel hang up the phone and rise from his desk. Mabel was back. Excitement tingled through her.

He came out of his office. "Ready to go?"

She nodded and finished what she was entering on the computer. "Are we walking?"

"Yep. The park is down the block. On the way I want to stop at the diner and pick up the food I ordered."

"So the diner does picnic lunches," Mabel said,

bending over the stroller to smile at Josh and touch his cheek.

"Nope, not usually. They're doing me a favor."

"Oh, boss, I don't know if that's a good idea." Mabel straightened, winked at Rebecca, then turned to Gabriel, presenting a stern facade. "What will the townspeople think of you, currying favors like that?"

"I insisted on paying extra for the picnic lunch."

Mabel punched Gabriel in the shoulder playfully. "I'll tell you what they'll think. That it's about time you came to your senses and started dating again."

"But—" Gabriel cleared his throat.

Rebecca's cheeks reddened. "This isn't—"

"Are you two pretending you aren't dating? If so, it isn't working. I've heard through the grapevine that you've already been on your first official date last Sunday night."

Gabriel and Rebecca looked at each other. "Bess!"

"Did you really think you'd keep it a secret in a town like Oakview?" Mabel shook her head, tsking. "Boss, you should know better than that. If you want, I can keep Josh while you two go eat lunch."

"That's okay. I'm sure you have a lot of work to do," Rebecca said, gripping the handle of the stroller as though Mabel would rip it out of her hands.

"If I don't get through, I'll stay this evening until I finish."

"I can't let you do that." Rebecca glanced at Gabriel for some help. He shrugged.

"What do I have to do at home? I live by myself with no obligations."

The loneliness Rebecca heard in Mabel's voice stirred her compassion. Until that moment Rebecca hadn't thought of Mabel as being lonely. "If you're sure—"

"Go. Enjoy your lunch. Josh and I have some serious talking to do." Mabel took the stroller and headed for her desk before Rebecca changed her mind.

Outside the police station, Rebecca paused and looked in through the picture window at Mabel taking Josh out of the stroller and holding him close to her. The whole time the woman was talking to Josh as if he understood every word she was saying. Rebecca's heart expanded, and she fought the emotions threatening her composure.

"I was so wrong about Mabel. Did you hear her teasing you in there?" Rebecca asked.

Gabriel placed his hand at the small of her back. "Mabel never married, but she has lots of nieces and nephews. Most of them live in other parts of Oklahoma and Texas, but the ones who live here she dotes on. I think she's just adopted your son as another of her charges."

"Speaking of adopting, I suppose you're aware of Peter adopting Bess as his grandmother. Did you come up with that idea for the Cougars?"

"Peter didn't tell you?"

"No, what?"

"That adoption scheme was all his idea. He orga-nized the Cougars with David's help. You have quite a son there. Actually you have quite a family." Gabriel stopped outside the diner. "You wait here. I'll get our food."

While he was gone, Rebecca scanned Main Street and noticed a few of the people on the sidewalk staring at her. She waved to them, and they waved back. One young mother from church paused when she passed Rebecca and told her about a meeting of the young mom's group on Saturday. Clara encouraged Rebecca to join them. As Clara strolled away, Rebecca drew in a deep breath of spring air and thought about how content she felt. In a short time she had become a part of this town, even a part of the church. She had never experienced this feeling of belonging when she lived in Dallas even though she'd lived there over seven years.

"Let's go," Gabriel said, grasping her hand and walking toward the park a block away.

"A basket and everything."

"I told them I wanted only the best."

At the park, Gabriel chose a picnic table under a big oak tree. He opened the basket, and spread a cloth over the stone table. Container after container came out of the basket, and Rebecca's mouth fell open.

"You must have been hungry."

Gabriel glanced at all the food, and a sheepish look entered his eyes. "I guess I went overboard. We can take the leftovers to the station. They won't last long if I put them out for everyone to take some."

"Yes, I noticed the policemen who work for you have hearty appetites. Those cookies Rose baked for them the other day didn't last an hour." Rebecca tilted her head. "Come to think of it, most of them were gone after you were alone with the plate."

Gabriel grinned. "Okay. I confess I probably took more than my share. In my defense, I can only say chocolate does crazy things to me."

"To be fair to the others, I need to tell Granny to bake oatmeal or sugar cookies next time."

Gabriel produced two large slices of the diner's famous French silk pie. "Well, in that case I ought to eat both of these."

Rebecca snatched a plate from his hand. "I don't think so." She put it out of his reach on the bench next to her.

She filled a plastic plate with fried chicken, potato salad, coleslaw and a roll with butter dripping off it. Gabriel sat across from her and piled his plate even higher.

After a bite of chicken, he said, "Next to home cooking—" his gaze caught hers "—yours in particular, this is the best food around these parts."

She laughed. "Okay. You must want something. You're buttering me up more than these rolls are. Spit it out, Stone."

"Another home-cooked meal would be greatly appreciated. And—" he picked up a paper cup of iced tea "—I would love to have you sing the solo at next week's service."

Rebecca dropped her plastic fork. "Sing in front of the whole church by myself?"

"That's what solo means." He leaned over, his expression intense, and seized the hand that had been holding the fork. "You've got a beautiful voice. I want everyone to hear how beautiful it is."

"But I can't—"

Gabriel held up his free hand. "Hold it. Don't say no yet. Think about it. What better way to celebrate what God has given you than by celebrating Him with a song?"

There was a part of her that wanted to accept the invitation, but there was a part that was afraid, that still wasn't sure where she stood with her faith. How could she celebrate God when she had doubts? "I'll think about it, Gabriel. Please give me more time."

His grasp on her hand tightened for a moment before he released his hold. "Rebecca, you have all the time in the world. I'll never force you to do anything you don't want to. You just say the word, and I'll give you the floor." He took a bite of his roll and chewed slowly, his regard fixed upon her face.

She dropped her gaze to her plate, feeling his probing look, and searched for a safe topic of conversation. "I'm picking Bess up this evening and bringing her to Peter's first game as a player. She's quite excited about seeing him play."

"And Peter's quite excited about playing. He tries not to act like it means anything, but the last two practices he has asked me to stay and pitch to him afterward."

"I wondered why he was late, but he wouldn't say anything. What if Peter doesn't do well?"

"He'll do fine, Rebecca. I promise."

"I know you pride yourself on always keeping your word. But Gabriel, you don't have control over this. Peter's the only one."

"I know your son's abilities. He can do it."

"But I don't know if he realizes that. I watched my son over the years slowly shut down because Craig demanded perfection."

"No one is perfect, especially ten-year-old boys." Again Gabriel's gaze captured hers. "Rebecca, you're just gonna have to believe in Peter and me. If he fails, I'll help him through it."

"That's my job," she immediately said.

His look sharpened. "There you go again, not wanting to share. You're not alone, Rebecca, and the sooner you realize it the easier things will be for you." Gabriel spread his arms wide. "You have a whole town that cares about you."

What about you? Rebecca wanted to ask, but didn't. She didn't know if she could handle his answer. "I realize I'm not alone."

He lifted a brow. "Do you?"

She straightened on the stone bench. "But I am Peter's parent."

"And I'm not?"

"You're Peter's coach. Of course, his playing is your concern, but—" Her words dried up.

"But that will be all I ever am?"

She swallowed around the constriction in her throat.

"I don't want to get into this, Gabriel. We need to get back. I still have physical therapy exercises to do with Josh." She reached for her pie. Rebecca focused on it rather than the intent look on Gabriel's face, which incorporated anger as well as sadness.

Rebecca shifted between Alicia and Bess. Peter walked to home plate and took a few practice swings. Rebecca's heartbeat accelerated. Biting her nails when she was nervous was a habit she had worked hard to break several years before. When she found herself starting to resort to the old habit, she quickly sat on her hands.

"Oh, isn't this exciting," Bess said in Rebecca's right ear.

Alicia said in her left one, "He's gonna do fine. Don't you worry."

But worry nibbled at Rebecca's composure. She caught her breath as Peter took his first swing and missed. She cringed when the ump shouted, "Strike one." When the ump announced the second strike, she chewed on her lower lip and closed her eyes. She didn't want to see the next pitch. She pried one eye open and saw her son swing at a ball that was outside and too low. The sound of it hitting the catcher's glove reverberated through her mind as the ump's words did. "Strike three. You're out."

She started to rise, to go to her son. Both Alicia and Bess placed a hand on her arms and held her down.

"You don't want to do that, my child," Bess said, pointing to Peter stalking to the dugout with a frown carved deep into his boyish features. "Let the coach handle it."

"But he's hurting."

"It won't be the last time. Gabriel will help him shake it off." Alicia patted Rebecca's arm and released her hold. "I sometimes think this game is harder on the parents than the children playing."

Rebecca watched her son plop down on the bench and hang his head, tuning out everything the other boys said to him. She knew he was drawing in on himself, berating himself for failing. She was afraid he wouldn't try to bat when his next turn came. She wanted to go to him so badly and put her arms around him, hugging him to her and telling him that it would be all right.

When Gabriel knelt in front of Peter and spoke to him, her son looked at his coach, shook his head and straightened on the bench. Peter watched the rest of the batters as they played, then, when the teams changed places, he snatched up his glove and headed for the outfield.

"See? I told you Gabriel knew just what to say to him. He'll be all right."

Rebecca was beginning to believe Alicia might be right about her son. She settled in for a long evening.

"Is this Josh?" Clara asked.

Nodding, Rebecca prepared herself for the questions that usually followed.

"He's adorable. As I told you earlier, you should join

us for the young mom's group on Saturday and bring him to play with the others. We don't leave our children at home. They're a part of the group, too."

Rebecca started to say no, but the word wouldn't come out.

"That would be perfect, Rebecca."

Rebecca shot Bess a bewildered look. Perfect? "Josh doesn't play much," she finally said to the woman in front of her.

"We have all ages ranging from a few months to four-and five-year-olds. Alicia can tell you all about it." The woman patted Josh's cap-covered head, then made her way to her husband who was sitting a few rows back and to the left.

"You know, I think she's right. The young mom's group would be great for you. It would give you a chance to get involved with the church. They do all kinds of projects, from sponsoring a huge garage sale every spring to a carnival in the fall to raise money for the Sunday school."

"I'll have to think about it. I need to start Josh in some more therapy in Tulsa, and Saturday may be my only day to do it."

As the game progressed, Rebecca reflected on her changing role as a working mother. She would like to join the group, but she didn't know if she had the time to do that, take care of Josh's therapy, be a mother to Peter and hold down a full-time job. She was finding there was only so much time in a day.

When Peter stepped up to bat two innings later, Rebecca felt the tension in her neck. She'd seen Gabriel whisper something to her eldest, pat him on the back and send him out. Again Peter swung at the first pitch and missed. He looked at Gabriel, who gave him a thumbs-up sign.

A light, cool breeze ruffled her hair. Sweat was rolling down her face, stinging her eyes and leaving salty tracks. Rebecca breathed deeply to ease the pounding of her heart and watched as Peter tapped his bat against home plate then positioned himself.

Peter hit the ball, and it went sailing into the outfield. He ran toward first. Pumping his legs as hard as he could, he rounded first and headed for second, then on to third, sliding into the base as the ball was caught by the third baseman.

"Safe," the ump called, and Rebecca jumped to her feet, screaming and clapping.

When she sat again, she noticed all the spectators' eyes were on her and she flushed, then shrugged and said, "That's my son."

Everyone applauded her and smiled.

She was tempted to bow but didn't. She sat, feeling the heat on her cheeks. She caught Gabriel staring at her, and her blush deepened. His grin widened and he winked, giving her a thumbs-up.

"Okay, restraint isn't one of my virtues."

"I like it," Alicia said. "I personally like an excuse to act like a maniac every once in a while. Very therapeutic, if you ask me. Just wait until David comes to bat."

When the game was over, Rebecca asked Bess to watch Josh for a moment while she headed for the group of boys. She wanted to comfort Peter. The Cougars had lost, and she was worried he would blame himself. She paused a few feet away and listened as Gabriel congratulated the team on playing a good game. Then he had them bow their heads while he said a prayer of thanks to God.

"Practice next Monday after school. See you all at Pizza To Go in a few minutes," Gabriel announced to the team, then clasped Peter by the shoulder while the rest of the boys filed away. "I'm pleased by your first performance. Four times at bat. One triple and another single."

"But I struck out twice."

"Remember, focus on the positive. No one—professional ball players included—has a hit every time at bat. You're an asset to the team, Peter. No doubt about it."

Rebecca listened to Gabriel target what Peter had done that was right, not wrong. Peter beamed under Gabriel's attention and words. His small chest puffed out, and he walked with his head held high toward her when Gabriel was through. If Rebecca hadn't seen the game, she would have thought the Cougars had won. No berating and yelling about the mistakes made.

"Did you see my triple, Mom?"

"Yes, I did. Quite a play."

Peter looked around Rebecca toward Bess. "I'll be

back in a minute." He raced to the older lady and sat next to her.

Rebecca watched her eldest for a few seconds, then faced Gabriel. "Between Granny and Bess, that guy has all his bases covered as far as grandparents go."

"Speaking of Rose, how is she?"

"Better. She wanted to come tonight, but I'm making her stay home and rest."

"I didn't think anyone could make Rose do anything she didn't want to."

"I promised her I would come by and get her for the pizza. She agreed to the compromise, which tells you she wasn't feeling well at all today. Even Josh is a little fussier these past few days. I hope his ear infection isn't returning. I'm so glad tomorrow is Saturday, and I don't have to work."

"I think I should be upset. After all, I am your boss." Gabriel walked toward home plate to retrieve a bat left by the last player.

Rebecca followed. "Who has work to do when he's at the station. You shouldn't have to spend your day giving Josh physical therapy."

"But I wanted to. There was no emergency I had to go to. Besides, it was only thirty minutes."

"But it's not part of your job description."

"Coming to townspeople's rescue is part of my job."

"I didn't need rescuing."

Gabriel stopped in the middle of the baseball diamond. "Are you so sure about that?"

Rebecca put her hands on her hips. "Gabriel Stone, I am not a fragile woman who needs a man to rescue her."

He laid his hand on her arm. "From where I stand you've lost your way and you're trying to find the path back to God. Am I wrong?"

A tightness in her throat burned and made it difficult to answer him. Finally she said, "Is that the way you see our relationship?" Suddenly she didn't want to hear his response. She pivoted and strode toward her family. She needed to get away before she broke down in front of everyone.

Gabriel grasped her and spun her toward him. "I want to help you not only find God again but find what you want in your life. Until you do, how can there be anything lasting between us? I want to be your friend and—" he sucked in a deep breath "—and more, but your life, and I'm finding my life, aren't settled. We both have issues that make it difficult for us to commit to another."

She shook his hand off her arm and continued toward her family, desperately wanting to deny his words but knowing he spoke the truth, as usual. Until they got their own separate houses in order, they couldn't become one family.

Chapter Eleven

"Child, what do you think about us working on a quilt for the carnival in the fall?" Granny stopped in front of Rebecca, leaning on her cane.

Rebecca inspected her grandmother's features, glad to see some color in her cheeks after the week she'd spent fighting off her allergies. "You and Bess?" she asked, turning to the older woman.

"And you," Bess added. "I think a quilt with different scenes from the Bible would be perfect for the auction. We could start with Adam and Eve and tell the story of the Old Testament."

"I like that."

"If we start now, we should be through in six months." Granny looked around for a chair, found one and eased into it. "I do declare these old bones creak at times."

Bess took the chair next to Rose. "At least you have a sharp mind. I keep forgetting things I know I shouldn't."

Rebecca left the two ladies talking and went in search of Gabriel, who had taken off with Josh the second she had arrived at the church social. In less than two minutes she found him in the midst of the children on the playground. The stroller was in a corner by the church building. He held Josh in the crook of his arm so her son could see everything that was going on. Gabriel pointed to a group of children playing on the jungle gym, one little boy hanging upside down.

When she walked up to Gabriel, he smiled and said, "We should plan Josh's birthday. Rose told me it was coming up soon."

We? That pronoun more than anything made her heart lurch and her hope soar. She liked the sound of it on his lips, but she had to remind herself not to get too excited. He still wore his wedding ring, which in her mind represented a high wall around his heart and indicated he was not ready to commit to anyone.

"I just thought we would have a quiet family get-together."

"Nonsense. I think we should invite the kids from the church nursery and have a gala event. It's not every day a child has his second birthday."

"Well—"

"Let me plan everything. I thought I did a pretty good job with Peter's."

"Yes, but—" Again her words lodged in her throat.

"Okay?"

"Yes," she finally said, taking her son into her arms

and hugging him close. "It's time for his afternoon nap. He's been sleeping more than usual lately. I think he might be trying to catch something. Did you say Mabel was going to be in the nursery?"

"Yep."

"It's probably better if Josh lies down rather than cat-napping in his stroller. I'll be right back."

Gabriel watched Rebecca enter the church building, a feeling of emptiness engulfing him as she moved away. When she disappeared from sight, he stared at his left hand and the wedding ring he still wore. What was holding him back from removing it? He cared a great deal for Rebecca and her family. He touched his wedding ring and slid it almost all the way off his finger.

A child's laughter penetrated his thoughts, and he slid the ring back on. What if she was right about him only wanting a family? What if his feelings for her weren't the real thing but just a knee-jerk reaction to not having what he wanted most with Judy? He had to be one hundred percent sure before he made any commit-ment to her. He would not be responsible for hurting her. Rebecca deserved the very best. He wasn't sure he was able to give his best.

Gabriel strode toward the barbecues that were lined up ready to cook hamburgers and hot dogs. Dashing by, Peter waved hello and continued after David and another boy on the Cougar team. Gabriel realized he did love Rebecca's two sons and would hate not being a part of their lives. How did he separate his feelings for her two sons from the feelings he had for their mother? They were a package deal.

"Hey, Gabriel, come settle a little disagreement for us. We need to know how you arrange your charcoal to get the best fire going," the reverend called, gesturing him to a group of men in front of one barbecue.

Gabriel started for them, but a motion out of the corner of his eye caught his attention. He turned toward the movement and froze. George McCall shut his car door, then walked toward the table where the food was set out. He carried a plastic bowl. Gabriel fisted his hands at his sides.

After George placed his bowl of food on the table, he scanned the crowd, avoiding eye contact. Hesitantly George approached two people not far from the table and started talking to them.

Gabriel opened and closed his hands, trying to control his emotions. But he couldn't. Everything faded but George, alive and well, calmly carrying on a conversation as though nothing had happened three years before to destroy Gabriel's life.

He took a step toward George.

Reverend Carson blocked his path. "Think before you do anything you'll regret."

"Did you know he was going to be here today?" Gabriel heard the seething tone of his voice and didn't care. Anger consumed him, with a touch of guilt thrown in.

"Yes, Gabriel, I did. He's a member of this church, too."

"Why didn't you tell me?"

"Because you wouldn't have come to the social."

"You're right about that."

"George intends to be an active member of our church again. He needs us. He's changed, Gabriel. He hasn't had a drink since the day of the accident."

Gabriel flexed his hands. His emotions boiled beneath the surface, ready to erupt. "I don't know if I can attend the same church as that man."

"Forgiveness is important in God's scheme of things. I can't choose between two parishioners. Don't ask me to."

Gabriel looked at George. The man glanced at him, a cautious expression on his face. "You should have told me he was going to be here, Samuel. I had a right to know. I feel like I've been hit by a semi."

Throwing one last glare at George, Gabriel stalked toward the church. He needed a quiet place where he could think, could get a grip on his emotions, which were rampaging out of control. He was afraid of what he might do if he didn't get that control. With a hard shove, he pushed open one of the double doors and nearly collided with Rebecca.

"I'm sorry it took—"

"Excuse me, Rebecca." He hurried past her before she demanded answers he didn't have.

Stunned by Gabriel's abruptness, Rebecca watched him storm away from her. What had happened in the short time she was in the nursery? She thought about following him into the sanctuary but discarded the idea immediately. The cold look on Gabriel's face completely shut her out. He wanted her to share her emotions, but he had a hard time doing the same. Earlier she had felt hope about the direction their relationship was going. Now she wasn't so sure.

When she went outside, she knew what had sent Gabriel into the church. George McCall. She knew his face from a photograph in his file at the police station. She shouldn't have looked up the information, but her curiosity had gotten the better of her.

Rose motioned for her to come over. Rebecca covered the distance quickly, aware of a buzz of gossip.

"Did you see Gabriel?" her grandmother asked.

"Yes, briefly."

"Did he say anything? Is he going inside to clean out his locker in the choir room?"

"Clean out his locker? What do you mean?"

"Well, Bess heard him tell Samuel he couldn't remain at a church where George was."

"He went into the sanctuary. I don't know anything beyond that."

"You two are close. Go talk to him. We can't lose him."

"I got the distinct impression he wanted to be left alone." Remembering the look on his face, Rebecca shivered in the warmth of the sun.

"Nonsense. He's been left alone too long. Go to him.

Be there for him. He needs someone even if he doesn't know it. You said so yourself."

But was she the person he needed? Rebecca asked herself, not for the first time.

"Shoo, child." Granny waved her toward the church.

Rebecca reluctantly headed to the church. Cautiously she inched open the door to the sanctuary and peeked in. The only light was what streamed through the stained glass windows, ribboning the hardwood floor and pews with multicolored lines as though in celebration of the Lord.

She saw Gabriel sitting in the first row with his head bent and his shoulders hunched. Her heart twisted at the sight of him, and all she wanted to do was hold him close. Her love for him propelled her into the sanctuary, the quiet click of the door echoing through the silence.

He raised his head, stiffened but didn't look around.

She proceeded toward him, her heart pounding, her pulse thundering in her ears, her loafers clacking against the floor. Slipping into the pew next to him, she waited until he spoke. His glance was sharp as it skimmed over her, leaving her in no doubt that he wasn't happy she was there. She felt the barrier between them as though it were an impregnable wall.

She gripped her hands together so tightly that her knuckles whitened. The faint aroma of lemon-scented furniture polish lingered in the air. Strips of color danced across the floor, reminding Rebecca of a ka-

leidoscope. And the silence ate away at her composure.
But still she waited.

"You saw him?" Gabriel finally asked, his voice
husky, almost a whisper.

"Yes."

"He destroyed my family and he's standing out there
enjoying himself as though nothing happened while…"

The strong slope of his jaw attested to his anger. "Do
you really believe that, Gabriel? Do you think he wasn't
changed by what he did?"

Gabriel buried his face in his hands. Rebecca's heart
wrenched. More than anything she wished she could
make him whole again.

"Let it go, Gabriel. Give over your anger and guilt
to God. It is destroying you—and your chance at happiness." His faith had sustained him through so much.
It could help him through this trial.

"If only I had stopped the man earlier that day, my
family would be alive today."

"But you didn't. You had no reason to. We all have
great hindsight."

"But he intends to come back to this church, to be a
constant reminder of my loss if I attend."

"You know the story of the prodigal son. This
reminds me of that story Jesus told. George was lost and
now he is found. Isn't that what everything is about—
forgiveness and acceptance of all God's children?"

"I don't know if I can do what the Lord wants. I feel
I've let Him down."

Rebecca laid her hand on Gabriel's shoulder. "Read the story in the Bible and pray for guidance. The Lord was there for you through Judy and your son's deaths. He will be there for you now. Don't do what I did."

Slanting his head to look at her, he asked, "Do you mean what you just said?"

"Of course."

"Then you have accepted God again?"

Rebecca blinked, nonplussed. "Yes," she whispered, then in a stronger voice, "yes, I have. When I look at what He has done for you, I know He was there for me. I just closed my heart to Him and wasn't listening when He spoke. Don't make the same mistake I did."

Rebecca rose. Gabriel needed time to come to terms with his feelings. He needed time with God to work out his anger and guilt. She quietly walked away, feeling lighthearted at the prospect of the Lord being in her life again. She turned at the door and looked toward the altar. Her heart flooded with love and acceptance, feelings she hadn't experienced in a long time.

She whispered, "Dear heavenly Father, please help Gabriel to see the way and to accept George McCall into his life. Please give him the strength to forgive himself and George. And thank you, Lord, for leading me back to You."

For the first time in a long while she felt a complete peace. She went out into the sunshine with her head lifted toward the light.

* * *

"Three more weeks, and summer vacation will be upon us. Have you figured out what you're gonna do this summer to keep yourself busy?" Rebecca poured Peter a glass of milk and slid the plate of home-baked cookies toward him.

"I want to work with Mrs. Wiggles and teach her some tricks."

"How about some manners, too?"

Peter took a bite of his sugar cookie. "I'm sorry about the shoe."

Rebecca remembered the hole the puppy had chewed in one of her favorite navy pumps. She learned quickly to make sure closet doors were kept shut and everything of importance was off the floor. "What else do you want to do?"

"I'm gonna help Miss Bess train Peepers. I'll have more time this summer to help her. Her eyesight isn't so good, so I told her I'd read more to her. There's a baseball camp Coach told me about and there's a church camp, too." Peter gulped half his milk, and when he put the glass on the table, he had a milk mustache.

Rebecca handed him a napkin. "It looks like you've got things figured out. You do need to save some time for Josh and chores around here."

"Sure. I already told Granny I would help with Josh while you're at work. Josh and me have been practicing real hard on his exercises. He'll walk in no time."

Rebecca wished that were true. She remained quiet.

She didn't want Peter to lose hope. And anything was possible where God was concerned.

When the phone rang, she said, "See if Josh is up from his afternoon nap. We need to go to Miss Bess's soon."

As Peter raced from the kitchen, Rebecca lifted the receiver, hoping it was Gabriel. He had been at church this morning but hadn't said more than two words to her. She wanted to talk to him about George's appearance at the worship service.

"Hello."

"Rebecca?"

"Yes, Craig," she said, her hands tightening on the phone.

"I'm glad I caught you. I have something I want to tell you and Peter."

Rebecca sat. "What is it?"

"I got married yesterday. Can you tell Peter for me?"

Numb, she loosened her grip on the receiver and shifted it to the other ear. "Yes, I will. Congratulations. I hope you're happy." As she said the words, she suddenly realized she meant them, and that surprised her. When had she forgiven Craig for leaving her and the boys? She knew the answer—when she had reconnected with the Lord.

"You mean it, Rebecca?"

"Yes, I do, Craig. Good luck." She hung up the phone, her hand lingering on the receiver for a few seconds while she thought about her newfound and exhilarating state of harmony.

"Mom, Josh is still asleep. Do you want me to wake him?" Peter came to a halt inside the doorway.

"Heavens, no. Never wake a sleeping child unless absolutely necessary. I suspect he didn't sleep much at the church nursery this morning. When he's around Mabel, he likes to stay up. She's so entertaining, I don't think he wants to miss anything." She removed her hand from the receiver.

"Who was that on the phone?"

"Your father."

Frowning, Peter tensed. "What did he want?"

"He got married yesterday and wanted us to know."

"I'm sorry, Mom." Peter threw his arms around Rebecca's neck and gave her a hug.

"Why are you sorry?"

Peter stepped back. "Doesn't it make you sad he's remarrying?"

Cocking her head, Rebecca replied, "You know, Peter, it doesn't. I'm glad he's found someone to make him happy." As she spoke, there was a part of her that was amazed by her words. But she meant them, and that surprised her even more. "How do you feel about it?"

Peter shrugged. "Kinda the same way. I wish Dad was around more, but even when we lived in Dallas, he wasn't, very much. I'm just not the kind of son he wants."

"That's not true," she said automatically, not wanting her son to feel that way.

"I never could please him. I tried. I just couldn't."

The sadness in her son's voice tore at her. She pulled

him to her and held him close, fighting the tears threatening to flow. "You know, son, that's your father's problem, not yours. He expects people to be perfect, and we aren't."

"Coach has told me the only way we really learn is by our mistakes."

"Well, I know one thing, young man. You're the son I want. I'm lucky to have you and Josh." Her arms tightened about him.

"Mom! I can't breathe."

Chuckling, she released her hold on Peter, and he quickly backed away. "Sorry. I got carried away. Moms do that from time to time."

"Just don't let the guys see you. I'd never live it down."

"I'll remember that. Seriously, Peter, are you okay?"

"Sure. Look at all the people who care about me. There's Granny, Miss Bess and Coach. And I have lots of friends now at school and church. I'm lucky."

Even though her son's words were said in a cheerful tone, she knew underlying them the sadness still lingered. His eyes lacked a bright sparkle, and there was a slight slump to his posture. His sorrow wouldn't go away overnight, if ever, but she realized living in Oakview would help Peter forget his father's indifference. The good people of Oakview weren't indifferent to anything, and she was beginning to appreciate the small town, where everybody knew everything about everybody else.

Glancing at her watch, Rebecca frowned. "You know, Peter, Josh has been down longer than usual. He's been fighting a cold for the past few days. I'd better check on him."

"Remember not to wake him," Peter called as she made her way up the stairs to her bedroom.

Peering into the crib, she half expected to see Josh with his eyes open, amusing himself by watching his brightly colored fish mobile. She saw neither. He was still asleep. Something was wrong. His breathing was wrong. His color was pale. She shook him.

Alarm bolted through her. She couldn't wake him up. Snatching him, she held his limp form in her arms. Panic took hold.

"Peter," she shouted, placing Josh on the floor and tilting his head back to open his airway. "Call nine-one-one."

Peter came running. "Mom, what's wrong?"

She checked Josh's pulse in his neck. "Call nine-one-one," she repeated as the steps of the lifesaving procedure clicked through her mind.

When Rebecca breathed into Josh's mouth, she noticed his chest didn't rise. Her hot air blasted her face. Blocked airway. Quickly she pressed with one hand on his stomach several times, then she began breathing for him, praying as she had never prayed before. *Please, dear God, don't take Josh. Please, please save my son.*

After several breaths Josh started screaming, and relief trembled through Rebecca. *Thank you, heavenly Father.*

Chapter Twelve

Rebecca paced from one end of the waiting room to the other, every few seconds checking the doorway for the emergency room nurse. Her heartbeat pulsated in her ears with each quick step she took. The antiseptic smells she associated with hospitals made her stomach churn. The sound of upbeat music over the intercom system grated on her nerves. The glare of the bright fluorescent lights gave her a headache.

Memories of other times she had spent in an emergency room waiting for a report on her youngest son flooded her mind, heightening her sense of aloneness. She glanced toward the doorway and stopped in her tracks. Gabriel stood there, his expression filled with anguish. She took one look at his face and rushed into his embrace.

"What's wrong with Josh, Rebecca?" Gabriel's hand stroked her back, his touch soothing, his voice caressing her soul.

"He wasn't breathing. I did CPR and he started breathing again, but I was so scared. The doctor is checking him over right now." She leaned back to look into his face. "How did you find out so fast?"

"Mabel heard Peter's call. She radioed me. What can I do to help you?"

Those words, never spoken by her ex-husband, underscored how different everything was in Oakview. You can help me by never letting me go, she thought.

She drew in a deep, fortifying breath, refusing to waste another second dreaming of what would never be. "Granny doesn't drive after dark. Could you bring her and Peter to the hospital? I imagine by now they are beside themselves. I told them as I was leaving with the ambulance that I would call when I talked with the doctor, but I know Granny. She would rather be here waiting than at home."

"Of course, I'll get them. Anything else?"

"Hold me." The words came out without her thinking about what they might imply. She desperately needed to feel a spiritual and physical connection to someone at the moment. That feeling of being alone that she had gotten often in Dallas had inundated her while she had fought to give Josh his next breath and on the short ride to the hospital. She needed to wipe it away before it consumed her again.

His arms about her tightened, and she laid her head on his chest, listening to the strong beat of his heart, its steady rhythm a balm. When she was in his embrace, she felt anchored. She cherished the feeling for a few precious moments before she pulled away.

"Thank you." She viewed him through a shimmer of tears.

He framed her face. "You aren't alone, Rebecca. I'm here for you. God's here for you. I won't be gone long. I'll bring Peter and Rose back."

She watched him leave, and a feeling of bereavement descended as though a part of her had left. The tears pooling in her eyes spilled down her cheeks, and she wiped them away. When she finally did get to see him, Josh mustn't sense her distress. She had to be strong for him and Peter.

She walked to the picture window and followed Gabriel's progress across the parking lot to his Jeep. She had a few minutes before her family would be here. She made a decision.

She hurried into the hall, then asked the lady at the reception desk, "Where's the chapel?"

The woman gestured with her right hand. "Down that way, third door on the left."

"If anyone is looking for Rebecca Michaels, that's where I'll be."

Rebecca followed the receptionist's directions and went inside. The small room had two rows of pews and an altar bearing a simple wooden cross. The grating canned music in the waiting room was refreshingly absent. The bright lights were gone, replaced with soft illumination that offered a tranquil dimness. Here, in the

Lord's house, peace prevailed over chaos, filling Rebecca with a quiet strength. She'd come to the right place. The Lord would know what to do.

Sitting on the first row, she clasped her hands in front of her and bowed her head. "Please, Lord, forgive me for turning away from you. I now know I was wrong. Please help me to find the strength to weather this latest crisis and show me the way back into Your arms. You have given me so much, and for a time I had forgotten that. Josh is just a baby. Please don't make him suffer for my mistakes."

Rebecca stayed for a few minutes, letting her mind go blank while she absorbed the serenity of her surroundings. When she stood, she felt whole and no longer alone. God was with her as she walked from the chapel to find her family. He would be with her through this crisis.

Gabriel escorted Granny and Peter through the double doors. Rebecca's son spotted her and ran to her, throwing his arms around her waist. He buried his face against her body and squeezed tightly.

"Josh will be fine, Peter. God will take care of him." She caressed her eldest son's hair.

Granny leaned heavily on her cane with each weary step, concern in her expression. "Have they told you anything yet?"

"No, but it shouldn't be too much longer."

As they started for the waiting room, a doctor came toward Rebecca. She paused, clasping Peter's shoulder.

"Mrs. Michaels, Josh will be all right. I want to keep

him overnight, and if he's okay tomorrow, he can go home then. He has bronchitis. I'll give you some medicine for him. You can go in now and see him before we transfer him to a regular room."

"Can I see Josh, too?" Peter asked.

"Sure. Don't stay long. I want to get him settled into a room soon," the doctor answered, indicating the way.

When Rebecca entered the room, followed by her family and Gabriel, a woman turned from the bed and said, "I'm the respiratory therapist. I just gave him a breathing treatment. He's hooked up to a pulse ox machine to measure the oxygen saturation of his body. That's what this is." She showed them Josh's finger, which looked like it had a Band-Aid on it. "And he has an IV."

Rebecca thanked the therapist, glad for the explanation. Josh looked so small in the hospital bed with tubes in him and a mask on his face. His eyes were closed.

"He's sleeping now. He's had quite a night, as I'm sure you all have," the therapist said.

Rebecca took Josh's free hand and held it for a moment while Peter stood next to her. Granny and Gabriel moved to the other side of the bed. Rebecca said a prayer of thanks, then released Josh. She motioned for everyone to leave. Granny bent and kissed Josh's forehead, then she walked to the door. Gabriel whispered something into Josh's ear and followed Granny out of the room.

Peter remained by the bed. "Josh, wait until you get

home. You won't believe how much Mrs. Wiggles is getting into everything. She ate one of your favorite toys, which I promise to replace." His voice grew thick. "It fell out of your bed—she found it on the floor."

Standing behind him, Rebecca placed both hands on Peter's shoulders. "This looks worse than it is. You heard what the therapist and the doctor said. He will be fine."

"It isn't fair that bad things keep happening to him." Peter whirled and pressed himself against Rebecca, his arms clinging to her. The sound of her son crying ripped through her, momentarily making her feel helpless. Then she remembered how much the Lord loved them all, and she found the strength to deal with her son's anguish.

She sat in the chair next to the bed and clasped her son's upper arms. "Honey, bad things happen to everyone. Just as good things do, too. What's important is how we handle those things. Josh is a trooper. That makes him even more special than he already is. I think he's pretty lucky. He has you as a brother."

Peter sniffed. "You think?"

"I wouldn't have said it if I didn't. I told you once I wouldn't lie to you, and that won't change."

"Are you still mad at God?"

"No, honey. I was wrong to be angry at God for what happened to me. I didn't handle things very well, but that will change. I have learned from my mistake."

Peter hugged her. "Mom, I love you."

"I love you, honey. Now let's get out of here so they

can move Josh to a regular room and we all can get some sleep tonight."

"Are you gonna stay with Josh?"

"Yeah. I'm going to have them set up a cot in his room so I can be there when he wakes up."

"Can I stay the night with you two?" Peter asked while they walked into the hall, where Granny and Gabriel were standing.

"You've got school tomorrow. I'll call you in the morning and let you know how the night went with Josh before you go to school." Rebecca caught Gabriel's intense gaze on her. "Would you please take them home?"

He nodded.

Gabriel hung back while Peter and Granny headed for the double doors that led outside. "Are you okay?" His touch whisper soft, he grazed her cheek with the pad of his thumb.

She smiled, warmed by his presence more than she cared to acknowledge. "Yes." She clasped his hand. "Thank you for taking care of Granny and Peter for me."

"I told you you weren't alone."

"I know that now."

He bent and gave her a quick kiss that left her stunned. Sunlight flooded her system. Angels sang. It had only been a peck, but sensations deep inside made her toes curl. She couldn't imagine what would happen if he really kissed her.

* * *

Rebecca rested her head on the back of the cushioned chair and stared unseeingly at the ceiling in Josh's hospital room. She listened to the quiet reigning on the floor and relaxed.

The sound of the door opening brought her up in her chair, and she twisted to see who was coming into the room. Gabriel entered, and her heart soared. He offered her a tender smile that had the ability to dissolve her apprehension. She remained where she was. She was afraid if she tried to stand she would collapse from exhaustion.

"You didn't have to come back."

"I know, but I wanted to see how Josh was doing—and how you were doing."

"We're both fine."

Gabriel covered the distance to the bed and stared at Josh, who was lost-looking in the white sheets. Myriad emotions—from worry to relief to joy—flittered across Gabriel's face, each one making Rebecca's pulse race. There were few people who cared and loved her son as the man before her was showing in the tender glow of his eyes.

"When Mabel called to tell me that Josh was being rushed to the hospital, I thought—" He shook his head. "I thought I might lose him."

Rebecca rose and placed her hand on his shoulder to comfort him. "As you can see, he will be all right."

He pivoted toward her, clasping her hands. "Rebecca, I want to take care of you and your sons."

Her heart stopped beating for a second, then began to pound a mad staccato against her chest. Her palms became sweaty, and her throat went dry.

"I would be a good father and husband to you, Josh and Peter."

She opened her mouth to reply, but no words came out. Her mind went blank. Her body trembled.

"Say something. Anything."

She moved back, needing to sit down before she collapsed. "I don't know what to say."

He took two steps and drew her against him. "Think about it, at least. I would never abandon you or your sons. Never."

His mouth came down upon hers, and his kiss robbed her of any rational thought and stole her breath. She felt cherished and capable of floating on a cloud high above the earth. His arms wound about her while his possession deepened to claim her. Her length meshed into his as though they were one.

When he moved back and looked at her, she thought she was dreaming, that somehow she had fallen asleep and would awaken at any moment. He cupped her face and started to kiss her again.

But Rebecca felt the coldness of his ring against her cheek and sobered to the situation. She pulled back. "Why do you want to take care of us? What does that mean?"

"I want to marry you. When I thought I might lose Josh, I went a little crazy. It made me realize I might have run out of time. Your boys need a father to love them."

"I agree, and I need a husband to love me. Is that what you're saying?"

"I love you, Rebecca."

"Then why do you still have your ring on?"

"I forgot—no, that's not quite right." He backed away, combing his hand through his hair. "I don't know why. I know I have deep feelings for you. I want us to be a family. That was made clear to me tonight."

She stood straight, as though a rod had been placed down her back. "Maybe until you forgive yourself and George, you feel you need to wear that ring as a symbol of what you imagine is your sin, like in *The Scarlet Letter.* I don't see us having a future until you deal with your past. My son is fine. There is no hurry." She sank onto the chair, desperately trying to hold herself together. "Good night, Gabriel. I won't be in to work tomorrow."

When the quiet swish of the door indicated he had left the room, Rebecca finally showed her emotion. She felt her face crumple, her body sink in on itself. He had kissed her like a man who had believed in a future, but he still wore a part of his past like a brand. He had helped her through her problems. Why couldn't she help him through his?

Rebecca stared at Gabriel's house.

Only one light shone in the living room window.

And somehow that one light symbolized the loneliness in her heart. Was Gabriel lonely, too?

She shouldn't be surprised that she'd gone for a walk and ended up at his place. He'd been on her mind all day. She'd managed to avoid talking to him on the phone because she would have felt awkward after the night before when he had asked her to marry him.

But they needed to talk.

She couldn't go on like this. While spending the day at the hospital with Josh, she'd had a great deal of time to think.

She was so tempted to accept Gabriel's proposal and hope that he would resolve his problems concerning his wife and child's untimely deaths. But what if that never happened? What if all he really felt for Rebecca was compassion and pity? She couldn't—wouldn't—base a marriage on that, no matter how much the man loved her children, and there was no doubt he loved them very much.

Squaring her shoulders, she marched up the steps and rang the bell. A few minutes later Gabriel swung the door open, his tired, grim expression dissolving when he saw her. His weak smile tilted her world while steeling her resolve. She wanted all of him—not only his breathtaking smile but his heart.

"Rebecca."

Had she ever heard her name said so sweetly? The sound on his lips coaxed her to forget what was at stake. That would be the biggest mistake, because she would be settling for less than she wanted, deserved.

"I thought you were George McCall."

"Why?"

"He called me at the station. He wanted to see me. I told him I was leaving to go home and didn't want to see him."

Her heart wrenched. George would be a constant reminder of the past to Gabriel until he dealt with the man.

"Please, come in. I just got home. It's been a long day. I was going to come by, but I wanted to change out of my uniform first and grab something to eat. How's Josh doing since you brought him home this afternoon?"

"Fine. The medicine is helping, and his breathing seems to be okay. I have a monitor on him when I'm not in the room. He's sleeping right now, and Granny is listening for any signs of trouble." Rebecca patted the pocket of her jeans. "I have my cell phone if there's a problem. I just needed to get out and get some fresh air. I started walking and ended up here." She listened to herself chatter a mile a minute and realized she was nervous. She had never confronted a man about loving her—not even Craig.

"Would you like something to drink or to eat?" Gabriel led the way into the kitchen. "I was just about to warm up something for dinner."

She shook her head. "Granny had a feast for me when I came home from the hospital with Josh. She declared I probably lost at least a few pounds from not eating, so she was determined to make sure I made up for it all in one meal."

"Did you?"

"Nope. I've lost my appetite."

"Why?"

She looked him directly in the eye. "My stomach is tied up in knots."

"Why?"

"Because all I thought about today was your proposal."

He arched a brow. "And?"

"And nothing. I don't know what to do anymore."

He closed the space between them but didn't touch her. She was glad, because that would have totally unraveled her. As it was, her composure was held together by a thin thread. His commanding presence was doing enough to her nervous system. She had never been so drawn to a man and yet so afraid to act on that attraction.

"Rebecca, I didn't mean to make matters worse for you. I want to help."

"Why?"

"Because I care for you."

"That's not enough, Gabriel. I'll never settle for less than all of a person ever again. Can you truthfully say you can give me that?"

He fingered his ring, twisting it. Then he yanked it off. "There. Is that what you want? I should have done that a long time ago."

Her shoulders sagged as though a great weight were pushing her down. Indeed, all she wanted to do was sink into the floor. "I want you to mean it. I can tell by the expression in your eyes you haven't yet made peace with yourself."

He clenched the ring. The cold metal dug into his flesh, painfully reminding him of the cold past he couldn't forget. "What do I have to do to prove my love to you?"

"I—"

The sound of the doorbell cut into tension-fraught air. Gabriel growled his frustration and went to answer the bell. Rebecca followed, intending to escape before she fell apart in front of him. His finger might be ringless, but his heart was still burdened.

Gabriel wrenched the door open and froze. George looked from Gabriel to Rebecca then back to Gabriel, determination in his eyes. Gabriel gripped the edge of the door and fought the urge to slam it in George's face.

"I told you I didn't want to talk," Gabriel said, his body taut.

"I think we need to."

"I have nothing to say."

"But I have something to say to you. May I come in?"

"No."

Rebecca laid a hand on his arm. "Gabriel, I think you should listen to what the man has to say."

He glared at her, shaking off her touch. "You do?" He heard the sarcastic edge to his voice but didn't care. He was tired of people telling him what to do where

George McCall was concerned. He could wallow in self-pity if he chose to. It was no one else's business.

"Please, Gabriel."

The pain reflected in her gaze tore at the barrier he had built around his heart. He could see in her eyes that he had shut her out again and that there could be no future for them until he could open his heart totally to her. One brick fell, then another. "For you."

"No, Gabriel, for yourself," she murmured, and left him alone with George.

With Rebecca's every step down the stone path, Gabriel felt abandoned. Why had she left him alone with his tormentor? It was easier not to face the past, to bury it deeply and not deal with the pain. Gritting his teeth, Gabriel slowly pivoted toward George, drilling his glare into the man.

Yet in the face of Gabriel's anger, George's expression softened with understanding. "Believe me, I know there's nothing I can say that will bring your family back. I'll pay for that the rest of my life."

"You came all the way over here to tell me that?"

"One of the things I promised myself in prison was that I would seek you out and apologize—no matter how difficult it was. I am so sorry for what I did. I replay that afternoon in my mind every day."

"So do I," Gabriel said, then realized that wasn't true anymore. Ever since Rebecca had entered his life, he had thought less and less about the day of the accident.

"I hope one day you can forgive me. I've made my

peace with God, but it's important that I try to make my peace with you, too. All I can say is that I'll spend the rest of my life trying to make up for that mistake."

"Why did you come back to Oakview?"

"This is my home. The only people I know live here. I have a problem that I'm coping with, but I need people who care around me. I'm not as strong as you."

His statement slammed into Gabriel, humbling him. If he was as strong as George thought, he should be able to forgive the man and move on with his life, open his heart totally to another—someone who deserved only the best. The sadness he'd seen in Rebecca's expression added salt to his open wound. It festered and bled.

"I came here today to beg you not to leave our church. I need their support, but you're an intricate part of that congregation. Your loss would be felt by so many, and I don't know if I could handle that on top of putting my life back together."

"Who said I was going to leave?" Gabriel asked, surprised by the man's plea.

George shrugged. "You know the rumor mill in our town."

Our town. Those words made Gabriel realize he didn't own Oakview. Nor did he have a say on who lived there. "Yes, but I never said that. I don't know if I could give up the support of my church, either."

"Then you understand what I'm saying."

"Yes," Gabriel reluctantly admitted, hating the fact

he did know how George felt. That realization took him one step closer to forgiving the man.

George strode toward the front door, pausing before opening it. "Please think about what I said. I'll try to stay out of your way as much as possible. I don't want to make this any harder on you."

The click of the door closing echoed through the empty house. Gabriel gripped the back of the chair until the tips of his fingers whitened. Exhaustion weaved its way down his length. In a split second three years before so many lives had been changed. Until this moment, however, he hadn't thought of George's life being altered. He had only thought of himself. Gabriel sank onto the wing chair, resting his head on the cushion, his eyes closed.

Thoughts swirled in his mind, making a jumbled mess. But from the chaos came the picture of Rebecca smiling at him, touching his arm, connecting with him on a level beyond friendship. She needed him; he needed her.

His eyes snapped open. She was right. If he didn't deal with his past, there could be no real future with her and her sons. His hatred would fester until it consumed him, defining his life.

Gabriel saw his Bible on the table next to him and picked it up. Remembering what Rebecca had said to him in the church a few days before, he flipped through the pages until he came to the story about the prodigal son. He read it, absorbing each word, taking it into his mind and delving beneath the words to seek the true meaning. It was a story of forgiveness, of giving a person a second chance.

"And he said unto him, Son, thou art ever with me, and all that I have is thine. It was meet that we should make merry, and be glad for this thy brother was dead, and is alive again; and was lost, and is found." Gabriel read the parable from St. Luke 15:31. Could he welcome George into the church and forgive him for what he had done against Gabriel?

He closed his Bible and prayed for the guidance he needed to rid his mind and soul of the anger that threatened to destroy him. As he said the Lord's Prayer, he felt a tranquillity wash over him, cleansing him of his rage. A balance was restored.

He drew his wedding ring from his pocket, rose and went to his bedroom. He opened a keepsake box, put the piece of his past inside, then closed it. God had taken Judy from him, but in His wisdom, He had given him Rebecca. Now, all he had to do was convince Rebecca that he loved her as well as her children.

Chapter Thirteen

Rebecca hated calling in sick for a second day in a row, but she wanted to make sure Josh was all right before leaving him while she worked. She chuckled when she hung up from talking with Mabel. She had to convince the woman not to come over and help her with Josh. Their relationship had come a long way in the few months she had worked at the police station. Gabriel had been right about Mabel being a softie.

Gabriel had been right about a lot of things. When Josh had been in the hospital, she hadn't turned away from God but had grown closer to Him. She felt whole again, as though a part of her wasn't floating around unattached.

Gabriel and the people of Oakview had shown her the way back to the Lord. Why couldn't she help Gabriel deal with his past? If they were to have a meaningful relationship, he would have to open his heart to her support.

Her heart ached when she thought about the scene at Gabriel's house the evening before with George. Gabriel had closed off an important part of himself. Not being able to forgive George had fueled Gabriel's anger, his ties to his past. Memories were important but not when they dominated a person's life and kept him from truly opening himself up to another.

The sound of the doorbell startled Rebecca. She hoped Mabel hadn't ignored what she had said and come anyway. She felt bad enough not going in to work without the whole office staff being gone. And knowing Mabel, she probably had ignored her.

As Rebecca threw open the door, she opened her mouth to tell Mabel to go back to work, but the words died in her throat. Craig, a beautiful woman dressed in a neat pair of slacks and a silk blouse, and two children stood on her front porch. My ex-husband's new family, she thought.

Rebecca forced a smile to her lips. "I wasn't expecting you, Craig." Her tight hold on the doorknob made her hand ache, but she didn't release her grip.

He tried to smile but failed. "I know I should have said something on the phone Sunday, but I wasn't sure I would accept the job."

"What job?" Apprehension washed over her. She wasn't going to like what Craig had to say.

"I'm starting a new job at a bank in New York City in two weeks. We're moving and decided not to wait once I made the decision to take the job." Craig gestured toward his car, which was packed full.

"That's awfully fast." She strongly suspected it had been a fact when she had talked with him a few days before, but she didn't have the energy to call him on it. Frankly, she found it didn't matter except that the boys would be farther away from their father. Of course, if he didn't want to see them five or five hundred miles wouldn't matter.

"I thought I would stop by and say goodbye to Peter."

"How about Josh? Peter's at school." Surprisingly the slight to her youngest son didn't arouse her anger. If Craig chose not to be in his two sons' lives, then that was his loss.

"Josh, too. When's Peter coming home?" He peered at his watch, his face pinched into a frown.

"He should be here in an hour. Since Josh has been sick, Peter wants to make sure he's okay and has been coming home for lunch."

Craig looked at his new wife, and she nodded. "Then we'll wait for him to come home. We can't stay long since I want to make St. Louis tonight."

His response didn't surprise Rebecca. He had never cared to ask about Josh when they had lived together. But the fact he again showed how he really felt hurt. "That's a long drive. Are you sure you should wait?"

"Yes," he said on a long sigh.

"Then come in and wait in the living room." Rebecca swung the door wide and waited until the family filed into the house before following them inside.

"I'm Rebecca Michaels," she said to the beautiful

woman with long auburn hair and a face perfectly made up to enhance her two best features, her blue eyes and high cheekbones. Rebecca noted that after several hours in the car the woman's blouse was still tucked into her neatly pressed slacks. Looking at her jeans and T-shirt, Rebecca inwardly groaned.

"I'm Laura Michaels, and these are my two daughters, Mandy and Sara."

Hearing the woman say Craig's surname reminded Rebecca of her failure to keep her marriage together and shook her self-confidence, which she had worked so hard to rebuild. "It's nice meeting you. Please have a seat."

Rebecca greeted each of the little girls who appeared to be six and eight years old. They were perfect little replicas of their mother, with long auburn hair brushed back from their pretty faces. They wore matching dresses with few wrinkles, the soft burgundy fabric complementing their creamy, smooth complexions.

Mandy and Sara quietly sat on the couch, their backs straight, their hands folded in their laps. Rebecca thought of Peter, who couldn't sit on a couch for more than a minute before he started to wiggle or talk. Or Josh, who until very recently couldn't sit up by himself. Far from perfect, but they were her sons, and she loved them dearly.

"May I get you something to drink?" Rebecca started for the kitchen, needing something to do while they waited for Peter.

"No, we're fine," Craig said, stopping her in her tracks.

Rebecca turned and glanced at the clock on the mantel, its ticking filling the quiet. Slowly she walked to a chair and sat. While she searched her mind for a topic of conversation, she listened to the ticking of the clock. What would the couple across from her do if she ran from the room screaming? She decided she wasn't much better than Peter at sitting still and being quiet.

"Oakview hasn't changed, I see," Craig finally said.

"I like the fact it hasn't." Rebecca winced at her defensive tone. Craig had always hated coming to see Granny, and when they had come to visit, he had made sure they hadn't stayed long.

"What do you do for fun around here?"

"It isn't that small. There's a movie theater with first-run movies. The town is big on sports, and there is great fishing in some of the streams and rivers nearby."

Another lengthy silence tautened Rebecca's nerves until she thought they would snap and she would go running from the room screaming. The doorbell sounded, cutting into the tension. She leaped to her feet and ran to the door, opening it without even looking to see who it was. It didn't matter. Anyone was better than her present guests.

Gabriel greeted her with a smile.

She returned his smile and sagged against the door, relieved to see a friendly face. The tired lines about his mouth and eyes drew her attention. She wanted to smooth them away, to ask how the night before with George went. She held onto the door to keep from reaching out to him. This wasn't the time to discuss George or their relationship.

"Am I glad to see you!" Rebecca exclaimed in a voice barely audible.

"You are?"

"Yes, of course."

"I thought after last night you wouldn't be."

"Craig and his new wife and family are here," she whispered, nodding toward the living room.

"We need to talk. How long is he going to be here?"

The venom behind the word *he* was clear to Rebecca. She relished the protective ring to his voice. "Too long. Until Peter comes home for lunch, which is in—" she glanced at her watch "—thirty minutes. What do you want to talk about?"

"It will have to wait."

"Please come in." She tried to keep from sounding desperate, but she needed moral support.

"I don't think I should. I might not be very nice to him."

Rebecca grabbed Gabriel's hand. "Sure you can." She tugged him into her house and closed the door before he changed his mind and escaped.

When she entered the living room, she introduced Gabriel to Craig and his new family. "Gabriel, our town's police chief, is my boss since I started working at the police station."

"Who takes care of the boys?" Craig asked after shaking hands with Gabriel.

Since when have you cared? That was what Rebecca wanted to say, but she forced herself to count to ten before answering, "Granny takes care of them."

"Do you think your grandmother should take care of Peter and Josh? That seems like an awfully lot of work for an old woman."

"This *old* woman can handle it just fine. Not that you've ever cared if I lived or died." Granny came into the room with Josh in her arms. "I heard you down here and thought you might like to say hello to your son." Granny thrust Josh into Craig's lap, then moved to sit in her rocking chair.

Craig clasped Josh before he toppled over and held him gingerly, as though he didn't know what to do with the child. He surged to his feet, gripping Josh under the arms and holding him away from his body. Quickly Craig covered the distance to Rebecca and gave Josh to her.

"I think he needs changing." Craig's nose wrinkled, a frown marring his features.

Rebecca seized the chance to escape the room, knowing that Granny would have changed him before coming downstairs. "I'll be back in a moment."

"I'll help you," Gabriel added, trailing behind Rebecca.

Upstairs in her bedroom, she laid Josh on her bed and checked to see if she needed to change his diaper. She didn't. She felt Gabriel's gaze on her as she buttoned Josh's pants. Suddenly she was all thumbs.

"When did Craig get married again?"

"I just found out about it right before Josh was rushed to the hospital."

"How do you feel about this?"

"Craig's getting what he wants, his perfect little family."

"You didn't answer my question."

"I'm sad that he's turning his back on his sons, but beyond that I don't feel anything. I refuse to waste any more energy trying to change something I can't change."

"No anger?"

She shook her head. "I guess I'm mellowing. How about you?" she asked in a casual tone. Inside she was anything but casual. She held her breath while waiting for his reply.

"I'm mellowing, too. Must be catching."

She noticed his wedding ring was still off his left hand, but she wasn't going to say anything about it. Seeing Craig with his new family didn't arouse her anger, but it did make her leery about any relationship a person wasn't committed to one hundred percent. She had to protect her heart and her children from being hurt again.

"I guess I've stalled changing Josh's diaper long enough. I probably shouldn't have left Craig with Granny. They never got along before, and now he definitely isn't on her favorite people list."

"Here, let me." Gabriel took Josh and swung him high.

The sound of her son's laughter dissolved some of her anxiety. Josh had a way of putting her life in perspective, of teaching her what was important. And having Gabriel hold her youngest gave her a sense of satisfaction. She knew he was trying in his own way to make a point with Craig, but she wasn't sure her ex-husband would get it.

When Rebecca entered the living room, the tension hit her like a brick wall. She looked from Granny to Craig then back to Granny. Her grandmother smiled so sweetly Rebecca knew she'd had her say while Rebecca was gone and Craig wasn't too pleased by it.

Craig stood, throwing her grandmother a narrow eyed look. "I think we'll wait outside by the car."

"Well, if you're sure that's what you want to do. Peter will be here in a few minutes."

Craig, with family in tow, stalked to the front door.

Rebecca peered at Granny, who shrugged and appeared innocent. "They're our guests."

"I didn't invite him here. Did you?"

"No, but he wanted to see Peter. I'll never deny him that."

Granny huffed. "It seems to me there are people in this town who are better fathers to that boy than his own." After looking pointedly at Gabriel, she headed toward the kitchen.

"No one can accuse my grandmother of being subtle. I'm sorry, Gabriel." She avoided his gaze, afraid of what might be in his eyes.

"She's right. I want to be a father to Peter and Josh."

Rebecca wasn't sure he was aware of the pain that laced his words. She knew he wanted to be a father, but at what cost? "I'd better get outside for when Peter comes home. I don't want him hurt any more than necessary." She started for the front door.

"Rebecca, I put my wedding ring away for good."

She stopped, her hand on the door, her back to Gabriel.

"I'm working on forgiving George. I wish I could say I have completely. I've lived with this anger and guilt for a long time, but with God's help I will forgive."

Her grip tightened. "Gabriel, I can't deal with this right now. I don't know how Peter will react when he sees his father and his new family."

"My proposal still stands. I want to marry you."

She shivered. Suddenly she was so cold. She pivoted at the door and faced Gabriel, who was still holding Josh. "Me or my children?"

"You. I love your children, but you're the woman I want to marry."

"I can't answer you right now." She pulled the door open.

"I think you're the one who is afraid, Rebecca. You're scared of being hurt again. It's easier to make it seem like my problems are what is keeping us apart. It's easier for you to shut off your feelings than to risk getting hurt again."

She quirked one of her brows. "Oh, and you didn't

shut off your feelings? So now you're the expert on relationships?"

Gabriel watched Rebecca flee outside. He shook his head. "I don't know, Josh, about your mother. Have any suggestions on how I can reach her?"

"I do."

Gabriel turned toward Rose, who stood in the entrance to the living room, using her cane to support her. These past few days had been difficult on Rose—on everyone.

"Don't take no for an answer, son."

"That's all?"

"Craig's just stirred up some feelings she's been having a tough time dealing with. She'll come around after he leaves."

"She demanded I come to terms with my problems, and I have. But she still hasn't completely faced hers."

"Give her some time. She will. You're a mighty powerful persuader." Granny walked to the front door and started to close it. "Come on into the kitchen, and we'll talk over some coffee."

Rebecca heard the sound of the front door closing behind her and almost hurried to push it open and escape inside where she was accepted for who she was. Instead, she gripped the porch railing and observed Craig and his family standing by the car. Craig's arms were folded over his chest, and his thunderous expression slashed his eyebrows and mouth downward. The three females remained quietly lined up next to him. In that moment she pitied Laura.

When Peter came running down the sidewalk, Rebecca straightened, praying that Craig would let their son down gently.

Peter stopped short when he saw Craig. Rebecca listened to Craig introduce Peter to his wife and her two daughters. There was a note of pride in Craig's voice that made her grip the railing tightly. *Lord, please give me the strength to handle this, to be there for Peter after his father leaves.*

She didn't have to hear the conversation to know exactly when Craig informed Peter he was moving to New York. Her son frowned, his teeth digging into his bottom lip. He had been okay with his father remarrying, but this was different. She wanted to go to her son and hug him, but she knew her presence would only compound the situation with Craig. Ten minutes later, Craig patted Peter on the head and told him goodbye, that he would call him soon.

As Craig climbed into the car, Rebecca descended the steps and walked to her son. Placing her hands on his shoulders, she squeezed and whispered, "I love you."

Craig's car disappeared from view before Peter said, "I know, Mom, but why can't Dad love me, too?"

She turned her son to face her. "He does love you, honey. If he didn't, he wouldn't have come by and told you personally about him moving. Some people have a hard time showing their love. Your dad is one of those people, but it doesn't mean he doesn't love you." She pulled him toward the steps and sat. "You should have seen the first time he saw you and held you. The look of wonder on his face was priceless."

"Really?"

"Yes. You were a beautiful baby."

"Mom! Boys aren't beautiful."

"Sorry, I meant handsome. And remember the time you learned to ride your bicycle? He was there helping you."

"But he has a new family now."

"People are capable of loving more than one person. He'll have room in his heart for all of you." She prayed that was true, but if it wasn't, she would be there to pick up the pieces.

Her son's stomach rumbled. He laughed. "I guess I'm hungry. We worked hard this morning at school."

"And you need to get back. Let's see what Granny cooked for lunch."

They mounted the steps to the porch. Rebecca was aware that Gabriel was still inside with her grandmother. She didn't want to see him right now. Craig's surprise visit left her feeling vulnerable, wounded, and she needed time to sort through the emotions swirling inside her.

"I bet Granny fixed ham and cheese sandwiches with tomato soup."

"You think?"

"It's Tuesday. She does every Tuesday for the lunch I take to school."

In the kitchen Gabriel sat at the table, cradling a cup of coffee while he spoke with her grandmother. He fell silent when she and Peter entered the room. A blush stained her cheeks. She obviously had been the topic of conversation. If she hadn't been so preoccupied with Peter the past few minutes, her ears would have no doubt been burning.

Gabriel pushed to his feet. "I need to get back to the station. I've played hooky too long. I'm afraid Mabel might come and hunt me down. Walk me to the door, Rebecca."

Reluctantly she led the way. When she reached out to open the door, Gabriel grasped her hand. The touch nearly sent her into his arms. Then she remembered Craig's visit and stepped back, their fingers still laced together.

"I know today hasn't been easy for you, Rebecca, but I'm not leaving without at least telling you I love you and doing this." Gabriel tugged her flat against him, and his mouth descended to claim hers.

Tingling sensations rocked her resolve to keep her distance, to wade through the emotions she was feeling. She gripped his shoulders to keep herself upright. Her legs felt like rubber and her heart felt on fire.

"Remember that. I'll see you tonight. You and I need to have a long talk and work all this out."

Gabriel left her standing in the middle of the entrance with her quivering fingers grazing the lips he had kissed so thoroughly. I love you. His words sang loud and clear in her mind, declaring his intentions.

* * *

Dare she take another chance on love? Rebecca wondered as she finished putting the last dinner plate in the dishwasher. She had been wrong once and was still paying dearly for it.

"Rebecca?"

She hadn't heard him enter the kitchen. Slowly she turned to face Gabriel who stood across the room—too far away yet too close. She felt as though she teetered on the brink of something important.

He strode toward her, determination in his gaze. To coat her suddenly dry throat, she swallowed several times, but she didn't move an inch. She felt trapped by his possessive look, which skimmed down her, laying claim to her.

"I'd hoped to be here earlier, but Susan reported Bess missing."

"She did? Why didn't you call me? Where is Bess? Can I help?"

Holding up his hand, close to her mouth but not touching her, he chuckled. "Bess is fine. She was asleep in someone else's room. Thought it was hers and took a nap."

Relieved, Rebecca eased back against the counter, aware of his nearness, which caused a fluttering in the pit of her stomach and siphoned the energy from her legs. "There are days I forget she has trouble with her memory from time to time, then something like that happens."

"We found her when Peepers wanted out of the room and began to yelp."

"She wasn't supposed to have the puppy inside during the day. Why am I surprised she did?"

"Bess isn't one for the rules. Everything's okay now. I even got Susan to overlook the puppy being inside."

With each moment he stood in her kitchen, her heart beat a shade faster until she was afraid she would become light-headed. She needed to put some distance between them. She ran her hand through her hair, then gestured toward the table. "Do you want something to eat? I could fix you a plate."

"There's only one thing I want."

"What do you want?" she asked, her voice a weak thread, her throat constricting.

"I want you to be my wife." He captured her face between his hands and stared into her eyes. "You're the one I love above everyone else. Yes, I love your sons, but it's you I'm asking to marry me. I want to make that perfectly clear right up front."

"I don't—"

He stopped her words with a fingertip pressed against her lips. "I am *not* Craig. Give me a chance to prove that. I know you're wary of committing to someone else. I was until I met you, but we can make this work."

"I'm so scared. I was wrong once. Seeing Craig again today only made me think about how wrong I was. I can't go through that again."

"I'm not asking you to." Gabriel stroked his fingers through her hair and brought her close to him, cuddling her head against his chest. "Do you hear that? That's my heart breaking."

The loud thumping sounded in her ear. The soothing touch of his hand riveted her attention. His scent of soap and pine engulfed her.

"I see that you have two choices here. You can embrace life with zeal or you can continue to hide and run away. Which is it gonna be, Rebecca?"

She heard the ticking of the clock on the wall as it echoed through the room, proclaiming her indecision. The stroking of his hand stopped, conveying his mounting tension. *Lord, I'm scared to risk my heart again. Help me.*

When her silence continued, Gabriel pulled back and stared at her. "I sign on, Rebecca, for life."

She opened her mouth.

"Mom! Mom!"

Peter burst into the room. Rebecca jumped away from Gabriel, feeling the heat creep up her face.

"Mom, come quick. Josh is standing on his own."

Everything evaporated from her mind except one thing—Josh. She hurried into the living room right behind Peter and came to a halt when she saw her youngest son taking a shaky step toward her grandmother. Stunned and in awe of what her son was doing, Rebecca froze, tears flooding her eyes and streaming down her face unchecked.

"Thank you, Lord," she whispered as Gabriel took her hand.

The feel of his fingers around hers, his arm touching hers, made the moment perfect. Josh stumbled, and before she could move to catch him, Peter whisked him up, laughing and shouting his joy.

"Who's my man? Josh is my man. I knew you could do it," Peter said, swinging his brother around and around.

Rebecca grasped Gabriel's other hand, compelling him to look from Josh to her. The tenderness in his gaze melted any doubts she might have had. "Yes, I'll marry you, Gabriel Stone. Name the day. I'll be there."

He grabbed her in a bear hug and swung her around, shouting his joy. When he placed her feet on the floor, he glanced over her shoulder at her grandmother and Peter. "Rebecca has just agreed to be my wife."

"This indeed is a wondrous day. Praise the Lord." Rose pushed herself to her feet and came to them.

Peter stood Josh next to him and slowly they made their way toward Rebecca. When the pair was a few feet away, Gabriel scooped Josh up into his arms and faced Peter.

"Will you give your blessing?" Gabriel asked her eldest.

Rebecca held her breath. Peter liked Gabriel, but would he accept him as a stepfather?

A serious expression marked the boyish lines of Peter's face as he thought about Gabriel's question. Cocking his head, he finally replied, "Can I be your best man?" A grin split his mouth.

Epilogue

Breathing in the scent of pine always brought a smile to Rebecca's lips, but on this magical night, the scent reminded Rebecca yet again that she'd come home. Home to Gabriel. Home to the Lord.

At the end of the Reverend Carson's touching service, Alicia switched off the overhead lights, leaving only the softly wavering candle flames on the altar to light the sanctuary. Instantly, Rebecca knew what it must have felt like that night in Bethlehem. A dark, cold night when the cry of a newborn babe had been all it took to warm the people's hearts and souls, a cry that proclaimed a new beginning for everyone.

In the shadowy darkness, Rebecca rose with the choir to sing the last song of the Christmas Eve service. She looked at the sea of faces before her and felt a wealth of love and good fortune.

Gabriel, standing next to her, took her hand in his and gave her a reassuring squeeze. "You ready?"

"Yes, my love."

Tears of pure joy pooled in her eyes as she flashed him a brilliant smile. It seemed her whole life had been about this moment. He picked Josh up. She tightened their family's bond by taking Peter's hand, and with the four of them linked together, they moved as one to the front of the choir. Together, as a family, they sang "Silent Night." The singing was a gift Rebecca wanted to offer to the Lord for all He had given her. Gabriel's deep voice complemented Peter's and hers as they paid tribute to Christ. They finished the song with their voices blending as one, just as over the past months they'd blended as a family.

When the lights came on, washing the church in a rich brightness, everyone began filing out of the sanctuary. Gabriel didn't release Rebecca's hand. Instead he pulled her around so she stood in front of him, much as she had the day she had agreed to be his wife. He brushed a kiss across her forehead.

"Have I told you how much I love you today?" Gabriel asked, taking her other hand and holding them between their bodies.

She tilted her head and thought for a long moment. "Mmm—let me see. Nope, I don't think so. And you haven't missed one day since we married five months ago. My, Gabriel Stone, you seem to be slacking on the job."

He pulled her closer, laughter deep in his eyes. "You didn't hear me when you were waking up this morning."

"So that's what you were whispering into my ear. I had other things on my mind. You know me first thing in the morning."

He smiled, the lines at the corners of his eyes deepening. "Yes, I do. You're a touch grumpy, Rebecca Stone."

"You would be, too, if you were carrying around an extra ten pounds."

His eyes softened. He laid his hand on her rounded stomach. "You're exceptionally beautiful in the morning—in the afternoon—in the evening."

"You're just saying that because I'm carrying your child." His compliments never ceased to bring a full flush to her cheeks. She felt the love in his voice to the depth of her being and marveled that one man could make her feel so special and complete.

"Highly unlikely, since I've thought that from the first day I saw you."

"If you two lovebirds can quit cooing, it's time to cut the birthday cake for Jesus," Granny said behind Rebecca.

"Did you hear something, love?" Gabriel winked at Rebecca, his gaze never leaving her face.

"You know how sound carries in the church, Gabriel."

"Funny, you two. I know that Josh and Peter are hungry for some cake."

"Well, in that case, let's get a move on it. We don't want to be last in line for our piece of cake." Gabriel began ushering his family toward the door.

George McCall, with his sister and her three children,

stood several people in front of them. Rebecca slipped her arm through Gabriel's and leaned against him, watching closely as he spied George a few feet ahead of them.

"I think it was wonderful that you talked to Ben about giving George a job," Rebecca said, slanting a look at her husband.

"Everyone deserves a second chance. I got one, thanks to you."

The love for this man flowed through Rebecca, expanding her heart to encompass all. "You have shown me what a family should be. You guided me back to the Lord and helped me to find my faith again. I love you, Gabriel Stone."

* * * * *

Dear Reader,

For many years I have worked with students with special needs. When I came up with the idea for this book, I felt as though God had given me a mission. This is a story to celebrate the beautiful children I've been fortunate to teach. Every day I go to work I'm the one who feels special because I get to teach them, prepare them for their future. They give me an appreciation of life and make me look forward to going to work. I thank God for giving me the chance to teach students with a zeal for life and an unconditional love for others.

I hope you enjoy this story of Gabriel and Rebecca and the blessings a child with special needs can bring to a family. I love hearing from readers. You can write me at P.O. Box 2074, Tulsa, Oklahoma, 74101.

May God bless you,

Margaret Daley

THE COURAGE TO DREAM

Trust in the Lord with all thine heart and lean not unto thine own understanding. In all thy ways acknowledge Him, and He shall direct thy paths.
—*Proverbs* 3:5–6

To my son, Shaun, and his new wife, Katie.
May you two have a long and wonderful marriage.

Chapter One

"I wondered when you would finally show up, Rachel." Michael Hunter stopped several feet from her on the river landing.

There was none of the remembered warmth in his voice, and Rachel Peters shuddered in the heat of the day. "I came as soon as I found out." Everything around her seemed to come to a standstill, the breeze, the flow of the river, the chirping of the birds, her heartbeat.

"We couldn't wait for you. We buried Flora yesterday."

"I was working halfway around the world as a guest chef on a cruise." The tightness in her throat prevented her from explaining further. She'd only found out the day before about Aunt Flora's death. Her aunt had been like a mother to her. It had taken more than a week for the message from the family lawyer to finally catch up with Rachel. She hadn't even had time to think about her aunt's death, much less grieve properly. Swallowing hard, Rachel asked, "How are Amy and Shaun?"

"Do you care?"

The hostility in his question sparked her anger, but she was determined not to let him see his effect on her. "Where are my sister and brother?" she asked in an even voice, suppressing her rage.

Michael gestured toward the riverboat. "They're with Garrett. Why?"

"Why? Because I've come to take them home."

"Whose home? Aunt Flora's or yours, wherever that may be?"

"I don't have to defend myself or my lifestyle to you."

The harsh glint in his eyes intensified. "They've been through a lot this past week. I think it'll be better if they stay with me for a while."

"You!" Her anger began to infuse her voice, her expression.

"Yes, me. I know Amy and Shaun. Can you honestly say the same?"

"They're *my* family."

"And that automatically gives you the right to decide what's best for them?"

"Yes."

"Where were you when Shaun broke his arm or Amy went on her first date?"

Rachel clamped her teeth together so tightly that pain radiated down her neck. "They're my responsibility now. Take me to them—please," she said in a slow, deliberate voice.

For a long moment he stared at her, his gaze hard, unyielding. Pieces of their past came together in her mind like a patchwork quilt. There had been other times when their gazes had clashed in silent battle and times when they had connected in friendship and mutual affection. The blare of a boat's horn startled Rachel, the pieces of the quilt unraveling. Blinking, she looked away from Michael.

"Don't bother. I'm sure I can find them." She headed for the gangplank, more resolved than ever to remain in control and not let Michael get to her.

"They're in the main salon."

Rachel kept walking, feeling the scorch of his regard on her back. All she wanted was to get her sister and brother and leave. She'd known when she returned to Magnolia Blossom, Mississippi, that she would probably see Michael again, but she hadn't been prepared for the emotional impact of their meeting.

Remembering the location of the main salon, Rachel went straight to it. She paused in the doorway to scan the room that had once been beautiful and grand. Amy, Shaun and Michael's son, Garrett, sat at a table, their voices low, their heads bent together. When Amy glanced up and stopped talking, Rachel entered the salon, realizing the next few minutes might be even more difficult than the last ones.

It had been almost a year since she'd seen Amy and Shaun. She'd talked to them on the phone, but it wasn't the same. They've grown up a lot in that time. I don't know them very well, she thought, fighting a surge of panic. Once or twice a year isn't enough time to know what they're feeling, thinking, to be a family.

"Hello, Shaun. Amy." Rachel attempted a smile that quivered at the corners of her mouth, the tension in the air as thick as the humidity that draped her. When neither one said anything, she turned to Michael's son, hoping he would break the taut silence. "I'm Rachel Peters, Amy and Shaun's sister."

"I'm Garrett. Nice to meet you." The young boy stood and extended his hand.

The similarities between father and son disarmed her. It was as though she was staring at a younger version of Michael, more relaxed, more carefree—like he had once been around her. Then she remembered his marriage to Mary Lou and the betrayal she'd felt when she'd heard about it. She realized she had no right to feel that way, but sometimes emotions weren't easy to control. The memory gnawed at her composure until she determinedly pushed it away.

"What are you doing here?" Amy's question cut into the silence like a sharpened butcher's knife into a piece of thick meat.

Rachel looked at her sixteen-year-old sister. Amy's expression was defiant, and for a moment Rachel didn't know how to answer her. "Aunt Flora asked me to take care of you two if anything ever happened to her. I promised her I would."

At the time she hadn't thought she would ever really have to take care of her brother and sister. She had only been concerned with making her aunt feel better.

Amy shot to her feet. "We're doing just fine the way things are now. Michael doesn't mind us staying with him. Go back to wherever you came from. Shaun and I don't wanna leave."

Rachel glanced from her sister to her eight-year-old brother then back to her sister, not sure what to do. "I'm not going back just yet. I've come to take you to Aunt Flora's."

Amy pushed back her chair, its scraping sound reverberating in the silence. Standing behind Shaun, she placed her hands on his shoulders. "We don't need your help. I'm sure you have better things to do than baby-sit us."

Michael walked into the salon, sharpening Rachel's awareness of the hostility in the room. Her nape tingled, and the humid air felt even heavier and more oppressive. "Let's go home and we'll discuss everything there. I'm not going to make any decisions without talking it over with you two first."

Amy began to say something, but Michael interrupted. "I think that's a good idea. Your sister has come a long way, and y'all have a lot to talk about."

Amy clamped her lips together in a pout.

Shaun looked at Garrett, who nodded. Shaun rose, touching Amy's arm. "C'mon, I need to check on my fish anyway."

Amy didn't move. Her pout deepened as she folded her arms across her chest.

"This was your aunt's wish," Michael said in a gentle tone. "Y'all are welcome to visit anytime. My home is always open."

When Amy's bottom lip started to tremble, she bit it. Drawing in a long breath, she said, "Oh, all right—for the time being." She rushed past Rachel and Michael.

As the two boys followed Amy from the salon, Rachel started to thank Michael, but the sight of his hard stare caused the words to die in her throat. His gaze cut through her as though she were beneath his consideration.

"I didn't do it for you, Rachel. Amy and Shaun don't need to feel any more torn apart than they already are. But my offer still stands. They're welcome to stay with me and Garrett anytime."

"We'll do fine once everything settles down." She stopped short of telling him that they didn't need his help. Since returning to Magnolia Blossom, she wasn't sure of anything.

One brow arched as he studied her. A slow, chilling smile appeared on his face. "I hope so—for Amy and Shaun's sake."

Michael had once been her best friend, but she didn't know this man before her now. The realization saddened her. Puzzled by her feelings, she hurried toward the door. "I'd better go. I don't want to keep them waiting."

"No, I wouldn't do that."

The condemning tone of his voice stopped her at the door. He had always been able to provoke her. She couldn't afford to let him incite her. Over the years she had learned to control her emotions. Gripping the doorjamb, she calmly murmured goodbye, then left the salon to find her sister and brother.

Amy and Shaun stood on the landing below. Her sister still had her arms crossed over her chest with a frown lining her brow while her brother was skipping rocks across the water with Garrett. Observing them, Rachel was overwhelmed. She was not only trying to come to terms with the death of her aunt, whom she loved dearly, but with the fact that she was the only person her younger sister and brother could depend on. Since leaving Magnolia Blossom she'd had her life planned. Now she had no earthly idea what the future held. The thought scared her to death.

When Michael came out onto the deck behind her, she felt his regard and shivered in the warm air. With no more than a glance at him, she hurried down the stairs.

Michael watched Rachel stop on the landing to gather her sister and brother. Anger held him rigid, his hands gripping the railing. Until he had seen Rachel, he hadn't realized how angry he was. He'd thought he'd gotten over her years before, but the memory of her last day in Magnolia Blossom assailed him. She'd walked away from him and the town and had never once looked back. He had to find a way to get past his anger because he loved Amy and Shaun and wanted to be there for them in their time of need.

Lord, help me to overcome this sudden feeling of anger at Rachel. She's a part of my past, where I want to keep her. I need to be strong for Amy and Shaun, but I'm afraid I can't do it without Your guidance.

"Rachel, Flora knew you would do what was best for Shaun and Amy," the family lawyer said as he closed the file and leaned back in his chair.

Rachel rose, feeling sorrow, pain, confusion. "But that's the problem, Robert. I don't *know* what's best."

"Give it some time. Don't rush things."

Rachel smoothed a strand of black hair that had strayed from her compact French braid. After gathering her clutch purse, she shook Robert Davenport's hand. "I don't think Shaun or Amy will let me do anything but take it slowly. I'm finding my sister and brother are as strong-willed as Aunt Flora was."

"Then I guess you'll be staying a while."

"Yes." The one word sounded like a death sentence.

"I'll be out to the house in a couple of days. There are some more papers you'll need to sign. We'll need to work out guardianship. From conversations with Flora, living with your parents isn't an option for Amy and Shaun."

Her control faltered, emotions constricting her

throat. The enormous responsibility she had agreed to take on hit her with overwhelming force. "No, my parents don't live in a place conducive to raising children. I tried reaching them, but I haven't gotten a response from their base camp in the Amazon."

When Rachel stepped outside Robert's office, a hot blast of summer air fogged her sunglasses. She moved them down the bridge of her nose and took a moment to scan the small, sleepy Southern town, nestled along the banks of the Mississippi River near Natchez.

An old man across the street waved to Rachel, and she returned the greeting. A couple passed her on the sidewalk and offered her their condolences. Everyone knew everyone. For two short years as a teenager she had been a part of this town, made to feel welcome because of her aunt. Rachel's chest tightened, and she drew in several deep breaths.

Magnolia Blossom—stifling, confining. She hadn't wanted to be a part of this town. She had left ten years ago because she'd refused to put down roots.

A bright yellow sign caught Rachel's attention. Helen's Southern Delight. Suddenly Rachel needed to be with a person who cared. Helen had been there for her in the past.

When Rachel entered the café with its booths along one wall and a jukebox on the other side, Helen came from behind the counter to hug her. "Well, sugar, it's 'bout time you stepped into my place."

Sitting at the counter, Rachel felt as though she were

eighteen again and seeking Helen's advice about going to Paris to study cooking. She scanned the café where her dreams had been cultivated and realized in all these years Helen hadn't changed the fifties decor.

Helen stood back from the counter, eyeing Rachel in her no-nonsense manner, placing her hands on her plump hips. "I'll certainly say you don't eat all that delicious food I hear you've learned to cook. You're skin and bones, sugar."

"I can always count on you to speak your mind. I'm glad some things haven't changed in this world."

Helen smiled, the corners of her eyes crinkling. "Hey, maybe you can show me one of your fancy recipes while you're here. I hear that you do divine things with chicken."

"I doubt there's anything I could show you about cooking, Helen. The basis of all my recipes came from working with you at this café."

Helen stared at Rachel with one of her probing looks. "I'm sure proud of you, sugar. I knew you had the talent and drive to make it big. Now I tell all my friends I know a famous chef who has been written up in some of those fancy magazines. You must have seen some pretty exciting places. I bet you've seen over half the world by now."

"You know me. My home is where my suitcase is."

"Sugar, that might be fine and dandy for some people, but for myself and most folks round here, being gone from Magnolia Blossom for more than a week is long enough."

"Actually, if everything goes according to plan, I'll be settling down in New York and opening my own restaurant soon."

"Your own place?"

Excited, Rachel leaned forward. "I've got a proposal before some investors. If they agree, I'll be working for myself."

"When will you hear?"

"Hopefully in late July."

Helen glanced toward the kitchen then at Rachel. "How do you think Amy and Shaun will like living in New York?"

Rachel frowned. "Given time, they'll see the advantages of leaving Magnolia Blossom."

"Then you've decided to leave for sure, even if the restaurant deal falls through?" Helen scrubbed a particularly clean spot on the counter.

"I don't know what I'm going to do. That's what's so frustrating. So much depends, of course, on whether I can open my own restaurant. I've dreamed about that for a long time. I'm not usually an indecisive person, but I don't know the first thing about raising children."

"Now, I've never had any children, but from all I've seen I'd say you take it one step at a time."

"I suppose my first step is to call New York and see about the schools available for Shaun and Amy."

Helen cocked her head. "The first step? Don't you think the first step is getting to know them? It's been pretty long since you've spent any real time with them. They have a full life here."

"I know. Everything's a mess." Rachel sighed. "But my life isn't here."

"It was once."

"No, it wasn't, Helen. Magnolia Blossom was only another temporary stopover. Longer than most, but temporary just the same."

"Well, sugar, I'm sure you'll do what's best for everyone concerned." Helen started filling the saltshakers, her glance straying toward the kitchen several times. "You know I saved that magazine with your name in it. Let me see, what did that magazine writer call you?" She snapped her fingers. "The Cajun Queen."

"Sounds like a riverboat, doesn't it?" The second Rachel said riverboat, a vivid memory of Michael's steamboat flashed into her mind and her resolve to forget their confrontation fled. She had instinctively known that if she paused for even a moment she would dwell on him, experiencing again the bittersweet emotions of seeing him. If she stayed in Magnolia Blossom for even a few weeks, she would be inundated with Michael Hunter's presence. Could she risk stirring up old emotions?

"Maybe that's what Michael should call his boat. 'Course, it needs more than a new name. Several coats of paint. A new interior. I think he's considering fixing it up." Helen paused. "Hey, sugar, I'm sorry for bringing up Michael. I forgot that y'all were once an item."

Years of experience had taught Rachel to hide pain and loneliness behind a mantle of deceptive calm, and she utilized that now. "Friends, Helen. That was all."

"Sugar, I was there when you needed to talk."

"He's in the past where he belongs. We've both changed, moved on with our lives."

Helen stared at her for a moment. "Can you honestly say your feelings for him are dead?"

After the scene at the riverboat, Rachel was left with no doubts about Michael's feelings. "Yes." She stood, her mantle of calm slipping. "I need to run. Thanks, Helen—for everything," she whispered, her voice raw, her throat tight. For years she'd struggled to present a strong, invincible facade to the world, but right now she was having a tough time keeping it in place.

As Rachel hurried from the café, tears crowded her eyes. Again she was accosted by the scorching summer heat, but this time she left her sunglasses on to conceal her glistening eyes. Emotion felt like a coil wrapped about her chest, squeezing the breath from her. She inhaled deep gulps of hot air.

She didn't usually indulge in tears. She hadn't cried when she had been forced to leave friend after friend as her parents had moved from one place to another. She hadn't cried when her mother had left her and Amy with Aunt Flora. But now she felt her world changing, her life in shambles. She experienced all over again the same hurt she'd felt when her mother deposited her with Aunt Flora. She remembered the confusion of falling in love with Michael while she wanted to pursue her dreams. In the end she had chosen to leave—that was the only thing she knew how to do.

At the only stoplight in town, she sat, indecisive about which way to turn. For one fleeting moment she wished she could turn to Michael as she once had.

Where was Amy? Rachel wondered as she stared at the kitchen clock. It hadn't been that long ago that she had been sixteen, and yet Rachel felt generations apart from her sister. She had been trying to reach her younger sister, to get to know her better, but all she got for her efforts were pouts and Amy's back as she stormed from the room.

Dinner was in the oven, ready for the past half hour. Rachel had been waiting for her sister's return from no telling where. Amy hadn't left a note. That would change the minute she came home, Rachel decided as she checked her Cajun chicken dish.

Rachel thought about eating without Amy, but she really wasn't hungry and didn't look forward to eating yet another meal alone. Earlier Shaun and Garrett had raced into the kitchen, taken one look at the meal she was preparing and fixed peanut butter and jelly sandwiches to eat while playing computer games.

"Isn't a family supposed to sit down to dinner and eat together?" Rachel muttered to herself, not knowing exactly what to do about the situation.

She poured herself a glass of iced tea. The sound of

pounding sneakers filled the kitchen as Rachel shut the refrigerator door. Shaun and Garrett came to a screeching halt inches from colliding into her. She eyed the two plates in Shaun's hand, happy this time they had made it to the kitchen.

"We're going out." Shaun started for the door.

"Where?"

Shaun shrugged. "Just out."

"It'll be dark soon. I want you back by then."

"But *all* the kids can stay out later. Garrett doesn't—"

"By dark."

"How 'bout nine-thirty?"

"By dark," she repeated, her voice firm.

Shaun started to argue the point, took one look at her, and instead mumbled something under his breath— which she was glad she didn't hear—and shuffled out of the kitchen with Garrett following.

Rachel watched them leave, her head pounding like their sneakers against the floor. As she massaged her temples, she thought about all the training she'd had to go through to become a chef. She had absolutely no training to become a parent. In only a few short days, the self-confidence she had painstakingly developed had been shaken to its very core.

On the patio, Rachel sank onto the thick red-and-blue cushion on the chaise longue and sipped her tea. Aunt Flora and she used to come out here after dinner and talk. Those had been special times. Her parents had always been too busy to listen. For the two years Rachel had lived with her aunt, she'd glimpsed what it would have been like to have been raised in a normal family, one that didn't pick up and move all the time, one where both parents weren't always working on research that was more important than their children.

The setting sun splashed the darkening sky with vivid colors. Rachel blanked her mind of all thoughts and relished the serenity that settled over the land right before the sun went down. Closing her eyes, she could still see the streaks of mauve, rose and gold weaving in and out of the blue tapestry.

As she let the beauty of the dying day seep into her mind, she relaxed her bone-tired body. Her exhaustion, combined with the humidity, cloaked her like a heavy mantle. A sound penetrated the lassitude that enveloped her. Amy was home. Even as that realization registered, Rachel knew she couldn't face her sister just yet. She needed the restful tranquillity she felt at the moment to give her the strength to remain patient when dealing with Amy later.

The screen door opened then closed. Rachel sensed someone was staring at her and suddenly realized it wasn't Amy or Shaun. Her eyes flew open, and she looked right into Michael's face, devoid of all expression. Tension vibrated in the air between them as he stepped away from the screen door and closer to her.

"Hello, Rachel."

She felt at a disadvantage, lying on the chaise longue, and quickly rose. "Hello, Michael."

As if he needed something to do with his hands, Michael fitted them into the back pockets of his black jeans. Rachel followed his movements, mesmerized by actions that conveyed a smooth athletic prowess. Slowly her gaze trailed upward, lingering momentarily on the bulge of muscles beneath the short sleeves of his black T-shirt. His body was wiry, tough, every lean ounce of him sculpted with a male strength that transmitted leashed energy and supple command. When she finally looked into his dark brown eyes, her pulse sped through her. Memories of their past nibbled at her fragile composure.

"What brings you here?" she asked, thankful that her voice worked, desperate to think of anything but their past.

"I want to discuss Amy with you."

Rachel stiffened and furrowed her brow. "Amy? Is she with you?"

"Yes, I followed her home from Whispering Oaks. She's in her bedroom."

Rachel started for the screen door. "Why was she at your house? Is something wrong?"

"No—yes."

Rachel halted, her hand falling away from the metal handle. She turned, her gaze immediately drawn to his. "What's wrong?"

As Michael moved toward her, Rachel automatically took a step away until she encountered the screen door. She tilted her head in order to look him in the eye, the gesture subtly defiant.

"Amy's concerned about having to leave Magnolia Blossom."

"Why didn't she come to me about her concern?" Rachel asked, and silently wondered, Why did she have to go to you instead?

"I think you know the answer to that."

The rough edge to his voice made her defenses go up. "But I'm her sister."

"Who never came home."

"This isn't my home."

"You're right. I forgot that. You made it perfectly clear that you wanted nothing to do with Magnolia Blossom or…" His jaw clamped shut; his gaze hardened.

"Or what?"

"Me."

Chapter Two

Coldness was embedded in his voice.

He was only inches away, the clean scent of his soap strong and powerful. His nearness made Rachel forget what she was going to retort. Instead, her gaze fastened on the cleft in his chin. She remembered how she loved to caress the dent and run her fingers through his thick brown hair, which held touches of sunlight.

"Why are you here now?" Rachel asked, unnerved by his presence more than she would ever admit.

"Amy overheard your conversation earlier this afternoon with Helen about schools in New York, and she wanted me to convince you not to leave Magnolia Blossom and take her and Shaun away." His laughter was humorless. "Of course, Amy doesn't realize I'm the last person in the world to convince you of that."

"Why does she want to stay here?" Rachel already had a good idea why her sister and brother wanted to stay in

Magnolia Blossom, but she wanted to center the conversation around her siblings and not her feelings for Michael.

"Because this is her home. Because she has only one year left of high school and wants to finish here. Because all her friends are here."

"But New York offers so many opportunities."

"Who are you talking about, yourself or Amy?"

"Both."

"Please, don't kid yourself. Amy isn't interested in New York. When you make your decision, I hope you'll at least consider your sister's needs, too."

"So now you not only know what's best for me but for Amy and, I suppose, for Shaun, too."

"I never tried to tell you what was best for you, but I'll tell you taking those two out of Magnolia Blossom isn't best for them." There was a quiet strength in his voice as he stared at her with a frosty regard. "I care about them."

"And so do I. There are some good schools for Amy in New England or Switzerland where she can make new friends. Those kinds of schools can open so many doors for her. Those places aren't the ends of the earth."

"Now you're talking about Europe! What are you going to do—dump Shaun and Amy in different schools on different continents?"

"If we leave Magnolia Blossom, they'll have a say in what school they'll go to."

"I see. After *consulting* them, you're going to dump them in different schools."

She was reminded of what her parents had done with Amy and her twelve years before, then later Shaun. All her suppressed feelings of abandonment and insecurity surfaced. Her parents hadn't wanted to be burdened with children who got in the way of research. Leaving them with Aunt Flora had been the best thing for them, but the abandonment still hurt, and no amount of logic took the pain away.

"Don't you see, Rachel, both Amy and Shaun need stability right now, not a major upheaval."

"I moved around when I was their age. I survived."

"What's good for you is good for them? Not all people like to pick up and move at a moment's notice. Not all people are as accomplished as you are at leaving friends."

With a flinch she pushed away from the screen door to put some distance between Michael and her. "What I do with them is none of your business."

"Amy has asked me to make it my business. I hope you won't rush a decision because of what happened between us."

"Isn't that presuming a lot?"

A nerve in his jawline twitched as his gaze narrowed on her face. "Then use this time to see things from their viewpoint. You traveled around a lot as a child. They didn't. This is the only real home those two have known. Their friends are important to them, even if they aren't to you."

His words cut deep. She wanted to deny the feeling; she couldn't. There had been a time in her life when she had wished she had a real home with doting parents and lots of friends—a long time ago. "I think you should leave now," she managed to say in an even voice.

He leaned close. "I hope you'll really think about what I said tonight."

She looked him in the eyes and said, "Contrary to what you believe, I do care what Amy and Shaun are feeling. Their feelings will be considered when I make my decision."

Amy opened the screen door and stepped onto the patio, turning to Michael. "Did you talk with her?"

"Yes, he did," Rachel answered.

Amy looked at Rachel. "Well?" she asked, her pout firmly in place.

"I haven't made any decisions and when I do, you, Shaun and I will sit down and discuss them."

Amy stared at Rachel for a long moment, her expression hostile, intense. "Discuss it with us? Don't you mean tell us?"

"I need to head home," Michael said.

"No! Please stay for dinner. Rachel has fixed one of her famous dishes. There's plenty for all of us."

"Sorry. Not tonight." Michael started for the screen door.

Rachel hadn't realized she was holding her breath until he'd declined the offer. Relief trembled through her. He aroused emotions in her that made dealing with everything else more difficult.

"Rachel?" Amy whispered. "Ask him to stay."

Rachel saw none of Amy's earlier hostility in her expression and was tempted to ask Michael to join them for dinner, but the words wouldn't come out. They lumped in her throat, her mouth dry, her palms damp. She couldn't face another moment in his presence, even to please her sister.

While he strode to the front door, Amy spun and glared at Rachel. "I thought he was a friend. Here in Magnolia Blossom we ask friends to dinner. You must do things differently where you come from."

The sound of the front door closing filled the air with renewed tension. "Amy, it's late and—"

"I'm not hungry anymore." Amy flounced into the house, banging the screen door behind her, then the front door as she left.

Rachel started to go after Amy and try to explain. But *how can I explain my feelings toward Michael to my sister? I can't even explain them to myself.* She sank down on the chaise longue, feeling defeated and alone.

When darkness settled around her, Rachel went inside, deciding to check on Shaun before going into the kitchen to eat an overcooked dinner. She knocked on his bedroom door, but he didn't answer. Opening the door, she glanced about the room to confirm her suspicions. Shaun was still outside.

She looked toward Amy's closed door. It boasted a new sign that read Do Not Enter. Glancing at Shaun's room, she saw total chaos—as though a hurricane had recently swept through. Silence magnified Rachel's feeling of loneliness as she walked into the living room to wait for her family's return.

Rachel sat in the darkened living room waiting for her younger brother. There was no sound of pounding sneakers to alert her to Shaun's presence. This time the sneakers were silent as he came into the house. When he was in the middle of the living room, heading for his bedroom, she switched on the lamp. Shaun froze as if he were playing a game of statue.

Rachel didn't say a word.

Suddenly her eight-year-old brother swung around and launched into his explanation. "We were playing a game of hide-and-seek and no one could find me. I had the best place *ever* to hide. I couldn't come home till the game was over."

For Shaun's sake Rachel was thankful that she'd had an hour to cool off or she would have grounded him for the rest of his life, which she realized was absolutely ridiculous. "Did you win?"

Shaun blinked, nonplussed by the question. Then he flashed Rachel one of the smiles that must have gotten him just about anything from Aunt Flora. "Sure. No one found me. Finally, they all gave up."

"Lucky for you that they gave up so soon." Rachel glanced at her watch. "Let's see. You were an hour late. I figure a fair trade-off is an hour for a week. You're grounded for the next week. I'll let you go to church as well as your baseball games and practices, but that's all.

No TV. No phone calls. No friends over." Rachel rose and started for the kitchen to clean up her ruined meal, which still smoldered in the oven.

"But Aunt Flora didn't care if I stayed out after dark. This isn't New York. Nuthin's gonna happen to me after dark here."

Rachel continued walking.

"That's not fair. A week! What am I gonna do in this place for a whole week? I'll die of boredom!"

Rachel pivoted. "You should have thought about that when you were hiding. You had plenty of time to come up with some ideas."

"Who are you to tell me what I can and can't do? You aren't my mother." Shaun's face reddened with anger.

Patience, she reminded herself. "I won't argue with you, Shaun. We'll discuss who I am later."

"But—"

Her younger brother snapped his mouth closed, then stomped off to his bedroom and slammed his door shut. First thing tomorrow morning she would go to the library in Natchez and hope there was a good book on parenting that she could check out.

The ringing of the doorbell a few seconds later made Rachel jump. When she opened the door to find Helen standing on her front porch, she was pleasantly surprised. "How did you know I was at the end of my rope? Did you hear the doors slamming all the way downtown?"

"No, but Amy paid me a visit as I was closing up tonight."

"Oh, she did." Why does my sister talk with everyone in town except me? "I can just imagine what she had to say if you decided to come by after a long day at work."

"I'm concerned, Rachel. I've never seen Amy so unreasonable. The whole time she was in the café she ranted and raved about what she was and wasn't gonna do. The bottom line is she won't leave Magnolia Blossom." Helen's smile was sad as she continued. "That was said as she stormed out of the café without letting me finish a sentence, which is very hard to do."

"Where did she go?"

"She didn't say."

Rachel clenched her teeth. "She thinks she can come and go as she pleases without saying anything to me. I have no idea where she is or what time she'll be home. Surely Aunt Flora didn't let Shaun and Amy do this."

"No, but then Flora never threatened their security."

"You think I should give up everything and stay here?" Wasn't it enough that she had agreed to take care of her brother and sister? Did she have to give up everything?

"It would be easier for Amy and Shaun in the short run. I can't answer beyond that, nor can I tell you what's best for you, sugar. That's your decision."

"I feel like I've been cast in the role of an ogre."

Helen rolled her shoulders. "I'd better be going or I'll be worthless tomorrow." At the front door, she turned and hugged Rachel. "Sugar, would staying here for a year be too much? You could open a restaurant later. Think about it."

"Night, Helen."

As Rachel closed the door, her anger pushed all other feelings to the side. Her life was already turned upside down with the unexpected responsibility of taking care of her sister and brother. First Michael and now Helen wanted her to forget all she'd worked for.

She went into the living room and sat on the couch to wait for Amy's return. They had to talk. But as Rachel waited, her temples throbbed with a headache. She couldn't stay in Magnolia Blossom, not even for Amy.

A persistent ringing gnawed at Rachel's dreamless sleep. All of a sudden her mind cleared, and she bolted up on the couch, snatching up the phone. "Hello."

"Rachel, this is Michael."

Her hand tightened about the receiver as she glanced at the clock on the mantel. Twelve-sixteen. "What's wrong?" The pounding of her pulse thundered in her ears as she tried to calm the racing of her heart.

"Shaun's here with Garrett."

"What?" She rubbed her hand down her face to try to clear her groggy mind.

"On my way to bed I passed Garrett's door and heard voices. Shaun was with him."

"I'll be over in a few minutes."

"Rachel, let Shaun stay till morning. Whatever you

have to say to him can wait till then. They've both finally gone to sleep."

"I'm coming. He disobeyed me." Without waiting for Michael to say anything else, Rachel slammed down the receiver, berating herself for falling asleep when she should have been alert. Maybe then Shaun wouldn't have sneaked out of the house.

She snatched her purse and started to leave when she remembered Amy. She quickly checked to see if her younger sister was home yet. When she didn't find Amy anywhere in the house, she made a mental note to get Shaun then go looking for her sister.

As Rachel hurried to her car, her thoughts churned with worry. What did Shaun think he was going to accomplish by running to Garrett's? Why couldn't he accept his punishment? Where was Amy at this hour?

When Rachel pulled into the lane that led to Michael's house, she pressed her foot down on the brake. The palms of her hands were sweaty as she stared at the two-story antebellum house ahead. She knew she couldn't barge into Michael's home and start yelling at Shaun, even though that was her first impulse.

Slowly she eased her foot off the brake, and the car crept forward. She couldn't let Shaun think he could do what he pleased. She could remember wishing her mother or father had set limits for her. Instead, they had allowed her to go anywhere she wanted with little supervision. She had often spent hours away from their temporary base, playing in the jungle or on a beach, usually alone. Her parents hadn't cared enough to ask where she'd been when she'd returned to the campsite. Rachel wasn't going to make that mistake with Amy and Shaun. They needed limits.

When she parked the car in front of Michael's house, the door swung open to reveal him standing in the entrance. "Come in." He stepped aside for her to enter.

She started to demand to see Shaun, but the expression on Michael's face stopped her. The air pulsated with his anger as they stared at each other.

"Where's Shaun?" Rachel finally asked, scanning the foyer, alarmed at how easily he could evoke strong emotions in her.

"Asleep."

"Then I'll get him." She turned toward the staircase, aware that she had no idea where Garrett's bedroom was, but nothing would be accomplished staying and dealing with Michael. She still needed to handle her siblings.

As she placed her foot on the first step, Michael grabbed her arm and swung her around. "We're going to talk first."

He dragged her toward the den and shoved her into a chair by the fireplace. Rachel couldn't believe his Neanderthal attitude. "I have nothing to say to you."

"Then listen, *really* listen for a change."

She began to rise, but when he put both hands on the arms of her chair and leaned toward her, she sank into the cushion. She felt trapped, surrounded by him. She closed her eyes, wishing she could block his image from her memory; she couldn't. She sensed his gaze drilling into her face and slowly opened her eyes, trying to remain in control.

"The only parent Shaun has really known was Flora. With her death his life has changed drastically. He doesn't understand your coming in and setting down all these rules he's not used to."

"So you think I should let him do anything he wants?" She allowed her rising anger to fight Michael's effect on her.

"No, but move slowly with him. Give him time to adjust to you."

"In the meantime he runs around town wild, going where he wants, coming in when he wants." Rachel shook her head. "A child needs rules to follow."

"Reasonable ones."

"Coming in by dark is reasonable."

"Maybe in New York City, but in Magnolia Blossom that's when all the kids his age play hide-and-seek in the park. Shaun's always been a part of that. The kids aren't doing anything wrong. They're having fun. It sure beats them sitting around watching TV."

"When we talked about his curfew, he never said anything about playing hide-and-seek in the park with the other kids. All he said to me was that he was going out." Michael's clean male scent accosted her, and she wished he would move away. She didn't want him so close, producing strange sensations inside her.

Stepping back, Michael directed the full censure of his gaze at her. "Sit down with Shaun. Talk to him. Tell him what you expect of him in concise, concrete terms."

"What in the world do you think I've been trying to do with both Amy and Shaun—tap-dance?" She stood with both hands planted on her waist, her anger escalating as quickly as the temperature. "It's kind of hard to talk to a person when all you see is his back as he's leaving the room."

"Talk to or at?"

"Talking is talking!" Her voice rose several levels. Her head began to throb again. "I ask a question, I expect a straight answer. I say something, I expect to hear something back, not a door slamming."

"Talking to a person is more than you saying words. It's also listening to him when he's talking and letting him know you've listened, maybe by paraphrasing what he's said."

"I know how to carry on a conversation."

"I'm sure you do with an adult, but..."

Rachel hated to admit she had the same doubts, but she was an intelligent woman who loved her sister and brother. Somehow she would work everything out with them.

"Will you please get Shaun for me?" She met his dark gaze with quiet dignity.

His mouth thinned into a slash. "Rachel, why is it so hard for you to accept help from another person?" He grasped her arms. "Believe it or not, I want this to work with you, Shaun and Amy. I care for those two."

All Rachel could focus on was his closeness. She wouldn't be drawn into his world again!

"Was that help you were offering me? Strange, that's not the way I heard it." Her gaze lowered to his hands still clasping her. "Please let me go."

He released her. His look flattened into a neutral expression as he pivoted and strode toward the stairs without another word.

Rachel held herself taut until Michael disappeared up the stairs. But once he was gone, the trembling started in her hands and spread like a brushfire through her. She hugged her arms to her, rubbing her hands up and down to warm her chilled body.

Rachel had little time to compose herself before Michael appeared with Shaun behind him. Shaun's pout rivaled Amy's as he came to stand in front of Rachel.

"How did you think you'd get away with this?" she asked in a tightly controlled voice.

"What did you expect me to do?" Shaun's belligerent eyes became slits as they locked with Rachel's.

"I expected more of you than this."

"Well, you're not my mother. I'm not doing what you say." He straightened as though ready to fight for what he had declared.

"No, I'm not your mother, but I'm the one taking care of you, and you'll do as I say whether you like it or not. Understand?"

"No, I'll never mind you!"

"I guess you don't think being grounded for a week is long enough."

"I hate you!" Shaun whirled and ran from the room.

Stunned by the violence in Shaun's last look, Rachel was immobile until she heard the front door slam shut. She started toward it.

"I know you're angry at Shaun right now."

She spun as fast as Shaun had seconds before. "Are you going to tell me I shouldn't be?"

"No, everyone has a right to their feelings—"

"Oh, thank you for that." She cut in.

"But I hope you'll think about postponing any further discussion concerning the night's escapade till tomorrow. Give yourself a chance to calm down. As you can see, Shaun needs it, too." One corner of Michael's mouth quirked upward. "Heaven knows, I learned that the hard way. I've said things to Garrett that I've regretted after I had time to think things through."

His half smile affected her senses. For a few seconds she felt as if they had something in common. A strong urge to seek comfort in his arms swamped her. It took all her willpower to stay where she was. She had agreed to be her sister's and brother's guardian and suddenly she realized how ill-equipped she was for that role. Would it be so difficult to ask for help?

"Let me talk to Shaun," Michael said as he walked past her, then stopped.

For an instant Rachel saw regret in his eyes. She blinked, trying to understand the look he was giving her, but as quickly as it appeared it vanished. He continued toward the front door, leaving Rachel alone to gather her composure.

Her life was not in Magnolia Blossom. It was that simple and that complicated. Even if she didn't get the backing for her restaurant, she had every intention of going to New York at the end of the summer. She would give her sister and brother time to adjust to her as their guardian, then close up the house here. She had been crazy to consider staying in this small town where everyone knew everyone.

When she went out, she saw Michael talking to Shaun near her car. Their murmuring voices drifted to her on the jasmine-scented air, but she couldn't make out what they were saying.

As Rachel approached the pair, Shaun looked at her, hostility still apparent in his expression. He mumbled something to Michael, then rounded the front of the car to climb in on the passenger's side.

Rachel faced Michael, uncertain what to say or do. Her inadequacies concerning Shaun filled her with fear. She didn't want to fail with Shaun or Amy. She didn't want them to grow up feeling as she had, unloved, unwanted, frightened to get close to anyone.

"Rachel, just as adults say things they don't mean, so can kids when they are angry or scared. Please give both of you some time to cool off before you decide what you're going to do about tonight. Find out why he stayed out."

"Isn't that obvious? He wanted to defy me."

"I'd rather his reason come from him."

An overwhelming desire to be held by Michael inundated her. If only she could drop her defenses for a while. Because he was standing in front of her waiting for her to say something, she murmured, "I'd better go," but she didn't move toward her car door.

She stared into Michael's face, illuminated by the light from the veranda. Lifting her hand slowly, she touched the cleft in his chin.

Clasping her hand, he stilled the movement.

"It's late. I really should go."

"Uh-huh." He bent his head toward hers.

Chapter Three

The blare of the car horn parted them instantly. Rachel jerked away from Michael. She quickly opened the door, murmuring goodbye, a flush heating her cheeks. Safely in the car with her sanity restored, she was thankful that Shaun had sounded the horn.

On the ride to the house silence dominated the confines of the car. Rachel thought about what Michael had said about waiting to talk to Shaun. Her first impulse was to get it over with and move on, but maybe Michael knew what he was talking about. He *had* been a father for the past seven years.

Rachel entered the house and tossed her purse on the table in the entryway. "We'll talk about this in the morning after we've both gotten a good night's sleep." She slanted a look toward Shaun, who had his arms folded over his chest and a frown on his face.

"Why don't you just get it over with now? You're gonna ground me anyway."

"Frankly, Shaun, I don't know what I'm going to do until I've had time to cool off and listen to your side."

When a puzzled look replaced the anger in Shaun's expression, Rachel knew Michael was right about waiting. For the first time, she felt she had a chance with Shaun.

As Rachel watched her younger brother walk toward his bedroom, she caught sight of Amy's door. She started for her sister's bedroom but stopped when she heard a car pull into the driveway. Rachel stood in the entry hall, trying to remain calm as Amy let herself into the house.

All her good intentions fled when Rachel saw Amy's defiant look. "It's almost two in the morning. Where have you been?"

"Around." Amy began to walk past Rachel.

Rachel grabbed her arm to stop her. "I won't have you going out at night without telling me where you're going."

Amy shook loose. "I'm not Shaun. I'll be seventeen in a few weeks and can do what I want."

"When you're on your own, you can do what you want. Until then you live by my rules."

"And what if I don't?"

"I want the keys to Aunt Flora's car." Rachel held out her hand.

For a tension-fraught moment Amy stared at Rachel before shoving the keys into her hand.

"You'll get these back when you're willing to follow a few simple rules. I want to know where you're going.

You'll be in this house by twelve. I'm responsible for you and Shaun now."

"I didn't ask you to be. I can take care of myself." Fury filled Amy's eyes. "Why don't you leave us alone like everyone else has?"

Before Rachel could reply, Amy whirled, ran to her bedroom and shut the door. Rachel stood for a few seconds, shocked by her sister's words, spoken in anger but suffused with pain.

The sound of Amy locking her door propelled Rachel forward. She knocked on her sister's bedroom door. "Amy, we need to talk. Please let me in."

For the longest moment Amy said nothing, then finally she shouted, "I want to be left alone. I don't need you or anyone else."

How many times had she said those very words? Leaning against the wall, Rachel trembled at the intensity of emotions coursing through her. Listening to Amy, Rachel felt as if she had traveled back in time and was reliving the pain of being left in Magnolia Blossom by her parents.

Michael stared at the large white sign that proclaimed June eighth Founders Day in Magnolia Blossom. It had been over a week since he'd talked to Rachel, but in that time he hadn't been able to get her out of his mind. *Lord, why did she have to come back to Magnolia Blossom?* Everything had been all right as long as he thought he'd never see her again. He didn't want her in his life, even temporarily. He didn't need that kind of reminder of what could have been.

Michael searched the field where the townspeople were setting up the tables for the annual picnic and found his son talking with a friend. Garrett looked at him and waved. The heaviness in Michael's chest increased when he remembered the phone call he'd received. His ex-wife had walked out on him and Garrett years before, declaring she wasn't ready to be a mother, that she needed to pull her life together—without them. Now she wanted to share custody of their son after all these years. He felt the edges of his life coming apart.

Heavenly Father, give me the strength to deal with this new problem. I've been there for my son from the beginning. Give me the knowledge to follow Your path in all things.

Garrett raced up to Michael, coming to an abrupt stop inches in front of him. "Dad, have you seen Shaun? We're supposed to practice for the game."

"No. They haven't arrived yet."

"Are ya sure?"

"Yes." Because I've been looking for Rachel ever since I came.

"We're gonna beat the pants off you grown-ups today."

"Wanna make a little bet on that?"

"Yeah. I don't have to do the dishes for a week if y'all lose."

"And when *you* lose, you have to keep your room clean for a week. Nothing shoved under the bed. Deal?"

Grinning, Garrett shook his father's hand. Perplexed, Michael frowned as he watched his son join a group of children and head for the river. He had the feeling Garrett knew something concerning the annual softball game between the kids and the grown-ups, something that swung the odds in the kids' favor.

"I need your help," Helen said, scurrying to Michael. "Max is sick and won't be able to coach our team. Not only is he the best coach we've had but our best player, too."

Michael chuckled. So that was it. Garrett knew about Max because Max's son hung out with Garrett and Shaun. "What do you want me to do?" He had a clean room at stake and had no wish to lose the bet with his son.

"Will you be the coach?"

All except that. "I don't think—"

"C'mon, Michael."

"Why don't you do it?"

"Remember three years ago when I did? Afterward, the town council banned me from ever filling that position again."

"Oh," Michael murmured, recalling the free-for-all during the fourth inning between Helen and one of the base runners who didn't follow the right signal. "If I accept, will I get combat pay?"

"I'll give you one of my pecan pies to take home."

"Two."

"Two it is." Helen lowered her voice and leaned closer. "I do have a few tidbits for you." She began to tell Michael where to put everyone on the team, what the batting order should be and what each player's strengths and weaknesses were.

After ten minutes of listening to Helen, Michael laughed. "Helen, isn't this game for fun?"

"Fun? No way! Not when we're playing the *children.*" She stressed the word *children* as if that explained everything.

No wonder she was banned from being the team's coach, Michael thought as Helen marched off to help prepare the food.

"My boy, you're braver than I thought," Robert Davenport said as he approached Michael and clapped him on the back.

"I guess we all have our moments of insanity. This is one of mine," Michael replied while scanning the crowd for Rachel. Speaking of insanity, why couldn't he get Rachel Peters out of his mind? When she'd left Magnolia Blossom ten years before, he had wiped her from his mind out of necessity. Now all of a sudden he couldn't stop thinking about the woman.

"Michael, someone approached me about your riverboat again."

"I want to back off from selling the boat right now. I've been reminded how important roots are. That riverboat is part of my family heritage." Michael plowed his hand through his brown hair, his gaze tracking Rachel as she walked toward the food tables. "I've been kicking around an idea lately. What if I fixed the boat up for short cruises on the river? It could have a restaurant that served lunch and dinner."

Robert looked in the direction Michael was staring. "You'll need someone to help you with the restaurant. Have anyone in mind?"

Michael furrowed his brow. "Do you?"

"We both know that Rachel would be perfect as a consultant. Of course, I get the feeling she's just biding her time until she leaves for New York."

The mention of New York produced a stab of pain in Michael's chest, reminding him again of what had happened ten years before. "It would keep her here for a while. That would help Shaun and Amy adjust to her."

"You'd have to work closely with her. Could you?"

What would his life have been like if Rachel had stayed in Magnolia Blossom and married him? Lately he'd asked himself that question, but as before he was determined not to pursue the answer. She was out of his system, and he intended to keep it that way.

"I don't know, Robert." Michael didn't know if he could work closely with Rachel knowing in the end she would walk away. His frown deepened. Again he tunneled his fingers through his hair in frustration while he glanced toward her. "It was just a thought. I haven't made up my mind yet."

Rachel placed her potato salad on the long table with the other food for the picnic. She hadn't been to this type of affair since she had lived here. When she looked up from inspecting the feast, she caught sight of Shaun racing toward the river. Since the night her younger brother had run away, their relationship had improved. She'd taken Michael's advice and listened to her brother's side. When she'd discovered that some of the older boys had taunted Shaun for having to come in early, she could understand why he had disobeyed her.

She could even understand why he had run away after she'd handed out what he considered an unreasonable punishment. She hadn't retracted the week's grounding, but she hadn't added to it, either. She still had a long way to go with Shaun, but he was more willing to talk to her now.

With thoughts of Michael weaving through her mind, Rachel found herself searching for him in the crowd. When her gaze settled on him, her heart missed a beat. Across the short distance she watched as Michael raked his hand through his hair, then massaged the back of his neck, gestures he used when he was upset. Frowning, he stared at the river for a long moment, then made his way toward the path that ran along the Mississippi.

Something's wrong. Rachel didn't think about the wisdom of following; she just did. She didn't like to see that vulnerable look in his expression.

As she hurried along the path, she wondered where Michael had disappeared. Rounding a bend in the trail, she collided with him and instantly backed away, her eyes wide with surprise.

"I'm sorry. I didn't see—"

"That's okay. I'm sure this trail is big enough for the both of us. I'll go this way. You go that way." He pointed in the opposite direction.

When he began to move past her, Rachel touched his arm. "Let's walk together."

One eyebrow rose. "Together? Has the heat finally gotten to you?"

Rachel laughed. "No. I came looking for you."

"Why?"

"I think it's time we talk."

"Why?"

"Because of what happened between us ten years ago. Because you know my sister and brother so well. Because I think you need to talk right now." That vulnerability she had glimpsed earlier flashed into his eyes, and she didn't wait for him to say anything. She took his hand and began walking along the path.

At the first lookout point on the path Michael stopped and gently tugged his hand from hers. "Rachel, I think it would be best if we went our separate ways. We hurt each other once, and I personally don't want to go through that again."

"Don't you mean I hurt you?"

He shook his head. "Lately, I've been thinking. I can see now that I demanded a commitment when you weren't ready to give one."

"We wanted two different things in life, Michael. I knew how important Whispering Oaks and Magnolia Blossom were to you, that you wouldn't want to leave them. And I couldn't stay." Rachel clasped his hand, marveling at the strong, warm feel beneath her fingers. "What happened is over, but we shouldn't let it stand between us now."

Again, he removed his hand from hers and strode to the edge of the bluff. "Let bygones be bygones?"

She joined him near the edge. "Exactly. We were best friends once."

"Before we started dating." He glanced at her. A smile touched the corners of his mouth.

She stared at him, memories tumbling through her mind. Vivid pictures of them together pushed all else from her thoughts. The remembered feel of his chiseled cheekbones and roughly hewn features beneath her hands produced tingling sensations in her fingertips as if she were running them over a piece of warm granite. His slow smile touched a part of her that she held in reserve. She was completely lost in the moment, the ten years that stood between them crumbling to dust.

"You want to be friends again?" Michael asked.

That was the only thing possible between them now, Rachel acknowledged to herself, and yet she couldn't quite let go of the intense emotions that had gone beyond friendship. She tried to inject some humor into her voice as she replied. "Well, at least not enemies. Amy and Shaun think the world of you. We should be on speaking terms for the children's sake." Her sentences were rattled off in rapid fire. She felt pulled toward him like the river toward the delta, her actions beyond her control.

"Only for their sake?" His gaze probed hers, stripping away the years of separation.

Disconcerted, Rachel turned away and tugged a leaf off a bush, crushing it in her hand, its fresh scent wafting to her. "No. For mine, too. I've got enough problems facing me here in Magnolia Blossom. I can't handle this tension between us, too. I need a friend." She had never admitted needing a friend to another person. Surprisingly, the admission came as a relief.

Michael placed a hand on her shoulder and kneaded her tensed muscles. "Amy and Shaun can be a handful."

Rachel laughed shakily, wanting desperately to lean back against him, but she'd walked away from having that right years ago. Instead, she stood stiffly in front of him. "That's the understatement of the year. It wasn't that long ago that I was Amy's age, and yet I feel so much older."

"She's extremely precocious and determined to have her way. She reminds me of someone else I knew years ago."

Her eyes closed as his hands continued to massage the taut muscles of her shoulders and neck. She wanted to give in to the delicious sensations flowing through her but realized she shouldn't, couldn't. Calling on a willpower that had helped her to succeed in a tough profession, she stepped away from Michael's entrancing caresses and turned toward the river as though she had never seen the Mississippi and was enthralled with its discovery.

"And Shaun. He's another story. I haven't been

around my younger brother much, and even though we're talking, I don't know if I'm getting through. He's such a—" No words of description materialized as she thought over the past two weeks with Shaun.

"A dynamo."

"Yes! If we could tap into his energy source, we could light half of Mississippi."

Michael's chuckle was low and warm like the night air in the summertime. "Shaun could talk Flora out of anything. In fact, he can talk just about anyone into doing what he wants."

"I can certainly vouch for that. There have been a few occasions I shouldn't have given in to him. He's a future con artist who definitely needs limits set for him."

"Rachel, it'll take time, but you can reach both of them. Your heart's in the right place."

She slanted a look toward him, their gazes embracing. When she saw the tenderness in his dark eyes, her throat contracted. She'd had so little tenderness in her life, a life she had purposefully chosen for herself, she realized. But sometimes it was difficult trying to be so tough and strong.

"Do your parents know what's happened to Flora?"

Rachel went rigid as if she had been hit and was bracing herself for another blow. "I've been trying to get ahold of my parents. Communications between here and the Amazon jungle aren't the best."

"But you haven't heard from them?"

"No. They're probably out stalking some rare

tropical plant and haven't returned to their base camp yet." Again Rachel was making excuses for her parents. Part of her was angry that she felt she had to. "They'll get in touch when they can," she added with more conviction than she felt.

Rachel had often wondered why they had bothered to have children in the first place. Neither her father nor her mother had been able to answer her satisfactorily. Eventually her parents would contact her about Amy and Shaun when they got the news about Aunt Flora. But she knew the outcome of that conversation. Even if they wanted to take Amy and Shaun, she knew that wasn't the best solution for her sister and brother. Her parents' living conditions were primitive and temporary. Amy and Shaun needed more stability than that, so the alternative was for her to take care of them. Even Aunt Flora had known that was the best solution. She had left money and provisions in her will for Rachel to take care of her younger brother and sister. Rachel wondered if her parents and aunt had discussed this at one time.

For a few minutes Rachel watched as a barge passed on the river below. She'd seen her mother a few years back when she'd been speaking at a conference in New York, and they had eaten dinner together. In the past four years Rachel had shared three hours of her mother's time. Why was saving mankind more important than her own children? Couldn't someone else do it for a while? Rachel had wanted to ask her mother those questions at dinner that evening. She hadn't. The conversation had been polite and insignificant, ending with a stiff hug reserved more for an acquaintance than a daughter.

"Rachel, are you all right?"

She swung around, pasting a bright, false smile on her face. "Of course, I am. I was just thinking about the softball game this afternoon."

Michael touched her arm, his hand sliding down to grasp hers. "It's okay to admit you aren't all right. You never talked much about your parents. I'm a good listener."

"I'm fine. Really," she quickly said. "Tell you a secret, though." She leaned closer, immediately realizing her mistake when her senses were deluged with his outdoor woodsy scent. She pulled back and whispered loudly, "I forgot how unbearably hot it can get here in the summertime. Since I've been here I've taken more naps in the afternoon than I have in the ten years since I've been gone. Come three o'clock I may just curl up in the bleachers and miss seeing the big event."

"You aren't playing?"

"Me! I wouldn't fit in. I haven't played in ten years. Surely the coach isn't counting on me."

"Not anymore."

Rachel laughed. "You're the one Helen duped—I mean, talked into being the coach."

"Afraid so."

"What persuaded you? I hear it's a thankless job."

"Someone has to do it."

"So you did it out of the goodness of your heart?"

"Yep."

Mischief prompted her to say, "Liar. She told me she was going to entice the lucky person with one of her pecan pies."

"Two."

"Oh, you are a shrewd bargainer. No one else in town would do it for less than four of them."

"I did it for the team."

"And not for your sweet tooth?"

"Well, that and to keep the peace."

Rachel shook her head. "Remember the time I baked you a three-layer German chocolate cake to get you to take me to New Orleans? You didn't want to go, but after eating the cake, you took me."

"That's what I wanted you to think so I could get one of your cakes."

"Oh, Michael Hunter! You may never get another cake from me again." Snapping her fingers, Rachel smiled. "Okay, how about that time I wanted to go to that new restaurant in Natchez?"

He grinned.

"The concert in Jackson?"

"That group was one of my favorites."

"I never thought you could be so devious. I can't let you get away with that."

"You can't?" A look of pure playfulness was in his eyes as he began to stalk her. She took one step back then another.

"I should have realized that when I saw one of their albums at your house. A friend's indeed." She chattered, her nerve endings quivering as she tried to push past him.

He blocked her escape, pinning her against the trunk of a live oak, the Spanish moss hanging on its branches concealing them from the world in a green drape. "You enjoyed trying to manipulate me. I just let you think you were and I got to satisfy my sweet tooth, too." His gaze snared hers as he bent closer. "Admit it. It was a game we both enjoyed playing," he murmured, his voice low, smoky.

She nodded once, trapped in a world where only she and Michael existed. She was seventeen again, he nineteen, and they had just discovered they were more than best friends. The kiss that had produced that revelation was still engraved in her thoughts.

Slowly, reverently Michael touched her throat. His eyes locked with hers. "We played a lot of games, you and I. I was always trying to discover what made you tick and never quite succeeding." He dropped his hand from her throat, his eyes clouding with bittersweet memories.

Rachel watched myriad emotions cross his face as he shoved himself away from the tree trunk, distancing himself physically and emotionally from her. He was different from the young man she'd fallen in love with. She was different, too. She didn't know this man before her. They were strangers with a shared past. It was a mistake to think she could afford to become his friend again. She stepped from underneath the hanging moss.

In the end she would leave him behind as she had all the other people before him.

As she stared at Michael's back, she didn't know if she could handle the next several months without some help. Whether she liked it or not, she needed Michael. Having decided she had to take the risk, Rachel approached Michael and laid her hand on his arm.

"I don't want to play games, either. I'd be kidding you and myself if I said I belonged in Magnolia Blossom, Michael. I have a business proposition before a group of investors. If they give me the go-ahead, I'll be opening my own restaurant in New York. I'll be gone by fall, but until then I need someone to talk to about Amy and Shaun. I'm out of my element with them."

He glanced over his shoulder and smiled, a sadness in his eyes. "I wondered when you'd quit pretending you might stay in Magnolia Blossom."

"Over the past two weeks I've been going back and forth on what I would do if my business proposal didn't work out. I've allowed myself to feel guilty about wanting to take my sister and brother and leave. Not anymore. You've made me see that. I have to look at what's best for everyone concerned, not in the short run but the long run. Leaving won't be easy for them, but people move around all the time."

"When are you going to tell them?"

"I want them to get to know me before we discuss leaving town."

"Don't keep this a secret from them. They have a right to know, Rachel, as soon as possible."

"You won't say anything until I tell them?"

"No, but you're wrong to keep it from them."

"Amy had a fit about the call to New York concerning schools. She's still not talking to me. If I say anything now to them about leaving, they'll close their minds completely to me, and I won't have a chance of making us a family."

"Is that what you're trying to do?"

"Yes, of course." Tension began to throb in her temples. Everything about her future, the children's futures, was so up in the air. She couldn't put anything into a neat, little package as was her custom.

"The longer you stay here and not say anything, the more they will think you aren't going to leave. You'll be giving them false hope."

"If they shut me out, I'll never be able to convince them there are advantages to leaving Magnolia Blossom."

"What?"

"The world has so much to offer. They can make friends at their new schools. We can travel as a family during the summers and holidays. They'll be able to see so many new things. I'll be able to open up a whole other life for them."

"When? Running a restaurant will require a lot of your time. Besides, is traveling, seeing the world what's best for them or you?"

"For all of us." She fired the words back, the tension

in her head intensifying. "At the moment, Michael, I'm all they have."

"They're involved in their church, this town. It won't be easy."

"Since when have I taken the easy route?"

His hard gaze bored into her as though trying to read what was deep in her thoughts. "I think we'd better head back."

Rachel needed the conversation to end on a light note. Every time she and Michael had been together since she'd returned they had argued. She attempted a smile she didn't feel and said, "Maybe if we stay out here long enough, Helen will recruit another coach."

"And lose my pecan pies! Never!" He started down the path toward the field. "You know I probably should have demanded those pies in advance. I may not be in any condition to accept them afterward. Thank goodness they've outlawed tarring and feathering."

"It's been ages since I had a piece of Helen's pecan pie. I'm sure you'll want to share it." Rachel snapped her fingers. "I've got it. Why don't you bring both pies over after the fireworks later tonight for some coffee and dessert? I'll supply the coffee." There was a part of her that was amazed she had asked him to the house, but the other part of her needed his help with her sister and brother.

Michael hesitated.

"I could use your help with Amy," Rachel added. She didn't want to spend another evening warring with her sister. Founders Day was a time for family in Magnolia

Blossom, and she was determined to observe it with her siblings even if that meant having Michael as a referee.

"Okay, I'll share the pies. After all, you'll be contributing to the adult team."

"How?" she asked, relief evident in her voice. Finding reasons to be around Michael wasn't the wisest thing. Surely if she looked hard enough, she could find someone else to help her with her brother and sister. But Michael knew what a family should really be. She'd always prided herself on seeking out the best advice and listening. That was the only reason she'd asked Michael over after the fireworks. Yeah, right, and the moon was made of cheese.

"You're refusing to play."

"I should be offended."

"I remember how you used to play."

"Now I *know* I'm offended." She frowned with a gleam in her eyes.

"Sports were never your forte, Rachel. You think a strike is something a union does when it wants more money."

"Well, it is."

Michael shook his head. "You're hopeless. When I tried to educate you, I almost lost my mind. I don't make a mistake more than once."

She heard the warning in his voice but chose to ignore it. She didn't want there to be any tension between them. "Are you going to hold that Atlanta Braves game over my head forever?"

"At least this time you got the name of the team correct."

"I was the chef for a party the owner had for the team. I had to learn real quick."

"Then there's hope for you, after all."

"I know that a player is out if he gets three strikes. I read up on the game when I found out I was going to do that party. I didn't want anyone asking questions I couldn't answer." Rachel was glad that Michael had picked up on her playful tone. "These games used to be fun. Since arriving here this morning, I get the distinct impression I'll be entering a war zone. What happened?"

"Helen took over."

"Oh." Rachel laughed. "I see now. Helen's one of the most competitive people I know."

"You're probably the wisest person in Magnolia Blossom today."

"How come?"

"'Cause you wouldn't allow Helen to rope you into being a part of the team."

A part of the team. Sometimes she had a hard time putting into words why she couldn't put down roots, was afraid to commit herself to anything that seemed permanent. This restaurant proposal was the first thing she had considered that would require her to stay in one place for any length of time. Maybe after ten years— no, twenty-eight years—she was tired of living a nomadic life. But never in her wildest dreams had she considered returning to Magnolia Blossom. The town was too small and too emotionally demanding. She had made her choice years before, and she was determined not to let herself become a part of this town—or a part of Michael's life.

Chapter Four

Rachel spread the blanket on the bluff that overlooked the river. Dusk settled around her as she waited for the fireworks display to begin and for her family to join her. The warm breeze, perfumed with the scent of mowed grass, caressed her face. The sound of the insects vied with the murmurs of people's voices as they prepared for the evening's activity. She closed her eyes and enjoyed the tranquillity.

"You won't believe that neighbor of yours." Helen plopped down on the blanket next to Rachel. "I went by your house to leave you your very own pecan pie and he almost ran me down with that big, gas-guzzling car of his."

"Who?"

"Harold Moon, who else?" Helen drew a quick breath and continued, "And when he almost backed into me, he didn't even bother to say excuse me or anything. He just drove away. Actually, he burned rubber like he was angry that I was in the street in *his* way. I should be the angry one."

"Maybe he didn't see you."

Helen gave her an exasperated look. "Not see me? Who are you kidding? I like my own cooking. You would have to be blind not to see me." She scanned the area. "Where is everyone?"

Glancing over her shoulder, Rachel saw Amy and her boyfriend, Kevin, strolling toward them holding hands. She indicated their approach with a toss of her head. Amy was paying close attention to something Kevin was saying, a look of rapture on her face. She was too young to be serious about a boy. She had too much to see and do before she settled down. Rachel was determined to make Amy see there was more to life than Kevin and Magnolia Blossom.

"Ah, and I see Shaun, Garrett and Michael coming, too," Helen announced as Amy and Kevin smoothed their blanket next to Rachel's and sat, Amy smiling at Helen but ignoring Rachel.

Rachel hadn't meant to search the people beginning to populate the bluff, but she did and immediately found Michael among the crowd. Sometimes she wondered if she didn't have a sixth sense when it came to him. There had been a connection from the first time she had seen him on the riverboat. It was powerful, compelling—frightening.

Dark shadows spread along the ground as Michael settled himself next to Rachel, stretched his long legs out in front of him and leaned back on his elbows. "Good evening, ladies. A perfect night for fireworks, don't you think?"

"Sugar, it's a perfect night for much more than fireworks."

"I do believe, Helen, you might be right about that," Michael said, his drawl more pronounced than usual. His glance strayed to Rachel, and he winked.

His impish grin generated a warmth in the pit of Rachel's stomach that expanded outward. She was remembering the night they'd spent on this very bluff— the night he'd told her he wanted to marry her. She'd left Magnolia Blossom one week later when she'd received the offer from the cooking school in Paris.

Rachel was thankful when the fireworks began. A spray of red and green streamed across the heavens like rubies and emeralds scattered across black velvet. Then another spray exploded above them.

The light from the display cast Michael's profile in golden splendor. He turned slightly, and his gaze seized hers for a long moment. The breath in Rachel's lungs caught and held while she was trapped in his look. Gone from his expression was any merriment. In its place was seriousness as though he, too, remembered that night when he'd given her his heart and she'd stomped on it.

She looked away as myriad colors splashed the darkness. Michael rose and walked away. She chanced a look and saw him stop by the line of trees where the cars were parked. He leaned against his truck with his arms and legs crossed while the fireworks continued to light up the night sky. His regard was riveted to her.

She strode toward him. They had to talk about that long-ago evening on the bluff, or it would be there between them anytime they were together. She needed to explain why she'd run away.

She halted in front of Michael. Words dried in her throat as she stared into his eyes. The hard set of his jaw and the tautness of his shoulders attested to his feelings.

"Remember the last time we were here?" he finally asked.

"I don't like to look backward." She knew it wasn't enough. The fireworks continued exploding above her. "My only defense is that I'm not good at relationships, Michael." She didn't explain herself often and had a hard time doing it now, but this was important. If they were going to be friends while she was in Magnolia Blossom she had to make him understand. "I never have been. I gave up after my fifth move as a child. It hurt too much leaving behind people I cared about."

"I'd hoped once that you would trust your feelings concerning us, or trust me at least. I'd hoped you could forget your past. You didn't have to leave me behind."

"Yes, I did. You weren't going to leave Magnolia Blossom for Paris. I had to see if I could do what I had dreamed about for years. You were already doing what you dreamed about. Your roots and soul were planted here in Mississippi."

"I would have waited if you'd asked."

"You didn't mourn me long, Michael. You have Garrett as proof that your life went on. He's nearly eight years old. I can add."

"Ah, so that's what's bothering you."

"No—yes. It didn't take you long to find someone else. Garrett was born a few years after I left." Rachel hadn't meant for the hurt to seep into her voice, but she heard it and knew that Michael did, too. She could remember the pain that pierced her heart when Aunt Flora had broken the news of Michael's marriage. Until that moment, she'd thought about giving everything up and returning to Magnolia Blossom and Michael.

He shrugged. "Think what you like. The bottom line is that it didn't work out between us ten years ago. I don't like to dwell in the past any more than you do. My future is Garrett and, yes, Magnolia Blossom. That hasn't changed. You're right about my roots being sunk deep in the soil of this place."

"Where does that leave us?"

"There is no us. We both agreed on that."

"Michael, if being friends is too difficult for you, then you don't need to feel obligated."

The final burst of fireworks lit the sky with a brilliance that made it appear as if the sun had risen. "I want to help with Amy and Shaun. I care about them. They have been a part of my life for a long time."

She wasn't alone in her battle. "Thank you."

"Don't thank me yet. I'm not worried about Shaun.

He'll adjust wherever he is. Amy is a whole different story. I'm not sure she's going to listen to anyone, including me. She's bound and determined to remain here. No telling what she's going to do. She doesn't have wanderlust in her blood like you do, Rachel."

"It's not a disease," she retorted, pulling herself straighter. "Not everyone is like you."

"And not everyone is like you," he countered instantly, pushing himself away from the bumper of the truck and standing a few inches in front of her.

Her heart responded to his nearness by speeding up. She swallowed several times and stepped back to a safe distance, where she didn't feel surrounded by him. "Touché. We agree that we are very different from each other."

"Are we?"

She heard the amusement return to his voice as he moved around her and started toward his son. She whirled and watched him walk to Garrett and tousle his hair, then hug him. The love between father and son was so evident it touched a place in Rachel's heart she didn't think anything could affect. Garrett was lucky to have a parent like Michael.

Pain buried long ago oozed to the surface. Clutching her arms to her stomach, she pressed inward, resolved not to let the tears flow. She didn't cry anymore, had stopped doing that long before she had come to Magnolia Blossom to live with her aunt.

She swallowed the lump in her throat and straightened. She depended on no one, and having to depend on Michael for help was leaving her feeling vulnerable. As soon as she was able to leave Magnolia Blossom and get on with her life, everything would be all right. But first she had to win her sister and brother to her side.

She started for the group and arrived by Helen's side in time to hear Amy mutter, "I'm not going to the house."

"That's too bad, Amy. I was counting on you showing me that new CD you told me about." Michael reached down, scooped up his blanket and began folding it.

"You're coming to the house?"

"Who do you think is supplying the pecan pies? I worked hard for those pies and I don't share them with just anyone."

Amy glanced at Kevin, who nodded. "Well, since Helen made them, I guess I could have one piece."

Helen helped Rachel shake out her blanket, then fold it. "I love hearing people talk about my pies like that."

"Why don't you come over, too?" Rachel asked, realizing that if Helen was there Rachel would never have to be alone with Michael.

"It's been a long day. Winning is exhausting. This is your party. Enjoy. I'm going home to bed and dream of our victory." Grinning as though she had a secret, Helen waved goodbye and strode toward her car.

Rachel fought the urge to run after Helen and beg her to come to the house. Rachel suspected her friend was up to her old matchmaking tricks.

"I want to ride with Garrett. Can I? Can I?" Shaun asked, hopping from one foot to the other as though he had so much energy he could barely contain it.

"If it's okay with Michael," Rachel answered, longingly watching Helen as she drove away.

"Sure. We'll follow you to your house."

With the plans settled, Rachel headed for her car, aware that Michael and the boys were right behind her. She felt self-conscious as she walked. Even though it was dark, she sensed Michael staring at her. Relieved when she slid into her sedan, she started it and backed out of her parking space.

She had a few minutes to compose herself before she had to entertain Michael. She looked in the rearview mirror and saw his headlights. Her palms were sweaty, and she rubbed first one then the other on her jeans. She was more nervous tonight than when she'd started dating Michael ten years before.

Once inside her house she quickly took the pies from Michael and prepared the coffee. "Anyone want vanilla ice cream with their piece?" she asked. The group sat in the living room, silent, staring at each other.

Shaun and Garrett said yes. Kevin declined, and Amy remained quiet. Deciding her sister's answer was a no, Rachel looked toward Michael. She wished she could accept his help without being in the same room with him.

He smiled, the corners of his eyes crinkling. "Pecan pie was invented specifically for vanilla ice cream. I'll help you."

That was not the kind of assistance she'd wanted. "Fine," she murmured when she couldn't think of a reason to refuse him.

Her hand quivered as she cut the pie. The kitchen was too small for her and Michael, the air charged with a finely honed tension that had nothing to do with Amy. Perspiration beaded on her forehead. She attempted to scoop some ice cream, but ended up bending the spoon, which clanged to the countertop. The sound seemed to echo through the kitchen.

"Here, let me try." Michael took another spoon from the drawer and ran it under hot water, then dipped it into the frozen dessert.

Rachel flushed. She knew better. She was letting him get to her—again. "I wish I had my utensils and equipment here. I didn't think to bring them. This wouldn't have been a problem."

"Do you travel with your own cooking utensils?"

"Yes."

"Then why didn't you bring them?"

"Because—" She hesitated, not wanting to voice her reason.

"Because you didn't think you would be here long?"

"Right. But Shaun and Amy's opinions made me reassess the situation."

Michael didn't say another word. His mouth firmed into a hard slash as he worked to get the ice cream out. After completing the preparations, he handed her two plates to take into the living room while he took the rest.

After the dessert was served to everyone, along with coffee or milk, Rachel sat on the couch next to Michael, the only empty place left in the living room. No one spoke while they ate, and she was glad for the reprieve while she collected herself.

"Now that school is out, Amy, what are your plans for this summer?" Michael asked as he placed his mug on a coaster on the coffee table.

Her sister shot Rachel a withering look. "That all depends on where I'll be. Why plan anything if we aren't gonna be here?"

"You'll be here." Rachel raised her mug to her lips, hoping the action would keep her from having to say anything further.

"Helen wants me to work at Southern Delight again."

"How about the summer arts program in Natchez?" Michael asked as he brought the last of his piece of pie to his mouth.

Amy shrugged. "I don't know if I'm gonna do it."

"What's that?" Rachel asked, again reminded she really didn't know her brother and sister very well.

Michael turned to her. "Amy is a gifted actress. For the past two summers she has gone through the program to hone her skills. Students from all over Mississippi attend for three weeks in July. Last summer they did *The Diary of Anne Frank* at the end of the session. Amy played the lead role."

"I didn't realize. You should do it, Amy," Rachel said, wanting to encourage her sister.

"Why? What difference does it make?"

"It's an honor to be invited to attend." Michael took a sip of his coffee. "Besides, I look forward to seeing you up on the stage again."

Amy stared at her hands, which were folded in her lap, and mumbled, "I'll think about it."

"The theater is one of the things I love about New York. You can't get any better than Broadway." Rachel finished her coffee, satisfied that at least her sister was talking.

Amy's head shot up, and she speared Rachel with a look that was meant to freeze. "I want to go to Hollywood. That's where *everyone* goes, not New York."

Rachel realized mentioning New York had been a mistake. Amy seemed to think Rachel had thrown down the gauntlet. Her sister was determined to find fault with the city no matter what.

Amy bolted to her feet. "Just because I've done some work on the stage doesn't mean I want to leave Magnolia Blossom. Everything I want is here. Come on, Kevin. We're late to meet the rest of the gang."

"You need to be back by twelve," Rachel called as Amy stalked to the front door with Kevin following her.

Amy jerked open the door while Kevin said, "I'll have her home by then."

After the couple left, quiet reigned for a few minutes in the living room while the two boys finished their pie and Michael drained his coffee. Rachel stood to take the empty plates into the kitchen. Tension knotted her stomach. She didn't think she would ever get used to these skirmishes between her and Amy.

"Can I go outside and play flashlight tag in the park?" Shaun jumped to his feet with a hopeful look on his face.

"Can Shaun spend the night?" Garrett asked, leaping out of his chair with the same hopeful expression.

"That's okay with me if Rachel says it's okay."

"Sure." She drew in a deep breath to calm herself. Every time she was around Amy she was left feeling wrung out. Of course, with Michael sitting only a few feet away from her, the tension was heightened, and she couldn't blame all her exhaustion on the confrontation with her sister.

"I'll pick y'all up at the park in an hour. That should give you enough time to play."

The boys raced for the front door and were gone before Rachel could blink. She sighed and looked at Michael, who still sat on the couch, relaxed as though he had not a care in the world.

"I hope you weren't expecting a miracle with Amy," he said with a lopsided grin.

"No. She stayed longer than I thought she would. Frankly, I wasn't sure she would last two minutes. At least she got the piece of pie eaten." Rachel stacked all the plates and started for the kitchen, needing to stay busy.

Michael followed. She realized she might have to entertain him for another hour until he picked up the boys. The knot in her stomach tightened into a fist, and a band contracted around her chest. In her world she was used to entertaining, but this was different.

"I'll help you clean up."

"Oh, no, that's okay. If you have something else to do before—"

"I don't, Rachel. I helped you make this mess. I'll help you clean it up," he said in that lazy Southern drawl of his.

"Fine. You can dry. The towel is in that drawer."

"It always amazed me that Flora resisted modern technology up to the end. I know that Amy kept trying to get her to buy a dishwasher, but she thought that was a waste of good money, especially since she had Amy and Shaun to do the dishes."

Rachel filled the sink with water and soap. "That was my aunt. Look how long it took her to buy a television. She didn't have one when I lived here. I think the kids went on a hunger strike before she caved in and got one."

Michael laughed. "She loved her radio."

"And her books," Rachel said as she placed the first plate in the drain. "I miss her, whether you believe me or not. I wish I could have made it to her funeral. I wish I could have said my goodbyes." Sadness laced her voice. She knew she was opening herself up in front of Michael and that was dangerous, but she hadn't talked about her aunt with anyone except Robert Davenport. She needed to talk.

"I know."

"Do you? Do you know how much she meant to me?"

Michael put the towel down and turned to her. "I'm sorry I said those things on the riverboat that first day. That was cruel. I know you loved Flora. We all did. She was a remarkable woman."

The tears threatened, but she was determined she wouldn't shed any in front of Michael. "She was like a mother to me." Rachel continued washing the dishes, her blurry gaze fixed on the soapy water. "She certainly was around more than my own mother ever was."

"That's how Shaun and Amy felt about Flora."

"Yeah, I can see why. Shaun has seen his real mother maybe four times since he was a baby and deposited with Aunt Flora. Amy is a little bit luckier, if you want to call it lucky. She was five when she came to live with Aunt Flora. Since that time she's probably seen our mother a dozen times."

"It's never easy for a child to be rejected by his mother or father. It's hard being shuffled back and forth between two parents, too."

Rachel slid a look toward Michael, noticing his tone of voice had changed. It held a sadness that had nothing to do with Amy and Shaun. Since she and her siblings had never been shuffled between their parents or their parents and Aunt Flora, she knew Michael was referring to something else, something that bothered him deeply. "What's going on?"

Chapter Five

The hardened line of his jaw emphasized the emotions Michael held locked inside. "Mary Lou called a few days ago. Now that she is remarried and lives so close, she wants to share custody of Garrett. She left us. Granted, she has kept in touch with Garrett *lately*, but our lives are just fine without any changes."

"What did you say to her?" Rachel finished washing the last plate and put it in the drain for Michael.

"My first impulse was to slam the phone down. I didn't. We're going to see her this weekend in Jackson."

The steel edge to his voice underscored his displeasure at the prospect of seeing his ex-wife. Rachel knew only a few tidbits about Michael's marriage to Mary Lou. When Amy or Shaun had wanted to talk about him, Rachel had changed the subject. She'd refused to let Aunt Flora mention him after his marriage. Rachel couldn't shake the feeling of betrayal she'd experienced. Even though Mary Lou and Michael's marriage hadn't worked out, he'd married her, loved her and had a son with her. Rachel emptied the water from the sink and kept her face averted, realizing she had no right to feel that way. Michael deserved to be happy, and Rachel had always known being a father and having a family were two important things he'd wanted in life. She couldn't begrudge him following his dream. She knew how important that was.

"How's Garrett feel about it?" Rachel remembered Mary Lou. She had been beautiful in high school and very popular. She'd grown up in Magnolia Blossom but had talked of moving to the big city after she graduated.

"I haven't said anything to him yet." One corner of Michael's mouth lifted. "I'm hoping the problem will go away. I don't trust Mary Lou. When she left us, she made it perfectly clear she didn't want to be a mother. Why is she suddenly wanting to change our arrangement? It's been working well."

"For whom?" Rachel asked, realizing she sounded like she was sticking up for Mary Lou.

Michael scowled at her. "Me! Garrett!" His voice was rough and grim. "Why can't things stay the same?"

Rachel wished she could control her life better, too. "That's not the way life is. You know that." She tilted her head so she could look at Michael. "What happened between you two?"

He slung the towel over his shoulder and began to

put the plates in the cabinet. His back was to her, his movements restrained. "It seems Magnolia Blossom wasn't what Mary Lou wanted. I have a habit of picking women who don't like small towns. She wanted more from life than what I or Garrett could offer her. She started drinking. Finally, after she nearly killed herself driving the car, she realized she couldn't stay any longer. She left to pull her life together."

"How does Garrett feel about her living so close?"

"He's excited to see her. That worries me."

Rachel faced Michael. "Are you worried he'll want to be with Mary Lou all the time?"

His smile was rueful "Yeah. Being a parent isn't easy. I have to be tough at times, set down rules."

"Tell me about it. I'm finding that out." She reached out and touched his arm, her fingers closing around it. "You're a great dad. He knows that."

"I don't want to lose him."

"You won't. Garrett knows who has stood by him." Suddenly aware that she was grasping him, she dropped her hand and stepped away.

Michael rubbed the back of his neck and shook his head. "Garrett's my life. I thank the Lord every day for him. I know God will provide me with the right answers when the time comes."

Michael's strong faith had always sustained him. When they had been friends years ago, he'd shown his love of God in many ways. And while in Magnolia Blossom, she'd believed she wasn't alone in the world and that she was one of the Lord's children, too. What had happened to her budding faith? "Are you still involved in your church like you used to be?"

"Yes. Amy and Shaun are, too. I hope you'll come to the service one Sunday. Reverend Williams is still the minister."

"I always enjoyed his sermons."

"Me, too. He has a strong belief in family. When I'm at church, I feel a part of a larger family. It helps to put my life in perspective. The people of this town are good people. My son and I can count on them in times of trouble."

Michael's words made Rachel wish she had that with her own brother and sister. It was her fault there was such a distance between her and her siblings. She had the summer to change that. "Well, right now I could use some pointers on being a parent. I wish parenting came as easily to me as it does to you."

"Came easily? Whatever gave you that idea? It's hard work, but I wouldn't trade my years with Garrett for anything. I want more children. I want to give him brothers and sisters."

Rachel didn't want to consider Michael remarrying and having more children. But she realized that was a purely selfish feeling because Michael was a great father.

He glanced at his watch. "It's getting late. I'd better go and pick up the boys."

"Thanks for your help tonight."

"I don't mind doing a few dishes."

"Not the dishes. With Amy."

"It was no big deal. I didn't need the pies, anyway."

"I hope that isn't because you feel you're over-weight? If so, the rest of us are in big trouble. There isn't an ounce of extra weight on you."

He chuckled. "No, I just don't need the sugar."

"But you used to love chocolate and anything else sweet."

"I still do. I just refrain from indulging too much."

Rachel eyed him. "Are you a health-food nut?"

"No, but I have to set a good example for my son. I try not to eat too much junk food."

"Now that's something all cooks love to hear."

He cocked his head, a tiny frown creasing his brow. "It really does fulfill you, doesn't it?"

"I think everyone needs a way to express herself. A creative outlet. Cooking is mine."

"No regrets then?"

"None." She answered too quickly, her throat closing at the intensity in his expression. How could she tell him the hardest thing she'd ever done in her life was walk away from him? But she'd made her decision ten years before and she would stick by it. Her life was her work. "I'll walk you to your truck."

"You don't have to. I know my way."

"That's the least I can do for you since you came tonight to help me with Amy." She began to move toward the front door.

"Tell her, Rachel."

His words halted her, and she turned to face him, the length of the kitchen between them. "You saw what happened when I mentioned New York. We've been through this, Michael. I need more time."

He held up his hand, palm outward. "Okay. I won't mention it again."

She quirked an eyebrow. "Really?"

"Really. You've made your point."

"This doesn't sound like the Michael I used to know. The guy I knew wouldn't have given up trying to convince me his way was the best way."

"Gee, you make me sound like a nag, or worse, a dictator."

"Never. Opinionated, yes. We did have some lively debates."

He crossed the kitchen and strode past her into the living room. "I guess raising a son has mellowed me. Besides, no one stays the same. People change, grow up. We were young back then."

"Yeah, babes in the woods."

Peering over his shoulder, he placed his hand on the front doorknob. "I see your cynicism hasn't changed."

"You forget that at the age of sixteen, when I turned up in Magnolia Blossom, I'd seen more of the world than most people, and the places I'd seen were not your typical tourist spots."

"Where? You've never talked much about your past."

"Because it is the past, and that's where it belongs."

It was one of her cardinal rules. She would not look back. It was a hard rule to follow, though, when a person returned home after being gone for a long time.

Michael stared at her for a moment, then yanked the door open. The air vibrated with his tension. Even ten years ago, he'd wanted to delve into her life as though he had a right to know every minute detail. She sighed and pushed the screen door open.

Out on the front porch, the night air was still hot and humid. It bathed her face in a blast of moist heat that, she kept reminding herself, was one of the reasons she liked living closer to the North Pole than the equator. She watched Michael descend the steps and head for his truck, his movements agile, fluid. She had always loved to watch him. That had not changed, she realized as she followed him to his truck.

With his hand on the door handle, he threw her a glance over his shoulder. "I'll bring Shaun home tomorrow afternoon."

"Fine." For a reason she couldn't account for, she didn't want him to leave just yet. "I realize we're two different people, that we've changed in the past ten years."

He pivoted, crossing his arms over his chest, and regarded her with the intensity she'd come to expect from him. "What you mean is that we don't know each other like we used to, that we're really strangers?"

"Exactly." She looked away, then at him. "But we can make this…friendship work."

"So long as I play by your rules?"

"Michael, you've never played by anyone's rules but your own. I know *that* hasn't changed."

He leaned on his truck. "I think that was a compliment."

She smiled, relishing the light breeze that had kicked up, cooling her flushed cheeks. "Yes. I've always admired your independence, your loyalty and honor."

"My gosh, you make me sound like a Boy Scout."

Rachel laughed. "Not you."

"Now, that didn't sound like a compliment. If I stay too much longer, I probably won't have an ego left. I need to go. The boys are waiting."

"Are you kidding? They haven't thought once about you picking them up."

"True. I'll have to drag them away and listen to them whine all the way to Whispering Oaks."

"The things parents have to put up with. I've come to the quick conclusion everyone who wants to be a parent needs to go to school, then take a long, exhausting exam before they can have children."

He dropped his arms to his side. "Tough, isn't it?"

"Yeah, tough." She hadn't meant there to be a note of vulnerability in her voice, but she heard it and so did Michael.

He took her hand in his and pulled her closer, brushing a strand of hair behind her ear. "I'll help you for as long as you need me to."

Her heart fluttered. "I appreciate it."

His hands tightened about hers. A warmth suffused

her. The world spun, and she leaned into him to steady herself.

"Are you okay?" He gripped her by the arms.

"I'm fine. Just not enough sleep. Amy gets in late. Shaun gets up early." She would never tell Michael his nearness still did strange things to her insides.

"I've spent a few sleepless nights worrying about Garrett, and he isn't even a teenager yet." Michael drew her into his embrace. "I'll walk you to the house."

She shook her head against his chest, said, "Really. I'm fine," but she didn't move out of his arms. Instead, she listened to the strong beat of his heart, its tempo increasing. The realization that she was having an effect on him made her bolder and probably, she would decide later, foolish. She wrapped her arms about him and tilted her face to look into his eyes. The illumination from the street-light cast shadows on his features, but she could read the concern in his expression.

He threaded his fingers through her hair, his gaze fastened on to hers. "You need to take care of yourself."

"I will," she murmured, licking her dry lips. "Strange bed. Strange house."

"Flora's?"

She nodded.

Silence engulfed them.

Her leaving Magnolia Blossom would always stand in their way. Suddenly, she didn't want that between them, at least not at the moment. She could get very comfortable in his embrace. That knowledge sent a bolt of panic through her, and she pushed away.

An electrified silence crackled between them like heat lightning.

Finally, he opened his truck door and slid inside. Hugging herself, she stood in her aunt's driveway while he backed out and drove toward the park. Coldness embedded itself in the marrow of her bones. She wasn't sure if she could make it to the end of summer living in the same town as Michael. He made her feel things she was determined she would never feel. He made her remember—something she tried very hard not to do.

Rachel rolled over and peered at the clock on her bedside table. Five in the morning. She groaned and snuggled under the covers, hoping to go back to sleep. Fifteen minutes later she gave up and climbed out of bed.

She slipped on a robe and headed for the kitchen to fix a large pot of coffee. She had a suspicion she would need it. She'd only had a few hours of sleep. Thoughts kept tumbling through her mind, and she couldn't stop herself from thinking—about Magnolia Blossom, Amy and Shaun, but, most of all, about Michael.

She switched on the light in the living room and gasped. Amy sat on the couch in the dark, a surprised expression on her face before her usual sullen countenance fell into place.

"What are you doing up?" Amy asked, bringing her legs to her chest and hugging them.

"I was about to ask you the same thing."

Amy wrapped her arms about her legs. "I like to sit in the dark."

Rachel came farther into the room. "It's soothing, isn't it?"

"Yeah, well, it's time for me to go to bed."

"You've been up all night?"

"Yeah, what of it?" Tension whipped through Amy's words.

Rachel shrugged. "Nothing. Just wondering."

"Well, you can stop wondering if I snuck out of the house. I've been right here for the past few hours."

"I wasn't wondering."

"Why are you up so early?"

"Couldn't sleep. In fact, I was heading into the kitchen to make some coffee. Do you want to join me? We could talk. We haven't—"

Amy jumped to her feet. "I'm tired. I'm going to bed."

She hurried toward her bedroom, leaving Rachel standing in the middle of the living room wondering if she'd even had a conversation with her younger sister. Maybe she had been dreaming, Rachel thought as she padded toward the kitchen and that pot of coffee she so desperately needed.

As the coffee brewed, its wonderful aroma filling the air, Rachel sank onto a chair at the kitchen table and rested her chin in her palm. Her eyelids drooped. The blare of the phone caused her to shoot to her feet, nearly toppling over her chair.

She snatched up the receiver. "Hello, Rachel speaking."

Static greeted her words.

"Hello, is anyone there?"

"Rachel, it's me, your mother. Sorry about this connection. It isn't the best in the world. Is everything all right?"

Through the bad connection Rachel heard the question and closed her eyes. *No, my world is changing.* "Aunt Flora died a few weeks ago."

"I know. I received your letter and the lawyer's. That's why I'm calling."

"Are you coming back to the States?" *When are you and Daddy going to be the parents?*

"Not for a while. I don't know when I'll be able to get away, but I'm sure you're taking care of everything. I know I need to sign some papers about guardianship and I will as soon as I can. I'll call you and let you know when I can come."

Rachel's grip tightened. "But, Mom—"

More static. "I don't have long before I have to head back to camp. We're moving it to another location. What are your plans?"

This woman was my role model. No wonder I can't make a commitment or stay in any one place for long. No wonder I'm afraid to be a mother. "We're staying in Magnolia Blossom until the end of the summer. Do you want me to wake Amy and Shaun so you can speak to them?"

"Can't." The static on the phone got worse. "I'll talk

to them another time. We're heading out now. Goodbye, Rachel."

"Goodbye, Mother," Rachel said to a dead line.

Her hands quivered as she replaced the phone on the wall. She was so cold. She hugged her arms to her, feeling the anger building inside her. She had been discarded twelve years ago and rarely thought about since. She felt as though she had lost more than Aunt Flora.

Rachel closed the oven door, set the timer on the stove, then began to stack the dirty dishes by the sink. Cooking was her therapy, she thought as she ran her finger around the inside of the metal mixing bowl and popped it into her mouth to savor the chocolate batter. She had been cooking for a long time and still loved to lick the bowl.

As she placed the dirty bowl into the water, she heard the front door bang open, the pounding of sneakers on the hardwood floor, then the door to a bedroom slam shut. Rachel shook her head. Quiet didn't exist in a household with children, something she would have to get used to.

She picked up a paring knife and was about to wash it when she heard pounding on the front screen door. She raced into the living room and saw a giant. A giant with a look to kill and a baseball bat in his hand.

"Where are those two brats?" Harold Moon's words filled the space between them like thunder filled a stormy sky.

"Who?" she squeaked.

"Your brother and that Hunter kid."

"What's the problem?"

"The problem is those two." His face red, Harold raised the baseball bat as though he was going to smash the screen door.

Show no fear, she chanted silently while she looked to see if either of the boys had at least thought to lock the screen behind them when they had fled into the house. No, there was nothing between her and Harold but a piece of flimsy screen with its latch unhooked.

"If you'll just put that bat down, we can talk about this calmly and rationally," she said, pointing with her knife.

He glared at her, the bat still in his hand. "Only if you get rid of that knife, lady."

"Knife?" Peering at her hand, she saw the parer and was surprised by the fact she had it in her grasp. They must look a sight, she with her small knife and he with his big baseball bat. Finally, she found some humor in the situation and smiled. She stepped to the table in the entrance hall and placed the parer on it. "Now it's your turn," she said in a soothing voice meant to placate a raging bull.

After tossing the bat into the yard, he turned, a frown etched deeply into his face. "Those two boys hit a ball through my picture window and missed hitting me by mere inches." A vein in his temple throbbed, the red flush in his cheeks deepened, and his already loud voice was getting louder with each word.

"Please come in and let's discuss this calmly." She managed to speak around the dryness in her mouth.

He stormed into the house, his bulk making the entrance hall awfully small. "Where are they?"

Now that she was facing him, she could see no humor in the situation. She didn't know if she could appease this man and she certainly wouldn't be able to stop him from doing anything he chose to. She pasted a calm expression on her face and waved her arm toward the living room. "Let's have a seat in here and talk about this picture window the boys allegedly shattered."

"There is no allegedly about it, lady. I saw them. Plain and simple."

Rachel moved past Harold and sat on the couch, hoping he would do likewise. "Well, then, with that settled we can discuss how to fix it." Out of the corner of her eye she saw Shaun and Garrett peeking into the room.

"They should have to pay for it." He remained standing with his eyes narrowed to slits.

Thankfully, the man's back was to the boys. There was no telling what Harold would do if he saw Shaun and Garrett. "I totally agree with you, Mr. Moon. The boys will pay to have the window fixed. Please get it replaced and send me the bill." Her neck was sore from looking up at the man. She finally stood when she realized he was not going to sit. "I'll make sure it doesn't happen again." She heard the pounding sneakers making a beeline for Shaun's room as she and Harold approached the entrance hall.

The man started to go after the boys. She placed herself in front of him. Show no fear, she repeated as she felt the anger emanating off him in waves.

"I believe we have concluded our business. I'll be expecting the bill, Mr. Moon. Good day." She began inching herself and him toward the front door.

He threw one last glare toward where the boys had been only a moment before, then stalked to the screen door. "I will. It will cost you a pretty penny."

"I'm sure it will," Rachel muttered as she watched the man storm across the street.

She gripped the screen to steady her trembling body. Shock was definitely setting in as the seconds of silence ticked away. She used the silence to calm her nerves. She glanced at the gaping hole in Harold Moon's picture window.

"I can't believe you stood up to him, Rachel," Shaun said behind her.

Slowly, she turned. Garrett stared at the polished hardwood floor by his feet as if he could see his reflection and was amazed with the discovery. Her brother's eyes were round, a look of awe on his face.

"He was gonna kill us." Garrett's gaze remained fixed on the floor while he scuffed the toe of his tennis shoe into the hardwood.

"Nonsense. I wasn't going to let him." Rachel closed the thick wooden door, locked it, then walked toward the couch before she collapsed.

"Yeah, I know," Shaun said in that awestruck voice.

Garrett finally looked up. "We didn't mean to hit the ball through his picture window."

"Of course not. No one intends to do that. But it did happen, and you two have to pay for it."

"How? My allowance is only five dollars a week. I'd be in debt until I graduate from high school." Shaun plopped down in the chair across from her.

Rachel smiled, relief finally sweeping through her. "Nah. Not that long. I'll talk with Garrett's dad, and we'll work something out."

"When?" Shaun asked, sitting on the edge of the chair.

"I don't know."

"Do it now," Garrett said. "I want to get this over with. Dad isn't gonna be too happy about this. It's best if he knows right away. Will ya tell him for us?"

Rachel wanted to groan. "I think you two should be the ones to tell him."

"We will, but please come with us," Shaun said as he jumped to his feet.

"We'll have to wait a few minutes until the cake is finished. I'll be there for moral support only. It's your job to explain what happened."

Both boys nodded.

As Rachel left the room to see about the German chocolate cake, she felt apprehensive about this meeting with Michael. Her emotions were still raw from the evening before and the phone call from her mother earlier that morning. She needed time between meetings with him in order to recuperate. But she couldn't turn down Shaun's request. The very fact that he'd made it gave her hope that she was making progress with her little brother. Now if only Amy would hit a ball through Harold Moon's picture window and live to tell about it.

Rachel pulled up to Whispering Oaks and parked in the circular drive. When she climbed from her car, she took a moment to look at the place that had once been a familiar favorite haunt of hers. Michael had taken good care of the plantation. The house was freshly painted, and the black fences that kept his horses and cattle in were well tended. The red azalea bushes that ringed his home were beautiful.

She turned slowly as memories inundated her. She could remember watching him ride a stallion in the paddock to the left. She could remember their first kiss on the veranda. From the beginning Michael had been very determined, knowing exactly what he wanted. Rachel looked away, and her gaze fell upon a stone bench in the rose garden to the right of the house. That was where he had told her he loved her. That had been where her panic began to grow. Those words had made her feel tied down to Magnolia Blossom. They had threatened her dream.

Rachel heard the sound of a horse approaching and swung around to see Michael riding toward her. He dismounted. While he strode to her, she shoved the memories to the back of her mind.

"What brings you out here? I thought Garrett was

spending the night with Shaun," he said, worry creasing his brow as he glanced at his son to make sure he was all right.

"Harold Moon paid me a visit this afternoon, and he wasn't too happy."

"The man never is." Michael removed his leather work gloves and tapped his leg with them.

"I'll let the boys tell you why."

Garrett stared at his left shoe, which he was digging into the dirt. Shaun looked away as though the horse in the paddock was the most fascinating creature he'd ever seen.

"Okay, what happened?" Michael asked with a sigh.

Shaun looked at Michael. "We were practicing. You should have seen Garrett's hit. The best ever."

"And where did that hit land?" Michael relaxed his stern expression, some of the tension siphoning out of him. "Garrett?"

Garrett quit digging the hole and mumbled, "Through Mr. Moon's picture window." He finally raised his head. "I got under that ball, and you should have seen it sail through the air."

"Yeah, right into someone's living room. Whatever possessed you two to toss a ball near that man's house?"

"You should have seen Rachel. Mr. Moon came over to the house furious. If she hadn't been there, no telling what he would have done to us," Shaun said, awe still in his voice.

Michael's jaw clenched, his regard on Rachel's face. "What happened?"

"Why don't you two go get the computer game you wanted earlier from Garrett's room?"

After the boys raced into the house, Rachel said, "Nothing happened. Mr. Moon was just a little angry that his window was broken. I took care of him."

"Harold Moon is always just a little angry about nothing, so I suspect it was more than a little." Michael shook his head. "They had no business in Harold's yard. They know he doesn't like anyone trespassing on his property."

"They weren't in his yard. They were playing in Aunt Flora's."

"Garrett hit the ball across the street? That's several hundred feet."

"Yeah," Rachel said, remembering she, too, had been impressed when she had pulled out of the driveway and had looked at the distance. The houses in the neighborhood sat on lots of several acres.

Michael whistled. "For him, that is far."

"Well, quit being impressed. We need to come up with a solution to how the boys will pay for the window."

He thought a moment, his head cocked. "I have some chores on the riverboat that need to be done. I was going to hire temporary help, but it might as well be the boys. But Shaun really doesn't have to do anything, since Garrett's the one who hit the ball."

"No, both of them were playing. Shaun pitched the ball to your son, so he's as guilty as Garrett. Besides, it won't hurt either one to do some work this summer."

"Then it's settled. I'll pay for the window, and they can work it off with me. Anything else?" Michael began to put his leather gloves on.

Wishing desperately for the ease they used to have between them, she looked toward the paddock, almost showing as much interest in the horse as Shaun had earlier. "Do you get to ride much?"

"Usually every day."

"I remember that time Ladybug threw me. My bottom was sore for a good week."

He lifted one eyebrow. "Rachel, I'm shocked. I can't believe you would dwell in the past. I thought it wasn't important to you."

She speared him with a glance she hoped conveyed her displeasure. "It's hard not to think about the past when you return home after ten years and every time you turn around you're slapped in the face with it."

"No one ever stopped you from coming back to Magnolia Blossom. Flora, Amy and Shaun would have loved it."

But not you? She wanted to ask but kept her mouth shut by clamping down so hard her jaw hurt. "It would have done no good," she finally said.

"Seeing your family or seeing me?"

Chapter Six

"Michael, I thought we agreed not to get into this. Remember, friends?"

"Yeah, you're right. It's been a tough day, and I'm taking it out on you. My apologies."

"What happened?"

In frustration he waved his glove-clad hand. "Mary Lou's making demands. Nothing I can't handle."

First Rachel had reappeared in his life, and now Mary Lou. His orderly routine was completely disrupted. He couldn't keep the anger from churning his stomach. He'd spent years coming to peace with how things had turned out for him and Mary Lou. Rachel had her dreams, but so did he. He had failed in his marriage and in his dream to have a large family. He would not let his son down. He would hold his small family together no matter what. And even though Mary Lou was Garrett's mother, Michael wasn't sure she was good for his son. He could still remember finding her drunk one afternoon while Garrett was crying in his crib. The memory shuddered through him.

Rachel placed her hand on his arm and drew his attention. "Maybe a friendly ear could help."

"I don't know if anyone could help me with this problem." Forgiveness was an intricate part of his faith, but he didn't think he could forgive Mary Lou in this case. That didn't sit well with his conscience.

"Now that sounds like me talking. We can all use a friend."

Remembering all the times he'd been shut out of Rachel's life, Michael clenched his jaw and shook her hand from his arm. He arched a brow. "Even you? I seem to recall you're not big on talking over your problems."

"I'm trying."

Hurt flittered across Rachel's face, but Michael hardened his heart to it. "I'd better get Avenger back to his stall. If he misses his dinner, he's one unhappy horse."

"Speaking of dinner, would you like to come over this evening? I've made a German chocolate cake." The second the invitation was out of her mouth she wanted to take it back.

A look descended on his face that chilled her in the humid, warm air. "No. I really must be going." He spun on his heel, walked to his stallion and vaulted into the saddle. "Send me the bill." He spurred his horse into a canter.

Michael disappeared around the side of the house, and Rachel felt as though he had slammed a door in her face. She wished she'd handled the baseball incident over the phone. She'd wanted to help him, but he had made it clear he didn't want her help. There was a time when he had turned to her. The past few minutes only emphasized how different they'd become.

Rachel stared at the table of food and wondered what army she was going to feed. Shaun and Garrett had begged off the beef Wellington she had prepared and had fixed themselves peanut butter and banana sandwiches. Armed with tall glasses of milk, the two boys had headed outside to eat on the patio since she had decreed no more food in the bedrooms.

After that she'd turned to Amy, hoping her sister would stay home long enough to eat a meal with her. But she should have known better, Rachel thought when she recalled the disdain on Amy's face at the very mention of spending any time with her older sister. So Rachel was stuck eating alone yet again and having mounds of leftovers. Cooking for her family was not doing her ego much good, Rachel decided as she carried a glass of sweetened iced tea to the table.

The sound of the doorbell demanded her attention. When she opened the front door, she was surprised to see Michael standing on the other side of the screen. "What are you doing here?"

"You invited me to dinner."

"And you declined."

"True, but a guy can change his mind."

She'd been crazy to ask him to dinner, and now she didn't know what to say. Her only defense was she'd thought that the two boys would be eating with them. She didn't want to share a cozy dinner for two with Michael, especially after their conversation at his house earlier that day. Forcing a smile, she opened the screen door and allowed him inside.

"When's it ready?"

"I was just sitting down to eat."

He walked into the kitchen and took in the table set for one. "Where is everyone?"

"They took one look at what I prepared and made a mad dash for the peanut butter jar. I guess I'm going to have to start experimenting with peanut butter in my recipes."

"Where are Shaun and Garrett?"

"Out back devouring their sandwiches."

"And Amy?"

"Out with Kevin. Those two are inseparable. I'm worried about what she'll do."

"She fancies herself in love."

"She's not even seventeen."

"Way too young to know what love is."

His sarcasm knifed into her. "I'll share my dinner with you if you can leave the past out. A deal?"

He tilted his head to the side and thought for a moment. "A deal. But you'll have to face the fact that your sister thinks she's in love with Kevin, and she doesn't want to leave Magnolia Blossom to see the world."

Rachel sucked in a deep breath, pressing her lips tightly together. The contrasts and similarities between her and her sister's lives were obvious to both her and Michael.

"We haven't sat down to dinner yet, and I'll have my say, Rachel. You're the one who brought up the subject of Amy."

"So you think she'll do something foolish?"

"That's always a possibility. Just remember when you were her age. You tell me what you think she'll do."

She shook her head. "I'm afraid I can't put myself in Amy's shoes. We're very different people. We want different things out of life."

"Are you so sure about that? Have you discussed this with Amy?"

"Discussed it with Amy? You know I haven't. She won't talk to me about anything."

"If she feels you're backing her into a corner, she'll come out fighting."

Rachel laughed, no humor in the sound. "That's all we do."

"She's trying to preserve the life she wants the best way she knows how."

"Like I did?"

"Yes. You wanted something different from me ten years ago and you went for it. What you have to ask yourself now is do you want the same thing?"

"To be a chef? Yes, of course."

"No. To avoid a commitment to another person."

Her breath caught in her throat, and her heart missed a beat. Michael had a way of striking below the belt and doubling her over with his words.

His eyes clouded with an expression Rachel couldn't read. "The commitment I'm talking about now is the one you need to make with your brother and sister. I know it's too late for us. We had our time ten years ago. Whatever we develop now wouldn't be the same thing."

No, it wouldn't be. She had been a teenager, a senior in high school. She was a young woman now. Rachel glanced away and gestured toward the food on the table. "If we don't eat soon, it'll get cold. I'll get you a plate."

"Rachel, your life has changed—"

"Don't, Michael. I'm trying."

"Remember the other day when you talked about getting help with parenting? Come to church this Sunday. Talk with Reverend Williams. He has five children and has dealt with many parenting issues. He's always listened to me when I've had a problem."

But she wasn't like Michael. She didn't open up easily to anyone. She'd spent all her life keeping her feelings bottled up. "I'm sure he has, but—"

Michael laid his fingers over her mouth to still her words. "Don't dismiss this. Church is a good place to start bringing your family together."

Rachel blinked, nonplussed by his touch. His gaze drilled into her as though he could convey silently how strongly he felt about his faith. When he dropped his hand, she stepped back. "Shaun said something about it to me. I'd already decided to attend next Sunday."

Michael smiled. "I'm glad. You won't regret it."

His smile, as usual, warmed her and flustered her. She pointed to the chair at the opposite end of the oblong table. "We'd better eat."

He sat next to her. That action affected the rest of the meal. Rachel was too near to him for her peace of mind. She had a hard time focusing on what he was saying. She was too busy watching him drink his tea, savor the food she'd lovingly prepared, smile at something she managed to say. By the time dinner was over, her nerves were as taut as a rubber band stretched to its limit. She wondered when she would snap from the strain.

"Let's do the dishes later. The sun's setting, and I know the view from Flora's patio is beautiful."

Rachel looked at the mess in the small kitchen and remembered the night before. "I have a better idea. I'll clean up later after you're gone."

"Sure you don't want my help?"

"Yes."

"I'd be nuts to pass up a chance not to do the dishes."

She was the one who was nuts for thinking they could be just friends. It was like jumping into a raging river to save herself from being burned.

Michael refilled the glasses of iced tea and handed Rachel hers. As she walked to the back door that led to the patio, she felt as though she were walking to her doom. The air was warm, laced with the scents of gardenia and honeysuckle, a gentle breeze stirring enough to keep things cool as the sun dipped toward the horizon. Shaun and Garrett, as she knew they would be, were gone to the park to play with the other kids. She and Michael were alone with a riot of colors splashed across the sky, offering a beautiful backdrop to the evening ahead.

Warily, Rachel sat in a chair and took several sips of her tea, relishing the coldness as it slid down her throat. Normally, she enjoyed silence, but right now the quiet eroded what composure she managed to have. "You're going to have Shaun and Garrett work on the riverboat. Have you decided to finally do something about it?"

"Yes." He lifted his tea and sipped. "The boat is a sound one. The repairs it needs are cosmetic. I've decided to renovate it and use it for short trips on the river. There'll be a restaurant on it." He cradled the glass in his large hands and stared into her eyes. "Will you help me design the kitchen while you're here this summer?"

Her hands trembled. She nearly dropped her drink and had to place it on the table. "Why me?" she asked, shocked by the offer.

"Why not? I don't know of anyone more qualified than a chef who is making quite a name for herself. I'll pay you for your services. Strictly business between us."

For a brief moment she was tempted to accept. She couldn't. She would be in constant contact with Michael, and that was a temptation too risky to take.

"Rachel, I know this offer is a surprise. Frankly, it's

a surprise to me. But it makes a lot of sense if you think about it. It'll give you something to do while you get to know Amy and Shaun. Don't give me your answer right now. Promise me you'll think it over."

She nodded, still too stunned to do much else. Her mind swirled with the possibilities. The job would help her when she designed her restaurant in New York. Michael wouldn't be able to devote all his time to the kitchen. He was a busy man with a plantation to run and with the rest of the riverboat's renovation to oversee. But nevertheless, she would probably be around him every day.

"When did you decide to renovate the riverboat?"

"I'd been toying with the idea for some time. I need to do something with it. Keep it or sell it. I just couldn't sell it. It was my legacy from my grandfather."

"Just like you can't sell Whispering Oaks?"

"Yes." He finished the rest of his tea in two swallows and put his glass next to hers on the table. "When I ride over the land, I think back to the past and imagine my great-grandfather doing the same thing, or one of my great-uncles working in the field as a young boy. We all had to learn about the plantation by working it right alongside the farm hands."

"A family tradition?"

"Yes. My family has a lot of them. I like the feeling of belonging. I've tried to pass that on to Garrett."

"My immediate family doesn't have any traditions unless you count knowing the best way to pack a suitcase."

With memories of her phone call with her mother, Rachel stared at the sky, the few ribbons of color left merging with the darkness. She was determined not to let her mother destroy the serenity of the moment. Rachel pushed the memories away. She felt insulated from the world as the night edged closer, and for a few minutes she allowed herself to forget her problems and savor the evening's beauty.

"Traditions have to start somewhere, Rachel. You can start some with Amy and Shaun." Michael cut into the silence.

"They'll have their own families soon."

"Shaun still has a few years to go." A chuckle added a richness to his words.

"Hopefully, so does Amy. What kind of person is Kevin?"

"He's a good kid. Plays on the football team. He's part of the same youth group that Amy belongs to at church. He was also on the debate team that won state this year. I think he'll get a scholarship to Ole Miss."

"For football?"

"No, academics. Actually, the way they started dating was he tutored Amy in math last semester."

"Ah, so she's inherited my ability for math," Rachel said with a smile.

The night completely surrounded them now, and the only light to illuminate the patio was what streamed through the living room window. But Rachel didn't have to see Michael's expression to know he was staring at her. She looked toward the dark sky, trying to ignore his intensity. "I didn't realize it was getting so late."

"Yes, and I'd better be going. Are you sure you don't want help with the dishes?" As he rose, Michael picked up the two glasses.

"Yes, you're off the hook. I'm just glad that I had someone to share my dinner with. Eating alone is lonely sometimes."

Rachel followed Michael into the kitchen and stood by the door while he placed the glasses on the counter. He glanced at her and caught her staring at him. Her cheeks flushed and she backed into the dining room as he came toward her.

"The more I think about you designing the kitchen on the riverboat, the more it makes sense. Is there anything else I can say to persuade you to design my restaurant?"

Rachel's steps were halted by the dining room table. "I don't know when my restaurant deal will come through. I might not be able to finish your project."

"If that happens, then you're free to leave. You know me. When I do something, I like the best."

She blushed even more at the compliment. "I'll be gone for sure by the end of summer."

"Then we'll need to get started as soon as possible. Most of the kitchen can be done by then, possibly the whole thing. That's over two months away." He grasped her upper arms and pulled her close.

She breathed in his scent and relished it. She touched

her hand to his chest, intending to push him away, and marveled at the steady beat of his heart while hers was pounding. The rhythm of his heartbeat began to increase the longer she stayed in his embrace.

"I can give you a tour of the boat tomorrow morning. How about nine?"

She nodded. She would have agreed to anything as long as he was touching her.

Michael grinned. "Good. You won't regret helping. I'll see you tomorrow at nine."

Rationality slowly returned, and his words sank in. "Nine?" She gripped the back of a dining room chair for support.

"For the tour of the boat."

"Oh, that." Oh, no, she had agreed to help him with his kitchen! One part of her knew that and was elated; the other part was appalled.

"Yes, that," he said and turned to leave.

She indulged herself in what was becoming her favorite pastime, watching him move. She couldn't do it. Look what happened to her willpower just being near the man. She'd agreed to do something she knew was wrong for her. Tomorrow morning she would have to tell him she couldn't design his kitchen.

Michael stood at the railing of his riverboat and watched Rachel pull her car into the parking space next to his. After spending a sleepless night, pacing from one end of his bedroom to the other, he'd finally decided he wasn't totally crazy to have asked her to help him design the kitchen for his restaurant. Only half-nuts, he thought with a derisive laugh. The plain and simple truth, though, was he had never been able to resist Rachel when she had really needed him, and she needed him— even if she was completely unaware of that fact.

Somewhere around three in the morning he'd come to the conclusion that he'd given her the chance because he knew she would have to have something to work on while she was here or she might leave sooner than she had announced. That wouldn't be good for Shaun and Amy. Somewhere around four he had known he had to see if there was anything left between him and Rachel because every time he was near her it felt like there was something between them. But memories of what had happened ten years before wouldn't vanish. How could he trust her not to stomp on his heart again? Somewhere around five he'd decided he could be her friend and keep their relationship strictly professional. And some-where around six he had declared himself a fool.

They'd had their chance, and for whatever reason, God in His infinite wisdom had decided the two of them wouldn't work. As friends, maybe. As a couple? A bittersweet laugh spilled from his lips.

As she walked toward the riverboat, he watched her long-legged strides. She was beautiful, talented and scared to care about anyone for fear that person would leave her. She liked to do the leaving first. She had spent her life avoiding roots while he had spent his trying to build a stable, grounded life tied to a community, church and family he loved.

If he was going to prove to himself he wasn't a total fool, he had to make this partnership work. Besides, for Amy's and Shaun's sake, he wanted this to work.

Dear Heavenly Father, please guide me and help Rachel to see that making a commitment to her family isn't a bad thing. Commitments are what make life worth living.

Michael focused on her expression and knew she had come to tell him she had changed her mind. He had expected that. He affected her whether she wanted him to or not. That would scare her, threaten all she thought she wanted. Now all he had to do was convince her not to change her mind. She was an excellent choice to design his kitchen.

As Rachel made her way to the riverboat, she set her jaw in determination. She would tell him she couldn't do the job, then leave before he could persuade her otherwise.

She had seen him at the railing on the upper deck, but by the time she arrived at that location, he was gone. She began her search in the main salon. As she passed through the large area, the size of two ballrooms, she saw such possibilities that she almost stopped to appraise it more thoroughly. She had to remind herself she was on a mission. She couldn't think about the beautiful carved moldings, the brass fixtures, the picture windows that afforded a clear view of the river and land beyond.

She headed toward the back of the boat, toward what she knew had once been the kitchen. She came to a stop just inside the doorway. The room was huge, and that would be the only thing she would keep. The rest of it would have to be gutted. There was nothing salvageable, from the antique stoves to the cabinets with missing doors. She visualized the kitchen as it should be. She put a halt to her musings when she pictured herself stirring something on one of the new stoves, everything clean and shiny in the brand-new kitchen.

This was a mistake. She took a step back, intending to call Michael about her change of heart. She should never have come to the riverboat. With another step backward she hit a solid wall of human flesh. Hands gripped her arms to steady her, then turned her.

Her heart plummeted when she saw the endearing grin on Michael's face. She was doomed if she didn't do something fast.

"You're right on time, Rachel. Let me give you a tour. Then we can talk about where you want to start."

"That's not why I'm here." She had to remain strong even though his smile warmed her.

He released his hold on her and started to guide her toward the front of the riverboat.

She halted, forcing him to stop. "I can't do it."

"Are you backing out? Rachel, we have a verbal agreement." He stepped closer.

She tried to move away and found herself trapped between Michael and the doorjamb. "I'm breaking it."

"Why?"

"I don't have the time."

"What are you doing with your time while you're here?"

"Taking care of Amy and Shaun. That can be a full-time job."

"Is it?"

She dropped her gaze and murmured, "Well, no, but only because they have their own lives with not much room for me. I hope to change that."

"Why can't you start on the kitchen design until they want to include you in their lives? I know you, Rachel. You'll go crazy in Flora's house without some kind of direction."

"I'm experimenting with some new dishes."

"Not enough."

"I'm cleaning and boxing up Aunt Flora's things."

"Still not enough."

"Helen wants me to get involved in the church again. I thought—"

He placed his fingers over her mouth to still her words. "I'm all for that, Rachel, but you can do that and still design my kitchen. You've always liked to be kept busy. What better way than doing something you'll enjoy?"

She sighed, knowing when to admit defeat. "Promise me it will be strictly business between us," she said, desperate for him to be the strong one.

"I can promise you nothing will happen that *you* don't want to happen. You are in control." He backed away.

She looked from him to the antiquated kitchen. "Okay. I'll design the kitchen, but as soon as my financing for my own restaurant comes through, I'll quit. You may have to find someone to finish the project."

"You won't back out until then?"

She nodded, feeling as though she had just agreed to her own prison term. "When do you want to start?"

"How about now? Let's take a tour, then we can talk in the main salon."

"I've been on the boat before. We don't have to go on a tour."

"But it's been over ten years, Rachel. I want you to see it, to get a feel for the place before you start your designing. I want to explain some of the plans I have for this old steamboat."

"Okay," she murmured, her interest piqued.

"When the boat's ready, we'll start with lunchtime cruises on the river. The customers will get a chance to eat good food and see some of the beautiful scenery. I plan to stop at a couple of the plantations for tours, too. If that takes off, then I want to do nighttime cruises. Make it romantic, evenings meant for two." He gestured for her to go down the hallway where the staterooms were. "Of course, I always have the option of never leaving the pier, but the engines are in good shape."

Rachel opened one of the doors to a cabin. "What are you going to do with these?"

Michael entered and made a full circle. "Nothing at the moment. Later I could have weekend cruises."

"Then are you going to redo these?" She looked at him and wished she hadn't.

"Yes." He walked toward her.

She had meant to move out into the corridor but felt snared by the intensity in his eyes.

"I want to furnish these rooms with period pieces. Make people feel like they've stepped back in time to the days when steamboats reigned on the river. I have some furniture in storage at Whispering Oaks. The rest I'll acquire. What do you think?" he asked in his Southern drawl that could melt her insides.

Thinking was impossible, she wanted to shout, but her throat was too parched to speak. Time came to a standstill, and all that mattered was Michael. It's happening all over again, she thought with a sense of panic.

The sound of boys laughing forced Michael's attention away. He stepped into the corridor as Garrett and Shaun came to a screeching halt outside the doorway.

"We're ready to work, Dad."

"What do you want us to do?" Shaun asked, looking at Rachel with a perplexed expression.

With a flush staining her cheeks, she brought her hand up to smooth her hair. While Michael gave Garrett and Shaun their instructions, she tried to compose herself enough to make it through the rest of the morning. She and Michael working together was an impossibility that she had to make work, because despite her misgivings, she wanted to design the kitchen.

When the boys raced away, Michael turned to her. "What do you think about all this?"

Rachel took the opportunity to move into the hallway. "I like your plans. You're not biting off too much at once, which is smart. The only thing I want to interject here is if you think I will design a kitchen like the one in this boat's heyday, then you'd better get someone else."

"You mean you don't want to cook on a wood-burning stove?" he asked with a chuckle.

"Afraid not."

"You should use whatever modern conveniences you need. Only the best. I can afford it."

She realized they were talking as if she would be the chef. She needed to make it clear that would never happen. "Do you have any idea who you'll get to be your chef?"

"No, do you have any suggestions?"

"You could advertise in the New Orleans and Jackson papers."

"That's a possibility. Or, Rachel, you could be my chef."

"No," she said instantly. "I have my own plans."

"I know, but I did want you to know you were the first person I thought of for the job."

"Thank you, but the answer is still no," she murmured and strode toward the main salon. She needed to be around other people before she found herself accepting his job offer.

She stopped in the doorway and watched her brother and Garrett removing chairs from the room. They were giggling and talking in lowered voices, and she suspected they were talking about her and Michael. The second the boys saw her they clammed up, but they were having a hard time not grinning.

"How did you two get here?" Rachel asked, hoping to divert their overactive imaginations.

"Our bikes. We ride everywhere." Shaun carried a chair outside.

"Dad, where do you want the lumber?" Garrett picked up the last chair to take to the stern.

"Put it on the lower deck at the back of the boat."

Rachel enjoyed her safety in numbers all of two minutes before the boys disappeared down below and she was left alone with Michael again. She pretended a great interest in the main salon, walking the length of the room, appearing as though she was taking note of the cornices above the windows, the ornamental molding. Her mind, though, wasn't on her surroundings.

She was aware of Michael's every move as he, too, made an inspection of the main salon. She saw him run a hand along the brass fixtures on the counter, then look at her in the large mirror on one wall. He winked.

A dog barked several times, followed by three splashes. Rachel dragged her gaze away from Michael.

"I'd better see what the boys are up to now." She hurried from the room.

She looked down and found Garrett and Shaun swimming in the river next to the boat with a big black dog. Leaning on the wood railing, she heard Michael behind her and knew she couldn't deal with him at the moment. She scurried down the stairs to the bottom deck and bent over the railing, shouting, "Whose dog is that?"

Shaun treaded water near her. "Don't know. He just followed us from town."

"Does he have a collar?"

"No. Can I keep him?"

"I don't know, Shaun."

"Please. Aunt Flora didn't like dogs. Only cats."

"I guess you can until we find out who owns him, then he'll have to go back to his owner."

The whoopee that greeted that announcement could have been heard clear to downtown Magnolia Blossom.

"I think you've totally won Shaun over, and it didn't take but a few weeks."

Rachel tensed. "He's the easy one. Of course, he won't be happy when the owner claims the dog."

"Maybe he was abandoned."

Rachel cocked her head to the side and studied the black Labrador retriever. "No. He's in great shape. Someone has been taking care of that dog."

"Then you can get Shaun one of his own."

Rachel faced Michael, who had donned dark sunglasses that kept his eyes hidden. "No. It's too hard to have a dog in New York City."

"Thousands of people do."

"I think a dog, especially a big one, should have a yard to run in, not a small apartment."

"It would be a nice way to allow Shaun to take something from here when he leaves."

The sun beat down on her, and she was forced to shield her eyes from the glare. The hot breeze tangled itself in the strands of her hair, whipping them across her face. "You know I shouldn't be surprised by your advice. That's what's so special about small towns. I would appreciate it *if* I was looking for advice."

Shrugging, Michael grinned. "Sorry. You asked me for my help. Part of that help is advice on what is best, in my opinion, for Amy and Shaun. Darlin', you can't have it both ways. It's all or nothing."

It always had been that way with them. He'd wanted everything from her, and she hadn't been able to give that to him. She dug into her purse in search of her sunglasses. "I'll think about a medium-size dog."

"What happens if no one claims this Lab? What are you going to do then?"

"Give the dog to you as a present?"

"Nope. I've got two already. Don't need another one."

She found her sunglasses and plopped them on her nose. "Then I'll face that problem when the time comes. I have too many problems ahead of that one to get too concerned at the moment."

"Well, then, I'd better warn you that Amy is worse than Shaun when it comes to animals."

"She is?"

"You can always hope the dog is gone before she realizes it's at your house."

Rachel wished she could wipe that grin from his face. He was enjoying her dilemma way too much. "I suppose I could hide him. Since she's rarely home, it might work."

Michael chuckled. "Anything's possible when you want it bad enough."

"Does that sum up your philosophy of life?"

"Sure does."

The dog's barking drew her attention to the end of the pier. "Are the boys through for the day?"

"Yep, until I get things started, then I'll use them more."

"Good. I'll have them follow me home and make posters about the dog. After that, I'll start working on some preliminary plans for the kitchen. I should be able to show you something in a few days."

"I'll be by to pick up Garrett a little later, then."

"Just let him spend the night again."

Michael drew himself up straight, his hands flexing at his side. "Can't do that. I have to take Garrett to Jackson early tomorrow morning."

"To see Mary Lou?"

He nodded, a frown carved deeply into his features.

"You can pick him up early tomorrow morning. I'm usually up by six."

"Okay, if you're sure," Michael murmured, tension threading through his words.

Michael leaned against the railing and watched as Rachel stopped to talk with Garrett and Shaun. His memories of his relationship with Rachel and his failure to keep his marriage together strengthened his desire not to get involved with Rachel again. Even though he'd always wanted a large family, he wouldn't put himself through that kind of pain ever again. He just had to remember that over the next few months.

Chapter Seven

The aroma of coffee brewing greeted Michael when Rachel opened the door to her house. Her hair was wet as if she had just gotten out of the shower. She wore a pair of shorts and a white T-shirt with Born To Cook in big red letters. She looked good to his tired eyes.

She smiled and gestured for him to come inside. "I hope you're hungry. The boys are finishing up their blueberry pancakes."

Michael yawned. He hadn't slept the night before. "All I want is a big cup of coffee. Preferably the whole pot."

"Now, Michael Hunter, I didn't get up thirty minutes early just so you could drink coffee and be on your way. You can have at least one of my pancakes."

"You shouldn't have gone to all that trouble."

"When someone is invited to breakfast, a person has to fix something to serve. Pancakes are easy, and they're something the boys will eat."

"As opposed to beef Wellington?"

"Yes," she said with a laugh. "I'm learning. Last night I fixed a pizza, and they didn't leave one piece." She headed for the kitchen.

As Michael entered the room, Garrett jumped out of his chair, downing the rest of his milk in the same motion. "I'm ready, Dad."

"But I'm not. Sit. Rachel is making me eat breakfast."

"Yeah, did she tell you that it was the most important meal of the day?" Shaun asked while spearing another pancake from the serving platter.

"No, but I did read that somewhere."

"Bet she didn't have to twist your arm much." Garrett grinned, displaying his milk mustache.

"Just about anything Rachel fixed would be tempting." Michael sat in a chair between the boys.

"Just about? What won't you eat?" Rachel handed him a large mug of coffee, then went to the stove to flip the last batch of pancakes.

"Well, let me see. I was never partial to snails. I'm sure you learned to prepare them in Paris."

"Ugh!" Garrett screwed his face into a frown. "Snails? People eat them?"

"I did learn how to prepare escargot, which is really a fancy name for snails. They are very good."

"I think I lost my appetite," Shaun said, scooting his chair back. "Let's play a video game until your dad gets ready to leave. First one in the living room gets to choose."

"Shaun—" The rest of her sentence would have been spoken to thin air as the boys raced from the room. Rachel shook her head. "Do they even know how to walk? Every time they go someplace it is always a race to see who'll get there first."

"Makes me tired just looking at them." Michael put several pancakes on his plate, plopped a square of butter on top, then lavished maple syrup all over them. He bowed his head and said a silent prayer.

Rachel sat in the chair farthest away from him and sipped her coffee. "Will you be all right today?"

"Yeah," he said with little conviction.

"Remember, Garrett loves you. She can't take that away."

He finished his coffee and went to the counter to pour himself more. "When Mary Lou left us, I prayed she would return. I didn't want Garrett to grow up without a mother like I did. But then Mary Lou didn't—" He swallowed hard, remembering the nights and days being both mother and father to Garrett.

"And now you don't think she has any right to be in Garrett's life?"

"Yeah. She chose to leave and find another life. I know in my heart I need to forgive her, but it isn't easy."

"Forgiveness doesn't always come easily, especially when you've been hurt."

"I'm more concerned about Garrett's feelings than mine. He was the one who was hurt."

"Are you sure that's the case?"

He stabbed her with a narrowed look. "Yes, of course."

"Have you forgiven me for leaving you?"

Silence hung in the air between them, thick, emotion-filled.

"Have you, Michael?" Suddenly she wanted to know more than anything.

"I'm trying, Rachel. That's the best answer I can give you."

She tried not to let his words hurt her, but it was hard. "Perhaps you should talk with Reverend Williams. He may be able to help you."

Michael didn't reply but sat down and took a bite of his pancakes. "This is delicious."

"Thank you. I never tire of hearing people say that about my cooking," she said, sad that he was doing what she did so well—avoiding his feelings.

"Don't tell Helen, but I think these beat hers."

"No way would I say that to her. I value her friendship."

"It's nice to hear you say that."

Rachel stiffened. "What's that supposed to mean?"

"Nothing." He stuck his fork in the last piece of pancake and brought it to his mouth.

"I care about Helen. She's the best friend I ever had."

"I'm sorry, Rachel. I'm tired. I didn't get much sleep last night, and I said something I shouldn't have." Michael rose, taking his plate and mug to the sink. His head was beginning to throb with tension. He turned to leave.

She stood in his way. "Maybe you shouldn't have said it, but it is the way you feel. I may not live here, but that doesn't mean I haven't kept in touch with Helen."

Michael wanted out of there, but short of physically moving Rachel out of his way, he wasn't going anywhere. "A card now and then is not keeping in touch."

Her eyes widened. "I've called her."

"Yeah, on her birthday. That's once a year. And since we're on the subject, you haven't done much better with your own sister and brother."

Rachel sucked in a deep breath. Lines of anger scored her features. She opened her mouth to say something but then clamped it closed.

His head ached, and his pulse hammered against his temples in a maddening beat. "This was not a good idea." He clasped her upper arms and moved her to the side, then he stepped around her and left the kitchen before he made the situation worse.

"Let's go, Garrett," he called, not breaking stride as he headed for the front door.

He strode to his truck and got in, deliberately keeping his gaze averted from the porch. He could feel Rachel watching him. Tapping a fast rhythm against the steering wheel, he waited for his son to climb into the passenger side, then he backed out of the driveway, barely managing not to screech his tires.

His son must have sensed his mood. He remained quiet as they drove out of town. "Are you mad at

Rachel?" Garrett finally asked when they were on the highway to Jackson.

"What makes you think that, son?"

"Gee, Dad, maybe the way you left her place."

Michael's grip on the steering wheel tightened. "We had words. Nothing important."

Garrett stared out the side window. "Dad, Mom wants me to come visit more now that she lives so near."

The words tore at Michael's heart. For years Garrett had been the center of his life. Now he had to share his son with Mary Lou. Mary Lou's timing was awful—not that there would ever be a great time to give up custody of his son, but with Rachel back in town his emotions had taken a beating.

"We'll work something out for the summer, son."

For a long moment Garrett was silent then he asked, "Dad, why did Mom leave?"

Michael sucked in a sharp breath. He wasn't sure how to answer. "We got married too young. We weren't ready." The steering wheel, where he gripped it, was wet with his sweat. He couldn't tell his son about Mary Lou's drinking problem.

"Do you think she'll come to one of my baseball games if I ask her?"

"Sure," Michael answered, trying to be positive. He might be angry at Mary Lou for walking out on them, but he never wanted Garrett to feel his mother didn't love him.

"Then I'll ask her today. Maybe I'll be able to hit a

home run. Of course, this time it won't go through Mr. Moon's window."

"Please remember that in the future. That's one man I don't want mad at us."

"Why is he so grumpy?"

"I think, son, he wants to be left alone."

"Maybe someone hurt him in the past."

"That's a possibility."

Garrett chewed on his lower lip, thought for a moment, then slanted a look at his father and asked, "Did Mom hurt you?"

"Our marriage didn't work out because we weren't right for each other," he answered, feeling as though he were balanced on a tightrope and any moment a stiff wind would whisk him off.

"Can I play one of my CDs?"

Michael nodded, relieved that his son didn't pursue the topic. He wasn't quite eight and certainly didn't need his illusions tarnished.

Garrett played a CD Michael hadn't heard. After several songs he didn't want to hear it ever again. But for the next half hour he endured the album, draining his mind of all thoughts.

By the time Michael pulled up in front of Mary Lou's two-story house, he was feeling better about the meeting. Maybe everything would work out.

Mary Lou opened the door when Garrett rang the bell. She smiled at her son, then drew him to her and hugged him. Michael hung back and watched the scene between mother and son, trying not to feel as though he was losing his son to Mary Lou. Anger he'd held bottled up escaped, carving a frown into his features.

"Y'all come on in." Mary Lou waved them into her house. "We'll have lunch out on the patio by the pool." She took Garrett's hand to show him the way.

Michael followed. The glass table on the patio was already set for three even though lunch was several hours away. Mary Lou indicated that they have a seat, but Garrett headed for the large kidney-shaped pool.

"You have a slide *and* a diving board. Wow!"

"I should have had you bring your swimming suit today. Next time you should," Mary Lou said.

Michael tensed. His frown strengthened into a scowl.

Mary Lou walked to where Garrett stood. "You know we have some time before lunch. I think I can find a suit that will fit you. Do you want to go swimming?"

"Can I, Dad?"

Michael nodded, not trusting himself to speak. His headache had returned, the pain behind his eyes intensifying.

While Mary Lou took Garrett into the house to change, Michael prowled the patio, too restless to sit. Mary Lou wanted to have a relationship with her son. After nearly six years, she suddenly wanted to share him equally. She hadn't been there when Garrett had gotten the flu last year or when he had gotten into a fight with a boy at school or— Michael shook the angry thoughts from his head. He had to deal with Mary Lou being back in Garrett's life. He had to deal with the anger and mistrust eating at him.

Lord, please give me the strength to deal with Mary Lou. I can't do it without You. I know I should forgive her. But I can't. I can't forget what she did to Garrett. She wasn't there for him when he needed a mother.

When Garrett shot out of the house and raced for the pool, Michael said, "Slow down, son. You know there's no running around pools."

Two feet from the water Garrett came to a halt, then proceeded to walk the remaining distance to the slide. At the top of it, he waved then plunged into the pool.

"You've done a good job with him, Michael."

He stiffened at the sound of Mary Lou's voice. Pivoting toward her, he managed to keep himself from scowling at her. "I had no choice."

"Please have a seat." Mary Lou gestured toward a chair while she sat down. "I thought for this first meeting, Tom shouldn't be here, but later he certainly wants to be involved in Garrett's life."

"Garrett has a father."

"I know that."

"What do you want?" His anger was apparent in his voice.

"Direct as usual. I know you have a right to be angry with me. I walked out on you and Garrett."

"You left without letting me know where you were. For days Garrett cried for you. I thank God every day he doesn't remember that. But I do."

"I was twenty-one and not prepared to be a mother. I couldn't stay any longer."

"And you think I was prepared to be a single father?"

"Michael, you've always been grounded. I knew you would do what needed to be done."

"And that's supposed to make everything okay now?" He looked toward where his son was swimming. His throat constricted with memories of the struggle he had gone through dealing with a two-year-old, trying to be the best father *and* mother his son could have. He'd tried to make his marriage with Mary Lou work even after he'd discovered her drinking problem. He'd made a commitment to her, and their son needed both of them. He knew he could forgive Mary Lou for walking out on him, but he didn't know if he could forgive her for leaving Garrett without a mother. He remembered growing up without his mother and the loneliness he'd felt.

"I'll ask you again. What do you want, Mary Lou?"

"As I told you on the phone, I want partial custody of Garrett. I'm able to take care of him now. I have a good home and a good husband. I have my life together. I haven't taken a drink in over a year."

"No." Michael shook his head to emphasize his answer. "You can see him with me present, but that's all."

"I'll go back to court if I have to."

The threat hung in the air between them. The pounding of his heartbeat roared in his ears. "Is that what you want—a fight?"

"Hey, Dad, Mom. Look at this." Beaming with a grin, Garrett waved again, then did a flip off the diving board.

"If that's what you want, I can't stop you from going to court," Michael said, a tightness in his chest that threatened to seize his next breath.

"I want to spend some time with him. Tom and I want to have him stay with us some weekends."

"No." Michael clipped the word out, then clamped his jaw shut.

Garrett pulled himself out of the pool and came over to the table, water dripping off him. "Mom, I'm playing baseball next Saturday. Will you come see me?"

Michael clenched the arms of the chair, wanting to snatch the invitation away.

"Of course, I will. Tom and I will be there ready to root for you."

The smug smile on Mary Lou's face caused Michael to cringe. Short of making a scene, he would have to endure Mary Lou and her new husband's presence at the ball game. First thing Monday morning he would pay Robert Davenport a visit concerning his ex-wife's demands.

"Helen, what a nice surprise." Rachel let her friend into the house. "Do you want some iced tea?"

"Sounds divine, sugar. I'm parched. It's so hot I could fry eggs on the sidewalk outside my café. Of course, I'd probably lose some customers if I did."

"What brings you by?"

"Do I have to have a reason?"

"No, but who's minding the store?"

"Amy is, and she's doing a nice job."

In the kitchen Rachel poured the tea into a glass full of ice, then handed it to Helen. "I'm glad she's working full-time. Keeps her out of trouble."

"If you say so."

"What aren't you telling me?"

"What's she doing with the other forty or so hours a week? When she isn't sleeping or working?"

"Helen, spill it. What's happening?"

"I just hear things from time to time."

"About her and Kevin?"

"They're getting mighty serious." Helen tipped her glass and took several long sips.

"I can't follow her every place she goes."

"No, I reckon you can't. But maybe you should talk with her."

"You know, the problem with that is she won't listen to me."

Helen rubbed the back of her neck. "Yeah, you do have a problem there."

"Maybe I should try to follow her. It would probably be easier."

Helen walked to the kitchen table and looked at the drawings scattered all over it. "Are these for Michael's boat?"

"Yes. I'm almost finished."

"Have you seen him lately?"

"I saw him briefly at church, but we didn't talk." Rachel recalled the way Michael had kept his distance after being the one to encourage her to attend the service. When she'd glanced at him, a look of vulnerability had touched his eyes before a shutter fell in place.

"You know Mary Lou's coming this weekend to see Garrett play baseball."

"No, I didn't," Rachel said, disappointed that she had to hear the news from Helen and not Michael. She knew he didn't owe her any explanations, but the hurt was still there. "I haven't seen Garrett much since he came back. He came over this morning to play with Shaun. But he raced through here with Shaun so fast I'm not even sure what he's wearing. They're out in the backyard right now with the dog they found."

"So you haven't found the owner of the Lab yet?"

"No, I'm beginning to feel the dog will be ours. I had the boys put up posters, but no one has called."

"Well, you know part of the problem is where the boys put up those posters. One is on a telephone pole, but a bush hides it from everyone's view. Another is in my window, but down in the corner behind the newspaper bin."

"Why am I not surprised?" Shaking her head, Rachel took a chair at the table.

"What's going on besides your problems with Amy?"

Rachel ran her hands down her face. "What can I say? Lack of sleep wreaks havoc with one's body. It all boils down to one person. Michael. I shouldn't have come back at all."

"I don't think you had much choice, Rachel."

"And I'm not making the best of this situation. Do I stay away from the man like my common sense keeps telling me? No, instead, I tell him I'll work with him on his riverboat. What's wrong with me?"

"Do you want the truth or do you want me to lie to you?"

"Michael Hunter is just a friend. He isn't even the same person I knew ten years ago, and I'm certainly not, either." With her eyes closed Rachel massaged her temples. Tension clung to every part of her like spiderwebs to a haunted house.

"I think you're falling for him all over again."

Rachel rose, gripping the edge of the table. "I won't do that to myself. I won't do that to Michael, either. We're just *friends*."

Helen bent over the table. "Fine. Then what's this problem you're having with sleeping?"

Rachel was so intent on Helen and their conversation that she jumped when she heard the pounding on the front door. "I sure hope it isn't that man again. He doesn't know how to use the doorbell."

"Who?"

"Harold Moon." Rachel started for the door.

"Hold it. Let me answer it. I've been meaning to have a few words with that man since he almost ran me over."

Rachel couldn't have stopped Helen if she had wanted.

Helen planted herself squarely in front of the open door. "Can I help you?"

Harold scowled and held up a poster. "This is my dog."

Helen huffed, shaking her head. "Do you honestly want us to believe you own a dog?"

The scowl lines in his face deepened. "I don't care what you believe. That's my dog, and I have the papers to prove it."

Helen put her hands on her hips, her eyes blazing. "I wouldn't turn any dog over to you without seeing those papers, and then I'm not sure I could do that to a poor defenseless animal."

"Look, lady, this isn't between you and me."

"I'm making it my business."

Rachel decided at that moment she better intervene. "May I help you, Mr. Moon?"

"Yes, get this—lady out of here, then we need to talk about Charlie."

"I'm not going anywhere. I wouldn't leave my friend alone with you if you were—"

Rachel placed her hand on her friend's arm. "Helen, why don't you go out back and get the boys? Please."

Helen stalked toward the backyard, glancing over her shoulder several times. When the door slammed shut, Rachel turned to her neighbor.

"Come in, Mr. Moon."

Harold hesitated before opening the door and coming inside. "All I want is to be left alone, and yet you and those kids keep getting into my business."

Rachel felt sorry for the man. He probably didn't realize how defensive his voice sounded. The touch of vulnerability in his eyes reminded her of Michael's look at church. "Is the dog named Charlie?"

He mumbled yes.

"How come we've never seen you with him?"

"Because there is a leash law in this town and, unlike some people I've seen, I abide by it."

"How long has Charlie been with you?"

"Two years. What does that have to do with anything?"

"I must be certain you're the dog's owner."

"Bring him here. I'll show you."

"That's an excellent idea, Mr. Moon." At the back door Rachel called to Helen and the boys to bring the dog inside.

The look on Garrett's and Shaun's faces made Rachel hope the dog didn't belong to Harold Moon. She had been afraid of this and wished she hadn't impulsively told Shaun he could keep the animal if they couldn't find the owner.

The two boys trudged inside followed by Helen and the dog. Shaun's head hung down, and his shoulders were slumped. Garrett didn't look much better.

Harold squatted and whistled. "Come here, Charlie."

The Lab's ears perked up, and he loped over to Harold, almost knocking the man back. The dog licked his face, his tail wagging.

Her neighbor glanced up. "Are you satisfied?"

"Yes," Rachel said before Helen could speak.

Tears glistened in Shaun's eyes as he said goodbye to Charlie, then came to stand next to Rachel, his chin touching his chest. She swallowed hard. "Mr. Moon, would it be possible for the boys to come over and see Charlie from time to time?"

Shaun's head snapped up, hopeful eagerness on his face. "We won't be no trouble."

Harold looked from Shaun to Garrett then at Charlie.

"Please. They have come to care about your dog," Rachel added, seeing the struggle in Harold.

"Okay. But not too much." He started for the door, called to Charlie to follow and was gone before Helen could recover.

The startled expression on her face was still in place as the door shut behind the man. "Did I hear right? He's invited the boys over. Are you out of your mind, Rachel?"

She shot her friend an exasperated look. "No, the man is lonely."

"How can you tell?"

"I can." Because I've felt the same way, she silently added, many times.

"Rachel, I don't know if we should go. He isn't too friendly." Shaun stared at the front door, his expression almost as shocked as Helen's.

"I grant you the man is not very social. He needs practice."

"Sugar, he needs more than practice. I don't think even Amy Vanderbilt could help him."

"You two will be playing with Charlie out in the

backyard. He has said you can come. The decision is yours."

Shaun conferred with Garrett, their whispers animated. "Okay. We'll try it."

When the boys left, Helen felt Rachel's forehead. "I think the heat has finally gotten to you. It's fried your brain."

"You know, Helen, small towns can be a closed society. Has anyone tried to reach that man?"

"Remember? I took him a pecan pie when he first came to town, and he refused it."

"Oh, my gosh, then he's a hopeless case."

"Okay. Maybe he did say something about being diabetic."

"There you have it." Rachel decided it was time to shake up her friend's life. "He's hurting, Helen. I can feel it."

"What are you? Psychic?"

"He's kind to his dog," Rachel explained, as if that said it all.

Helen walked to the front window and looked at Harold's house. "He does have one of the prettiest yards in town."

Rachel smiled as she turned to go into the kitchen. Helen had been alone for too long. And if her friend was busy with her own romance, she would leave Rachel be.

Rachel stared at Michael as he worked on his riverboat. She watched him move some lumber, sweat beading his brow. She felt the energy seep from her and she grasped the railing to steady herself. He picked up a canteen, took a sip, then dumped the rest over his head. Water dripped from his face, catching the fading sunlight and glistening. All she needed to complete the scene was to hear "Ol' Man River."

Michael looked toward her. He grinned and waved. Flushed from the warm greeting he sent her, she clutched her briefcase and strode toward him.

"I have the designs ready," she said in an all-business tone she was sure contrasted with the blush staining her cheeks.

"Oh, great! That was quick. Here, let me take a look." His hand touched hers on the handle of the briefcase.

She released her grip and stepped back, perspiration bathing her face. So much for presenting a business facade, Rachel thought. "If you don't like the design I've come up with, let me know what you don't like about it. I'm sure I can fix it."

He gave her a smile that doubled her heartbeat. "I'm sure you can. I have complete faith in you when it comes to cooking."

"Only cooking?" she asked, hearing the hurt tone in her question. She bit her lower lip, wishing she hadn't said anything.

His look drilled into her. "Let's go into the main salon and have a look. I have a table in there where I can spread everything out."

"How was your trip to Jackson?"

"I'm sure you've heard by now that Mary Lou is coming this Saturday to see Garrett play baseball."

But not from you. She nodded, careful to keep her expression neutral.

The main salon offered a slight reprieve from the afternoon sun. "My, don't you think it's unseasonably warm?"

Michael looked up from examining the designs. "It's the humidity. You'll get used to it."

"Most of the time I feel like a limp noodle."

"Mmm," he said absently, turning his full attention to the papers before him.

Anxiously, Rachel waited, perspiration rolling down her face. She wiped her hand across her brow.

"I like this design, Rachel. The only thing I would change is the area over here." Michael pointed to one wall. "I would move some of the cabinets to here and have the other preparation area along there so the two people don't have to stand so close together." His gaze trapped hers. "In the summer, even with air-conditioning, it can get awfully hot in a kitchen. I think spreading the people out might keep wars from erupting."

"I heartily agree," she said, brushing her hand across her brow again.

He straightened and removed a clean, folded handkerchief from his back pocket. He wiped it across her forehead, down her cheeks and along her neck. "I believe I heard we're having a heat wave."

"Isn't that a song?"

His thumb paused at the base of her throat. "Not any I heard of."

"Ah, yes, you used to be partial to rock and roll."

"Still am. And your favorites are classical and show tunes." He pocketed the handkerchief while the other hand remained on her shoulder, his thumb drawing slow circles where her life force beat beneath it.

"Yes. I see we still don't like the same music."

"But I can think of a few things we still have in common." His gaze linked with hers.

"Like what?" She took an unsteady breath.

"We both like chocolate." His impish grin caused her to think of the past, when he'd made her laugh.

"That doesn't sound like much."

"But it's a start," he replied with a wink.

Rachel laughed, relaxing for the first time since coming to the river landing.

A flash of red, a sound, pulled her attention from Michael. Amy stood in the doorway with a sullen look on her face.

Rachel's tension returned. "Hello, Amy. Did you need me for something?"

"I came to talk to Michael." Her sister peered at Michael as if Rachel weren't there. "Kevin needs a summer job. We were wondering if you needed people to work on the boat." Amy glanced at the door and motioned for Kevin to come inside.

"Good to see you, Kevin," Michael said, shaking the

teenager's hand. "I could use some help with painting, sanding, moving heavy stuff."

"That's sounds great, Mr. Hunter. I was supposed to work at the gas station, but Bob's nephew is going to spend the summer with him."

"Well, then, the job is yours. You can start tomorrow morning at seven o'clock."

"I'll be here." Kevin started to leave, but Amy remained.

"Thank you, Michael."

Amy refused to look at Rachel. "Will you be home for dinner?" Rachel asked.

Her sister arched one of her brows. "No, I'm helping Helen at the café. I'll be home later."

"When?" Rachel hated dragging information out of Amy bit by slow bit.

"Twelve."

When Amy left, Rachel sagged. "I have to keep repeating Reverend Williams's advice to have patience."

"You talked to him?"

"After church. I looked for you, but you were gone when I came out."

His gaze shifted away, then back. "It was a rough weekend."

"And you didn't feel like talking to a friend?"

"Is that what we are?"

"I hope we are."

Michael dragged his hands through his hair. "If you

say so. Frankly, I don't know what I'm feeling anymore. My emotions have taken a beating lately."

She looked him straight in the eye. "Then we have something else in common."

Chapter Eight

"Dad, where's my uniform? You cleaned it, didn't ya?" Garrett yelled from the laundry room.

Michael sauntered into the kitchen, poured himself another cup of coffee and faced his son, who looked as if his whole world was about to fall apart.

"I put it on your bed this morning."

"Oh."

Garrett started to leave when Michael said, "When we talked after our trip to Jackson, everything was fine. Is everything okay now? You seem a little tense."

"Mom's gonna see me play today. I need to look my best. Dad, I need to get dressed or we'll be late. We can't be late!"

Michael drew in a deep, fortifying breath as he watched his son head for his bedroom. Michael took a sip of his coffee, then decided against another cup of caffeine. He was already wired from the six cups he'd had, starting at three o'clock this morning.

He pitched the coffee down the drain and rinsed his cup. Not only were Mary Lou and Tom coming to Magnolia Blossom, but after yesterday with Rachel on the riverboat, he was wound so tightly it wouldn't take much for him to slip over the edge.

The worst part of today would be seeing Rachel in the crowd of people at the ballpark. He ran his hand through his hair repeatedly. Today could be a very long day, he thought as he scooped up his keys.

"Ready, Garrett," he called to the second floor.

His son came bounding down the stairs. "How do I look?"

For the first time Michael could remember, Garrett had combed his hair and scrubbed his face clean without Michael telling him to do so. His uniform shirt was tucked into his pants. His son had never been concerned about his appearance until today.

"Great. Your mom will be impressed."

"She said her husband will be coming, too."

"Nervous?"

"Yeah, kinda."

Michael tousled his son's hair and hugged him to his side. "You don't have to be."

"Dad, you messed up my hair. Now I have to go upstairs and comb it again." He raced up the stairs. "We're gonna be late."

Michael heaved a deep sigh, thinking of the *long* day ahead.

* * *

Rachel stared at the massive front door, inhaled a deep breath and marched up the steps to Harold Moon's house. Her hand shook as she reached to ring the bell. The door swung open a minute later, and the man stood in the entrance as though he would fight anyone who dared to cross the threshold. And Shaun was somewhere inside. What had possessed her to ask him to allow her little brother to play with Charlie?

"Shaun said he was coming over here to see Charlie. He has a baseball game."

"He's in the backyard." Harold jerked his thumb in that direction, his usual scowl firmly in place. "Go around by the gate."

She stepped inside the yard and called, "Shaun, time to go."

Her brother glanced up from throwing a Frisbee for Charlie. "Just a sec." He hurried to the back door and knocked.

Her neighbor opened the door a crack. "Yes?"

Rachel's eyes widened at the man's tone of voice. It wasn't soft, but it wasn't gruff, either. And she could swear, even though the door blocked some of his face, that Harold Moon wasn't scowling. Of course, he wasn't smiling, either.

"I hope you can come see me play this afternoon. I'm pitching. We're playing our arch rivals, the Seahawks." Shaun puffed out his chest, proud of the fact that he was the best pitcher on the team.

"Probably not, kid. I have things to do around here."
Harold shut the door quietly.

"Why did you ask Mr. Moon to your game?" Rachel
asked as they were getting into the car.

"Ah, he's not so bad. You should see him with
Charlie. You know, he used to play minor league ball."

"He did?"

"Yep. He even showed me a new pitch."

"He did?"

"Yeah, and he helped Garrett with his swing."

"He did?" Rachel slanted a look at her brother, astonished.

"Boy, is Garrett nervous about today. His mom's
coming."

Rachel was very aware that Mary Lou was coming.
Rachel had tossed and turned last night with dreams
about Mary Lou and Michael. Rachel couldn't have
slept more than a few hours, and she was wrung out.

"Is he glad his mother is coming?"

"Heck, yes."

"Most kids would be angry with a mother who hasn't
been around much." Rachel thought about her situation
and knew she was speaking from experience.

"Garrett isn't like most kids. Besides, Michael explained everything to him a long time ago."

"What did he explain?"

"That his mom needed to find herself. That she had
been too young to have a child. That she loved him very

much because she left him in Michael's care and knew he would be fine."

Something in Shaun's voice made her glance at her brother. His brow was wrinkled as though he was thinking. "What about our mother?"

He looked at her, his eyes clouded. "Mom loves us. She left us with Aunt Flora. One day she'll come back just like Garrett's mom."

Rachel's heart swelled; her throat constricted. She wished she felt the way her brother did about their mother and father. Reality would hit one day, and he would learn their parents only cared about their work. Rachel was determined to be there for her little brother when it happened.

She pulled into the parking lot next to the ball field. The second she cut the engine Shaun was out the door and running toward the dugout. She remained in the car, gripping the steering wheel while she composed herself. The mention of their mother had been a mistake. It brought to the foreground feelings she didn't want to deal with today.

When she saw Mary Lou walk past the car, Rachel's grasp on the steering wheel tightened until her knuckles were white. Michael had married Mary Lou eighteen months after Rachel had left for Paris. That had hurt. She had wanted him to pine for her the way she'd pined for him.

You had no right to feel that way, a voice inside her head said.

This had nothing to do with rights and everything to

do with emotions. Rachel realized she had never been totally rational about Michael Hunter, and that had not changed. That was why she had run when he'd declared his love for her. She didn't want to feel intense, all-consuming emotion. Her parents had that, and they excluded everyone else from their lives.

Sliding from the car, Rachel looked toward the stands, which were filling up with parents and friends of the teams. Mary Lou was sitting between a man who must be her husband and Michael. This was going to be a *long* afternoon.

Michael watched Rachel climb from her car and look at him. Their gazes connected.

"Garrett looks good in his uniform."

Mary Lou drew his attention with her statement, and he reluctantly turned his head toward his ex-wife. "He especially wanted to look good for you today," Michael said, hearing the warning in his voice.

"That makes two of us. I think I changed four times before deciding on what to wear."

"Five, dear," Tom interjected with a wry grin.

Mary Lou glanced toward Rachel, who was walking to the stands. "I see I'm not the only one who has returned home."

"Rachel's aunt died a month ago."

"Oh, I'm sorry to hear that. Flora Sanders was always nice to me."

"She was nice to everyone. That was her way."

When Rachel started to mount the bleachers to sit on the top row, Michael snagged her hand and pulled her toward him. "Sit here." He didn't give her a chance to say no. He tugged her down next to him on the wooden seat. "Rachel Peters, I'd like you to meet Tom Bantam, and of course, you already know Mary Lou."

Rachel smiled and nodded toward both of them, but the look she sent Michael spoke of her displeasure.

"I'm sorry to hear about your aunt." Mary Lou leaned around Michael to talk with Rachel. "What happened?"

"A heart attack. Very quick."

The tight thread in Rachel's voice underscored her leashed anger. Michael realized he shouldn't have asked—okay, forced—her to sit next to him, but he didn't want to spend the whole afternoon listening to Mary Lou.

He bent close to Rachel's ear and whispered, "I need your help. Please."

When the edges of her mouth and the look in her eyes softened he knew she would help. He relaxed his tensed muscles and squeezed her hand, then quickly released his grasp.

"Oh, look, Garrett is first up to bat," Mary Lou exclaimed.

Michael shifted his attention to the field, comforted by the fact that Rachel was sitting on one side of him. Maybe this afternoon wouldn't be too bad, he thought as his son swung and missed the ball.

When his son struck out and tromped off the field,

Michael decided he probably should reassess his assumption that everything would be all right. He could taste Garrett's desire for a home run. He had swung at the first three pitches with everything he had. Michael needed to have a word with his son. He started to get up to walk to the dugout when Harold Moon beat him to it. The man pulled Garrett to the side and whispered to him. His son nodded a few times, smiled, then went into the dugout.

Michael frowned. "What's Harold Moon doing with Garrett?"

"Shaun told me he has been giving Garrett a few pointers on swinging the bat."

"He has?" Michael rubbed the back of his neck, shaking his head. "I don't believe it."

"I can't believe he actually showed up. Shaun invited him, but Harold said he had things to do around the house."

"Who's Harold Moon?" Mary Lou asked.

"My neighbor." Rachel didn't look at Michael's ex-wife but kept her gaze trained on the field. Shaun was coming up to bat.

Michael cheered when Shaun got a base run. Rachel's enthusiasm was interesting to observe. When he had played baseball in high school and college, she hadn't cared much for the sport. If she came to the game, she would applaud with everyone else, but that was all. With Shaun she jumped up, clapped and whistled. If Michael didn't know better, he'd have thought she'd changed.

When the Tigers took the field, Rachel straightened,

clasping her hands so tightly in her lap that Michael laid his over hers and said, "Shaun's good. He'll be all right."

"I know. It's just that the last time the Tigers lost and Shaun was pitching he blamed himself. I couldn't get him to see that no one person was to blame for losing."

"Shaun has always been more competitive than Garrett."

"Tell me about it. I actually played one of his video games with him the other night. I have great eye-hand coordination, but there was no way he was going to lose."

Rachel grew taut as Shaun threw the first series of pitches. She began to breathe easier when the first two batters struck out. She relaxed even more when Helen sat next to her.

"Sorry I'm late. Some customer had a mix-up that I had to see to personally. How's it going?"

"Zero to zero," Rachel replied as the third batter hit the ball, and it went sailing out into left field.

When Garrett caught the fly ball, Mary Lou leaped to her feet and yelled, "That's the way to go. Three up. Three down."

Helen leaned close. "So, is this not cozy?"

"Shh." Rachel grinned and mouthed the word *behave*.

"Who me? I always do," Helen whispered.

Rachel rolled her eyes and hoped she got through the afternoon unscathed. Between dealing with Michael and Mary Lou and watching Shaun play an important game, she was sure her nerves would be shredded like pieces of confetti by the time the game was over.

By the ninth inning Rachel had bitten two fingernails down to the quick. She glanced at the scoreboard for the hundredth time. The score was still tied, five to five. Nothing magical had changed while she wasn't looking.

"I don't know how much more of this I can take. No wonder I never liked to watch you play, Michael."

He chuckled. "Relax."

Again, he took her hand. She kept telling herself to withdraw it from his, but she couldn't. She enjoyed the contact but wished she didn't.

Garrett was getting ready to bat. Rachel noticed Harold motioning the boy to the fence and saying a few words to him. Garrett grinned and went to the plate. She felt the tension in Michael's grip as his son swung at the first pitch. The sound of the bat hitting the ball reverberated through the park. Rachel stood next to Michael as the ball soared over the playing field. She shouted and clapped when it landed on the other side of the fence.

"A home run! He did it!" Michael wrapped his arms about Rachel and spun her around and around.

When he placed her on the ground, she was dizzy, and that would be her defense if anyone asked why she allowed Michael to kiss her in front of half the town. He pressed her against him and settled his mouth over hers, not in a quick congratulatory kiss but in a long one that curled her toes.

When he pulled back, his gaze captured hers, and for a brief moment everyone else faded from view. They were the only two people in the whole ballpark. His look melted her insides.

"Hey, y'all sit down in front. The game isn't over. Some of us would like to see the rest of the game."

Rachel blushed when she glanced at the people in the stands, every eye on them. She sunk to her seat, wishing she could crawl under the bleachers to hide. Whereas Michael was grinning from ear to ear. The only thing he didn't do was give everyone a high five.

The rest of the inning passed in a blur. The next batter struck out, and the Seahawks came up to bat for the final time—if the Tigers could hold them to no runs. She was aware of everything happening around her, but she felt as though she were in a vacuum, observing the situation from afar.

When the game was over and the Tigers had won, all Rachel wanted to do was get Shaun and head home before someone asked her about the *kiss*. The whole town would have her engaged to Michael before the night was over.

When Mary Lou started talking to him, Rachel saw her chance to escape without having to say anything to Michael. She backed away a few paces, then turned and hurried toward the parking lot. She would wait for Shaun inside the safety of her car.

Turning, Michael started to say something to Rachel, but she was gone. He searched the crowd around the boys but didn't see her. Then he looked toward her car and found her sitting behind the steering wheel with the engine running. He grinned and waved. She glanced away.

Garrett ran up to Michael. "Did you see me?"

"You were awesome, son."

"I was very impressed," Mary Lou said.

Garrett straightened, a big grin on his face. "I've been practicing."

"Tom and I would like to take you out for some ice cream."

"Can we go, Dad?"

"Sure," Michael said, feeling trapped into spending more time with Mary Lou and her husband.

Garrett and Tom walked ahead of Mary Lou and Michael. He was sure she'd maneuvered it that way. He could tell she had something on her mind.

She slowed her step. "I see that Rachel is back in your life. Do you think that's wise?"

"Rachel needed my help with Shaun and Amy."

"I don't want to see Garrett hurt by all this."

"I find your concern just a little late, Mary Lou."

She winced. "Let me say one more thing, then I'll keep quiet on the subject of Rachel. Think long and hard before you fall in love with her again. Has anything really changed with her? Can she stay in Magnolia Blossom? I can't see you any other place but here. Do you want a repeat of ten years ago?"

He ran his hand through his hair and massaged the back of his neck. He was very aware that Rachel wouldn't make a commitment or settle down in Magnolia Blossom. That was why he was protecting his heart against her. The kiss had been a lapse in good judgment. That was all.

Sheltered under the overhang, Rachel stood at the back of the riverboat and watched the rain fall in gray sheets. A thin layer of perspiration blanketed her whole body as she inhaled air laced with the clean, fresh smell of a summer shower.

It had been almost two weeks since the baseball game, and life moved forward, Rachel thought, peering over her shoulder at the beehive of activity in the main salon. The sound of an electric saw and hammering dueled with the sound of the falling rain.

She hadn't seen Michael much since the game and she never saw him alone, which she suspected he arranged purposely. She welcomed the crowd of people who demanded his time. She was able to come to the boat, supervise the renovation of the kitchen, which was progressing nicely, and leave with her emotions intact. It couldn't have worked out better if she had planned it.

"I love to look at the river when it rains, to listen to it hit the water. Soothing. Calming. Something I need right now."

At the sound of Michael's voice, Rachel closed her eyes for a few seconds, realizing her reprieve had ended.

He came to the railing and leaned back against it, facing her, one corner of his mouth lifting in a smile. "I need a break. I've been so involved in these renovations that I feel like I'm meeting myself coming and going."

"There does seem to be a lot going on around here these days."

"I wanted the boat ready before the end of summer. I think I'll get my wish, but at what price?"

"Why the push? You've had the boat for years."

"You know me. When I get something into my head, I don't like to wait." He crossed his arms over his chest, his back against a post.

"I feel the same way. That's why I've been on pins and needles waiting to hear from the investors about my restaurant." She realized she had brought up the subject of her restaurant as a reminder to him—and herself— that her stay in Magnolia Blossom was temporary.

Michael's expression went neutral, and a subtle tension sharpened the air between them like the atmosphere right before a storm. "When do you expect to hear?"

"Within the month. A couple of them are out of the country right now."

"What do you think your chances are?"

"Good."

"Then you'll leave?"

"Yes." Thunder sounded in the distance, and Rachel jumped. The tension between them had honed her nerves to a keen edge.

"Looks like the weather is taking a turn for the worse." Michael faced the same direction as she did, his arm brushing hers.

The casual contact sent a jolt through her as if lightning had struck her body. "How are things going with you and Mary Lou?"

Michael sighed. "We had another big discussion about Garrett. It didn't go well."

For a few seconds his emotions lay exposed. She placed her hand over his on the railing, wanting to comfort and give something to him. He had given her so much.

"Does Garrett know you two are arguing about custody?"

"I haven't told him yet. I didn't want to fight a legal battle over him, but I don't trust Mary Lou." He stared at the rain, the weather a reflection of his mood. He hadn't intended to come out on deck and talk with Rachel, but before he'd realized it, his feet had taken him to her and his mouth had opened and spoken.

"You won't be able to keep this from him for long."

"So I guess we both have secrets we're keeping from our families," he said with a bitter edge to his voice.

"I've decided to tell Amy and Shaun soon, even if I haven't heard from my lawyer about the restaurant proposal."

"When?"

"After her birthday next week. I don't like keeping secrets. You were right."

"Which is your way of saying I'd better tell Garrett about what's going on?"

"He doesn't realize what really happened when

Mary Lou left, does he? He doesn't know about her drinking problem?"

"He was too young. I could never disillusion him by telling him the truth about his mother. I'm not putting my son in the middle of this."

"But aren't you doing that with this custody battle? Maybe Mary Lou has changed. Is she drinking any-more?"

"She says no, not for a year."

"But you don't believe her?"

He stiffened. "No—yes. I don't know, Rachel. I want to believe her. It would make things so much easier. She sees Garrett on a limited basis with me around."

"But not alone."

"No."

"What are you afraid of? That she will run away with him? Isn't her husband established with a medical practice in Jackson?"

"Mary Lou was always unpredictable."

"Contrary to you?"

Michael pressed his lips together and continued to stare at the gray sheets of rain. The sound on the water usually soothed him, but now he was wound so tightly he was afraid he would snap in two pieces. He let the silence between them lengthen, hoping that Rachel wouldn't pursue the topic of Mary Lou. He was all talked out.

"What are you going to do for Amy's birthday?" he finally asked.

"I'd like to organize a birthday party. What do you think?"

"It's worth a try. I'll even help you. You can have the party on the boat. A lot of the work has been done."

"Thanks. I want it to be a surprise."

"This from the woman who hates surprises?" Michael arched a brow.

"If it wasn't a surprise, I'm afraid she might not agree to me giving her one."

"Aren't things better between you?"

"A little, this past week. She actually had breakfast with me this morning."

"Speaking of breakfast, don't forget the pancake breakfast at the church. Amy is one of the organizers. Great way to be around your sister and help the youth group, too."

"I'll be there," Rachel said, realizing she would also be around Michael.

"We need more pancakes," Kevin called from the doorway of the church kitchen.

"Where are all these people coming from?" Rachel asked, stirring another batch together.

"They heard you were making the pancakes and they couldn't resist sampling your cooking, sugar." Helen flipped over some pancakes on the griddle.

"I'm not the only one. You're cooking, too."

"But, sugar, they've tasted my pancakes at the café. You're a mystery to them."

"Quit chatting, ladies, and get busy. You have a

hungry crowd out there in the parish hall." Michael slid another serving platter toward Helen.

Perspiration beaded Rachel's brow. "And this is for charity?" She felt like a piece of wilted lettuce.

"Yep. The youth group is raising money for their mission trip to Mexico," Michael said, then left the kitchen to give the full platter to a teenaged server.

Amy dashed in and grabbed another pitcher of orange juice. "Two more families just showed up. Kevin is seating them now."

"When you're through pouring the juice, we could use another cook." Rachel slid the mixing bowl to Helen. "We're running low on bacon."

"Be back in a sec."

Rachel stared at her sister as she slipped from the kitchen. "Did you hear that?"

"Yeah, she'll be back in a sec. What's wrong with that?"

"Nothing. It was actually said in a perfectly normal voice. I may needlepoint those words and frame them."

"There's only one problem with that. You don't needlepoint."

"True. But I could take it up."

Helen nearly choked on her laughter. "You sit still long enough to do something like that?"

"Do what?" Michael asked, coming up behind Rachel and snatching a piece of bacon.

She thwacked him playfully across the knuckles with a spatula.

"Ouch!"

"You have to wait like all the other workers until the paying customers have eaten."

"You wield a mean spatula, Rachel Peters."

"And you just remember that the next time you try to eat before it's your turn."

"Oh, look, what's Amy doing?" Michael pointed toward the door into the parish hall.

Rachel started to turn but stopped and whirled in time to see Michael snitching another piece of bacon. He had it halfway to his mouth when she said, "I'm ashamed of you, Michael Hunter. You're the youth director. What kind of example are you setting by taking that bacon?" The corners of her mouth twitched as she tried to suppress her laughter.

Michael hung his head and offered the piece to her. "It's hard to resist your cooking." He slanted a glance at her through lowered eyelashes, a sheepish look on his face. "I'll try to resist, but I can't promise anything."

Rachel rolled her eyes. "I don't want that bacon. You touched it, you have to eat it."

"Oh, really." His expression brightened. He popped the piece into his mouth, an impish grin gracing his face. "It's a sacrifice, but I'll do it."

"Will you two get back to work? We'll never get everyone served—at least not before lunch. And I have a café to run, customers who might want to see me before the end of the day." Helen stood with her hand on her waist, a lethal-looking spatula in her grasp.

Michael saluted. "Yes, ma'am." He grabbed another plate of pancakes and headed for the parish hall, whistling as he went.

That set the tone for the rest of the pancake breakfast. Even Amy relaxed and smiled more than usual. By the time Rachel mixed the last batch of pancakes, exhaustion clung to her, but it was a pleasant feeling. She leaned back against the counter and surveyed the kitchen. The scent of frying bacon and pancakes still laced the air. She felt at home. The sensation took her by surprise.

Kevin entered the kitchen with a tray full of dirty dishes. Amy followed with several empty platters stacked on top of each other. Their laughter filled the room with a warmth that heightened Rachel's sense of belonging.

"Okay, is it our time to eat?" Michael asked, bringing in more plates.

"Yes," Helen announced. "Everyone can grab some food. We'll clean up after we eat."

Several teenagers scrambled to be first in line for the remaining pancakes. Helen patiently doled them out. Kevin and Amy brought up the end of the line, taking their breakfast and following the rest of the youth group into the parish hall.

"There'd better be some left for us adults." Michael held up his plate.

"Don't you mean me?" Helen asked, slipping a stack of pancakes on his plate.

"No, I mean me."

Rachel laughed. "You two are giving me a head-ache."

When Helen, Michael and Rachel came out of the kitchen to sit with the youth group, Reverend Williams stood up. "This fund-raiser was a rousing success again this year. We owe it all to the hard work of everyone in this room. Having Rachel as one of our cooks was an added treat. I heard members would like to have another pancake breakfast next week. I never knew pancakes could be so delicious. Thank you all for making this a success."

Several teenagers glanced at Rachel. She blushed while applause erupted in the parish hall.

Michael leaned over and whispered, "Looks like you won the reverend's heart as well as the youth group's. Anytime you want to help me with this group, let me know."

"Sorry, I'll have to pass. The only hearts I need to win over are Shaun's and Amy's."

"Shaun's you have in the palm of your hand."

"But not my sister's," Rachel whispered. "Not yet, at least."

"Amy has volunteered to say the blessing." Reverend Williams sat while Amy came to the front of the room.

"Heavenly Father, bless this food we are about to eat and help provide for those who are less fortunate than we are. Guide us in our mission to spread Your word and show us how to reach out to those who need us. Amen."

Her sister's prayer filled Rachel with a sense of

peace. Amy's sincerity and generosity touched Rachel's heart. Even though she and Amy weren't getting along, her sister was a good person whose strong faith would help her adjust to any situation. That realization made Rachel wish her own faith was stronger. Then maybe she would be satisfied with her life. Rachel pushed away that idea. She just needed to get to New York and her dream of having her own restaurant.

Chapter Nine

"Yes, I understand. I'll be there August tenth to sign the papers," Rachel said, jotting a note on the pad next to the phone. "Thank you, Frank. This is wonderful news and sooner than I expected." She hung up, her hand lingering on the receiver.

Wonderful news? Then why wasn't she happier about getting the money for her restaurant? She should be jumping for joy. Instead, she was wondering how she was going to tell everyone the *good* news.

Amy's surprise birthday party was this evening on the riverboat. Rachel couldn't say anything until after that. She had a month before she had to be in New York to sign the papers, then a couple more weeks after that before she had to start the plans for the restaurant. She had some time. She would wait until the moment was right.

"Rachel, I'm leaving for the boat," Shaun called.

Taking her mug of coffee, she walked into the living

room. "I'll be down later. Did you get all the invitations delivered?"

"Yeah. She doesn't suspect a thing. She thinks she's coming to the boat to pick up Kevin after work. He told her that his car was having some problems."

She went with her brother onto the porch, taking a deep breath of the fresh air. "It's a good thing she's doing that summer arts workshop in Natchez or I don't know how we could have kept this quiet."

Rachel watched as Shaun rode his bike away from the house. He would be all right about the move, but that still left Amy. Sighing at the task ahead of her, Rachel took a sip of her coffee, then retrieved the mail from the box. As she entered the house, the phone rang. She hurried into the kitchen and snatched up the receiver.

Breathless, she said, "Hello."

"Rachel, it's your mother. I wanted to let you know I'll be coming to the States in a few weeks to testify before a congressional committee on funding for medical research. I thought I would stop in Magnolia Blossom and sign those papers."

Rachel sank onto the chair next to the phone, her hands trembling with anger. Her mother's life went on as if nothing was different, and she supposed, for her mother, it wasn't. She didn't have to worry about her children. That was Rachel's responsibility. It shouldn't be.

"Rachel? Are you there?"

"Yes, Mother."

"I won't be able to stay long because your father and

I are at a crucial time in our research. I wanted to take care of the legalities as soon as possible because I have no idea when I'll get back to the States."

Rachel's anger mounted. "How convenient for you that I'm here to take care of your children."

"You know it wouldn't be a good situation to have Amy and Shaun live here in our camp."

"For whom? You and Dad or Amy and Shaun?" Rachel's hand tightened around the receiver until her knuckles turned white.

"For everyone."

"Why did you have children, Mother? You certainly aren't around enough to know what is good for us. First Aunt Flora and now I will take care of *your* responsibilities."

"I thought you were okay about this?"

"How? Did you ever really talk to me about it?"

"I've got to go. The boat's leaving to go back upriver. We'll talk when I get to the States."

Before Rachel could say, "Don't bother," the line went dead.

Tears pooled in Rachel's eyes as she stared at the phone. She didn't understand where the tears were coming from. She had long ago given up crying over a situation that would never change. She and her siblings were a burden. She just hated having it confirmed again. Why was she still trying to have a relationship with her mother when it was obvious that wasn't going to happen?

"Rachel, where are you?" Helen called from the living room.

Rachel rubbed her hand across her wet cheeks, hoping to erase any evidence that she cared what her parents thought or did.

"There you are." Helen stood in the doorway into the kitchen, her eyes narrowing on Rachel. "You've been crying."

"No, I just got something in my eye." Rachel hurriedly stood.

"When you're ready to tell me, I'm all ears. Is it Michael?"

Rachel shook her head.

"Amy?"

Rachel turned and leaned against the counter, her hands grasping its edge. "You aren't going to let this go until I tell you?"

"Confession is good for the soul."

"I'm not ready yet." She had a hard time telling anyone that her parents had rejected her and wanted nothing to do with her, Amy or Shaun.

Helen threw up her hands. "Okay. I'll mind my own business."

"Now, that will be a first."

Helen glanced at all the food ready to go. "I'm sorry I'm late, but I got held up at the café." Helen picked up a box of food. "Here, the least I can do is help you load this into your car. I'm sure there's a lot to do at the boat. We only have a few hours left."

After Helen helped load the car, she followed Rachel to the pier. Michael came down to the landing and started carrying the boxes of food to the main salon.

"Where's Kevin?" Rachel asked after everything was on the boat.

"He went to pick up some of the kids," Michael said. "He didn't want a lot of cars near the landing. Do you have everything you need for the party?"

"All except Amy and her friends."

He stared at her, his gaze intent, probing. "Something's wrong. What is it?"

Her eyes widened. Michael had always had a sixth sense when it came to her moods. No matter how hard she tried to hide her feelings from him, he could tell. Rachel's teeth dug into her lower lip as she debated how much to tell him. She decided to reveal part of the problem. "I received a phone call from my mother today."

"Is she coming for Amy and Shaun?"

Rachel shook her head. "No, but she's coming to sign the papers Robert told her were necessary for me to be their guardian. She doesn't want them to live with her and Dad. Of course, this shouldn't come as a surprise. Amy would really protest that move, and the conditions my parents live in aren't the best." Her chest constricted, and her lungs burned.

Suddenly, she needed some fresh air. She escaped to the deck and took a deep breath. Michael's hands settled on her shoulders, and he drew her against him. He felt strong, capable—steady. He was a man who would never turn his back on his family. He would do anything for his child.

"Is there something else?" Michael asked, his fingers kneading the tightness in her shoulders.

She flinched and was glad he couldn't see her expression. She wasn't ready to share her good news about the restaurant deal. "Isn't that enough?"

"Are you going to tell Amy and Shaun about the call?"

"No, I don't want them to be hurt."

"Like you?"

"Yes, like me," she murmured, realizing she was finally speaking about her feelings concerning her parents.

Even Aunt Flora hadn't realized the depth of Rachel's despair over her parents' rejection. She'd always tried to put up a brave front when the subject of her parents had come up. She was tired of denying her hurt and anger. Over the past weeks Rachel's idea of family had shifted. It wasn't okay that her parents didn't have time for their children.

"The day my mother brought Amy and me to Aunt Flora's was one of the saddest days of my life. At the time I didn't realize that my aunt would be the best thing for Amy and me. All my life I had been shuffled from one place to the next, never able to make friends because I didn't stay in one place long enough. Then my mother left us with Aunt Flora, expecting us to settle down and be happy and content to make our home with her older sister. It never happened for me. I didn't know how to settle down. I had never learned how to." Tears cascaded down her cheeks.

Not saying a word, Michael continued to massage her tensed shoulders.

She knuckled her tears away, but they still flowed. "As a little girl I used to dream of the Ozzie and Harriet type of family, but I gave that dream up a long time ago. I'm not cut out to be part of a family like that."

He turned her to face him. "Why not?"

"Because I can't make that kind of commitment. You, of all people, should know that."

He took a handkerchief from his back pocket and wiped her tears from her face. "Then what do you plan on doing about Amy and Shaun?"

"What I'm doing now. I'll love them the best way I can and hope it's enough. I'm just not very good at this sort of thing."

"That's how I felt when Mary Lou left me to raise Garrett all by myself."

"Then there's hope. Look at you now. You're a great father. He adores you."

"But it wasn't easy."

"Is that why you're so angry that Mary Lou is back in Garrett's life?"

Surprise flashed in his eyes. "Yes, I think that's part of it. She wasn't around for six years and now she wants to waltz right back in and pick up where she left off without having done any of the hard work it takes to raise a child."

Rachel cupped his face with one hand and with the

other urged him closer to her until their mouths touched. His kiss was a gentle reminder of what kind of person he was. He was a good man who deserved a woman who could love him with no reservations, who could totally commit to him. Times like this she wished she could be that woman.

"You know, we're more alike than you and I ever thought, Rachel. For years after my mother died, I fought my feelings of abandonment. At six she was such an important part of my life that I couldn't understand why God took her away from me. I needed my mother. I was angry at God for a while. Then my father made me realize that my mother would never be gone as long as I could remember her. She was with God, and I would be reunited with her one day."

Rachel pulled back and stared into Michael's eyes, filled with a sadness she'd glimpsed from time to time. "But your mother never had a choice. Mine does. She chooses not to be a part of our lives. And you had your father to comfort you."

"Yes, but when I was six, none of that mattered. My mother was gone. I realize our situations are different, but the emotions are the same."

"And I made everything worse. I left you not six months after your father passed away. I'm sorry." She clenched his shoulders, hoping to convey in her touch how much she wished she hadn't hurt him all those years ago.

He blinked, erasing any evidence of sorrow. "My

point in telling you this is that you'll have to deal with your parents' abandonment or it will haunt you and influence everything you do."

"Is that experience talking?"

His nod was curt. "I'm still working on it."

"Because of me and Mary Lou."

"My dream was to put down roots here in Magnolia Blossom and raise a large family—the more children the merrier."

"Whereas I've always run from commitment because of my childhood."

The smile he gave her was mocking. "I guess we've handled our issues of abandonment differently. But, Rachel, praying has helped me through the rough times."

"Our guests are arriving," Helen announced from the doorway into the main salon.

Michael rested his forehead against Rachel's, his hands buried in her hair. "I know you'll do what's right for Amy and Shaun. They're lucky to have you for a sister. We'll talk some more later."

Rachel stepped away from the comfort of Michael's touch. She wished she had his kind of faith. She wished it were as simple as turning to God to erase the feelings churning inside her. Maybe praying could help her, too, Rachel thought, grasping on to a seed of hope and holding tight.

When Amy walked into the main salon thirty minutes later, Rachel realized all her hard work had been worth it. After her initial shock, Amy had a big grin on her face as her friends swarmed around her congratulating her. Rachel had never seen her sister so happy.

One of the teenagers cranked up the volume on the CD player, and the sounds of pop rock bounced off the walls. Rachel stood back from the group and watched her sister interact with her friends. None of Amy's hostility was evident, and Rachel wished it could be different between her and her sister.

"Do you want to dance?" Michael all but shouted in her ear.

"I never learned to dance."

"There's not much to it. You move to the beat. Anything goes." He tugged on her arms. "Come on. Besides, I bribed them to play a slow dance right about now."

The music changed to a soft melody that Rachel would have called music. Michael pulled her into his arms and began to move to the slow beat. Rachel locked her arms about his neck and allowed the rhythm to flow through her body as she swayed.

"See, this isn't so bad. We can carry on a conversation without shouting." He leaned back slightly to look at her. "I'd have thought you would have learned to dance by now."

"Never had the time."

"What have you been doing with your time besides cooking?"

"Not much else. Sometimes when I'm in a new place, I sightsee, sample the local foods, that sort of thing."

"Have you ever been serious about anyone?"

"No. I'm never in any one place long enough."

"You have been running fast. What's going to happen when life catches up with you?"

Rachel stiffened within the circle of Michael's arms. "It's not going to. I'm very good at evading."

When the music changed to a fast tempo, Rachel slipped from his embrace and made her way to the refreshment table.

Following her, Michael picked up a half sandwich and took a bite. "This is my dinner, I'm afraid."

"You didn't eat before?"

"When? I was too busy getting this place ready. Did you?"

"No, I was too busy getting the food ready."

"Michael, thank you for this party. I was so surprised." Amy gave him a kiss on the cheek.

"Actually, all I did was supply the place. Rachel did all the work. It was her idea."

"Thanks," Amy murmured in a less than enthusiastic voice. "In another year I'll be able to do anything I want. I'll be eighteen and won't have to answer to anyone."

Even though Amy spoke to Michael, Rachel knew the comments were directed at her. She had felt that very same way when she was seventeen. "Well, that may be true, but you still have a year to go."

Amy lifted her chin. "I know some seventeen-year-olds who are on their own."

Rachel regretted being pulled into Amy's argument.

She bit the inside of her cheeks to keep from saying anything. Michael gripped her hand and pulled her to his side, his support quietly conveyed.

"And how well are they doing?" Michael asked, squeezing Rachel's hand. "Striking out on your own is a big step."

"They're happy," the teenager declared, louder than necessary. "Kevin's friend Patrick has a job at the supermarket in Natchez. He has an apartment with two other guys. He's doing fine."

"Is that Patrick Johnson?" Michael asked.

Amy nodded.

"When I talked with his dad last week, he was worried about Patrick. He isn't going to finish high school because he has to work two jobs to pay the rent. He's thinking about moving back home."

Amy grabbed Kevin's hand. "Let's dance. This is our song."

Rachel watched the young couple move onto the dance floor. "Thank you, Michael. If I had said anything else, this boat would have been declared a war zone."

"There's trouble brewing."

"I know."

"Why don't you leave her in Magnolia Blossom? She can stay with me."

"No. I won't abandon her. She's had to deal with that one too many times. She'll adjust. Besides, Shaun, Amy and I are all we have. We're family."

Michael twisted to face her. "A month ago I wasn't sure you felt that way."

"I've always felt Amy and Shaun were my family."

"I think you knew it in your head but not your heart. Now, you know it in your heart."

The truth of his words hurt. She had run from the idea of a family most of her life. She couldn't run anymore. "We'd better take up our battle stations before some of these teenagers slip out of here for dark places on this boat."

For the next two hours Rachel stood by the door, feeling like a warden in a prison. She had to turn several couples away from exploring the boat. Another hour, and the party would be winding down, she thought, and began to relax until Helen scurried over to her.

"They're gone!" Helen declared in her melodramatic way.

"Who?"

"Amy and Kevin. They walked onto the deck to get some fresh air, which I've been letting the kids do. I've been keeping an eye on them. Well, I turned to speak with a young man, and that must have been when they slipped away. I can't find them on the deck."

Rachel tensed. "Do you think they left the boat?"

"No, Shaun and Garrett are playing on the lower deck by the gangplank. No one has gone past them. They're here somewhere."

"Where's Michael?" Rachel asked, worried that Amy would do something foolish and end up hurt. It wasn't that long ago that she had felt the tender emotions a first love produced. And look at the pain her relationship with Michael had caused both of them.

"He's coming."

Rachel looked beyond Helen and saw Michael striding toward her. Relief shimmered through her. "You know?"

"Let's check all the cabins first. I have the master key."

Fifteen minutes later she and Michael had opened and locked every cabin door on the second deck. They climbed to the upper level, Rachel's heart hammering faster each minute. As they walked by the wheelhouse, Rachel heard a noise. She stopped and pointed toward the door, which was slightly ajar.

Michael came up and whispered in her ear, "I'll handle this."

She shook her head. "She's my sister. I will."

Taking a deep, fortifying breath, Rachel slid back the wheelhouse door and stepped into the room. Silhouetted against the moonlight streaming through the large windows were Amy and Kevin, standing very close together. They were so intent on each other they didn't hear Rachel come in until she coughed. They jumped apart.

"Excuse me, Amy, but I believe some of your guests are starting to leave. You need to say goodbye to them." Rachel was amazed her voice was level and calm, because inside she quaked.

Amy didn't say a word but stomped past Rachel and

Michael, who was still standing outside the wheelhouse. Rachel was glad she couldn't read her sister's expression because she was sure Amy was furious. Rachel could tell by the rigid way her sister held herself as she left.

Michael came up behind Rachel and gripped her shoulders. "This, too, shall pass."

She sighed. "I hope so. Another reason I couldn't leave her here is that I don't want anyone else to have to deal with Amy's volatile emotions."

"That's being a teenager. Up one minute, down the next."

"Amy's issues go deeper than that."

He drew her against him and cradled her in his arms. Their strong feel dimmed her worries for a few seconds. She allowed herself to forget her troubles, to forget that she needed to tell Michael the restaurant deal had gone through. She would soon.

"How could you embarrass me like that?" Amy asked the next morning in the kitchen.

Surprised her sister was up so early, Rachel glanced up from reading the papers concerning her restaurant proposal, which her lawyer had faxed her. "It's called being a responsible chaperon."

Before Rachel had a chance to turn over the legal papers, Amy plopped down in the chair next to her, her gaze straying to the documents. "What's that?"

Rachel drew in a deep, calming breath. "Details about my restaurant deal in New York."

Amy scowled, her eyes narrowing on the pieces of paper as if she could ignite them with her gaze.

"The investors said yes. They want to meet with me in August. I'll sign the papers then."

"When were you going to tell us?" Amy's voice rose.

"I just found out yesterday myself."

Sleepy-eyed, Shaun shuffled into the kitchen. He halted, took one look at Amy and said, "I think I'll skip breakfast."

"Stay. This concerns you, too." Amy flexed her trembling hands. "When are *you* leaving?"

Rachel inhaled deep breaths that did nothing to calm her speeding heart. "Shaun and I will go to New York on August tenth so I can sign the papers while you're in Mexico on your mission trip. Then we'll return and pack up the house. I want both of you in New York by the start of school."

"I'm not going." Amy's pout descended.

"I can't. Garrett and I have a basketball clinic at school that week."

Both her sister and brother faced Rachel, accusations in their expressions. In that moment Rachel realized she would rather face an angry mob of strangers than her own angry family. "Shaun, don't you want to check out New York before you move there?"

"No." Tears welled into his eyes.

"I know you don't understand now—"

"You got that right," Amy interrupted, rising and putting an arm around her brother as though she would protect him from their older sister. "When were you going to discuss this with us like you promised? Right before you had to leave? The only reason you told us now is because I saw you reading those." She flipped her hand toward the papers in front of Rachel.

"I want us to be a family. We can't be one if we live in different cities." Rachel knew anything she said at the moment wouldn't really be heard by either one.

"Your idea of discussion is quite different from mine. You led Shaun and me to believe we might actually have a say in our own futures."

"I suppose I could go and sign the papers, Shaun, without you. That way you could still go to the basketball clinic."

"How big of you. We're staying come September." Amy shot the words back.

"We're a family. We do this together." After talking to her mother on the phone, she was more determined than ever to keep this family together. She wanted to give her siblings something she'd never had—a real home.

Amy took a step then another until she was only inches from Rachel. "I will not leave Magnolia Blossom. Ever." She brushed past Rachel and hurried out of the room.

The slam of Amy's door reverberated throughout the house like a gong. Rachel winced.

With tears streaming down his cheeks, Shaun yelled, "I'm not leaving, either." He, too, raced from the kitchen and slammed his bedroom door shut.

Rachel started to follow Amy and Shaun, but when she stood in the hallway, staring at the closed doors, she felt the wide rift between her and her siblings. She didn't know if she would ever be able to close it. She had to try. She would give them some time to calm down, then she would talk with each one and try to make them understand.

Rachel sat in the living room in the dark, trying to bring some order to her life. The whole day, her sister and brother had given her the cold shoulder. Neither had left their bedrooms, not even to eat. When she returned to New York, she was sure everything would settle down and her life would be like before—except she would be responsible for Amy and Shaun, and there would be a part of her left in Magnolia Blossom, the part that wished she could make a total commitment to Michael.

She had given Amy and Shaun time to digest her news. She needed to talk to them and get them to understand. She knocked on Shaun's door, then waited until he said to come in. He was at his computer, playing a game. He didn't look at her as she entered and sat on his bed behind him.

"We should talk about this." Rachel watched him kill a few aliens and wondered where she should begin.

When his man died, he switched the game off. "I don't want to leave Magnolia Blossom. My friends are all here. Garrett is the best friend a guy could have."

"I know. But my work is in New York, not here."

"Amy says you can cook anywhere."

She'd heard those words before—from Michael, years ago. "Yes, but I'll have my own restaurant. That's something I've been planning for ten years. It's one of my dreams. Do you have dreams, Shaun?"

His lower lip stuck out. "Yeah, I want to pitch a no-hitter."

"That dream is important to you. Well, my dream is important to me. You'll be able to make new friends in New York and you can come visit Magnolia Blossom and Garrett. He can come see you and you can show him all the neat things there are to do in New York. He'd probably love to see a Yankees game."

His lower lip quivered; tears pooled in his eyes. "I don't want to leave. I'm scared."

Rachel went to her brother and hugged him. "I know. Change is scary. But I want us to be a family, to be together, not separated. I love you, Shaun. Please give this a chance."

He leaned back, swiping the tears from his face. "I love you, Rachel."

"I promise you can come visit every summer. I know that Michael or Helen would love to have you."

He pulled away, straightening his shoulders. "Do you think I could see the Yankees play? They are one of my favorite teams."

"Sure, and when the Braves come to town, I have connections. I think I could get you in to meet the team."

"You can?"

"Yep, anything for my little brother." Rachel tousled his hair.

"I don't have to go away to school, do I?"

"Not unless you want to. There are plenty of good schools in New York City."

Shaun turned to his computer and began to play the game again.

"Don't stay up too late," Rachel said as she left Shaun's bedroom.

She halted in front of Amy's door, not really ready for the confrontation. She knocked, her heart beginning to beat faster. Her palms were damp as she lifted her hand to knock again. Nothing. She shouldn't be surprised. Amy was ignoring her, as usual, but they had to talk about this sometime.

Rachel eased the door open. The room was empty, and the window was wide-open. Panic began to nibble at the edges of her mind. Quickly she made a search of the house to assure herself that Amy wasn't around. She wasn't.

Rachel returned to her sister's bedroom and looked at the mess. Then she walked to the open window and stuck her head out. The drop to the ground was only four feet, and the bush under the sill was trampled. Amy was gone, and Rachel's panic burst forth. She knew in her heart that her sister had run away.

Chapter Ten

Rachel couldn't keep her hands from shaking as she punched in Michael's number. All she could think about was that her baby sister had run away—possibly with Kevin.

As soon as he picked up, she asked, "Michael, do you know where Amy is?"

"What's wrong?"

"She climbed out of her window tonight and is gone. I have no idea where she is and it's now an hour past her curfew." Rachel glanced at her watch as though that would change the time.

"Did you call Kevin?"

"Yes, he was the first person I called. He's not at home. His mother *thinks* that he's out with Amy." Rachel sat at the kitchen table, her legs too weak to support her.

"It's probably nothing. Amy has lost track of time before."

"You don't understand. My lawyer called yesterday morning. My restaurant deal came through, and Amy knows about it." Even to her own ears she heard the hysterical ring to her words.

"It did? And when were you going to tell me?"

The accusation in his voice cut deep. "I started to tell you last night, then Amy and Kevin were missing and the opportunity passed." Her voice sounded heavy with emotions she wished she could control, but Michael could always expose her feelings faster than anyone else.

"I see."

She heard the distance in his voice as though he were barricading his heart against her. "I'm scared. What if something happens to Amy?"

"I'll be over."

He hung up before Rachel could tell him no. She called him back, but there was no answer. She knew he was ignoring her. After the gentle tone of his voice at the end of the conversation, Rachel wasn't sure she could handle him showing up. Her control was fragile at best.

She placed a call to Helen. "Amy's gone. Do you have any idea where she would be? When she's been at work, have you heard her talking about a place she might go when she's upset?"

"No, sugar. I'll be over to help you look for her. Have you called the police?"

"Yes, but Henry said there wasn't much he could do since she is a runaway. He's doing some checking for me, but I just can't sit here waiting to hear something. I think she's with Kevin."

As she got off the phone with Helen, the doorbell rang. Not wanting to alarm Shaun, she hurried to answer it. He had finally gone to sleep at twelve, and she would prefer he didn't worry along with her.

Michael, with Garrett beside him, stood in the doorway, his appearance disheveled as if he had dropped everything and rushed over. She knew she'd awakened him, and he must have thrown on whatever was near at hand. His shirt didn't match his pants, but to her he looked wonderful. Against her better judgment she was glad he was here. She stepped to the side to allow him and Garrett into the house.

"Thanks for coming. I hate dragging you out at this hour, but—" Rachel swallowed hard. "I'm sure I'm worrying for nothing. She'll probably come strolling in here with some excuse that Kevin's car ran out of gas."

Michael turned to his son and said, "Why don't you go back to sleep in Shaun's room?"

"Is he still up?" Garrett asked Rachel.

"No. He finally went to bed an hour ago."

Garrett shuffled toward Shaun's bedroom. "I won't wake him."

After his son left, Michael combed his fingers through his mussed hair, then rubbed the back of his neck. "I've got a feeling Amy was serious when she told you she didn't want to leave Magnolia Blossom."

"Then where could she have gone?"

"We'll check some of the teen hangouts."

"We'll have to wait until Helen shows up and can stay here with Shaun and Garrett. Do you want some coffee until then? I know I woke you up."

"Sure." He walked with her to the kitchen. "How did Shaun take the news about the move?"

"Okay. He wasn't happy, but we talked about it."

"You realize when we do find her the situation will still be the same."

"Yes." Rachel poured him some coffee, trying to keep her hand steady as she gave him the cup. "I didn't want to break up the family, but since I've been waiting for her, I've been thinking. I guess I'll have to see if she can stay with someone here in Magnolia Blossom for her last year of high school."

"As I said before, she can always stay with Garrett and me."

"Thanks. I'd hoped that Amy and I would get to know each other all over again, but that doesn't look possible now."

"Rachel, it doesn't have to be like this. The option of you staying is always open."

The doorbell sounded again. Rachel used the excuse of answering it to avoid replying to Michael's statement. She was relieved to see Helen on the porch. Rachel pulled her into the house.

"I'm so glad you're here. Can you stay with Shaun and Garrett while Michael and I go look for Amy?"

"So you called Michael?"

"Yes. I thought she might have gone to see him."

"Sure, Rachel. Haven't you noticed whenever something goes wrong you call Michael? Who did you call first, him or me?"

"Not another word, Helen. I don't need you to play matchmaker now."

"You called Michael. Just as I suspected." Her smile was way too smug as she strode into the kitchen and greeted Michael.

"We're going to try the turnoff on Miller Road. I also thought the park and the bluff nearby. Any other places you can think of, Helen?" Michael asked, downing his coffee in several swallows.

"The dock at the end of the Old Farm Road, your riverboat."

"Helen, if Amy comes home, call me on my cell phone. I don't know when we'll be back." He put his hand on the small of Rachel's back to guide her toward the door.

The dim light of dawn grayed the landscape as Michael pulled his truck up to the bluff that overlooked the Mississippi River. "It doesn't look like anyone is here."

"Let's check around just to make sure. This is the last place. If she's not here, where is she?" Rachel felt weariness in every part of her body. The night had been long and unproductive, and she felt as though she'd lived through a month's worth of nights instead of one.

Michael turned, sliding his arm along the back of the seat. "Rachel, you may have to face the fact that she has left Magnolia Blossom."

"But she wanted to stay. That's what this is all about."

He opened his door. "We'll take a look."

Rachel heard the resignation in his voice and knew he thought searching the bluff was futile. But the alternative was going to Aunt Flora's and admitting defeat. She couldn't do that just yet. Right now she would give anything to find Amy safe and sound.

After making a careful inspection of the area, Rachel met Michael at the truck. The sun peered over the horizon, casting its rosy hues into the blue sky like long fingers reaching for something unattainable. The warm air smelled of grass and pine. Birds sang in the trees along the bluff as though there was nothing wrong in the world.

Rachel couldn't bring herself to open the truck door. "If Amy stays here, I've failed to keep the family together. I didn't realize how much that would bother me until now."

"You have been away for years. Why is it so important to you now?"

She flinched at the question that pierced her armor. "I don't want them to feel they have been totally abandoned by their family. I want them to feel that at least someone cares about them, especially now that Aunt Flora is gone."

"You're talking about your parents?"

"Yes. It's hard to accept that your mother and father don't want you around. I've been there. I wanted to make it better for Amy and Shaun."

"So you want to be their mother and father."

"I guess something like that."

"But you aren't. Be a sister to Amy, not a mother. Aunt Flora filled that position quite well. And sometimes no matter what we do we can't shield our loved ones from being hurt. Both Amy and Shaun have a strong faith. That will help them through this."

"But I don't? You've always had a way of getting right to the point."

"God is with them. He is with you. Your parents may have abandoned you, but God hasn't. You are never alone."

"I feel that way right now."

"Then maybe you need to turn to the Lord. Let God be there for you."

She wanted to. Something was missing in her life. She realized she needed help. "Let's go back to the house. I want to be there when Shaun wakes up so I can explain what happened."

Rachel remained silent on the ride to Aunt Flora's. She thought over what Michael had said to her. She knew she couldn't be her sister and brother's parent, that she couldn't erase what their mother and father had done to Amy and Shaun. She did feel she could ease the hurt, be there for them. But Amy wanted nothing from her. The gulf between them was as wide as the one between Michael and her. She was good at keeping people at a distance. She had learned from a master, her mother.

Lord, help me to reach Amy. I love her and want us to be a family. I don't know where to begin. Please guide me in what to do.

Shaun and Garrett came onto the porch when the truck pulled up. A troubled expression creased her brother's brow.

"No rest for the weary. I was hoping to shower and change before I had to talk to Shaun about Amy." Rachel climbed from the truck, feeling both physically and mentally exhausted.

"Helen told me Amy didn't come home last night. Where is she?" Shaun chewed on his lower lip, trying desperately not to show how worried he was.

But Rachel saw it in the lines that marked his young face, in the distressed tone of his voice. She placed an arm around his shoulders and guided him into the house. "That's true, Shaun. Amy's left, and we don't know where she is. Do you have any idea where she would have gone?"

He shook his head. "She doesn't tell me much, especially lately."

Rachel listed all the places Michael and she had searched. "Any other hangouts we didn't go to?"

Shaun snapped his fingers. "The church. She has gone there before when she was upset."

"It's worth a look. Rachel, why don't you stay here with Shaun? If she is there, I'll call."

"But I should come with—"

"Rachel, Shaun needs you," Michael said in a low voice. "He's worried about Amy. Your presence will help him. Let me check first."

While Michael headed for the door, Rachel proceeded into the kitchen. "Let's get some breakfast while we wait. Helen, do you want to stay?"

"Yes, sugar. I'll even help cook."

"No, you're a guest. Besides, cooking will take my mind off my troubles. You sit and entertain Shaun and Garrett."

Rachel immersed herself in the food preparation, fixing enough to feed an army. She kept mixing and cooking to take her mind off where Amy could be. What was she doing? Rachel remembered the impulsiveness of youth and the feeling of being invincible. The combination of those two things could get a person into trouble.

You are never alone. Michael's words came to mind. Rachel thought of this summer and how she had become involved in the church and in the town.

Oh, dear God, please let her be all right. I need You.

When the phone rang, Rachel grabbed the receiver so fast she was sure she surprised everyone in the kitchen. "Yes?"

"Rachel, she's here at the church," Michael said.

"I'll be there. Please keep her there." Rachel hung up before Michael could talk her out of coming. She had to see that her sister was all right with her own two eyes.

At the church she jumped from the car and rushed up the steps to the large double doors. If Amy hadn't wanted to stay, it would have been difficult for Michael to keep her. Rachel prayed he was able to persuade Amy to stick around because Rachel had been going out of her mind with worry about her baby sister.

Michael met her at the doors into the sanctuary. "She's sitting in the back. I'll make sure y'all have some privacy while you work this out."

"Did you talk to her?"

"Yes. She knew I was calling you."

"She did?"

"Actually, it was her idea. I think y'all need to talk."

"I've been trying to."

"She's ready now, Rachel."

The foreboding tone to his words made her apprehension mushroom. "What happened, Michael, to change her mind?"

"Just talk to her." He stepped to the side to let her pass.

When Rachel entered the sanctuary, she wasn't sure what to expect. She halted inside the doorway and searched the back pews for her sister. At first she thought Amy had fled despite what Michael had said. Then Rachel found her sister in the corner, sitting on the floor, looking forlorn. The ache in Rachel's heart expanded, constricting her breathing as she stared at Amy, lost and alone.

Her sister glanced up and saw her. A mutinous expression immediately descended on her face. Amy might be ready finally to talk, but Rachel knew this wouldn't be easy.

She walked over to her sister and sat cross-legged on the floor in front of her. "Are you all right?" She wanted to touch her, pull her into her arms and hug her. Her sister's expression forbade her to do any of those things. The ache in Rachel's chest sharpened.

"No." Tears shone in Amy's eyes, and she immediately blinked them away as though she was determined not to show any emotion to Rachel.

"What happened? Did someone hurt you?" Rachel forced her voice to remain calm while inside she was trembling so badly she had to clasp her hands together in her lap.

Amy laughed, the sound a bit hysterical. "You've hurt me, sister. Everything I care about is here in Magnolia Blossom, and you want me to leave it behind just like that." She snapped her fingers in front of Rachel's face. "I can't. And I don't know how to change that." Amy's voice cracked on the final sentence.

"I realize that Magnolia Blossom is important to you. I was wrong to try and force you to leave. I didn't want to break up the family, and I can't stay."

"Why not?"

Amy's chin tilted at that defiant angle that Rachel had come to expect. The need to be totally honest with Amy—with herself—engulfed Rachel. She scrubbed her hands down her face in weariness, the past twenty-four hours so emotionally draining that she had to labor to put two thoughts together. "I don't know how to explain this to you. It's a long story." I don't know if I can do this.

"Maybe you should tell me. Everyone needs someone." Concern erased Amy's defiant expression.

Rachel stared long and hard at her little sister and realized she needed to start taking emotional risks or there would be nothing left for her. She glanced at the altar and remembered she wasn't alone. Michael was right; God was with her. She could do this. Peace descended.

"Maybe you're right." Rachel sighed. "For sixteen years of my life when I lived with our parents, we moved once or twice a year. We never stayed long in any one place, so it was difficult establishing friendships and making any kind of commitment to anyone because I'm basically a shy person. Moving about was the pattern of life I got used to. With each new place I withdrew further into myself, scared to open up to others, to expose my feelings. Then I came to Magnolia Blossom and actually stayed here for two whole years."

"I wasn't that young that I don't remember some of the moving. I hated it."

"So did I at first, then I slowly learned to accept it as a way of life for myself. Moving around isn't all bad. I've been doing it for almost my whole life." Rachel couldn't even remember how many countries she had visited in the course of her twenty-eight years.

"But coming to Aunt Flora's changed things?"

"For a short time. I began to make friends. I fell in

love with Michael. But I got scared of the feelings he created in me. I didn't want to depend on anyone for my emotional well-being. To do that was to give him a great deal of power over me. I couldn't do that a second time in my life."

"You're referring to our parents?"

A lump lodged in Rachel's throat, and she nodded.

"So you ran."

"Yes, but I ran toward a dream I'd had for years." Rachel moistened her parched lips with the tip of her tongue, then swallowed several times to ease the tightness in her throat. "I've always wanted to be a chef and to have my own restaurant."

"You are a famous chef."

"I'm getting there. This deal in New York for my own restaurant was just another part of my dream coming true."

"Sometimes dreams we have when we are young aren't right for us when we get older."

Rachel smiled, feeling every bit of her twenty-eight years. "When did you get to be so smart?"

"Aunt Flora's influence."

"Then our parents probably did the right thing leaving us with her."

The tears returned to sparkle in Amy's eyes. "But I'm the reason they left us with Aunt Flora. I'm the reason they abandoned us."

Rachel reached out and touched her sister's arm. Finally, and for the first time since she had come home, she felt there really was hope for her and Amy. "How can you say that?"

"Remember that day I wandered from camp and almost died? It wasn't a week later that our mother brought us to Aunt Flora."

Rachel drew Amy into her arms and stroked her hair, the ache within easing. For all these years her sister had carried that burden inside of her. "It wasn't you that was to blame. It was me."

Amy pulled back, tears streaking down her cheeks. "No, Rachel, you're wrong."

"I was supposed to be watching you. I should have done a better job of it. You could have drowned in the ocean if our father hadn't seen you."

"I sneaked off because I wanted to explore on my own. You aren't to blame."

Rachel brushed Amy's tears away with the pad of her thumb. "Let's make a deal. Let's decide that neither one of us was to blame. It was an accident. Accidents happen."

"Then you don't blame me for what happened?"

"Heavens, no. I never did. I love you. That won't ever change. We are a family. We'll stick together no matter what."

Her sister smiled, the moisture in her eyes making them glisten. "Yeah, we are a family, aren't we?"

"You bet." Rachel took her sister's hand. "Now, can you tell me what happened after you left last night?"

Amy took a long breath. "Okay. After I left the house, I walked to Kevin's. We came here to be alone and pray. He was the one who talked me out of running away."

Rachel squeezed her sister's hand. "I did a lot of thinking last night, and I think you should stay here in Magnolia Blossom. I know now that I can't take you away from your friends the last year you're in high school. You and I are a lot alike, but we are different, too. I couldn't see what I was doing to you because I have no reference to those kind of feelings. I kept telling myself I wanted the family to stick together above anything else, that you and Shaun would adjust because I always had."

"Who would I stay with?"

"Michael offered, and I'm sure Helen would. Of course, you might have a friend you could stay with."

Amy grinned. "You mean it?"

"Yes. I hope, though, you'll come visit Shaun and me in New York during school vacations."

"I've always wanted to go to a Broadway show."

"Then that's what we'll do." Rachel stood and offered her hand to her sister. "I'll be busy with the restaurant, but for you I'll make the time." Rachel put her arm around Amy as they headed for the door.

Before leaving, Rachel turned and stared at the altar. Light from the ceiling shone on the cross. Michael's words whispered through her mind. *Let God be there for you.*

Could she open her heart totally and let God inside? She realized that until she did she would have a hard time allowing anyone else in. Tears glistened in her eyes. *Heavenly Father, I have avoided making any kind of commitment. I have run from people all my life. Help me to open myself to Your love. Help me to love.*

"If your dream is to have your own restaurant, Rachel, why don't you open one here or in Natchez? You're willing to settle down in New York, why not Magnolia Blossom?" Amy asked as she pushed the door open.

"In New York I can get lost in a crowd. In Magnolia Blossom everyone knows when I sneeze," Rachel quipped, stating her usual argument against staying.

"Is that the only reason?"

Pausing on the steps, Rachel regarded Amy. She searched the area for Michael, but he was gone, driven away by her. She remembered his wariness about trusting her again. "The bottom line is that I couldn't stay here and be around Michael and not be a part of his life. I don't know if I can be what he wants or give him the family he deserves, but it would kill me to see him with another woman."

"Why does it have to be another woman?"

She didn't answer her sister's last question, but Rachel couldn't get it out of her mind on the drive to the house. In her profession she had taken one risk after another, but in her personal life she hadn't even taken one chance. Speaking to Amy honestly had been a small first step.

Shaun flew out the screen door and down the stairs when they pulled into the driveway. He threw his arms around Amy's waist. "You're okay."

"Of course, shrimp. What did you think?"

"That you ran away. That I'd never see you again."

"And leave you? No way. My main goal in life is to make yours miserable."

"Yeah, well, I want that CD you borrowed back."

Rachel followed the pair into the house, listening to them bicker. This was what family was all about. She didn't realize how much she needed this until she'd almost lost it. Could she take another risk on Michael?

Chapter Eleven

"Okay. Who sprayed me?" Whirling, Amy put her hands on her hips and looked for the culprit.

No one said a word.

With water dripping off her, Amy sighed, swiping her wet hair out of her eyes. "Kevin Robert Sinclair, I can tell it was you."

Kevin lifted his shoulders. "How?"

"You're still holding the hose."

The eight other teenagers laughed.

"She caught you red-handed, Kev," one of the boys said.

Kevin arranged his features into an innocent expression. "I thought you might be getting hot, so I was cooling you off. That's what friends do for each other."

Amy grinned. "Gee, thanks. Let me return the favor."

Rachel stepped over to Michael and whispered, "You better do something fast or they'll never get these cars finished. Six people are waiting. Thank goodness they're patient. Of course, they're parents, so they have to be."

Michael surveyed the cars lined up in the church parking lot. "Who said parents are necessarily patient?"

"Isn't that written down somewhere?"

"In your dreams."

Amy marched over to Kevin and held out her hand for the hose. The boy reluctantly passed it to her, but his hands remained around it. A tug-of-war began, with water spewing everywhere.

"You're her sister. Do something." Michael moved away from the group to keep from getting wet.

Rachel headed for the teens by the black sedan. Over her shoulder she said, "Chicken. I agreed to help because you said this would be a piece of cake."

"You agreed to help because I promised you ice cream afterward."

Michael watched Rachel step into the melee and wrestle the hose from Kevin and Amy. Thoroughly wet, Rachel proceeded to spray both of them.

"I'll control the water from now on, children. Chuck, put that other hose up. If any of you get out of line, you get sprayed. Let's get back to work before these good people make us pay them for the privilege of washing their cars. Remember, this is a fund-raiser for your mission trip. If no cars are washed, no money is made."

There were a few good-natured grumblings as the teens went back to work.

"I'm impressed, Rachel," Michael said with a chuckle. "You could be a drill sergeant with the best of them."

"My training is finally coming in handy. You ought to see me manage a kitchen full of temperamental chefs. There were times I wished I had a hose to cool them off."

"You and Amy certainly seem to be getting along."

A grin lifted the corners of her mouth. "Yeah. Since she ran away and we had that talk, things are so much better. Thanks for all your help. I'm not sure we would be where we are without it."

"Sure you would. Has she decided who she's going to stay with this next year?"

"Not yet. She's having a tough time deciding between you and Helen," Rachel said, a wistful tone in her voice. She still wished Amy would come with Shaun and her to New York in the fall, but she wouldn't say anything else to her sister. Amy knew how Rachel felt without her adding pressure.

"But you wish she was moving to New York?"

"You bet. I'll miss her. So will Shaun. I know she's gonna come visit during her school vacations, but it won't be the same."

"That was a tough decision for you to make."

"Yes." Rachel moved to the next car and rinsed it off so the teenagers could soap it down. "I'm still hoping I can convince her to come live with Shaun and me after high school. But it will be her decision."

"It wasn't that long ago you felt differently. I'm glad you changed your mind."

Rachel shot him a frown. "People can change, Michael." She sprayed another car, then stepped back to let the youths do their job.

"Maybe."

"You don't think people change?"

"Of course, they can change—if they want to badly enough. But that's the key. Do they really want to? Or are they fooling themselves and others into thinking they do, then revert back to their old ways the first time things get rough?"

"Chuck, will you take over with the hose?" Rachel asked, handing it to the nearest teenager.

"Yes."

When a gleam of mischief entered the tall boy's eyes, Rachel added, "And only spray the cars?"

The gleam vanished. "Yes, ma'am."

After Chuck took the hose and headed toward the next car in line, Rachel faced Michael, her back to the crowd in the parking lot. "Okay. What's going on, Michael? What are you afraid of?"

"What makes you think I'm afraid of anything?"

"Oh, maybe the fact you're not looking at me."

He directed his gaze to her. "I thought at least one of us should keep an eye on the kids. I can't believe you gave Chuck the hose."

"And I can't believe you're changing the subject on me. Besides, I'm all wet, so what's the worst he could do to me? Now you, on the other hand—"

"Why do you think I'm watching the young man? I would like to remain dry."

"Okay. Enough chitchat. What's going on, Michael?"

"Mary Lou has contacted a lawyer concerning custody and visitation rights. She wants equal say in raising Garrett. I don't think I'll be able to avoid a fight."

"And what do you want?"

He stabbed her with an intense look. "Frankly, I want Mary Lou out of Garrett's life."

Shocked, Rachel gasped. "You usually don't judge people so harshly."

"I don't trust her. It wasn't that long ago that she was drunk a good part of the day and could care less that Garrett was in the next room crying for her. That's not something I'll forget."

"Or forgive?"

"Yes." Michael clamped his jaws together, flexing his hands then curling them into a tight ball at his side.

"Is she drinking now?"

"No—or so she claims. She belongs to AA. She says all the right things, but I don't trust her."

Pain and anger laced his words. Rachel's throat constricted. "You suggested I should turn to the Lord for guidance concerning Amy. Maybe you should turn to the Lord about Mary Lou. If she has truly changed, don't you think she deserves a second chance? Don't you think Garrett deserves a mother? How does Garrett feel about all this?"

"He doesn't know what's happening between Mary

Lou and me. I haven't told him. I don't know how." Michael raked his hand through his hair, staring over Rachel's shoulder, a scowl knitting his brow.

She could tell he wasn't really looking at anything but was lost in his own thoughts. He was hurting, and she wished she could do something to help him. "Remember your advice to me? That I should tell Shaun and Amy about my decision as soon as possible? Well, I wouldn't keep this from Garrett for too long. He should hear it from you, not someone else. You know how small towns are. He'll hear it from someone."

Michael closed his eyes for a few seconds. "Yes, I know. He's been bugging me about spending the weekend with Mary Lou. They have a boat, and he wants to go skiing."

"And you don't want him to be alone with Mary Lou?"

"Yeah. I trust people totally until they give me a reason not to, then I find it hard to give my trust again."

The tightness in her throat expanded. She swallowed several times. They could be speaking about their relationship. Ten years ago he'd felt she had betrayed his love.

A shriek erupted behind Rachel. She jumped and nearly bumped into Michael.

He steadied her, then headed for the youths. "Now you'll see why Chuck was the last person to give the hose to."

There was one car left in the parking lot. The tall boy

wet it down, then turned the water on the girl next to him. She took the bucket of soapy water she held and dumped it over Chuck, who proceeded to chase her with the hose. Thankfully, the last car was cleaned before a full water war erupted in the parking lot. Rachel backed away and watched, still troubled by her conversation with Michael.

He came to stand beside her. "I guess this is one way to beat the summer heat."

"Does this happen often?" Rachel asked while Amy produced the hose Chuck had put away earlier.

"Let's just say these guys know how to enjoy themselves."

"How many car washes have you had?"

"Oh, five or six in the past few years."

Suddenly Rachel noticed the quiet. She looked toward the teens, all drenched from head to toe, all staring at her and Michael with silly grins on their faces. She didn't trust her sister's impish expression, nor the fact that Amy whispered something to Kevin who in turn whispered something to the petite young woman next to him. Quickly, whatever Amy had come up with spread to the whole group.

"I think we may be in trouble," Rachel murmured, sliding a step closer to Michael.

"I think you're right. Run," Michael said the second the teenagers started toward them.

The hoses were turned on Rachel and Michael. They didn't get three feet before they were drenched.

Laughter bubbled up inside Rachel while Michael tried to wrestle the hose from the teen nearest him. Finally, he managed to capture it.

"Scatter," Amy shouted to the group.

Before Rachel could blink the water from her eyes and flip her wet hair out of her face, the parking lot was deserted. Michael stood ready to do battle with no one to fight. He glanced at Rachel. The gleam dancing in his eyes warned her she was his next target. She backed away, scanning the area for the second hose. It lay five feet away—five *long* feet away.

Rachel dove for the hose and got hit with a spray of water. "You won't get away with that." She grasped the hose and aimed it toward Michael, squeezing the handle on the nozzle. Water dribbled out.

Michael laughed. "I won't? Looks like I might." He blasted her with the full force of the hose.

Rachel peered toward the building and saw Amy push Kevin out of the way then turn the faucet on before hurrying to the one that controlled the flow to Michael's hose. Rachel pressed her handle down and fired water at Michael at the same time Amy managed to shut off his flow, leaving him at Rachel's mercy. She covered him with water from top to bottom. Exasperated because his hose didn't work, he tossed it down and rushed her.

Rachel saw his intent, screamed, threw her hose down and ran for the church. As she wrenched the door open, she heard the giggles of the teens nearby, then the sound of Michael's pursuit. Inside the building she frantically searched for a place to hide.

Before she could move toward the ladies' rest room down the long hallway, Michael captured her. "Now I know where Amy gets her playfulness." He swung her around.

"Uncle. Uncle."

"But I haven't done anything."

"But you're thinking about it. I can tell." Rachel shivered in the coolness of the air-conditioned entrance. "Admit it."

Michael released his hold on her. "The thought did cross my mind—but only briefly."

"Sure. And pigs fly."

"Rachel Peters, are you mocking me?"

"Never." She skirted him, keeping several feet between them. "I need to thank Amy for her help."

"And I thought Amy was a friend."

"She is, but she's my sister," Rachel said over her shoulder as she went outside. Pride swelled her chest at the thought that she and Amy were finally truly sisters.

While she and Michael had been in the building, the teenagers had returned to the parking lot and begun cleaning up their mess. Rachel stopped dead in her tracks, amazed.

"You've done well, Michael. I thought you and I would have to clean this up."

"Well, thank you, ma'am. I'll accept that compliment."

When everything was put away, Amy came to Rachel and Michael. "Are y'all coming with us to get some ice cream?"

"Of course. That's the only reason I agreed to help today." Rachel gestured toward her wet clothes. "But what do we do about these?"

"Nothing. We can get our ice cream and eat outside at the picnic tables," Amy said, walking toward Carol's Sundries, halfway down the block from the church.

Michael and Rachel fell in behind the group of teenagers. Again, she felt that Amy was planning something. Whispers flew among the youths with a few knowing glances thrown toward Michael and her.

"There isn't anything they could do at Carol's Sundries, is there?" Rachel asked when Amy smiled at her.

Michael took a moment to answer. "I don't think so, but your sister is definitely up to something. The last time, I got drenched."

"We'd better be alert, then."

After Rachel and Michael got their ice cream cones, they left the shop to sit at the picnic tables across the street in the park. There was nowhere to sit except at a lone table under a live oak. The teenagers lounged all over the benches of the three tables clustered together, leaving no room for Michael and her.

Rachel smiled sweetly at Amy and marched to the lone table. "Now we know what she was planning."

"I think Helen is rubbing off on her," Michael grumbled and sat across from Rachel.

"Do you think? That's all Magnolia Blossom needs is another matchmaker."

Michael's expression went neutral. He concentrated on eating his chocolate ice-cream cone.

"Does that bother you?" Rachel asked, taking a lick of her peppermint ice cream.

He shrugged. "If she wants to waste her time, that's fine by me."

"Yeah, we're just friends."

Rachel slid her gaze away, afraid her feelings were reflected in her eyes. She shouldn't feel hurt, but she did. When had she wanted there to be more than friendship between her and Michael? She was leaving, which made it an impossible situation. She had a restaurant deal in New York waiting for her. She had a life outside Magnolia Blossom. She wasn't good at making commitments to others. She had little practice.

But while she ran through all the reasons it would never work between her and Michael, she kept thinking she wished that wasn't so. Would it be so bad if she postponed going to New York for a year to see what developed between them? That way Amy, Shaun and she would be able to stay together. Her restaurant deal could be renegotiated later.

"Yuck! I don't see why I have to go to this dumb play. Boys don't see *Romeo and Juliet*. It's for girls." Garrett squirmed in his seat in the back of the car.

Michael pulled into Rachel's driveway. "The last

time I checked, I'm male, and I'm looking forward to the play tonight. Amy is playing the lead, and she's a friend of ours."

"I have one thing to say. Yuck!"

"Well, then please keep your opinions to yourself. I don't want to do anything to ruin Amy's big night." Michael opened the car door. "You stay here. I'll go get Rachel and Shaun."

As he closed the door, he heard his son say, "Yuck! Yuck! Yuck!"

In the past Michael had been relatively assured that Garrett would behave himself at functions like the one they were attending. But lately he wasn't so sure. Garrett was angry a lot of the time. When Mary Lou came back into their lives, Garrett changed. All the more reason to fight her on the custody issue. She wasn't a good influence on Garrett.

Before Michael could ring the bell, the door flew open, and Shaun raced outside.

"He's faster than a speeding bullet," Rachel said from the entryway. She gathered her purse and stepped onto the porch. "He's been complaining about the play, but the second you pulled up to the house he made a mad dash for the door. Do children ever make any sense?"

Michael looked toward his car, the light from the dome illuminating his child's surly features. "Nope. The day we think we have them figured out is the day they are guaranteed to change again." He opened the door for Rachel, then rounded the front and slid in behind the wheel.

"And if I hear another negative word about this play from either one of you, we'll just come home afterward instead of going out to eat. I'll fix you both one of my specialties." Rachel flashed Michael a grin. "Let's see. If I remember correctly, the boys haven't tried snails. I think it would be a good opportunity to expand their palate. What do you think, Michael?"

"Sounds good to me."

"We don't have any snails," Shaun said from the back seat.

"I could go out in the yard and hunt some down." Michael threw the car into reverse and pulled out of the driveway.

"You wouldn't!" Garrett exclaimed.

"I think I saw something slimy out in our backyard the other day."

"Those were slugs, Dad. Yuck! Yuck!"

"That seems to be his favorite word lately," Michael whispered to Rachel, then said, "this is Amy's night. Be good, boys."

During the short drive to Natchez, Shaun and Garrett were unusually quiet. Rachel felt pinpricks in the back of her head, as though they were staring holes through her. Despite the boys' reluctance concerning the play, she was looking forward to this evening, not because Amy was performing, but because when Michael asked Rachel if she would like to go with him, it felt as if he was asking her out on a date—a crowded date with two young boys as chaperons but a date nonetheless.

At the community theater in Natchez, Michael led them to their seats. While Rachel settled down to watch *Romeo and Juliet,* the two boys wiggled and whispered to each other until she had to intervene and threaten extended grounding. Finally, in the second act, they calmed down, and Shaun fell asleep.

By the time the performance was over, Rachel was in awe of her sister's acting ability. She knew the story, had seen it performed in London by the Royal Shakespearean Company, but watching Amy in the part of Juliet made her realize what talent her sister had. Amy definitely needed to be exposed to Broadway and the theater in New York City.

Everyone crowded around Amy backstage after the play. Rachel's gaze sought Michael's as though it had a will of its own. While the group parted to let Amy see them, Rachel felt trapped by Michael's intense look, a look that told her she was missing out on life, that she was throwing away the best thing she could ever have by leaving Magnolia Blossom.

"What did y'all think?" Amy asked, her eyes alight with happiness.

"You were nothing short of brilliant. Where did you learn to act like that?" Rachel asked, her smile attesting to how proud she was of her sister.

Amy shrugged, suddenly embarrassed. "I just like to pretend."

Kevin came up next to her and took her hand. "Are you ready?"

"Hey, little brother, would you and Garrett like to go get hamburgers with Kevin and me?"

Rachel winced when she heard Amy name a fast food chain. "I was thinking we could celebrate at—"

Amy waved her hand in the air and laughed. "Don't worry, sis. I don't expect you to eat there. Kevin and I made a reservation for you and Michael at one of the plantations in town."

"But—"

"I hear the food is great. Since when would a chef pass up an opportunity to eat good food?"

"This is your evening. We're celebrating your play."

"And I want a hamburger. We're meeting some other kids there."

Michael arched a brow. "And you are voluntarily taking your brother and Garrett?"

Amy grinned. "They'll behave. I can't see them eating in a fancy restaurant after sitting through the play. I thought I would reward them for coming."

Rachel narrowed her eyes. "You're just too good to be true. It's not going to work."

"Sure it is." Amy checked her watch. "You have fifteen minutes to get there. Come on, Garrett and Shaun. You two better not give me a bit of trouble or y'all will be walking back to Magnolia Blossom."

"Amy!" Rachel exclaimed, ready to snatch the two boys back.

Amy glanced over her shoulder and winked. "Just kidding. Have fun."

As everyone filed out of the community theater, Michael whispered close to Rachel's ear, "I think we've been had."

"I think you're right. We can always go back to Magnolia Blossom. I think Southern Delight is still open."

"No. Your sister went to a lot of trouble to plan this. I wouldn't want to ruin this evening for her."

"And she's right. I would like to sample the food at this restaurant."

"Then we'd better get going."

Michael touched the small of her back as he guided her to his parked car. The light feel of his fingers sent a tingling sensation up her spine. Now tonight felt like a real date. She knew she would need to say something to Amy tomorrow about trying to match her and Michael, but for the rest of the evening Rachel intended to enjoy herself.

At the plantation house they were shown to a table set for two in a dark, secluded alcove. They each ordered something different so they could sample each other's dishes. When Michael held up his fork, Rachel leaned forward to taste the steak speared on it. The intimate gesture of sharing their meals heightened her awareness of the man sitting next to her. His clean, fresh scent surrounded her and pushed all other delicious aromas away. His deep, masculine voice centered her full attention on him while they discussed the renovations on the riverboat.

"So, do you have a chef for the restaurant?"

"No. I've interviewed several but haven't made up my mind yet. Maybe you could help me decide."

"Possibly," Rachel said, stirring some sugar into her after-dinner coffee.

"I'm leaning toward a young woman who's working in New Orleans right now. I think she's got a lot of possibility. She wants to strike out on her own."

A seed of jealously swamped Rachel, the sudden feeling disconcerting. She busied herself by taking several sips of her coffee while she wrestled with an emotion she had no right to feel. "Has she ever run a kitchen before?"

"No, but I like to give people a chance to grow. And she seems quite loyal. She's been at her present place for four years. She doesn't move around a lot. I like that."

His words held a hidden rebuke, directed at Rachel. He hadn't really forgiven her for what had happened ten years before. Loyalty had always been important to Michael. It went hand in hand with trust.

She took another swallow of her coffee to ease the constriction in her throat. "I'd be glad to help any way I can."

His gaze snared hers. "Then I'll set up a time for you to meet the applicants."

Candlelight danced in his eyes, drawing her in. For a few seconds she fought the desire to tell him she would be his chef. Then she remembered her plans and his earlier comment about trust and loyalty. She realized she loved him, always had, but could she make the kind of commitment he deserved?

"Well, what do you think, Rachel?" Michael sat at a table in the riverboat's newly redecorated dining room.

"I have to agree she has possibilities as a chef," Rachel said, shifting in her chair next to him.

"But?"

"But I'm concerned about her management skills. You'll need someone who can run your kitchen as well as be a good cook."

He tossed the pencil he'd been taking notes with onto the wooden table. "And Paul Fontaine earlier?"

"His experience is with making desserts, not entrées."

Michael rose and began to pace. "There's only one more I'm interested in. Marcus Davenport couldn't come till tomorrow."

"Then I'll be back. What time?"

"One."

"Good. I can oversee the final touches to the kitchen and sit in on your interview with Mr. Davenport."

Michael continued to walk from one end of the dining room to the other. Rachel could understand his uneasiness over hiring a chef, but something else was making Michael as restless as a caged animal.

"Michael, you're exhausting me. Sit. Tell me what else is wrong."

He didn't stop pacing. "I got served with the papers today."

"But you knew Mary Lou was going to go to court."

"Yeah, but I kept hoping she would tire and go away. Leave us alone."

"Have you told Garrett yet?"

He came to a halt a few feet in front of her. "No. I will tonight. If I don't, Mary Lou will."

"You and Garrett have a good relationship. He'll understand. Are you going to tell him about Mary Lou's drinking?"

Michael scowled. "I can't. He's not even eight yet."

"Then what are you going to tell him?"

He ran his hand through his hair repeatedly. "I'll think of something. I don't have any choice. I have to tell him now."

"Remember what you told me about God being with me. It's the same for you. The Lord is here to guide you, Michael."

"Right now I feel very alone," he murmured, his shoulders sagging as if he had the weight of the world bearing down on him.

Rachel stood and reached out to lay a comforting hand on his arm. Her cell phone rang. She touched Michael, intending to ignore the call. The jingle sounded again in the quiet.

"Please answer it," Michael muttered and stepped away from her.

She flipped open her phone. "Yes?"

"Rachel," Amy said in a tense voice. "You've got to come home now. Mom's here, and she wants us to pack."

Chapter Twelve

Rachel slammed on the brakes, jumped from the car and raced up the steps of Aunt Flora's house. Her heart hammered against her chest as she thrust open the front door and entered. She came to a halt halfway into the living room. Amy and Shaun sat on the couch, facing their mother, who stood by the fireplace, tall, stiff, frowning.

Shaun leaped to his feet and launched himself at Rachel. "I'm so glad you're home." His arms went around her.

Rachel placed her hand on his back and patted him. "Everything will be okay," she whispered, then looked at her mother. "Hello, Mother. This is a surprise."

"It shouldn't be. I told you I was coming."

Rachel walked with Shaun to the couch and waited until he was seated before facing their mother. "No, the surprise is the part about Amy and Shaun packing their bags."

Her mother's tanned features were pinched together in a deep frown. "Weren't you the one who a few weeks ago brought me to task for not doing my duty by my children? I'm here now to take Amy and Shaun back with me."

Amy shot to her feet, her arms ramrod straight at her side. "No, I won't go!"

Rachel gave her sister a reassuring smile. "Amy only has another year of high school left. She shouldn't leave Magnolia Blossom right now."

Her mother quirked a brow. "And you're staying here?"

Amy pushed past Rachel. "This is my home. You can't make me go with you." She left.

Shaun rose, tears brimming in his eyes. "Me, neither!" He ran from the room.

Her mother sighed. "I thought this would make everything better."

"How?"

"Weren't you the one who said I should take responsibility for my children? That's what I'm doing. Your father and I talked it over. They can come live with us."

"How generous of you."

"I don't need your sarcasm."

"Why did you have children?" Rachel desperately wanted an answer to the question that had been eating at her for years.

"Your father wanted a son to carry on his name. At least that's why we had you and Amy. Believe it or not, Shaun was an accident. By that time we'd realized raising children and doing our research didn't mix well. It wasn't safe for children in our camp. Our lifestyle didn't go well with parenthood."

"So you discarded us."

"I gave you the best home I could. My sister always wanted children and couldn't have any."

"And now suddenly the camp is safe for children?"

Her mother looked away, shifting her weight from one foot to the other. "It's better than before. I should be able to keep Shaun and Amy safe."

"That's not good enough. We're a family now."

"What do you mean a family? They've always been your sister and brother."

Rachel advanced toward her mother, locking gazes with her. "Until recently I didn't realize what the word *family* really meant. Now I know. For family you make sacrifices if you must. For family you stick together through the good and bad times." She drew in a deep, cleansing breath and added, "Yes, Mother, I am staying in Magnolia Blossom at least until Amy graduates from high school. Go back to the Amazon with a clear conscience. I want to take care of Amy and Shaun because we are family."

Her mother blinked, backing up several steps. "You want to stay in this town?"

Rachel lifted her chin and met her mother's direct look with one of her own. "Yes."

"But what about your plans for your own restaurant?"

"They can wait. Amy and Shaun come first." Not

until this moment had Rachel realized she'd committed fully to her siblings, and it felt as right as did her decision to stay.

Her mother squared her shoulders, snatched her purse and headed for the front door. "Then I'll sign the guardianship papers Robert has." She paused at the door and faced Rachel, a strained expression carving tired lines about her eyes and mouth. "If you're sure?"

"Yes, very."

She turned to leave.

And be ye kind one to another, tenderhearted, forgiving one another, even as God for Christ's sake hath forgiven you. The Bible verse popped into Rachel's thoughts, showing her what she must do to be at peace with herself. How could she expect Michael to forgive her if she couldn't forgive her parents? "Mother, why don't you stay for dinner?"

Tossing a glance over her shoulder, her mother hesitated. "Are you sure?"

"Yes, very. We don't get to see you nearly enough."

Her mother peered at her watch. "It'll have to be an early dinner. I have to make a late flight from New Orleans for the congressional meeting in Washington."

"Dad, Mom wants to take me deep-sea fishing this weekend. Can I go?"

Michael turned from staring out the window into the darkness. His son's eager expression faded to a frown as Michael wrestled with what to say.

"We get to spend the night on the boat. She even said I could invite Shaun to go with me."

"Not this weekend," Michael finally answered, bracing himself for the ensuing battle.

"Why not?" Standing in the middle of the den, his son stiffened.

"We need to talk, Garrett. Have a seat." Michael gestured toward the couch.

His son remained where he was, his frown deepening.

Michael heaved a sigh and moved away from the window. "Your mother and I—" He searched for the right words and decided there was no easy way to tell his son the truth. "We don't see eye to eye on some things. We're going back to see the judge to help us make some decisions."

"What kind of decisions?"

"When your mother can see you and how often."

"Why can't I see her whenever I want? Whenever she wants? She's my *mother.*"

Tension bore deep into Michael's neck and shoulders. "It's complicated. I'm not sure it's best that you stay with your mother a lot."

"Why not?"

Because she might start drinking again. Because she left you and me years ago. Michael couldn't say what he wanted, and no substitute words came to mind. "It just isn't."

"That's not fair! You have to let her see me. She

won't love me if she doesn't," Garrett shouted, then he spun on his heel and ran from the room.

Michael placed his hand over his chest to ease the tightness constricting it. Each breath he drew hurt his lungs, and his heart pounded a mad beat. He was losing his son and he didn't have any idea how to stop it from happening.

He started to follow Garrett but decided against it. Instead, he stood in the middle of the den. Mary Lou kept trying to see Garrett, knowing how Michael felt about it. At least he could be thankful she hadn't told Garrett about the custody hearing. Michael plunged his hand into his hair. But then maybe it would have been better if she had. He'd certainly made a mess of it.

The sound of the doorbell rang through the house. He wished he could ignore it. He had no desire to see anyone tonight, but it chimed again. Determined to send the person away as quickly as possible, he headed for the front door and wrenched it open.

The light from his veranda illuminated Rachel in a soft glow. She smiled, the gesture reaching deep into her eyes to enhance her natural beauty.

"I hope I haven't come at a bad time. I couldn't wait until tomorrow to talk to you."

Michael stepped to the side to allow her into the house. "What couldn't wait?"

She pivoted toward him. "I decided to stay in Magnolia Blossom this year while Amy's finishing high school."

"And then what?" He quietly shut the door, resisting the urge to slam it.

He walked toward the living room, needing its formality to remind him not to get too comfortable around Rachel. She moved to the sofa and sat. He remained by the brocade wing chair, his hands gripping the back.

"That will depend. I haven't made any plans beyond that. I only made the decision to stay this evening."

"Why?"

"Why am I staying?"

He nodded, his fingers digging into the brocade.

"Mother came today to see us. She was going to take Amy and Shaun back with her to the Amazon."

"That would be an answer to all your problems."

She flinched at the sarcastic bite to his words. "But it wouldn't be what's best for Amy and Shaun. Magnolia Blossom is their home. We're a family. I convinced Mother that I wanted to be their guardian and live here."

"And you really do?"

"What's wrong? I thought you would be happy about my decision. This is what you've wanted all along."

"Is that why you're staying, because I wanted it?" His anger infused his voice.

"No. I want it. But I would be lying if I denied you weren't part of this decision."

"How nice. And when you begin to feel trapped, you can blame me right before you leave again."

The color drained from her face. She rose, clasping

her hands in front of her. "Is that what you're worried about? That I'll blame you if something goes wrong? Or is it something else that's bothering you?"

"Oh, don't get me wrong. I'm ecstatic for Amy and Shaun. But what about your restaurant? What are you going to do this next year?"

She took a deep breath. "I'm putting my plans for a restaurant on hold." She paused and drew in another fortifying breath. "I was hoping you would offer me the chef position on your riverboat."

"What happens when you leave in ten months?"

She glanced away, then brought her gaze to his face. Her eyes shone. "I wanted us to start over. See if we could be more than friends."

"Again the question, what happens when you leave in ten months? Am I supposed to pick up the pieces of my life like I did ten years ago? Forget about you? Forget about any feelings I might have for you?"

She trembled. Hugging her arms to her chest, she said, "I know I haven't been very good at making a commitment, but I'm learning. I care about you, Michael. Very much. You're important to me, and I want to see if we have a future together."

He ached to hold her, to wipe away the haunted look in her eyes, but he couldn't. He remembered the anguish, the loss, he'd experienced when she'd left him. He knew his limits, and he'd reached them. He couldn't deal with losing Rachel on top of everything else happening in his life. "But I don't, Rachel."

Pain flickered in her eyes before she veiled them. When she looked at him, her expression was neutral. She'd always been good at hiding her emotions behind a mask. She hadn't really changed.

"If this wasn't so tragic, I'd laugh. You've always been willing to take emotional risks, whereas I never have. And here it is, our roles are reversed."

"I'm tired of exposing myself to those emotional risks you say I take." He pushed himself away from the wing chair. "I don't trust your sudden change of heart."

"That's what it boils down to. You don't trust me. You can't believe that I might have really changed. People do. And people deserve second chances, but of course, you have to forgive a person to give her a second chance."

With her shoulders back, she walked past him into the foyer. He wanted to stop her, to tell her—what? At the moment he felt as though his life were falling down around him. Each brick resounded with a warning to protect himself from further pain.

"You don't need to say anything else to me, Michael. Without trust and forgiveness we have nothing. Goodbye."

The sound of the front door closing echoed through the house, announcing to the world that he was letting go of the best thing that had ever happened to him. He shuddered, cold to the marrow of his bones. Kicking Rachel out of his life would only cause him to suffer more. But then denying Garrett his mother was causing his son to suffer. When Mary Lou had left them, the one thing he'd vowed he wouldn't do to his son was cause him undue pain.

He peered at the door, then up the stairs where Garrett had disappeared. Michael had to start putting his life back together. He suddenly remembered the nursery rhyme about Humpty-Dumpty and wondered if he could piece himself back together. The task seemed overwhelming. He trudged up the stairs, viewing his son's closed door and remembering the sound of Rachel walking out of his life. The coldness burrowed deeper into him.

Almighty God, ruler of all things in heaven and earth, hear my prayer for guidance. Strengthen my faith and help me to forgive those who have wronged me and to right the wrongs I have committed. Open my heart to Your love and mercy. Grant me the ability to love and show mercy, through Jesus Christ our Lord. Amen.

With each word he whispered, he drew nearer to Garrett's bedroom. As he knocked on his son's door, a calmness washed over him. God was with him. God would show him the way. Michael would be all right.

"Go away! I don't want to talk," Garrett shouted.

"I'm not leaving until we talk, son."

Seconds stretched into a full minute. When the door swung open, Garrett hid behind it. Michael stepped into his son's bedroom and pivoted toward him. Garrett shoved the door closed, the sound reminding Michael of Rachel's departure and the hurt stamped on her expression.

Where to begin? A momentary surge of panic flashed through Michael. The Lord was beside him every step of the way. He closed his eyes for a few seconds, visualizing peace and forgiveness.

"Being with your mother is important to you?"

Tears welled in Garrett's eyes. "Yes. I missed her while she was gone."

"You never said."

"Because you never liked to talk about her. I didn't want to hurt you."

Michael's heart expanded with all the love he had for his son. He could learn a lesson about forgiveness from Garrett. He never held a grudge for long.

His son plopped down on the nearest twin bed, his shoulders slumped, his hands clasped between his legs. "She needs me."

Surprised at Garrett's words, Michael blinked. "Why do you say that?"

"She wants to make up for leaving me. That's important to her."

"Did she tell you that?"

"Not in so many words, but I can tell. She did tell me that she did some bad things and that she had to ask God for forgiveness. If God can forgive her, why can't you?"

Michael sucked in a deep breath as though he had been punched in the stomach. "I—" He clamped his lips together and tried to think of the best way to reply to his son. "I don't know. I'm trying."

Garrett lifted his head, tears running down his cheeks. "I want to get to know her. Please let me."

For a long moment Michael stared at Garrett, frozen, unable to move or say a thing. Tears continued to fall from his son's eyes, unchecked, as they stared at each other.

Michael was across the room in two strides. He scooped his son into his arms and held him tight, tears misting his eyes. "I love you, son."

"I know that. I love you, Dad, but I love Mom, too."

"I can't promise I'll change overnight, but I'll call your mom and talk to her about you going deep-sea fishing this weekend with them. Okay?"

Garrett pulled back, wiping at his tears. "You mean it?"

Michael nodded, a lump the size of the Gulf in his throat.

"Do you think Shaun can go, too?"

"You'll have to ask him."

"I'll go call him right now." Garrett hurried toward the hall, stopped halfway to the door and said, "No, wait. You'd better call Mom first, then I'll talk to Shaun."

Michael smiled. "I'm going to. Don't worry. I won't change my mind."

Garrett blushed. "I know you won't. I just want to make sure everything is still on for the weekend before I invite Shaun."

"Do you want to talk to her after I do?" Michael tousled his son's hair as he passed him.

"Sure. Just let me know when you're finished."

Michael arched a brow. "You aren't going to listen?"

"No. I know you have things to talk over that are private. I'll wait here."

Michael paused in the doorway. "When did you get to be such a smart kid?"

With a huge grin on his face, Garrett shrugged.

"Well, that's done." Rachel replaced the receiver in its cradle and twisted to look at Amy. "And you know what? It felt good to tell my lawyer to hold off on the restaurant deal."

Amy downed the last of her soda. "Then you really don't mind staying in Magnolia Blossom this year?"

"No." Rachel fingered the newspaper at her elbow. "But I'll need to see about getting a job. I'll have to travel to Natchez or Jackson, possibly even New Orleans."

"What about Michael's restaurant on the riverboat?"

"He's interviewing someone else today."

After the evening before, working with him wasn't a possibility, Rachel thought with a touch of sadness. She couldn't be around him all the time in a work situation, or a situation of any other kind. The idea that he couldn't totally trust her hurt her deeply. Granted, she had given him reasons to feel that way, but she had changed. She had learned to make a commitment.

"Maybe it won't work out."

"Amy Peters, no more matchmaking. One Helen in Magnolia Blossom is enough. Besides, Michael isn't interested."

"Does that mean you are?"

Rachel held up her hand, palm outward. "Stop. Don't go there. Whatever we had once is over. Period. No more."

"Thou doth protest too much." Amy rose and put her glass in the kitchen sink. "Are you through with the renovations on the riverboat?"

"I'm going over later this afternoon to meet with the carpenter about a few last-minute details, then I'm basically finished." Thankfully, Rachel thought, trying to ignore the pain threatening to overwhelm her.

Amy leaned against the counter. "You know we didn't get to talk last night after Mother left. You ran out of here so fast you made my head spin. Are you sure about what happened?"

Rachel's smile came from the depths of her heart. "Yes. We're a family. It took me some time to really realize what that meant, but I must say, you, Shaun and Michael have helped me with that."

"Were you as surprised as I was about Mother's offer?"

Rachel laughed. "Shocked."

"Do you think she was serious?"

"Yeah, or believe me, she wouldn't have made the offer to take you two with her."

"Why did she do it?"

Rachel looked away from her sister for a few seconds. "I believe because I said something to her that last time she called about being your guardian."

Amy's eyebrows shot up. "But I thought you and Aunt Flora had talked about it several years ago."

"Yes, but I got angry at Mother for not doing what I thought she should as the parent."

"Oh." Amy hung her head, staring at the floor.

Rachel stood and went to her sister. "This summer I've done a lot of thinking. Getting involved in the church again has helped me to sort out my feelings concerning our parents. I've always felt abandoned by them, and in a way we were. But you know, Amy, I feel they did the right thing by leaving us with Aunt Flora. Their medical research helps thousands of people. I'm not excusing how they handle everything, but I understand. I can forgive them. I can move on."

The words, said out loud, felt so right. Rachel pulled her sister into her embrace and hugged her.

"I love you, big sis."

"I'm glad, because you're stuck with me. I'm not going anywhere."

Rachel stood on the landing, peering at Michael's riverboat. A man was positioned over the back of it, painting the name. So far there was a big black *C*.

She saw Michael's truck parked nearby and hoped she could meet Brandon, the carpenter, and leave without running into Michael. Her heart ached too much to see him right now. Maybe later, with time, she could feel as though she weren't coming apart if she met him on the streets of Magnolia Blossom. Somehow she had to pull herself together enough to live in the same small town for at least the next ten months. For Amy and Shaun, she would do it. She was through running away from her emotions and denying they existed.

With a heavy sigh she walked toward the gangplank. She would use the back way to the kitchen. In and out. Thirty minutes tops. Then her professional connection with Michael would be cut.

But never her emotional one, she thought as she climbed to the second deck. When she stepped into the kitchen, she was surprised to find it deserted. A feeling of coming home inundated her as she ran her hand along the gleaming stainless steel. She visualized herself standing in front of the stove, stirring one of her cream sauces, the scents and smells of a kitchen enveloping her. Onions sautéing. Bread baking. Coffee brewing.

She gripped the counter and leaned into it. She quivered with the vision she knew was just out of her reach. If only she had learned how to make a commitment earlier—ten years ago.

"Rachel."

With her back to the door, she slid her eyes closed, her breath bottled in her lungs. *Please not now, Lord. I can't handle seeing Michael.*

"I was afraid you weren't going to meet Brandon."

She spun. "I always finish a job, Michael. I have changed, but not totally."

Michael moved into the kitchen, his face no longer in the shadows.

Rachel sucked in a deep breath at the haggard lines

around his mouth and eyes. She wanted to smooth them away, ease what torment had put them there. She remained where she was, aware that a large wall stood between them, originally erected by her, reinforced by him.

"I told Brandon you would meet with him another day."

"Why?"

"Because we need to talk."

"I thought you had said all you wanted to last night."

"A guy can change his mind."

Hope vied with her natural wariness. Her hands on the counter tightened. "Yes, just as a gal can. What do you want to talk about?"

"Us." He took a step closer.

"There is no us. Haven't you said that enough these past few months? I've finally gotten it, Michael."

He tunneled his fingers through his hair. "I was wrong last night about a lot of things."

Her heart began to pound.

"I want you to be the chef on the riverboat."

"No."

"Why not? I thought that's what you wanted. Have you changed your mind about staying in Magnolia Blossom?"

"No."

He shook his head. "Then I don't understand."

"Ten years ago I ran because I couldn't give you what you wanted, and yet I knew I could never watch you fall in love with another woman, marry and have a family. I'm staying in Magnolia Blossom, but I won't work for you. I made a promise to Amy and Shaun, but I know my limitations."

The frown that furrowed his brow vanished. "You won't work for me because you have feelings for me?"

"I love you. I now realize that hasn't changed in ten years."

"Good." The tension in his body melted. He moved one step closer.

"Good?"

"I love you."

"But last night—"

He placed his fingers over her mouth. "When you came back to Magnolia Blossom, I fell in love with you all over again. With you as you are today, not ten years ago. What I feel for you now far outshines those feelings."

The pounding of her heart thundered in her ears. Her throat contracted, making it difficult to draw air into her lungs.

"I've been up all night, trying to work through my problems. I did some soul-searching with God's help and realized a few things about myself." He rubbed his fingers across her lips.

The sensations created from his touch made the world fade. Her every sense became centered on the man standing in front of her.

"I do trust you. I have from the beginning. You were the one I turned to when things were heating up with Mary Lou. The past few months I have opened my heart to you, and that's not something I've done in years. You know me better than anyone. That doesn't happen without trust, Rachel. I was just being too stubborn to realize that."

Tears flooded her eyes and spilled down her cheeks. Michael wiped them away, but more fell.

"You aren't supposed to cry."

"Tears of joy. I didn't think I would ever hear you say you trusted me. Does that mean you have forgiven me for leaving you ten years ago?"

"For a time I'd forgotten the power of forgiveness. You taught me how freeing it is to forgive another." He cupped her face, leaning closer. "Yes, I have forgiven you. Will you forgive me for being so pigheaded?"

"Mmm. I don't know."

He brushed his lips across hers. "Is there anything I can do to change your mind?"

"Perhaps."

He wound his arms about her and brought her against him. His mouth settled over hers. His kiss rocked her to the depths of her being.

When he pulled back, his eyes gleamed with happiness. "Well?"

"Not a bad start."

"Then I guess I'll have to spend the next thirty or forty years trying to convince you."

"Oh, it probably won't take *that* long." She laughed and tightened her embrace, drawing him close to her.

"Will you marry me?" He kissed her lightly on both sides of the mouth.

"I thought you'd never ask."

"Is that a yes?"

"Yes. Yes. Yes."

"Will you be my chef on the *Cajun Queen*?"

"The *Cajun Queen*?"

"I decided to name the riverboat after you." He grinned and snuggled closer, nibbling on her ear. "I want the very best, and you, my love, are that."

"How can I turn down a proposition like that?"

"You can't, since I'm giving you the *Cajun Queen* as a wedding present."

Rachel gasped. "Giving me the boat?"

"Do you honestly think I'll have the time to run the restaurant with my plantation and other business ventures?"

"But, Michael, it's been in your family for several generations."

"And you'll be family, so it will stay in it. It'll be something you can pass on to our children."

She knew how much family and traditions meant to him, and the gesture took her breath away. "I don't know what to say."

"How about yes? I started this riverboat project to give you a reason to stay in Magnolia Blossom. At the beginning I told myself it was for Amy and Shaun's sake. Now I know better. It was for me."

She leaned her head on his chest and listened to his strong heartbeat. "The only thing I can say is yes."

Epilogue

Two years later

Rachel searched the restaurant full of diners for Helen and Harold. She saw them in front of the picture window and strode to their table, so glad her best friend had given Harold a chance. He'd turned out to be such a dear man and perfect for Helen.

"I hope the dinner was to your satisfaction."

"Are you kidding?" Helen placed her hand over Harold's. "It was a delicious prime rib."

"Only the best for your first anniversary."

Helen smiled. "What are you going to do about your second one coming up in three weeks?"

Rachel laid her hand over her rounded stomach. "Hopefully, be in the hospital delivering this sucker."

"Are you sure you trust me in your kitchen while you're on maternity leave?"

"Well, it was you or Michael. And he told me in no uncertain terms he would be too busy taking care of me and the baby."

Helen squeezed her husband's hand. "Aren't men grand?"

"Harold, you better watch out. She wants something," Rachel said with a laugh.

"I've learned how to handle this woman." He winked at Helen.

"I think that's my cue to leave you two lovebirds alone."

Rachel headed toward the kitchen, stopping at tables on the way to say a few words to the customers. When she reached one couple, she smiled and said, "I'm glad you and Tom could come this evening, Mary Lou."

The woman returned her smile. "I thought it would be a perfect way to top off a great week, since we had to bring Garrett and Shaun back."

"I haven't seen them yet. Did they have fun at Disney World?"

Mary Lou's eyes sparkled. "I didn't realize how much energy they had. We were up at dawn and went all day— not *one* break. I believe I wore out a pair of tennis shoes."

Rachel laughed. "I know what you mean. Enjoy the rest of your evening."

Rachel paused at the entrance to the kitchen to scan her restaurant. Pride straightened her shoulders as she noted every table was full. People came from all over to sample her food. She and the *Cajun Queen* had been written up in the New Orleans and Jackson newspapers.

But all this wouldn't mean much without Michael and his love.

As she entered her domain, she was captured from behind and pulled against a hard body. She snuggled against the man holding her, his familiar, comforting scent wafting to her.

Michael buried his face in her hair. "Mmm. You smell like garlic and onions."

"I'm not sure that's a compliment."

"To a chef, I'm sure it is." He turned her around, his arms still loosely about her.

"You know I'm busy."

He looked over her shoulder at the workers in the kitchen and drew her to the side so a waiter could get through the door. "I won't keep you. I just wanted to check and make sure you were all right before heading home."

She cupped his face. She loved how he fussed over her even to the point that the riverboat had remained at the pier for the past two weeks and would until after the baby was born. "I realize you've been gone all day to Vicksburg, but honey, I have your pager number as well as your cell phone number. Believe me, if I go into labor, you'll be the first person I notify, even before the doctor."

"Do you think that's wise?"

"In this case, yes. You'd think this was your first child, not mine."

Michael placed his hand on her stomach, stroking it. He felt a kick and smiled. "He wants out of there."

"His mother wants him out of there, too. I think I've put on thirty pounds."

His gaze linked with hers. "You're the most beautiful woman in the world."

Tears thickened her throat. "You're going to make me cry, and I still have work to do."

"Then I'll leave. I'll be back to pick you up." He slid his hands into her hair and brought her mouth to his.

His kiss, full of all the emotions he felt, shook her to her very soul. Right in front of all the kitchen staff, she returned his kiss, her arms winding about her husband's neck.

When they parted, the staff clapped. Rachel blushed while Michael gave her another quick kiss, then left. Content and happy, she walked to the sink to wash her hands before cooking. She had everything she could ever want.

* * * * *

Dear Reader,

This was my fourth book for the Love Inspired line. I had so much fun writing it because it brought back memories of my childhood in Mississippi.

In this story I wanted to explore a woman's fear of opening herself up to love. Once Rachel allowed the Lord into her life, it wasn't long before she was able to see that she could love her siblings and a man. Love can be scary. We open ourselves up and sometimes we do end up getting hurt. But love is what makes life rich and wonderful—from the love of God to the love of a partner to share your life with.

I hope you enjoy Rachel's journey toward finding her soul mate. Michael is a hardworking man who has a strong faith and believes in family. Rachel learns some valuable lessons from him, but he in turn learns how to forgive, which is such an important part of our faith.

I would love to hear from you! If you want to be added to my mailing list, please write to me at Margaret Daley, P.O. Box 2074, Tulsa, OK 74101.

May God be with you,

Margaret Daley

REQUEST YOUR FREE BOOKS!

2 FREE INSPIRATIONAL NOVELS
PLUS 2
FREE
MYSTERY GIFTS

LoveInspired®

YES! Please send me 2 FREE Love Inspired® novels and my 2 FREE mystery gifts (gifts are worth about $10). After receiving them, if I don't wish to receive any more books, I can return the shipping statement marked "cancel". If I don't cancel, I will receive 4 brand-new novels every month and be billed just $4.24 per book in the U.S. or $4.74 per book in Canada, plus 25¢ shipping and handling per book and applicable taxes, if any*. That's a savings of over 20% off the cover price! I understand that accepting the 2 free books and gifts places me under no obligation to buy anything. I can always return a shipment and cancel at any time. Even if I never buy another book, the two free books and gifts are mine to keep forever.

113 IDN ERXA   313 IDN ERWX

Name	(PLEASE PRINT)	
Address		Apt. #
City	State/Prov.	Zip/Postal Code

Signature (if under 18, a parent or guardian must sign)

Order online at www.LoveInspiredBooks.com

Or mail to Steeple Hill Reader Service:

IN U.S.A.: P.O. Box 1867, Buffalo, NY 14240-1867
IN CANADA: P.O. Box 609, Fort Erie, Ontario L2A 5X3

Not valid to current subscribers of Love Inspired books.

Want to try two free books from another series?
Call 1-800-873-8635 or visit www.morefreebooks.com

* Terms and prices subject to change without notice. N.Y. residents add applicable sales tax. Canadian residents will be charged applicable provincial taxes and GST. Offer not valid in Quebec. This offer is limited to one order per household. All orders subject to approval. Credit or debit balances in a customer's account(s) may be offset by any other outstanding balance owed by or to the customer. Please allow 4 to 6 weeks for delivery. Offer available while quantities last.

Your Privacy: Steeple Hill Books is committed to protecting your privacy. Our Privacy Policy is available online at www.SteepleHill.com or upon request from the Reader Service. From time to time we make our lists of customers available to reputable third parties who may have a product or service of interest to you. If you would prefer we not share your name and address, please check here. ☐

LIREG08R

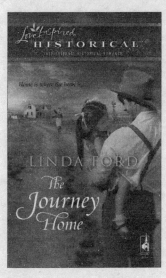

Love Inspired

David Ryland knows all about tough situations. When the father he never knew is suddenly revealed, he knows he'll need a different kind of bravery. A late war hero has confessed David's parentage in a deathbed letter—a letter that charity worker Anna Terenkov knows all about. Can David open up his heart to the truth, and find room for Anna?

Look for

Lone Star Secret

by

Lenora Worth

HOMECOMING
★ HEROES ★

Available August wherever books are sold.

Steeple
Hill®

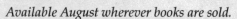